STUDIES IN THE HISTORY OF MUSIC 3

Lewis Lockwood and Christoph Wolff, General Editors

LAURENCE DREYFUS

Bach's Continuo Group

Players and Practices in His Vocal Works

Harvard University Press
Cambridge, Massachusetts, and London, England   1987

Publication of this book has been aided by a grant from
the Frederick W. Hilles Publication Fund of Yale University
and a grant from the Andrew W. Mellon Foundation.

This book is printed on acid-free paper, and its binding
materials have been chosen for strength and durability.

Library of Congress Cataloging-in-Publication Data

Dreyfus, Laurence Dana.
   Bach's continuo group.

   (Studies in the history of music ; 3)
   Bibliography: p.
   Includes index.
   1. Bach, Johann Sebastian, 1685–1750. Vocal
music. 2. Thorough bass. I. Title. II. Series:
Studies in the history of music (Cambridge, Mass.) ; 3.
ML410.B1D67   1987   784'.092'4   86-29593
ISBN 0-674-06020-2 (alk. paper)

Designed by Gwen Frankfeldt

To my parents

Acknowledgments

The research for this study was first undertaken in 1976 and, over the course of a decade, has incurred sizable debts. To Christoph Wolff in particular, who inspired me to undertake the research, who became a benevolent *Doktorvater,* who oversaw the early stages of this work, and who has encouraged me in countless ways ever since, words cannot repay my thanks nor adequately express my affection. I am also specially indebted to Hans-Joachim Schulze for so often pointing me in the right direction. To other members of the community of Bach scholars who offered much-needed corrections, criticism, and encouragement—Paul Brainard, Alfred Dürr, Don Franklin, Robert L. Marshall, Joshua Rifkin, William Scheide, Ulrich Siegele, and Peter Williams—I am also deeply grateful. The errors that remain are, of course, my own doing.

Without grants awarded me by the Deutscher Akademischer Austauschdienst (DAAD) and the International Research and Exchange Council (IREX) I could not have spent the academic year 1976–77 and the summer of 1978 in Berlin and Leipzig inspecting the original sources. I am also happy to acknowledge the assistance of the Society of Fellows in the Humanities at Columbia University, a faculty summer fellowship from Washington University in St. Louis, and a Morse Faculty Fellowship in the Humanities from Yale University. Without the gracious cooperation of Rudolf Elvers at the Musikabteilung of the Staatsbibliothek Preussischer Kulturbesitz (Berlin) and both Karl-Heinz Köhler and Wolfgang Goldhan of the Deutsche Staatsbibliothek Berlin (DDR), it would have been impossible to undertake comparative work on such a large number of manuscripts. I am also grateful to both institutions for their kind permission to reproduce materials from their collections in facsimile. I found the staffs at both Berlin libraries consistently helpful, and Heidrun Siegel and Eveline Bartlitz of the Deutsche Staatsbibliothek were especially good-humored even when attending to irksome requests for stacks of manuscripts. The former Bach-Archiv (Leipzig) was an especially pleasant place to work during a four-month stay, and I am grateful to Rosemarie Nestle for her bibliographic help. The Johann-Sebastian-Bach-Institut (Göttingen) graciously permitted me to dash in and out at will, combing through their photographic collections and catalogs. In addition, I wish to thank Paula Morgan for allowing me to use the excellent resources of the Princeton University library; William Scheide for showing me his priceless collection of Bach autographs; Harold Samuel and Victor Cardell of the Yale University Music Library for allowing such easy access to the rare book collection and for permission to photograph a volume in their collection; Susan T. Sommer of the New York Public Library for her help in the use of the Toscanini Archives; Frits Knuf of Buren (the Netherlands) for permission to reproduce pages from a published facsimile edition; the Kunstsammlungen der Veste Coburg and the Hessische Landes- und Hochschulbibliothek Darmstadt for permission to reproduce pages of manuscripts in their holdings; the Staatliche Museen zu Berlin (DDR) for permission to reproduce a drawing in the Kupferstichkabinett; Edition Peters Leipzig for permission to reproduce a page from a published facsimile edition; and the Germanisches National-Museum, Nürnberg, for permission to reproduce an engraving in their collection.

Among the friends who offered various forms of welcome support, I especially wish to single out V. Kofi Agawu, Michael Beckerman, Brigitte Borchardt, Maria Bräutigam, Volker Bräutigam, Richard Campbell, Lenore Coral, Hans Grüss, Horst Gurgel, Marlene Gurgel, Victoria Horn, Wieland Kuijken, Nicolas McGegan, Loretta Nassar, Carla Pollack, Curtis Price, Rhian Samuel, Judith Silber, Barbara Wolff, Mechthild Göckert Zimmermann, and the late Walter Eisen. Others who improved this book include Robert E. Anderson, Barbara Brewer, Donald J. Cohen, Reinhard Goebel, Ellen Harris, Christopher Hogwood, Ryan Kadri, Eva Linfield, Joel Newman, Ulrich Prinz, James Schultz, Jacob Willem Smit, Kerala Snyder, Philip Swanton, Richard Taruskin, Teri Noel Towe, and William Waterhouse. Edward Mendelson, friend and Bach devotee, was kind enough to read through the entire manuscript, offering much-needed criticism at every turn. And in the final stages of putting this book together, Marian Smith checked references and gave strongly worded advice on nearly every issue, for which I am very grateful. I also wish to thank both Margaretta Fulton and Mary Ellen Geer of Harvard University Press for their help and encouragement.

My wife, Nancy Elan, has borne marriage to a would-be author with unwarranted patience and enthusiasm. My most musical reader, she has insisted that historical work not wander too far into academic groves. Her unflagging confidence in the value of my work has remained a deep source of encouragement.

Contents

I Introduction 1

II The Organ and the Harpsichord 10

Keyboard Accompaniment in the Sacred Works 10   The Harpsichord
Controversy 12   Evidence of Harpsichords in Churches 23
Harpsichord Participation during Bach's Tenure at Leipzig 25
Cembalo Parts 32   Harpsichord Parts in Performances of Other
Composers' Works 44   Figured *Cammerton* Continuo Parts 48
Tacet-Indications in Organ Parts 58   Performance of Cantatas with Solo
Organ 63   Dual Accompaniment as Convention 68

III The Accompaniment of Recitatives 72

The Convention of Short Accompaniment in Secco Recitatives 72
Witnesses to the Convention: 1711–1750 76   Later Witnesses:
1750–1810 82   The Convention in Historical Perspective 88
Evidence in Bach's Continuo Parts 89   Bach's Recitatives and Their
Performance 105

IV The Bassoon 108

Two Views of the Bassoon 108   The Original Parts and the
Question of Participation 113   The Pitch of Bach's Bassoons 118
Weimar Parts 123   Leipzig Parts 125   The Bassoonist as Adjunct
Continuo Player 127

V The String Instruments in the Continuo Group 132

The Violoncello 132   The Problematic Identity of the Violone 136
Definitions of the German Violone: 1697–1752 137   Case Study: The
Brandenburg Concertos 142   Violone Parts from Mühlhausen,
Weimar, and Cöthen 151   Leipzig Violone Parts 156
Bach's Violone Types 165   The Viola da gamba 166   The Lute 170
The Violoncello piccolo and the Viola pomposa 172   The Bass Players
in Perspective 175

Guide to the Appendixes   179

Appendix A Catalog of Original Performance Parts for Bach's Vocal Works   183

Appendix B Bach's Continuo Parts Arranged by Date of Performance   208

Abbreviations   220

Notes   221

Index to Cited Works of Bach   259

General Index   262

BACH'S CONTINUO GROUP

CHAPTER I

Introduction

The basso continuo assumed a role within the early eighteenth-century ensemble that nearly eclipsed all other parts in importance. As the term suggests, the basso continuo functioned "continuously" throughout a piece of music. The continuo, however, was important not only because it was omnipresent but because it represented so much more than an individual part. In this connection, composers often referred to it by two related terms, *thorough bass* and *general bass*. The *Bassus generalis,* writes Johann Gottfried Walther in his *Lexikon* of 1732, is "so called because it encloses within itself the entire harmony of a musical piece."[1] Walther refers, of course, to a defining feature of thorough bass in which composers superimposed numerals above the music to denote the chords and, by extension, to imply the voice-leading of a composition. Amounting to a scaffolding of the complete harmonic design, the thorough bass could justifiably be said to include the "entire harmony."

The basso continuo (or simply "continuo") also signified the musicians assigned to realize it: that is, the organists and harpsichordists who could play the chords indicated by the figures above the bass line. Other bass players—such as the cellists, bassoonists, and violone players—also reinforced the continuo line; the difference was that they ignored the figures or played from separate, unfigured bass parts. Strictly speaking, the term *thorough bass* applied only to instruments that could realize the chords. As Walther points out, "An unfigured general bass should not actually be called a General-bass."[2] On the other hand, the doubling instruments participated as a rule throughout a composition: they were, in this sense, also continuous. Since, moreover, Bach and his contemporaries often entitled all instrumental bass parts *Continuo*—whether figured or unfigured—it has become customary to include both the keyboardists and the other bass players within the continuo group.

Although composers called for the basso continuo in nearly all Baroque ensemble music, they rarely specified which instruments should realize it. This shifting membership of bass players depended on factors such as genre, institution, and national tradition. Conceptually, composers thought of the continuo more as a sounding principle of composition than as a section of the ensemble to be orchestrated. To put it another way: the function of the continuo part was more important than the instruments that happened to play it. For this reason, those who have attempted a historical reconstruction of the continuo have been frustrated in their attempts to enumerate a definitive list of the musicians who participated in it. Though the purpose of the continuo remained constant, its membership fluctuated.

The tradition of basso continuo practice saw its culmination in the works of Johann Sebastian Bach, who was probably the last important composer to formulate his system of composition on an elaboration of thorough bass. In his eyes, thorough bass was profoundly metaphysical. According to Bach's rules for the general bass set down for the use of his pupils, "The end or final cause of all music, and also of thorough-bass, is the glory of God and the permissible enjoyment of the spirit. Wherever this is disregarded, there is no longer actual music but a devilish bawling and singsong."[3] It is no coincidence that, in a chapter defining thorough bass, Bach invokes the traditional Lutheran antinomies underlying human works. The strong language hints that the realization of a bass line involved more than a matter of good craftsmanship. Indeed, it suggests that, for Bach, continuo playing entailed an obligation to elevate man's station above the imperfections of a sinful world. Nevertheless, Bach's works also foreshadow the eventual dissolution of thorough bass. The use of textures that occasionally dispense with the continuo realization—*bassetto* accompaniments, organ parts with *tacet*-indications, obbligato harpsichord parts in trio sonatas—all point to the dawn of a new aesthetic that viewed chordal filler as unnecessary.

Thorough bass was not only a practical matter, but also the basis for composition. Bach's testimonial for a former pupil, Friedrich Gottlieb Wild, states that Wild had taken special instruction in "thorough-bass and the fundamental rules of composition based thereupon."[4] In this respect Bach differed from certain enlightened contemporaries like Johann Mattheson who, without attacking the continuo tradition, saw the root of musical practice in melody, a sensuous entity preferable to the more intangible stuff of harmony. For Bach, the harmonic realm never lost its importance.

Since the late nineteenth century, the desire to reconstruct Bach's basso continuo practice has presumed a special notion of historical fidelity—performing Bach *his* way. Before this time, most musicians acquainted with historical practices felt free to disregard them in the name of expressivity. It is clear, for example, that the editors of the Bach-Gesellschaft edition (1850–1899) wanted to clarify the historical record in their prefaces without attempting to dictate musical practice. Consider Julius Rietz (1812–1877), who edited the St. Matthew Passion for the Bach-Gesellschaft edition. When performing the work with the Gewandhaus orchestra in Leipzig, Rietz scored the secco recitatives for a trio of two solo cellos and a double bass, dispensing with the organ altogether.[5] Even where Bach had gone to the trouble of specifying all the secco recitatives in quarter-note values, Rietz orchestrated the parts in notes of varying lengths, both to enrich the color of the accompaniment and to underscore the drama of the delivery. His efforts to establish an authentic text thus had little effect on the interpretive activity of music making; here, expressivity overruled history. The idea, so influential today, that something essential in the music emerges in its original manner of execution had not yet become a regulative norm.

It took a scholar as devoted as Philipp Spitta, Bach's great nineteenth-century biographer, to raise history as an issue for performing musicians. Although practical performance receives scant attention in his two-volume biography—his index, for example, cites only five references to "musical practices of execution" (*musikalische Ausführungs-gebräuche*)—Spitta believed that a recovery of forgotten practices was essential to the Bach Movement. Moreover, the revival of basso continuo practice held the highest position on his agenda: "It is important to clarify Bach's fundamental principles underlying the execution of his accompaniments, for this, the loftiest bough in the art of that time, has now quite died out, and yet an essential part of the possibility of making Bach's works accessible in our time rests on its due reawakening." Although Spitta made a strong case for the revival of continuo playing, he was also greatly interested in restoring the organ to its former position of glory in German music and, despite a distaste for the "dry, ineffective tone of the harpsichord," even argued for its incorporation in the secular genres of chamber music. This is not to say that Spitta was a strict reconstructionist; he did not believe that Bach devotees should restore every material condition under which the composer worked. Indeed, part of Spitta's mission was to rescue Bach's work from what he termed the "few inadequate performances" given during the composer's lifetime.[6]

It was Charles Sanford Terry who most successfully expanded the notion of Bach's performance practice to include a detailed study of the instruments. "Of all the Masters whose art has continuing and unabated vogue," Terry writes in the preface to *Bach's Orchestra* (1932), "[Bach] especially spoke through voices silent in the modern orchestra."[7] To hear what Bach was saying, Terry argues, one needs to resurrect the obsolete instruments he used. Bach's performing forces, in other words, were uniquely suited to the expression in his music, so that any so-called modernization would only hinder understanding. Thurston Dart, summing up Terry's point of view, puts it this way: "Bach's music will be best served, first, by discovering his intentions, and then by obeying them as scrupulously as circumstances permit."[8] The search for these intentions motivated Terry's thoughtful compilation of documents and data that catalogued for the first time the sum of knowledge about Bach's ensemble. In his extended discussion of the continuo group, moreover, Terry critically examined all the known evidence published in the prefaces to the Bach-Gesellschaft edition. Relying on both Spitta's chronology of the vocal works—recognized as faulty only in 1957— and a great deal of common sense, Terry devised ingenious solutions to puzzling problems.

Following the bicentennial commemoration in 1950, most Bach scholars plunged enthusiastically into the philological projects mandated by the editorial board of the just-inaugurated New Bach Edition (the Neue Bach-Ausgabe, or NBA; the edition, the first volume of which appeared in 1954, is still in progress). Philology, of course, aimed to produce an authentic text by critically evaluating the original manuscript sources. In the case of the NBA, the philological method included not only diplomatics—cataloging and dating the papers and their watermarks—but also graphology—identifying the handwriting of Bach and his copyists. An important breakthrough occurred in 1957–1958 with the publication of Alfred Dürr's and Georg von Dadelsen's revised cantata chronology, whose landmark status placed an indelible stamp on subsequent Bach research.[9] The NBA editors—Dürr and von Dadelsen among them—were particularly concerned about editorial matters affecting practical performance, although their philological expertise, which set a new standard for scholarly editions, sometimes conflicted with the demands of historical performance. Indeed, the ideal of a fixed text to which all philology aspires cannot help but misrepresent Bach's constantly shifting working conditions. Nevertheless, many of the issues motivating earlier research on performance practice became clear only after one had sifted through the details of the original manuscripts. To a great extent, this is exactly what the critical apparatus in each volume of the NBA (the *kritischer Bericht* or KB) has accomplished. Although editorial policy has sometimes fallen back on philological conservatism, the high standard of textual criticism has added to work on Bach's performance practice a dimension not available to previous historians.

The present study, indebted to the scholars associated with the revised vocal chronology and the NBA, focuses on the original orchestral parts for Bach's vocal music in order to reconstruct the practices of the continuo group. The extant parts for some 175 vocal works that survive from Bach's own performances of these pieces present an impressive repository for research. Although relatively few parts remain from Bach's early years (1704–1713) or from those spent at Cöthen (1717–1723), many survive from works performed at Weimar (1714–1717) and Leipzig (1723–1750). The repertory includes not only the sacred and secular cantatas but also the passions, oratorios, motets, masses, and chorales that together constitute the vast majority of Bach's occasional compositions.

Four fundamental questions underlie the following chapters:

1. Which keyboard instrument accompanied Bach's sacred vocal works?

2. How did continuo players execute the bass parts in recitatives?

3. When did Bach use doubling bass instruments such as the bassoon, cello, and violone?

4. Did instruments such as the viola da gamba, the lute, or the violoncello piccolo ever play continuo?

Though the questions are modest, they raise many other issues. To talk about the harpsichord in sacred works invites a discussion of the nineteenth- and twentieth-century view that the harpsichord did not belong in church; to deal with Bach's recitative basses prompts a chronicle of eighteenth-century writings treating the question of note length in recitative accompaniments; to understand Bach's use of the violone entails a history of changing sizes and pitches of the lowest member of the string family. In general, I have favored questions that could be addressed directly by a study of the original musical sources.[10] For example, the manuscripts offer substantive evidence on the question of the length of bass notes in secco recitatives. On the other hand, they provide no evidence to indicate how keyboard players voiced the chords of the continuo realization. For this reason I have not discussed styles of continuo realization. Although historical documents (such as treatises on thorough bass) can furnish general answers here, the extant manuscripts say little. Whenever possible, however, I have endeavored to place the source evidence in historical context, drawing on writings and documents of the eighteenth century.[11]

What does one find in an original set of Bach's orchestral parts? A glance at the sources for a Leipzig cantata, BWV 40, provides a brief answer to this question.[12]

The original sources for Cantata 40, "Dazu ist erschienen der Sohn Gottes," consist of an autograph composing score (Deutsche Staatsbibliothek Berlin [DStB], Mus. ms. Bach P 63)[13] as well as a set of parts (Berlin, Staatsbibliothek Preussischer Kulturbesitz [SPK], Mus. ms. Bach St 11).[14] The paper on which both the score and the parts are written bears a familiar watermark "IMK." According to the revised chronology, this means that the first performance took place on December 26, 1723, that is, on the second day of Christmas during Bach's first yearly cycle (or *Jahrgang*) of weekly church cantatas at Leipzig.[15] Although no evidence in the sources confirms any later performances of Cantata 40, Bach surely reused the parts for this occasional work at several Christmas feasts during the subsequent twenty-odd years of his Leipzig tenure. The parts, numbered by the Berlin library, bear the following titles:[16]

St 11/1	*Canto*
2	*Alto*
3	*Tenore*
4	*Basso*
5	*Corno 1*
6	*Corno 2*
7	*Hautbois 1*
8	*Hautbois 2do*
9	*Violino 1mo*
10	*Violino 1mo*
11	*Violino 2do*
12	*Violino 2do*
13	*Viola*
14	*Continuo* [figured]
15	*Continuo* [figured and transposed]
16	*Continuo*

The principal copyist in this instance was the 20-year-old Johann Andreas Kuhnau, the nephew of the former Thomas-Cantor. Taking Bach's score as his exemplar, Kuhnau copied Parts 1–9 and 12–14, that is, a core set of vocal and instrumental parts which the other scribes could use as exemplars.[17] The duplicate parts, Parts 10–11 and 15–16, therefore include one copy each of the two violin parts and two copies of the continuo part. In the case of the violins, the duplicate part served the third (and possibly fourth) member of each section, which is similar to today's practice. (Considering the number of singers Bach had available to him among the pupils at the Thomas-Schule, in addition to the university students and others who studied under him, there is good reason to assume that, just like the string players, the singers also read more than one to a part.)[18] The duplicate first violin part was copied jointly from Kuhnau's exemplar by Christian Gottlob Meissner and another copyist, while another anonymous scribe copied the duplicate second violin part. Unlike other parts, the continuo parts did not generally specify which instruments played at a particular performance. One of the duplicate continuo parts—Part 15—was, however, clearly for the organ. Since the organ at Leipzig was tuned a whole tone higher than the conventional performing pitch, it required a continuo part transposed a whole step below the main continuo part. (The conventional tuning at Leipzig was at *Cammerton,* or "chamber pitch," while the transposed part was in *Chorton,* or "choir pitch.") Bach placed a copyist in charge of the transposition and afterwards, as was his custom, concerned himself with the continuo figures.[19]

The parts, much more than the autograph score, disclose details that help to reconstruct the original performance. The first horn part, for example, reveals that the horn player had to perform various movements at different transpositions, although the part makes no mention of the changes. While the horns play in F in the opening chorus and are therefore notated in C, Kuhnau left the first horn part untransposed in the final chorale. The player therefore realized that it would be necessary to transpose when he saw three flats in the key signature (or Bach may also have personally advised him about the change). In the case of the second horn part, the copyist, on Bach's instructions, omitted the two chorale movements and copied only the obbligatos. This might mean that Bach did not want to risk the inevitable problems of intonation that would result from two natural horns attempting to play *colla parte* with the chorus; it is also possible that the second horn player was occupied with another instrument (perhaps the violone) during the movements in which his obbligatos were not required. The first horn part therefore alludes to a convention which a contemporary player took for granted, while the second part clarifies a feature of orchestration about which the autograph score says nothing.

The continuo parts are also revealing. Although the organist, playing from Part 15, had figures in most movements (1, 3−7) to help realize the continuo, he had to make do with very sparse figures in Movement 2, a secco recitative, and without any in Movement 8, the final chorale. In the recitative, to compensate for the absence of a complete set of figures, the copyist provided the organist with a superimposed cue stave, that is, a textless copy of the vocal part he was to accompany. This means that the organist had to guess at the proper harmonies by comparing the bass with the melodic voice. (Even a practiced continuo player today would have trouble accompanying a recitative without the aid of figures.) Bach's organist had to follow the same procedure in the finale chorale, since he could not depend on the mere two figures that surface in the middle of the movement. Without any other cues, he had to gauge the harmonies by relying on his ear and his knowledge of the chorale tune.

The organist, moreover, was apparently not the only thorough-bass player, for Part 14 also contains continuo figures. In fact, the parts give us an indication of the time pressure under which Bach must have worked to produce two figured parts: instead of first figuring one continuo part and handing it to the copyist, Bach worked merely a step ahead of the copyist, as Table 1–1 reveals, apparently to speed up preparations for the rehearsal. Although one could imagine that, given two sets of figures, a copyist could have duplicated Bach's set at a later performance, the evident swap of bass parts between composer and assistant reveals that both were entered at the same time. This, in turn, suggests that someone else realized the continuo on an instrument tuned in *Cammerton*—such as the harpsichord—at the same time as the organ or that, for some other reason, a *Cammerton* part was furnished with a set of figures. The parts therefore help to reconstruct details of a par-

TABLE 1–1 Authorship of thorough-bass figures in the continuo parts for Cantata 40

	Part 14 (untransposed)	Part 15 (transposed)
Movement 1		
page 1	Bach	copyist
page 2	copyist	Bach
Movement 4		
staves 1–2	Bach	copyist
remainder	copyist	Bach
Movement 5	copyist	Bach
Movement 6	copyist	Bach
Movement 7	copyist	Bach

ticular performance at the same time that they allude to the tacit conventions of Bach's musicians.

How does a study of Bach's continuo group contribute to an understanding of the composer? First, one retrieves a sense of Bach at his workplace. As documentary evidence of daily life, the original parts bear witness to a wide variety of hectic circumstances as well as to Bach's remarkable flexibility in adapting to them—a flexibility that runs the gamut from fastidious concern to surprising neglect. On the one hand, there are indications of extreme care in Bach's preparation of his parts even for occasional works. On the other hand, there are, in certain orchestral parts, omissions of whole measures of music which Bach never saw fit to supply and which must have wreaked havoc at each subsequent performance. The parts tell a human story.

Second, the study of Bach's continuo group contributes to an understanding of practices that eighteenth-century musicians took for granted. The last twenty years have seen tremendous strides in the way Bach's music has been played, precisely because musicians have become increasingly familiar with historical conventions. Certain practices common to twentieth-century performances, however, require further clarification. The use of the organ as the only keyboard instrument in sacred music, the *sostenuto* rendition of secco recitative basses "as written," the presence of a bassoon wherever there are oboes, the inclusion of a 16-foot violone in any Bach work—all these practices contribute to an unconscious notion of how Bach sounds. This is why the restoration of forgotten conventions, if put into practice, poses such an exciting challenge: by refining, reformulating—and sometimes even refuting—twentieth-century notions about the performance of Bach, our sense of the composer and his works undergoes a subtle but decisive change. The conclusions reached in this book—that there was occasional dual accompaniment by harpsichord and organ, that bassists played the accompaniments in secco recitatives as detached quarter notes, that bassoons played only an adjunct role, that Bach's violone sometimes sounded at pitch—offer a fresh perspective on the ways Bach performed his works. Although these practices may not be deemed appropriate to every performance of Bach's works today, they nonetheless should stimulate thought about his intentions and the extent to which musicians today should realize them. Whatever choice is made, the interpretation of Bach's music can only gain in depth when we better understand how it was originally performed. And it is this extraordinary music, after all, that invites an ever-closer look.

CHAPTER II

The Organ and the Harpsichord

Keyboard Accompaniment in the Sacred Works

One of the most persistent controversies in Bach scholarship has re-volved around a simple question: Which keyboard instrument provided the accompaniments to Bach's sacred vocal music? Was it the organ or the harpsichord? Revived again and again in the literature over some seven decades, the controversy ran out of steam only in the mid-1930s when Arnold Schering published a lengthy study devoted in large part to Bach's keyboard practice.[1] Schering argued that Bach relied on the organ alone as the accompanying keyboard instrument in his church music, whereas he resorted to the harpsichord only to substitute for the organ during repairs or to accompany the traditional German motets. Although Schering never disputed Bach's use of the harpsichord to ac-company his secular ensemble music, he maintained that Bach excluded the harpsichord altogether from his sacred works—the church cantatas, passions, masses, and oratorios. It is no exaggeration to say that postwar scholarship not only has accepted Schering's conclusion but has ex-panded on it. As a result, the received wisdom regarding performances of Bach's works—organ for the church, harpsichord for the chamber—has acquired the status of an established fact, rarely subjected to serious scrutiny.

There are, however, good reasons to reexamine this question. First, the arguments banishing the harpsichord from the sacred works were never particularly compelling. The standard view, for example, had to dismiss documents stating that harpsichords played a role in church mu-sic. It also overlooked manuscript evidence not to its liking. By un-thinkingly accepting the neat division between two choices—*either* organ *or* harpsichord—scholarly argument maneuvered itself into an awkward corner. Even today the controversy remains embroiled in disputes extraneous to historical reconstruction. Debates over whether Bach is a colorful modernist experimenting with new forms or a severe traditionalist defending the faith—positions that inspired the conflict—are no longer relevant to modern-day performance practice. Yet remnants of this dispute exert a hidden influence on scholarly discussions by shaping the terms and tenor of the debate. Thus, when we take a fresh look at the question of Bach's keyboard accompaniments, an account of scholarly interest in the subject proves as relevant as a review of the historical record.

The argument in this chapter proposes a new theory for Bach's keyboard accompaniments, a theory that recognizes the primacy of organ continuo but at the same time takes account of the substantial role played by the harpsichord. The main advantage of this theory of "dual accompaniment" is that it explains more adequately than traditional views the documents and notational evidence attesting to the presence of the harpsichord in Bach's ensemble while retaining the strengths of the traditional argument favoring the organ.

Dual accompaniment rests on the claim that the organ was played in virtually all performances of Bach's sacred music. As Bach's pupil J. P. Kirnberger put it: "From time immemorial the organ has accompanied church music, providing the foundation and keeping the concerted music in good order."[2] Regarding Bach's Leipzig practice, the evidence for this claim is commanding. The organs in all Leipzig churches were constructed at the high *Chorton* (choir) pitch, largely to conserve on the metals used in their construction. The main body of the ensemble, however, played at the *Cammerton* (chamber) pitch, a whole tone lower. One can therefore easily distinguish the organ parts among Bach's orchestral sources, since they were always transposed down a whole step below ordinary performing pitch. Because *Chorton* continuo parts survive in the vast preponderance of extant part-sets for Bach's sacred works, the organ must surely have been a regular participant in those performances. This should come as no surprise: the close association in the Lutheran tradition between the organ and the chorale had already fostered the development of a rich solo repertoire, in which the instrument stood as the perfect symbol for the authority of the sacred realm. Even the apparently menial task of thorough-bass realization was imbued with theological significance. In sum, the association between the organ and the accompaniment of sacred music was never in any doubt.

The early eighteenth-century German harpsichord cannot compete with this rich iconography—nor should it have to. For without the organ/harpsichord dichotomy enforced by the controversy, Bach devotees might never have viewed the role of the harpsichord in sacred music differently from any other accompanying instrument. In other words, the harpsichord did not require a specific symbolic purpose in order to have enriched the divine service along with other instruments of the orchestra.

A composer would also have had a more practical reason for the inclusion of the harpsichord in performances of sacred music. Since the organist played with his back to the orchestra, the harpsichordist, sitting in full view of the whole ensemble, was in a far better position to guarantee its orderly cohesion. Moreover, with its sharp attack, the harpsichord could maintain a reliable link between the organist and the continuo basses as well as ensure communication between the instrumentalists and singers. Yet dual accompaniment does not mean that the harpsichord was a necessity in sacred music. Just like other nonobbligato instruments (such as the violone or the bassoon), the harpsichord was used intermittently during Bach's tenure at Leipzig (1723–1750) for a variety of practical, circumstantial, and aesthetic reasons. What the theory of dual accompaniment explains is a set of references to the harpsichord found both in the contemporary documents and in the Bach manuscript sources which otherwise proves baffling.

The Harpsichord Controversy

Current interest in the question of Bach's keyboard accompaniments rests primarily on the premises of modern historicism, which sees the composer's music in connection with the way it was originally performed. In other words, one asks what instruments Bach used so that his works can be performed authentically today. However, this premise did not inspire the original discussion. The roots of the controversy regarding the harpsichord are embedded in the polemics of the nineteenth-century Bach revival, polemics that now seem strangely arbitrary. Nonetheless, because echoes of these disputes continue to resound today, it is useful to reconstruct the debate in order to clarify why the seemingly innocuous matter of a church harpsichord should have become a matter for dispute in the first place.

The controversy began innocently enough when the composer Robert Franz, known today chiefly for his Lieder, published a set of modernized "practical arrangements" of Bach vocal works in the 1860s based on his own idiosyncratic performances. Franz was then director of university music at Halle, and took it upon himself to disseminate Romanticized arrangements, freely altering the original instrumentation to suit contemporary purposes. For example, Franz's continuo group for Cantata 106 consisted of a quartet of clarinets and bassoons which alternated with a richly layered organ part spanning three staves.[3] It was not long before these liberties came under vigorous attack as coloristic distortions by Franz's critics.[4] A sincere propagator of Bach's works, Franz took umbrage at this criticism of his efforts. He defended himself in an open letter to Eduard Hanslick in 1871, justifying his arrangements in this way: Since the old harpsichord, unlike the "monochromatic" pianoforte, had been capable of a wide variety of colors in its mixture of three registers, the updated arrangements preserved the spirit—if not the letter—of Bach's original conception.[5]

The most pronounced critique of Franz appeared the following year in a series of articles in the Leipzig *Allgemeine Musikalische Zeitung*. Here the medievalist Heinrich Bellermann framed his attack under the "scientific" banner of musicology. For Bellermann the debate centered on the question of color, particularly in the way contemporary composers employed it to achieve—in his view—cheap tonal effects. Applying this modernistic excess to old music, particularly the pure and objective polyphony of Bach, was the height of impropriety, according to Bellermann. His antidote was historical factualism based on the latest scholarship. Bach used the organ—Bellermann assured his readers—only in tutti sections of large-scale movements to support his weak choristers, while he used the harpsichord everywhere else. His authority was Friedrich Chrysander, who had described in an article published in 1863 the practice of alternating continuo accompaniments in performances of Handel's *Saul*.[6] Bellermann's antipathy for the organ—strange in light of later developments in the Bach Movement (*Bach-Bewegung*)—stemmed from its associations with coloristic decadence. With its manifold stops and registers, the organ was especially inappropriate for the black-and-white objectivity of Bach's music. Yet in his practical recommendations, Bellermann did not hesitate to recommend substituting the piano as the closest modern approximation to the harpsichord. Bellermann's criticism of Franz therefore dramatized a crucial moment in the nineteenth-century reception of Bach. Romantic arbitrariness was dethroned, and in its place, historical rectitude was to reign supreme.

When Philipp Spitta, the most imposing Bach scholar of his day, came to correct Bellermann's misguided ideas, he proceeded from nearly identical assumptions.[7] One difference was his more thorough research. From his intimate familiarity with both the Bach sources and the historical documents bearing on the organ and the harpsichord, he concluded that organ accompaniment was ubiquitous in Bach's sacred works. Spitta, however, held a contradictory view of the harpsichord. Although he took the trouble to cite all the known sources that pointed to its use, he then proceeded to deny that they had any significance. If only because Spitta's argument remained the *locus classicus* for the next hundred years of the controversy, it is worthwhile to sort out his motivations. This stage of the controversy took place in those significant years following German unification termed the *Gründerjahre,* or the "foundation years," of 1871–1873. This period—critical for the future of the Bach Movement—saw an immense surge of German national feeling that was channeled into Bismarck's "cultural struggle" (*Kulturkampf*), which condemned the forces of "progress, liberalism and modern civilization."[8] Just as Spitta's famous misdating of the chorale cantatas was based on a historiographic prejudice—Bach's supposed advance to the mature chorale cantatas—so his exclusion of the harpsichord from the sacred works betrays a bias that affects both the facts of the controversy and their interpretation.

This bias has both nationalist and theological components. Throughout his erudite biography of the composer (1873, 1880), Spitta emphasizes that because of Bach's historical stature, an appreciation of his work could help to reinstate the religious ideals native to the German people, to inaugurate a new epoch of national greatness and theological purification following the political events of 1871. The preface (1873), in which Spitta permits himself a personal statement, exhibits this attitude best:

I hold firmly to the belief in the ever growing significance of Bach for the German nation, to whom . . . he decidedly belongs in all his thought, deed and emotion. When my preliminary studies on Germany's greatest church composer began, I did not think that its publication would occur at a time which proves by its fierce spiritual struggles how deeply (despite all signs to the contrary) the religious need inheres in the German people. Even more than those sterling political triumphs, the mighty religious impulses stirring the deepest being of our people herald the approach of a new and great age. And just as religion always nurtures art, so too will religion now bear the seed from which music once sprouted her new ideals . . . Almost incomprehensible in scope and content, the great, sacred artworks of this man, whom we can easily call the personified musical genius of the German people, cannot have been put in the world to disappear without a trace after a few inadequate performances. These works must—they will—become alive in the people . . . If only I have contributed to such a mighty goal![9]

Consider this passage in conjunction with Spitta's first mention of the harpsichord controversy later in the first volume:

We have previously shown that the style of Bach's church music, with all its idiosyncrasies, resulted from organ music. In order to keep this feeling unrelentingly alive, the uninterrupted engagement of this power was necessary to govern and unite disparate elements. For it alone was capable of creating true church music. Although an attempt was made under Italian influence to introduce accompanying harpsichords into the churches, it is significant, if also self-evident, that Bach steadfastly used only the organ for his thorough-bass accompaniments. Remove the organ and the soul has gone: only a machine remains.[10]

Although this Italian influence is questionable, Spitta's dichotomy between organ and harpsichord could not be more striking. Whereas the organ represents the soul, the harpsichord represents a machine. This depiction reflects a similar nineteenth-century prejudice against the harpsichord which saw in its lack of dynamic range an absence of expression. But Spitta's harpsichord not only lacks a soul: it becomes morally tainted when introduced into church music. This is the same "Italian" usage which he later terms a "mongrel" or "hermaphrodite" practice *(eine zwitterhafte Praxis)* as well as a "wicked habit" *(eine Unsitte).*[11] Spitta's moral repugnance is such that he would have us believe in the complete incompatibility of the harpsichord with sacred music. The metaphors of "machine" and "mongrel" may appear mixed, but both express a powerful wish to banish the harpsichord from sacred music, a realm circumscribed by expressivity, propriety, and moral purity.

All the same, Spitta did not suppress evidence pointing to Bach's use of the harpsichord. On the contrary, in a remarkable appendix entry that accompanies the passage just cited, he vividly recounts evidence that directly threatened his conclusion. Unmoved, he assimilated all of it to his argument. The fact that Handel, for example, failed to regard the organ as central to his oratorios is chalked up to the influence of the Italians, "who transferred both their chamber music and their theatrical traditions to their church music." When Johann Mattheson recommended in 1739 that harpsichords be combined with organs in church music, he too was Italianate. As for a report by the Leipzig chronicler Sicul that Bach played the harpsichord in his performance of the *Trauer-Ode* (Cantata 198), this "only serves to prove that Bach did not usually employ it." A score to Cantata 80, "Ein' feste Burg ist unser Gott" (hardly an Italianate work), copied by Bach's son-in-law, supplies two bass lines, one "Violoncello e cembalo" and the other "Violone ed organo," and yet Spitta supposes "that the word 'Cembalo' [harpsichord] was used very loosely." Likewise, when Spitta quotes Bach's pupil Kittel as saying that pupils accompanied on the harpsichord whenever Bach performed church cantatas, he adds that "this of course can only mean (although imprecisely) a rehearsal." What about figured *Cammerton* continuo parts found next to figured organ parts for the same cantata? "Naturally this does not mean that both were played when the piece was performed," Spitta relates, but that the harpsichord part was used for "rehearsals which did not take place in church." [12]

Spitta's meticulous scholarship elsewhere is so legendary that his twisted argument must be seen in the context of his ideological prejudices. In his words: "[Unlike Handel or Mattheson,] Bach always adhered to the pure German principle and had as little to do with a harpsichord in church as he did with theater music . . . As Bach was the only composer who wrote in the true church style, it ought not to surprise us if he alone gave the organ its due." [13] Seven years elapsed before the appearance of the second volume of his Bach biography (1880). In the intervening years Spitta collected additional evidence pointing to the presence of the harpsichord, which forced him to amend his argument. Yet nowhere does he retract his statements from Volume 1. Indeed, the glaring contradiction between his two pronouncements seems to account for the subsequent longevity of the controversy. For all later arguments both for and against the harpsichord ultimately derive from two irreconcilable views in Spitta's text.

Spitta's new interpretation evidently followed his examination of Leipzig church expenditures. Here he found that both Johann Kuhnau, Bach's predecessor, and Bach himself had maintained harpsichords in the choir lofts of the Thomas-Kirche and the Nikolai-Kirche. Accordingly, he speculated that "from the thirtieth year of the century onward . . . it ceased to be the fashion for the conductor to stand and beat time all through the piece, and . . . it became more and more usual to conduct from the harpsichord . . . Thus order was preserved not only by mute signs but by audible musical effect." After a lengthy citation from Emanuel Bach on the advantages of conducting from the harpsichord— the younger Bach is not, however, discussing sacred music—Spitta concluded that "this is clear testimony that Sebastian Bach availed himself of this method." [14] One can only infer that Spitta thought that Bach practiced some form of dual accompaniment.

Nevertheless, Spitta obscured this inference in countless ways. Since the record of expenditures in the Thomas-Kirche was missing for the years 1743–1750, he concluded—unjustifiably—that the harpsichord had been removed from the church. This in turn prompted the statement that Bach turned away from the practice in his later years. In confronting a description by Gesner depicting Bach directing from the harpsichord or in reviewing Kittel's statement regarding a student harpsichordist at cantata performances, Spitta still insisted that these descriptions referred to rehearsals.[15] But even the suggestion that Bach might have used a harpsichord at the main Saturday rehearsals in church made him uncomfortable—for if someone played the harpsichord on Saturday, what would have prevented him from playing it on Sunday morning? Uneasy with his new disclosures, Spitta weakened his later stand on the harpsichord with spurious qualifications, thereby lending credence to his previous pronouncements banning it altogether.

The pendulum swung back to the harpsichord in 1904, when Max Seiffert offered a new interpretation purportedly based on a study of the manuscript sources. This paper, delivered at the 1904 Bach-Fest by an authoritative scholar, again raised the heat of polemic. The new facts in this case, either errors or misrepresentations, mattered less than the central fiber of the old debate: was Bach the symbol of theological rectitude or was he a precursor to Romantic expressivity? Seiffert, updating Robert Franz, inveighs against the purists: "I hardly need describe what passes for . . . a stylistically correct [*stilvolle*] Bach performance. Whoever dares shake the traditional, stuffy wig is branded . . . a state criminal by critics and pedantic colleagues. Instead, monotony, solemnity, [and] nothing extra—this alone is authentic!"[16] In this context, the reintroduction of the harpsichord into church accompaniments provides an antidote for antiseptic respect. To support this view, Seiffert claims—with entirely unwarranted conviction—that "so far as the performance materials to the Bach cantatas are preserved, one regularly finds, in addition to the required continuo parts for the bass instruments, a continuo part *pro Organo* and one *pro Cembalo* . . . Organ and harpsichord: these are the two keyboard instruments without which one cannot perform a Bach cantata."

Although Seiffert proposes dual accompaniment, he cautions that both instruments did not function simultaneously during a complete church cantata: this "would be as much a fundamental error as asserting that the organ is the only adequate accompanying instrument for the cantatas."[17] According to Seiffert, only in the opening chorus and closing chorale would both organ and harpsichord play together; otherwise it fell to the harpsichordist to accompany the recitatives and arias. His evidence consisted of, first, a statement recommending this practice by C. P. E. Bach, and second, the original parts for two cantatas (Cantatas 139 and 177) in which Bach supposedly made this practice explicit.[18] Considering that Seiffert ignored Spitta's well-known account of Bach's keyboard accompaniments, it is surprising that the former's weak argument carried as much weight as it apparently did. Although certain contemporaries knew that he had grossly misrepresented his sources,[19] Seiffert had evidently struck a sympathetic chord by arguing in favor of Bach as "expressionist." His argument thus became one with which historians reckoned until well into the 1930s.

The next stage of the controversy saw few original contributors.[20] Only Max Schneider, in an article from 1915, furnished the harpsichord question with a measure of sobriety during this period. Although he presented no new evidence, Schneider reviewed the contemporary reports and documents (Sicul, Wild, Kittel, Gesner, Emanuel Bach), which Spitta had already detailed, but left no doubt that Bach's sacred accompaniments made use of dual accompaniment. He concluded that:

1. Bach directed his ensemble as its first violinist and took over difficult accompaniments (at the harpsichord) on occasion.

2. Pupils regularly realized the continuo part on the organ and the harpsichord.

3. The use of the organ and harpsichord in church is a fact; no scheme exists for a division of labor between the two instruments. The (old) preponderance of the organ is proved by the surviving manuscript parts, whereas the harpsichord plays a substantially greater role than has hitherto been recognized.[21]

Although Schneider read the historical documents more dispassionately than his predecessors, his suspicion of the premises of the "strict" historical school led to the subsequent neglect of his findings. For this reason, despite his reasonable summation, the controversy did not end here. For Schneider remained unmoved by the imperatives of "authenticity," which equated aesthetic decisions with historical reconstruction; instead he supposed that one might conceive of various possibilities for Bach's thorough-bass practice. More important, he intentionally subordinated the historical question (how did Bach perform his sacred accompaniments?) to the pragmatic aims of contemporary performance (how might we realize them?). But in so doing, he unintentionally sabotaged his own influence on the wide circle of Bach devotees. To Schneider, the idea of resurrecting dual accompaniment made a "virtue of necessity," since it was no more than an auxiliary aid that Bach was forced to use. Moreover, he claims, Bach employed this method of accompaniment to maintain order in his poorly schooled ensemble and "without special regard for tonal beauty."[22] One can imagine the effect of such views on the early twentieth-century Bach Movement. To orthodox ears, Schneider's hasty dismissal of historicism placed him squarely in the camp of Romantic distorters. By revealing a point of view at odds with mainstream Bach studies, Schneider undercut the influence of his conclusions, quite apart from the fact that his historical argument for the harpsichord could be read entirely on its own.

The controversy took a new turn in 1932 when Charles Sanford Terry published his carefully documented study, *Bach's Orchestra*, which detached questions of history from those of modern practice. Although he subscribed to the German moral imperative—Bach should be performed according to the composer's intentions—Terry believed that a historian's job was to assemble the facts. He was the first to single out Spitta's bias against the harpsichord, although his criticism took issue with Spitta's shaky logic rather than his ideological allegiances. Terry pointed out several harpsichord parts among the original sources for the vocal works and noted Bach's request in 1724 that the Town Council repair the harpsichord in the Nikolai-Kirche before a performance of the St. John Passion, stating that "these instances, though not numerous, suffice to indicate that Bach's attitude towards the harpsichord was not antagonistic, as Spitta supposes."[23]

Yet Terry too opposed dual accompaniment. His rejection of it, however, invoked common sense instead of German ideology. That two figured continuo parts "were used simultaneously" he finds "an improbable explanation."[24] "A more reasonable explanation," he counters, "(is that the parts were employed alternately) . . . if we remember that Bach's cantatas received repeated performances, and that his organs, as has been shown, were not seldom undergoing repair." But even if Terry believed that this organ repair hypothesis explained the existence of the figured *Cammerton* continuo parts, he would still have to suppress a common-sense reading of the documents he had just cited: Kittel's student harpsichordist, harpsichord accompaniment in the *Trauer-Ode,* and the harpsichord repair preceding the Passion performance. Terry's objection to dual accompaniment was therefore primarily aesthetic, as if two continuo realizations necessarily led to pandemonium.

Of all the scholars embroiled in the controversy, Arnold Schering is undoubtedly the most passionate, for he devotes more than half of his influential monograph, *Johann Sebastian Bachs Leipziger Kirchenmusik—*

still a standard text in the field—to excluding the harpsichord from all but the most peripheral association with Bach's sacred music. Because of Seiffert, he claims, "opinion had again shifted in favor of the harpsichord,"[25] and he thereupon launches an elaborate argument of some 100 pages dedicated to clarifying once and for all the details of Bach's continuo practice. Schering had long held a vested interest in the controversy. As early as 1921, he dealt in a cursory way with the problem in an article on Bach's method of parody. How, he asks, can Bach have taken a secular cantata, exchanged the texts, and then used the same music in church? The answer, for Schering, lies in the sacred work's transformed meaning, caused primarily by the substitution of the organ for the harpsichord: "In the transplanting of an initially secular piece into church, the organ accompaniment compensates [for the work's origins]."[26] If Schering's attitude seems curious, it is because the sacred parody of a secular work endangered his own hermeneutic position, according to which "the meaning of a musical work, particularly a vocal work, is always singular." In short, a piece of music could not be both sacred and secular. Schering's philosophy, ringing with metaphysical overtones, dovetailed neatly with Spitta's allegory of the sacred organ and the secular harpsichord. Although Schering had disposed of the nationalist rhetoric, the theological garb shrouding the controversy remained intact.

Nowhere does this bias appear more prominently than in the 1936 monograph, which, Schering relates in his Preface, he would like to have called "Paths to Bach." These paths "lie neither in the aesthetic nor in the general realm of art-history, but rather where the great master even today is reachable both as human being and artist: in his daily work as cantor and director of church music." It comes as no surprise, then, when Schering—presenting the fruits of his painstaking research—rehearses and extends Spitta's arguments against the harpsichord. The stakes, again, were far higher than a mere historical determination of Bach's keyboard practice. Indeed, they threatened to undermine the very core of Bach's reception within prewar German culture.

Although Schering had researched the original sources and documents even more rigorously than Spitta, his starting point was identical. The nineteenth- and twentieth-century idea of harpsichord accompaniment in church, he insists, arose from mistakenly applying Italian and specifically Handelian practices to conditions in Leipzig. The frequently cited statement by Emanuel Bach calling for a form of dual accompaniment, Schering continues, can have nothing to do with his father's practice because an overwhelming number of corresponding harpsichord parts do not exist in the Leipzig sources. The practice of using the harpsichord in church simply "goes against German church custom." Why should this be so? As Schering puts it, paraphrasing Spitta: "It is very probable that with the sound of the harpsichord the image of secular, particularly operatic music emerged, arousing the suspicion that a sacrilegious element is intruding in church."[27]

Since the Leipzig chronicler had mentioned the harpsichord in the *Trauer-Ode* performance at the same time that he noted the "Italian taste" of this special work, and since Bach was contractually forbidden (as were all his immediate predecessors) to compose "operatic" music for the church, Schering supposed that Bach had theological grounds for neglecting the harpsichord in his sacred works. But if this were so, Schering must have found it strange that Johann Kuhnau (Thomas-Cantor from 1701 to 1722), well known for his opposition to the Leipzig opera, had petitioned the town council in 1710 for funds to maintain the harpsichords in both main churches, hoping to use them at cantata performances.[28] Although the absence of a large number of extant harpsichord parts in the Bach sources seemed to support Schering's view, he was unjustified in concluding that the use of the harpsichord in Leipzig sacred works was traditionally "sacrilegious."

Thus Schering knew that the harpsichords were present in the Leipzig churches but refused to consider that they might be intended for regular use in cantata accompaniments. This refusal ultimately structures his entire argument. Without following each deliberate turn, it is revealing to consider two new topics that Schering added to the controversy: the use of a small, portative organ to play the figured *Cammerton* parts, and the retention of the harpsichord to accompany the old German motets.

For those few Leipzig parts explicitly labeled "Cembalo," Schering was content to view them as exceptional cases for times when, in an emergency, Bach was forced to substitute the harpsichord for the organ.[29] But for the substantially greater number of figured *Cammerton* parts, which even Spitta and Terry had seen as harpsichord parts, Schering proposed a new solution. If Bach had been averse to the harpsichord in cantata accompaniments, he would more likely have used one of the portable organs from the Thomas-Schule to substitute for the main organ when it underwent repairs. The chief candidate here was the so-called portable *Trauungspositiv* which Kuhnau had purchased in 1720 for use at house weddings. Schering refers to a letter Kuhnau wrote to Johann Mattheson in 1717, in which the Thomas-Cantor stated that he had changed the performance standard of the orchestra from *Chorton* to *Cammerton*,[30] and guesses from this that Kuhnau probably had the *Trauungspositiv* built in *Cammerton* as well.

This claim is questionable on several counts. First, Kuhnau, who had changed the standard Leipzig performing pitch from *Chorton* to *Cammerton* (or as he calls it, high *Cornett-Ton*), conceded that the switch would inconvenience the organists, who would henceforth have to play from transposed parts. Second, there is no evidence that any Leipzig organ was tuned in *Cammerton* before 1756, when Bach's successor, Doles, noted that a new *Positiv* was to be tuned in *Cammerton*.[31] Third, there is cause to believe that the *Trauungspositiv*, like all other organs, was indeed tuned in *Chorton:* the original parts for the three wedding chorales (BWV 250-252) include a *Chorton* part labeled *Organo*. If, as even Schering supposed, Bach took the portable *Trauungspositiv* from the Thomas-Schule to the wedding service at a private home, then it was played from a transposed part.

If Bach maintained the harpsichords in the two main Leipzig churches but excluded them from cantata accompaniments, then what use, according to Schering, did he have for them? To answer this question, Schering proposed that the harpsichords accompanied the introit motets contained in the seventeenth-century collection *Florilegium Portense,* published by Erhard Bodenschatz in 1618 and 1621.[32] Known to have been sung in the Leipzig service, this printed set of traditional pieces by composers such as Calvisius, Hassler, Praetorius, Marenzio, and the two Gabrielis included a simple continuo part at pitch. Schering reasoned that, since no transposed parts in *Chorton* survive, the harpsichord must have accompanied the choir. But this theory does not really rescue Schering's conclusion, for he could not explain why the harpsichord posed a secular threat in the cantatas but not in the motets. Nor could he clarify why the Council would have appropriated annual sums for the maintenance of the harpsichords if they were only to play the most rudimentary bass parts in these simple introit motets. Most implausible of all, Schering's restriction of the harpsichord to the introit motets conflicts with the documents stating that the harpsichord accompanied sacred cantatas. This is why his argument first disposed of every positive sign of harpsichord participation before offering the transparent hypothesis of motet accompaniment. Only with this overpowering need to rescue Bach's sacred music from the taint of secularism could Schering have sustained such a protracted circumlocution.[33]

Thus, even though the "harpsichord controversy" did not mean the same thing to all its participants, it retained a coherence beyond its shifting concerns by framing the terms of the debate under a seemingly inescapable yet attractive opposition—organ versus harpsichord. But to all who accept this dichotomy, one must pose several questions. Is it historically justified to view the harpsichord as a sign of secularity antagonistic to sacred music? Do commentators in early eighteenth-century Germany associate the sound of the harpsichord with Italian opera? Do eighteenth-century writers question the propriety of harpsichords in church? Do eighteenth-century critics argue against the combination of organ and harpsichord in church music, or for that matter, against any duplication of instruments realizing continuo?

The controversy itself has clouded a historical view of the questions it pretends to answer. To attain any clarity about Bach's accompaniments, one must question the central analogy: that the organ opposes the harpsichord in the way that the sacred opposes the secular. To proceed in the usual manner—by reasoning inductively from the musical sources and then interpreting the documents—unwittingly retains the loaded apparatus from the past. Although it may seem paradoxical, a new chapter in the controversy over the harpsichord in Bach's sacred music can be written only after the motivations that sparked it have been laid to rest.

Evidence of Harpsichords in Churches

Already during the tenure of Johann Kuhnau as Thomas-Cantor (1701–1722), large harpsichords were installed and played in both main churches.[34] In a "Reminder by the Cantor regarding the School- and Church-Music" from 1709, Kuhnau points out: "It would be desirable to allocate funds for the upkeep of the two large harpsichords found in both churches, to which belongs at the very least the annual interest of 300 Thalers; for in case one wants to use them, they must be tuned anew for each cantata performance and in their present condition could hardly be put back in order for less than 6 to 7 Thalers."[35]

As a major center for Lutheran sacred music, Leipzig apparently set a fashionable tone in its use of church harpsichords. Johann Samuel Beyer (1669–1744), Cantor and Director of Music at the Freiberg cathedral, after first lending his own harpsichord for church use, petitioned the local authorities in 1726 (during Bach's third year at Leipzig) to purchase their own, because he deemed "most necessary a special accompaniment [*ein apartes Accompagnement*] with a harpsichord, as is usual in Leipzig and in other noble locales, also for their Passions, Resurrection pieces and most other solemn concerted works."[36] Whatever Beyer's motives may have been, the Leipzig practice was evidently notable enough to be emulated elsewhere.

Harpsichords also played a role in sacred music in northern Germany.

In his early work of 1713, *Das neu-eröffnete Orchestre,* Johann Mattheson makes it clear that he prefers harpsichords to regals in church. The harpsichord, he writes, is "an accompanying, almost indispensable foundation to church-, theatre-, and chamber music and it is really surprising that in the churches of this town people still use the snarling, loathsome regal; for the rustling, lisping harmony of the harpsichord—one can use a pair of them in special circumstances—has a far finer effect with the choir."[37] And in the final chapter of his *Vollkommener Capellmeister,* entitled "On Conducting, Direction, Production and Execution of a Concert," Mattheson even recommends dual accompaniment in sacred music. Discussing how difficult it is for a good music director to arrange his ensemble, he notes that "regals are of no use here [while] the . . . harpsichord is fine everywhere and is much nicer than the former. Though it would not be bad for a number of reasons if nice and quickly-speaking small positive organs without the reed stop could be united with the harpsichord in churches, or even if a pair of the last-named were present if there is a strong chorus."[38]

From Mattheson's recommendation it would appear that, in the interest of good ensemble, he did not make use of the principal church organ in concerted works: hence his proposed combination of the harpsichord with a small *Positiv.* Beginning with Spitta, Mattheson was discounted as a Handelian proponent of Italian opera, of secular influence, and so on.[39] But even if Mattheson cannot attest to Bach's practice, his text establishes a precedent for the performance of Protestant sacred music in which, first, the harpsichord found a rightful place, and second, it played simultaneously with an organ.

One practical reason for harpsichord accompaniments in church was that a conductor, seated at the keyboard, could lead singers and instrumentalists most easily when he had them directly in view. Coordinating the ensemble from the organist's bench was far more difficult. A document dating from 1724 makes this quite clear. An unsuccessful applicant for the municipal cantor's position in Weissenfels, Gottlob Christian Springsfeldt, registered a complaint with the civic authorities regarding what he considered to be an unfair audition. In the first place, he was given a piece to sing that lay far above the range that a normal tenor could manage. Moreover, in a piece he was to direct, "the accompanying fundamental instrument, played normally in addition to the organ [so sonst ausser der Orgel]," was taken away from him, and he was forced to conduct from the organ. The audition, he reported, would have gone far better if he could have stayed put "because from [the organ] the beat cannot be seen and observed."[40] If Springsfeldt's "accompanying fundamental instrument" is taken to be a harpsichord—and what other continuo instrument would be designated so abstractly?—then his testimony presents strong evidence for dual accompaniment in Saxon church music as well as explaining why it was desirable.

Harpsichord Participation during Bach's Tenure at Leipzig

Harpsichords in the Main Leipzig Churches

There can be no doubt that a harpsichord was in use in both the Thomas-Kirche and the Nikolai-Kirche during the greater part, if not all, of Bach's tenure as Thomas-Cantor. The records show a repair of the harpsichord in the Thomas-Kirche as soon as Bach arrived in Leipzig in 1723. Thereafter, the church records note tuning costs and adjustments every year through 1743. Although the entries in the Thomas-Kirche records for tuning and repairs are missing from 1744 until 1750, the allocated funds seem to have been paid through 1744 to Johann Gottlieb Neuhaus, who began tuning and adjusting the instruments in the Thomas-Kirche and the Nikolai-Kirche in 1739–1740, and from 1744 to 1751 to Christian Gottfried Eichlern, who also took care of the harpsichord in the Nikolai-Kirche. Expenditures appear once again for the years 1751 to 1756, after which a new instrument was acquired, "the old one becoming so unusable that it could not be repaired."[41] Thus, in all likelihood, the instrument that Bach used in the Thomas-Kirche continued to function until 1756, six years after his death.

More precise information is known about the harpsichord in the Nikolai-Kirche. Bach himself was reimbursed for repair and maintenance costs in 1723, and in subsequent years the instrument was generally kept in working condition.[42] Only for a brief period in 1724 did this harpsichord become unusable, and, significantly, the document recording this fact demonstrates Bach's eagerness to have the instrument repaired. Four days before Good Friday in 1724 the Town Council informed Bach that the Passion service would be held in the Nikolai-Kirche, not in the Thomas-Kirche, as had originally been planned. To this notification Bach responded:

> He would comply with same, but pointed out . . . that there was no room available and that the harpsichord needed some repair, all of which could be arranged at little cost; but he requested that a little additional room be provided in the choir loft and that the harpsichord be repaired . . .
>
> [The Council replied:]

The Cantor should, at the expense of the . . . council, have . . . the necessary arrangements made in the choir loft with the aid of the sexton and have the harpsichord [das Clav-Cymbel] repaired.[43]

This document describes preparations for the initial performance of the St. John Passion (BWV 245), Bach's first large-scale undertaking after arriving in Leipzig in 1723. Particularly striking is Bach's repeated insistence on the harpsichord repair, as if its presence were indispensable to the performance. The cantor would hardly have formulated his response to the Council's last-minute change in plans so forcefully if he had only required the harpsichord for rehearsals. Moreover, both Bach's request and the Council's reply display a matter-of-fact quality that underscores the ordinariness of the exchange. The document does not mention the organ, but there is no reason to doubt its participation in the performance. Unlike the 1736 version of the St. Matthew Passion with its two continuo sections, the St. John Passion requires only one continuo group, so that Bach's effort to secure the harpsichord in advance of the performance seems to indicate that both instruments took part in the continuo realization.[44]

The Organ Repair Hypothesis

The literature of the harpsichord controversy often makes reference to what can be termed the "organ repair hypothesis," in which the harpsichord is understood to have been used only when one of the main organs was unplayable.[45] Accordingly, evidence substantiating the use of the harpsichord—whether in the documents or in the musical sources— is attributed to an emergency substitution for a malfunctioning organ. One would think from this argument that periods of repair were frequent and extensive; in fact, they were exceptionally rare. Excluding repairs that took place during the *tempus clausum,* when concerted music was forbidden, only two major repairs were undertaken on Bach's principal organs during his entire tenure at Leipzig (1723–1750).

The first of these took place in 1725 on the instrument in the Nikolai-Kirche, while the second occurred in 1747 in the Thomas-Kirche. Yet only the second repair could have forced Bach to substitute the harpsichord for the organ. Riemer's *Chronicle* of 1725 relates that the organ in the Nikolai-Kirche "was played continuously despite the work being done on it."[46] And if the organ functioned in the midst of a major repair, it must also have functioned during a minor repair, such as the one Schering describes as having taken place on the Nikolai organ in 1726–1727. A cantata accompaniment, after all, required only minimal organ support—one or two registers would suffice. Even if one register were unavailable, the continuo player would surely have used another for the accompaniment. Admittedly, this recourse was impossible for a period of four months in 1747 when the Thomas-Kirche organ, according to reports, was totally unplayable.[47] In all, then, four months remain out of the twenty-seven years at Leipzig in which Bach must have relied on a secondary keyboard instrument to play the continuo accompaniment. Clearly, the organ repair hypothesis is untenable.

The Harpsichord as a Continuo Instrument

A 1727 letter of reference from Bach for his pupil Friedrich Gottlieb Wild offers compelling testimony regarding the performance of the harpsichord in church:

Whereas Herr Friedrich Gottlieb Wild, Cand. Juris, and noted musician, has asked the undersigned to furnish him with a letter of recommendation . . . I have thought it no more than my Christian duty to testify to the fact that the said Monsieur Wild, during the four years that he has lived here at the university, has always shown himself to be diligent and hard-working, in such wise that he not only has helped to adorn our church music with his well-learned accomplishments on the *Flute traversière* and the *Clavecin* [dass er nicht allein Unsere Kirchen Music durch seine wohlerlernte Flaute-traversiere und Clavecin zieren hellfen], but has also taken instruction from me in the Clavier, thorough bass and the fundamental rules of composition based thereupon.[48]

Wild, then, appears to have played the harpsichord during Bach's first four years at Leipzig, that is, when the composer wrote and performed the vast majority of his sacred cantatas.[49] If the harpsichord had been used merely to replace the organ on rare occasions, the text would scarcely describe this as "adorning our church music." Nor can the letter be taken to refer to the harpsichord as an obbligato instrument: the few harpsichord obbligatos in the cantatas are exceptional. Only if the letter refers to Wild's continuo playing at performances does it make any sense.[50] Since Wild made use of the letter to apply for a position at the Jakobi-Kirche in Chemnitz, it is probable that he wanted his continuo playing positively evaluated. Finally, there is no suggestion that this mention of Wild's harpsichord playing was in any way unusual or would have been thought inappropriate by the Chemnitz authorities. The very ordinary quality of the language undermines one of the central tenets of the harpsichord controversy: that Bach considered the use of the harpsichord in church a secular intrusion.

Even more explicit testimony regarding the student harpsichordists appears in a reminiscence written by one of Bach's last pupils, Johann Christian Kittel (1732–1809). Kittel had come to Leipzig as a young Thomaner chorister in 1748, two years before Bach's death, and wrote the following account in an organ treatise published in 1808: "When Sebastian Bach performed a piece of church music, one of his most capable pupils always had to accompany on the harpsichord. It will easily be guessed that no one dared put forth a meager thorough-bass accompaniment. Nevertheless, one always had to be prepared to have Bach's hands and fingers intervene among the hands and fingers of the player, and, without getting in the way of the latter, furnish the accompaniment with masses of harmonies which made an even greater impression than the unsuspected close proximity of the teacher."[51] This document, a perennial stumbling block to opponents of the harpsichord, reveals a good deal about the apparently informal manner of Bach's performances of church music. Although it is true that Kittel wrote down the anecdote at the age of 76, there is every reason to take him at his word. In 1748 he was already 16 years of age, certainly old enough to be impressed with such a fundamental detail. Moreover, his story makes particular sense in light of the Wild recommendation, which had already established a precedent for a student harpsichordist performing in church.[52]

But does Kittel's story in fact amount to what Spitta calls a "fantastic scene"? Hardly. After all, cantata performances took place in a choir loft, not a concert hall. Considering the amateur performers and the limited rehearsal time for such demanding music, it would be surprising if Bach had *not* intervened with constant cues and verbal directions. To suppose that a solemn formality prevailed in the choir galleries anachronistically imposes the atmosphere of awe attached to Bach performances by the Romantic tradition.

A further indication that Bach put up with consistently hectic conditions appears, curiously, in a footnote to a passage from Quintilian's *Institutiones Oratoriae,* edited by Johann Matthias Gesner and published in 1738. At the time a professor of classics at Göttingen, Gesner first met Bach at Weimar and later (1729–1734) became his colleague as Rector of the Thomas-Schule. Quintilian is speaking of the ability of a *cithara* player to do several things at once, such as singing, playing his instrument, and beating time with his foot. Gesner remarks:

You would think but slightly, my dear Fabius, of all these, if, returning from the underworld, you could see Bach (to mention him particularly, since he was not long ago my colleague at the Thomas-Schule), either playing our harpsichord [*polychordum*], which is many citharas in one, with all the fingers of both hands, or running over the keys of the instrument of instruments [*organon organorum*], whose innumerable pipes are brought to life by bellows, with both hands and, at the utmost speed, with his feet, producing by himself the most various and at the same time mutually agreeable combinations of sounds in orderly procession. If you could see him, I say, doing what many of your citharoedists and six hundred of your tibia players together could not do, not only, like a citharoedist, singing with one voice and playing his own parts, but watching over everything and bringing back to the rhythm and the beat, out of thirty or even forty musicians, the one with a nod, another by tapping the foot, the third with a warning finger, giving the right note to one from the top of his voice, to another from the bottom, and to a third from the middle of it—all alone, in the midst of the greatest din made by all the participants, and, although he is executing the most difficult parts himself, noticing at once whenever and wherever a mistake occurs, holding everyone together, taking precautions everywhere, and repairing any unsteadiness, full of rhythm in every part of his body—this one man taking in all these harmonies with his keen ear and emitting with his voice alone the tone of all the voices. Favorer as I am of antiquity, the accomplishments of our Bach, and of any others that there may be like him, appear to me to effect what not many Orpheuses, nor twenty Arions, could achieve.[53]

While fascinating in its flowery detail, this passage raises certain puzzling questions. Has Gesner described a rehearsal or a performance? From which instrument or position is Bach directing his ensemble? What does Gesner mean by "the most difficult parts" which Bach himself plays? The meaning of the text is not altogether clear on any of these points, so that any reading must remain hypothetical.[54] Schering reads the passage as a fantastic, atypical depiction of a rehearsal in the school, believing such antics during a worship service to be quite incredible.[55] Whether the conjured scene is a rehearsal or a performance remains unclear; more to the point is the fact that the passage details Bach's conducting from the harpsichord.

It also seems likely that Gesner is describing not one extended scene, but in fact two scenes. In the first (which begins "if . . . you could see Bach . . .") he depicts Bach as the famous keyboardist, either at the harpsichord or at the organ, where Gesner admires the agility, speed, and combination of sounds which "Bach alone produces." No ensemble is implied here; in fact, the description tallies with many others characterizing Bach as a solo player. In the second scene Gesner recalls Bach the director (beginning with a parallel opening, "If you could see him . . ."), not only comparing him to the citharoedist (who, in contrast to the citharist, sings and accompanies himself simultaneously) but also describing him as controlling as many as forty other musicians. There is no reference at all to the organ, only to the cithara. As a plucked string instrument, the cithara most closely evokes the harpsichord, earlier called the *polychordum* because of its strings, but especially because it was defined as "many citharas in one." But if Bach is directing from the harpsichord, can he merely be realizing the continuo? Gesner explicitly states a few lines later that Bach is "executing the most difficult parts himself." Although a nonmusician might think continuo playing a challenge (particularly with Bach's reported penchant for full-voiced realizations), calling it "the most difficult parts" still seems exaggerated. If Gesner is describing a harpsichord concerto at the Collegium musicum with Bach as soloist (a possibility, given the dates during which Gesner coincided with Bach in Leipzig), it is curious that Bach is singing pitches to various members of the ensemble: this happens more often with singers than with instrumentalists.[56] Ultimately, though, Gesner's classical comparisons for Bach's "accomplishments" would make little sense if he were merely referring to rehearsal techniques. This is why Gesner probably depicted—if somewhat impressionistically—usual occurrences resembling, in quality, the story told by Kittel. Pandemonium may have been the price Bach paid for writing such uncommonly demanding music.

Gesner was not the only one to witness the fact that Bach, at least on occasion, led church performances from the harpsichord. Such a scene was recorded by the Leipzig chronicler Sicul in his account of the performance of the *Trauer-Ode* (Cantata 198), composed for the memorial service honoring Queen Christiane Eberhardine in October of 1727. In *Das Tränende Leipzig,* he writes: "There was shortly heard the *Trauer-Music* which this time Capellmeister Johann Sebastian Bach composed in the Italian manner, with the *Clavi di Cembalo,* which Herr Bach himself played, organ, gambas, lutes, violins, recorders, transverse flutes etc."[57] As the description of an admittedly unusual event, the chronicler's account may not be relevant to Bach's conventional continuo practice. Eager to view the harpsichord as a secular intruder, both Spitta and Schering nonetheless seized upon Sicul's mention of the use of the harpsichord in the *Trauer-Ode* as an indication of its "Italian manner," suggesting that it was not used for ordinary cantatas. But this interpretation ignores the circumstances surrounding Cantata 198. As Werner Neumann has shown, the event was staged by both city and university officials to pay tribute to a Saxon Queen who, under duress, had remained true to the Lutheran Confession.[58] With music by the Thomas-Cantor (over the protest, in fact, of the University music director, Görner) and text by Johann Christoph Gottsched, the *Trauerakt* was hardly a "secular" affair. In light of Queen Christiane's significance for Protestant Saxony as well as Gottsched's own aesthetic proclivities, the service had both theological and nationalistic components.[59] What raised the chronicler's eyebrows—perhaps his hackles as well—had nothing to do with an unlicensed "operatic" harpsichord but rather with Bach's unauthorized tinkering with Gottsched's text. No longer a classical strophic ode, the work had been transformed into a cantata with alternating "Italian" arias and recitatives.[60]

This still leaves the matter of the harpsichord—indeed, of the entire fortified continuo section. Since the autograph score for the *Trauer-Ode* survives without its accompanying orchestral parts, it remains unclear how the continuo forces were ultimately deployed. Yet even from the instrumentation designated in the score, it follows that the two lutes played a simultaneous—that is, additive—continuo part at least in Movements 1, 7, 8, and 10.[61] To retain any scruples regarding the combination of organ and harpsichord in light of an already redundant continuo realization begins to seem a little foolish. For the present purpose it suffices to say that the evidence for dual accompaniment of organ and harpsichord coincides with the one surviving eyewitness description of a Bach vocal work. Sicul, as the university actuary and registrar accustomed to the practices of the university church, might be indicating that the harpsichord was not generally used there. But he might just as well have singled it out for special mention in the *Trauer-Ode* account because, as Werner Neumann points out, it happened to be played by Bach himself.[62]

Bach as Conductor

From which position, then, did the composer direct his ensemble? Certainly not from the organist's seat, where, with his back to everyone, he would have been in the worst possible position to oversee the orchestra. Carl Gotthelf Gerlach, organist in the Leipzig Neu-Kirche, confirms this when, in requesting additional funds for continuo players, he notes that: "On several different occasions I myself had to play organ without being able to conduct the cantata."[63] It also stands to reason that Bach would hardly have bothered to transpose parts in *Chorton* for the organ each week if he himself had been responsible for the organ continuo. Considering Kittel's tale of Bach's surprise visit to the harpsichord, it seems likely that he intervened from a nearby position where he stood conducting, perhaps with a paper roll, as was common in Germany.[64] Supporting the idea of Bach the conductor is the statement in his obituary: "In conducting he was very accurate, and of the tempo, which he generally took very lively, he was uncommonly sure."[65] On the other hand, contrary testimony is offered by Carl Philipp Emanuel Bach. Although himself in favor of directing from the harpsichord, he states unequivocally that his father "in his youth, and until the approach of old age . . . played the violin cleanly and penetratingly, and thus kept the orchestra in better order than he could have done with the harpsichord."[66] But against this testimony stands the report of Bach playing the harpsichord in the *Trauer-Ode,* which is the only surviving document describing the performance of any Bach vocal work. Even Emanuel Bach himself says: "Should someone hasten or drag, the keyboardist is the one who can most readily correct him."[67]

It is impossible—but also unnecessary—to harmonize these disparate views into a single definitive statement. Some researchers have taken this lack of consistency as a decree to remain skeptical. According to this view, the documents are too contradictory to answer conclusively exactly how Bach led his orchestra. Yet it does not seem unreasonable to conclude that, at one time or another during his Leipzig career, Bach played all the possible roles in directing his ensemble—hand-waving conductor, principal violinist, and continuo harpsichordist.

Cembalo Parts

The documentary evidence establishes dual accompaniment as a conceivable staple of Bach's performance practice. It remains to examine the surviving original orchestral parts in order to characterize the support they offer to the theory.[68] Although not every bit of evidence independently confirms the practice of dual accompaniment, the sum total endows the theory with an explanatory power unmatched by competing interpretations. It is therefore useful to specify and separate the various questions that can be applied to the continuo parts:[69] (1) Were organ and harpsichord parts copied for the same performance? (2) What kinds of parts count as harpsichord parts? (3) In which type of works do they occur? (4) Are only certain movements figured? (5) How frequently did Bach employ the harpsichord? (6) How necessary was it?

The continuo parts that Bach actually called "harpsichord parts"— those labeled *Cembalo*—provide the most obvious point of departure for an examination of the sources. Treated throughout the controversy as anomalies that require special explanations, the *Cembalo* parts, I argue, serve merely as more explicit equivalents of ordinary figured *Cammerton* continuo parts. There are, to be sure, only five such parts among

TABLE 2-1 Continuo parts labeled *Cembalo*

BWV	Part title	Date	Autograph figures in movements:	Copyist's figures in movements:
109	Continuo pro Cembalo	Oct. 17, 1723	1, 6	1–6
23	Basson. e Cembalo	Feb. 7, 1723	complete	
6	Cembalo	Apr. 2, 1725	complete	
244	Continuo pro Cembalo	1744–1748	complete	
245	Cembalo	1746–1749		1–39

the extant sources for Bach's own sacred vocal works. Yet the striking range of works in which they occur undermines the belief that they served some extraordinary purpose. On the contrary, it is more likely that the copyists, for circumstantial reasons, entitled these normal bass parts *Cembalo* instead of the more usual part-title, *Continuo*. To have written *Cembalo* on a figured *Cammerton* part, therefore, is analogous to having labeled a *Chorton* continuo part *Organo*. Both provide clarification, although not an absolutely necessary one (see Table 2-1).

Aside from the Passions (BWV 244 and BWV 245), in which it may be argued that Bach employed the harpsichord to maintain order in extraordinarily large-scale works, harpsichord parts (labeled *Cembalo*) are found in two pieces—Cantatas 109 and 6. Both are perfectly conventional Bach vocal works dating from the first and second cantata cycles. (Cantata 23, although not unusual compositionally, will be treated separately because it was Bach's audition piece for the Leipzig cantorate.) For both Cantata 109 and Cantata 6, the parts reflect dual accompaniment of harpsichord and organ at the first performance.

Consider first Cantata 109, "Ich glaube, lieber Herr, hilf meinem Unglauben," written for the 21st Sunday after Trinity and performed on October 17, 1723, during Bach's first *Jahrgang*. This cantata consists of an opening chorus, two recitatives (both secco), two arias, and a concertato setting of a chorale. The two figured continuo parts in *Chorton* and *Cammerton* include nearly identical sets of figures for all movements. Johann Andreas Kuhnau, the principal copyist of the original part-set, wrote out the *Cammerton* part, labeling both the enclosing wrapper and the first page of music *Continuo*. But on the wrapper, as shown in Facsimile 2-1, Bach has added the words *pro Cembalo*. Although he could conceivably have added the extra words at a later date, the figures must have been entered in this harpsichord part before the first performance:

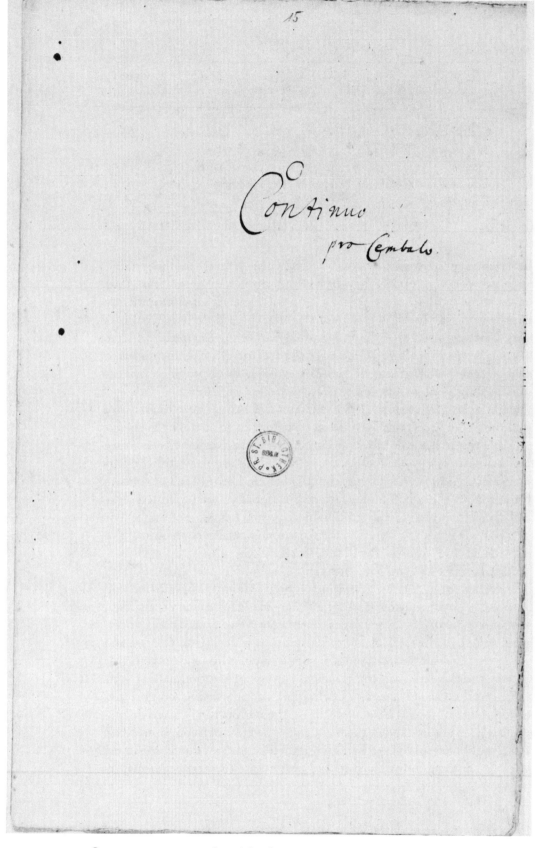

FACSIMILE 2-1 Cantata 109, wrapper to harpsichord part, Deutsche Staatsbibliothek Berlin/DDR, Musikabteilung, Mus. ms. Bach St 56 [St 56/15]

in his customary final review of the part (usually the last stage in the copying process), Bach placed dynamic markings above the numerical figures which a scribe had already copied from Bach's set in the organ part.[70] Since the figures parallel each other in all movements, it follows that the organ and harpsichord accompanied together throughout the cantata.

It is even possible to reconstruct the order in which these parts for Cantata 109 were copied and figured in order to gain a picture of a copying process that Bach employed for cantata performances during the first *Jahrgang*. As the primary copyist, Kuhnau first completed the core set of parts (that is, without duplicate parts for violins and continuo) from the composer's score. Christian Gottlob Meissner (later a principal copyist himself) then referred to Kuhnau's continuo part in order to transpose the organ part, labeling it *Continuo*. At this point Bach figured this organ part in its entirety (see Facsimile 2-2) and himself figured the opening ritornello in Movement 1 of the harpsichord part (see Facsimile 2-3). An anonymous copyist took Bach's figures as his exemplar and continued the figuring until he reached the last page of the part, which he left unfigured. He made only a few errors; for example, he sometimes ignored the transposition and forgot to change natural signs to sharps.[71] The complete part-set includes three continuo parts: a figured, transposed *Chorton* part for the organ, a figured *Cammerton* part for the harpsichord, and a third duplicate part. The organ part lacks dynamic markings. Since this part could not be shared with any doubling player who could have made use of dynamic markings, it did not require them. But since Bach entered dynamic markings in the harpsichord part, he surely intended another bass player—a cellist or violonist—to read his part over the shoulder of the harpsichordist. The other bass player(s) therefore read from the duplicate part. Dual accompaniment undoubtedly provides the simplest explanation for the evidence encountered here.

In Cantata 6, "Bleib bei uns, denn es will Abend werden," a piece for Easter Monday from the second *Jahrgang,* it was Bach who figured both keyboard parts and labeled the title page on the *Cammerton* part *Cembalo*. This is clear first of all from an identification of Bach's hand: the style is not inconsistent with Bach's hand in the 1720s and even closely resembles the same *Cembalo* marking in Cantata 109 from the year before. The figures in the organ part, thought by some to be copied by a scribe, can also be identified as the composer's, especially because the *Chorton* part contains numerous correct figures that do not appear in the harpsichord part. (What source would a scribe have for these?) Finally, an autograph *pizzicato* marking in Movement 2 seems to reveal that a

FACSIMILE 2-2 Cantata 109, organ part with autograph figures, Deutsche Staatsbibliothek Berlin/DDR, Musikabteilung, Mus. ms. Bach St 56 [St 56/14]

FACSIMILE 2-3 Cantata 109, harpsichord part, figures by Bach and copyist, Deutsche Staatsbibliothek Berlin/DDR, Musikabteilung, Mus. ms. Bach St 56 [St 56/15]

cellist shared the part with the harpsichordist. This practice is confirmed both by the evidence in the Bach sources and by contemporary iconography, which shows how frequently string players shared continuo parts with harpsichordists.[72] Although Alfred Dürr has taken pains to demonstrate that the two sets of figures do not imply dual accompaniment at the first performance, it is more likely that, given what the documents relate about the use of the harpsichord, they do exactly that.[73] Indeed, the historical evidence suggests that the burden of proof falls on those wishing to date one set of figures from a later performance. For even according to the most conservative rules of inference, dual accompaniment in Cantata 6 is the simplest explanation.

The complicated performance history of Bach's audition piece at Leipzig, Cantata 23, also reveals a good deal about his continuo practice. From the first performance of this work, "Du wahrer Gott und Davids Sohn," there remain five extant continuo parts:[74]

1. *Violoncello* (in C minor) [St 16/25]

2. *Violoncello* (a duplicate part in C minor) [St 16/22]

3. *Violoncello* (a duplicate part in C minor) [St 16/23]

4. *Basson.* [*é Cembalo*] (in B minor) [St 16/24]

5. *Continuo* (in A minor) [St 16/26]

Originally composed in C minor before Bach arrived in Leipzig, Cantata 23 was first performed at *Cammerton* pitch in B minor. The strings therefore tuned down a semitone. (Part 5 in A minor was copied at the conventional *Chorton* pitch for the organ.) As can be seen from Facsimile 2-4, Kuhnau had originally entitled Part 4 *Violoncello* after its exemplar; Bach later crossed this out and entitled the part *Basson*. From the lighter ink, it appears that he may have added the extra words—*é Cembalo*—at some later time, perhaps at the presumed second performance of the work in 1724.[75] Whether the figures stem from the first or second performance is uncertain, but in any event they were entered before Bach converted this part into a *Chorton* organ part in B♭ minor for a later performance around 1728–1731. (*Cammerton* then reverted to C minor.) At this later performance he deleted the sharps in the key signature and inserted flats, still visible in the adjusted continuo figures. The harpsichord thus accompanied simultaneously with the organ on at least one and probably two occasions for the initial performances of Cantata 23.

The sources for Cantata 23 yield yet another clue regarding dual accompaniment. In the last movement of Part 1 (copied at Cöthen) one

FACSIMILE 2-4 Cantata 23, *Basson. é Cembalo* [sic], Deutsche Staatsbibliothek Berlin/DDR, Musikabteilung, Mus. ms. Bach St 16 [St 16/24]

finds copyist's figures that can only derive from the *post correcturam* version of the *Basson. é Cembalo* part.[76] That is, after Bach transformed this into an organ part, he now lacked a figured *Cammerton* part. The figures later copied into the cello part (in C minor) are therefore an indication that the harpsichord accompanied even in the latest traceable performance of Cantata 23, suggesting that dual accompaniment occurred each time Bach is known to have performed the work.[77]

A figured harpsichord part for a performance of the St. John Passion (BWV 245) held in the late 1740s, mentioned earlier, echoes Bach's insistence years earlier that the harpsichord be repaired for the first performance of this large-scale work. Although the figures in this part display consistent errors of transposition (natural signs instead of sharps) and a certain number of mistaken readings, there is every reason to assume that the part was used.[78] Indeed, in a performance assembling an unusually large ensemble, the participation of the harpsichord does not seem very surprising. The use of the harpsichord cannot, in any event, be connected to the 1747 repair of the organ in the Thomas-Kirche; this repair took place in the Trinity season and was completed long before Passiontide of 1748. Although the church records state that before this major repair the organ was "almost unusable," this did not necessarily mean that the organ could not manage a continuo accompaniment.

By contrast, the *Cembalo* part in the St. Matthew Passion (BWV 244) suggests an instance in which the harpsichord replaced—rather than augmented—organ accompaniment. As Winfried Schrammek has shown, the 1736 performance (which first made use of two separate continuo groups) took place in the Thomas-Kirche with "both organs," as the Thomas-Kustos noted in his records;[79] these included both the large organ on the main West gallery as well as the older organ on the small East gallery (the so-called "Swallow's nest gallery"). This second instrument played the *cantus firmus* in the opening movement and was perhaps reinforced by a few sopranos. On the main gallery (the so-called *Schüler-Chor*), then, were the two orchestral groups and the two choirs. Since two *Chorton* parts are entitled *Organo,* it follows that the large organ accompanied one orchestra while a *Positiv* accompanied the other. There is no evidence that a harpsichord took part in this performance.

The later *Cembalo* part accompanying the second choir, therefore, must have substituted for the second organ at a later performance. Most probably a rendition of the St. Matthew Passion in the Nikolai-Kirche occasioned the use of the harpsichord, since the smaller loft could not have accommodated an additional *Positiv*. This disposition, Schrammek makes clear, follows from Bach's indication of the "sesquialtera" register of the *Rückpositiv* in the Organ I part. This marking can only apply to the instrument in the Nikolai-Kirche because the organ in the Thomas-Kirche lacked this stop. As the bass fundament for the second orchestra (which plays a far less demanding role than the first), the harpsichord would have played simultaneously with the organ only in the large choral movements and in the simple chorale settings. The disposition of forces in 1736 suggests that Bach sought to balance both orchestral groups with identical continuo forces. The contrast between equal contingents was therefore "geographic" rather than coloristic. Yet when circumstances dictated a modification of this scheme, Bach called on the harpsichord without any evident reluctance.

Considered together, the number of parts explicitly labeled *Cembalo* in Bach's sacred vocal works is indeed very few. Does this fact damage the theory of dual accompaniment? Was Bach's intentional use of the harpsichord at best infrequent? Answering yes to this question seems to rest on the claim that, as a rule, continuo parts specified the precise instrument for which they were designed. In fact, the opposite is true: instrumental bass parts of any sort were most often simply entitled *Continuo*. Parts entitled *Organo*, for example, are far from common during the Leipzig period, particularly when, as a rule, a copyist merely reproduced the main continuo part at a wholestep transposition. Consider, for instance, the performances of the second *Jahrgang*—June 11, 1724, through May 22, 1725—from which an abundant number of original sources survive. Of the forty-three *Chorton* continuo parts that are indisputably for the organ, only four are labeled *Organo*. (They are from Cantatas 26, 41, 124, and 125.) And of these four part-titles, Bach penned two himself (Cantatas 26 and 124), suggesting that the composer was more explicit in performance instructions than were his copyists. In another organ part written out by Meissner (Cantata 41), moreover, the part-title reads *Continuo: Organo,* showing that the specification occurred to the copyist after the generic designation. The part-titles to the keyboard continuo parts therefore provide only partial testimony regarding the presence of the harpsichord. One must instead imagine the situation in the choir loft. Given two available keyboard instruments and two figured parts marked *Continuo*—one in *Cammerton,* one in *Chorton*—the former undoubtedly was handed to the harpsichordist. The part-titles most likely spelled out what was in any case self-evident. While the *Cembalo* parts therefore provide important evidence for dual accompaniment, they must be considered in the context of the more significant number of other figured *Cammerton* parts.

Harpsichord parts were also unlikely to have been labeled so readily if the part were shared between the keyboardist and another bass player: whereas *Continuo* is inclusive, *Cembalo* is exclusive. An example of this

TABLE 2-2 *Cammerton* continuo parts containing the marking *tasto solo*

BWV	Catalog number	Date	Autograph figures in movements:	Copyist's figures in movements:
114	Thom 114/12	Oct. 1, 1724		1, 5
169	St 38/14	Oct. 20, 1726	complete	
29	St 106/22	Aug. 27, 1731	complete	
248^{IV}	St 112^{IV}/15	Jan. 1, 1735	36–42	36, 39, 40

practice of sharing (commonly depicted in contemporary iconography) is found in the sources for Cantata 23, discussed earlier, in which one of the continuo parts is labeled *Basson. é Cembalo*. An even more striking example occurs in the 1729 performance of the motet "Der Geist hilft unsrer Schwachheit auf" (BWV 226). Consider its group of bass parts:

Violoncello
Bassono
Violon e Continuo
Organo

Since there is a part for every regular bassist in Bach's orchestra, *Violon e Continuo* must be read as *Violone e Cembalo*.

Another group of *Cammerton* parts may count as harpsichord parts, although they too lack an explicit part-title:[80] these are continuo parts that contain the performance indication *tasto solo*. As Johann Gottfried Walther puts it in the *Lexikon,* "*Tasto solo* occurs in thorough bass and means that one should play the notes quite alone at this place without using the right hand."[81] In other words, the keyboardist temporarily suspends the continuo realization and plays only the bass line. As the Italian word for key, *tasto* refers only to a keyboard instrument. Table 2-2 lists the *Cammerton* continuo parts with this marking.

Consider the musical context in which the *tasto solo* marking occurs in the Christmas Oratorio (BWV 248^{IV}, Movement 40; see Example 2-1). At the end of this accompanied recitative with superimposed chorale, the upper strings provide a languorous postlude suspended over a pedal point in the bass. Although Bach entered figures in the organ part, he marked the corresponding passage in the *Cammerton* part *tasto solo*. It is, of course, conceivable that the conflicting readings reflect two distinct compositional intentions, if one insists—like Alfred Dürr—that the two markings date from different performances in keeping with the

EXAMPLE 2-1 Christmas Oratorio, Part IV (BWV 248), Movement 40, mm. 13–18

organ repair hypothesis.[82] But it is more compelling to observe how Bach has devised a particularly elegant orchestration for the passage. As the texture of dual accompaniment thins out to a single, sustained continuo realization on the organ, the languid ending literally fades away.

Harpsichord Parts in Performances of Other Composers' Works

Although explicit harpsichord parts are rarely encountered in Bach's own works, they turn up surprisingly often—if unaccountably so—in sources reflecting performances he gave of works by other composers (see Table 2-3). In addition to two cantatas by Johann Ludwig Bach,[83] pieces and arrangements of works by composers such as Keiser, Telemann, Kerll, Peranda, Pergolesi, and Palestrina include parts labeled *Cembalo*. The earliest such part in the Bach sources stems from the Weimar performance of the St. Mark Passion by Reinhard Keiser. Here Bach apparently substituted the harpsichord for the organ, since the organ was under repair at the time.[84] The parts from Leipzig, on the contrary, all point to dual accompaniment.

It is difficult to explain why these harpsichord parts appear in pieces representing such widely varying styles. Latin figural music in both *stile antico* and *stile moderno* as well as the contemporary cantata idioms of central and north Germany are found here. Nothing associates this group of harpsichord parts with a special, "foreign" performance prac-

TABLE 2-3   Bach's harpsichord parts in works by other composers

Composer	Work	Location	Part-title	Date	Extant organ part
Keiser	St. Mark Passion	DStB 1715516	Cembalo	1714	
J. L. Bach	Cantata 4	SPK, St 301	Cembalo	Feb. 24, 1726	x
J. L. Bach	Cantata 6	SPK, St 317	Cembalo	Apr. 28, 1726	x
Peranda	Kyrie in C	SPK 17079	Cembalo	1731–1742	x
Telemann	"Seliges Erwägen"	Göttingen	(Cembalo)[a]	1732–1735	
Handel/Keiser	Passion-Pastiche	private	Cembalo	1735–1750	
Palestrina	Missa sine nomine	DStB 16714	Cembalo	ca. 1740	x
Pergolesi	"Tilge, Höchster"	DStB 17155	Cembalo	1744–1748	x
BWV 241 (Kerll)	Sanctus in D	Coburg	Cembalo	1747	x
BWV Anh. 157	"Ich habe Lust"	Gdansk	Violono[b]	?	

a. *Cembalo* noted in score.
b. Contains *tasto solo* indication.

TABLE 2-4 *Cammerton* continuo parts for cantatas by Johann Ludwig Bach

Work	Source	Date	Figured *Cammerton* part	Corresponding *Chorton* part
BWV 15 (JLB)	SPK, St 13a	Apr. 21, 1726	x	x
JLB 1	DStB, St 310	Mar. 2, 1726	x	x
JLB 2	SPK, St 303	Mar. 10, 1726	x	x
JLB 3	DStB, St 302	Feb. 17, 1726	x	x
JLB 4	SPK, St 301	Feb. 24, 1726	*Cembalo*[a]	x
JLB 6	SPK, St 317	Apr. 28, 1726	*Cembalo*[a]	x
JLB 7	DStB, St 313	Jul. 28, 1726	x	x
JLB 9	DStB, St 314	Feb. 2, 1726	x[b]	x
JLB 12	SPK, St 316	May 5, 1726	x	
JLB 13	SPK, St 304	Jul. 2, 1726	x	x
JLB 14	SPK, St 306	May 19, 1726	x	x
JLB 15	SPK, St 307	Sep. 1, 1726	x	x[c]
JLB 16	DStB, St 312	Sep. 15, 1726	x	x
JLB 17	SPK, St 315	Jun. 24, 1726	x	x[c]

a. Unfigured *Cembalo* part.
b. Presence of a *tasto solo* marking.
c. Unfigured *Chorton* organ part.

tice. On the contrary, the cantatas by Johann Ludwig Bach, a cousin from Meiningen, do not depart significantly from the tradition in which J. S. Bach himself worked. The two *Cembalo* parts for the J. L. Bach pieces, moreover, should be considered in the context of the other sources for his cantatas performed at Leipzig (see Table 2-4). As the table shows, twelve other cantatas in this group contain figured *Cammerton* parts labeled *Continuo*. The part for J. L. Bach's Cantata 9, moreover, contains a *tasto solo* indication. There is evidence of dual accompaniment, therefore, throughout the entire set of works by Johann Ludwig Bach.

A particularly vivid example of dual accompaniment occurs in Bach's reworking of a Sanctus by Johann Kaspar Kerll (BWV 241) performed during the 1740s. The continuo parts include, among others, a figured *Cembalo* part and a figured *Organo* part, both in the hand of J. S. Bach (see Facsimile 2-5).[85] That Bach wanted both continuo instruments to play simultaneously is evident from the title page to his score (Facsimile 2-6). In this rare instance in which all the participating bass instruments are enumerated, Bach lists the following: *Bassono/ Violoncello/ Violono/*

FACSIMILE 2-5 Kerll, Sanctus (BWV 241), *Cembalo* and *Organo* parts, Kunstsammlungen der Veste Coburg, V, 1109, 1b

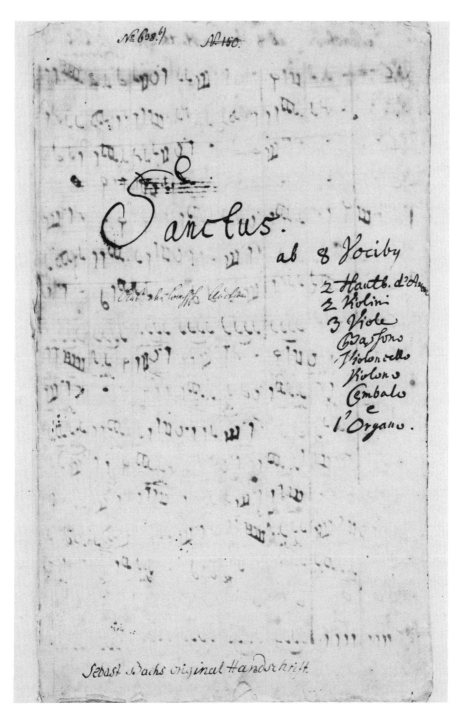

FACSIMILE 2-6 Kerll, Sanctus (BWV 241), score, title page, Kunstsammlungen der Veste Coburg, V, 1109, 1a

Cembalo/ e l'Organo. Even more striking is the fact that dual accompaniment was Bach's idea and not Kerll's. For the exemplar from which Bach copied the piece is still extant: it is a score in the collection of the Thomas-Schule. The instrumentarium lists only "con organo e Violone" for the required bass section. Bach therefore construed dual accompaniment as an added feature of his arrangement of the work. Admittedly, his intention to require both harpsichord and organ in BWV 241 may have depended on the presence of the large eight-part chorus. However, BWV 241 lays to rest any lingering belief that the harpsichord in church constitutes a "sacrilegious intrusion," or that the very idea of dual accompaniment "can only cause confusion."[86] When subsequently confronting an organ and harpsichord part, such as the autograph parts for Bach's arrangement of Palestrina's *Missa sine nomine,* one no longer has any reason to doubt that they reflect intentional dual accompaniment.[87]

Figured *Cammerton* Continuo Parts

Since dual accompaniment seems to have been a desired practice during at least some of Bach's performances, the question turns to its frequency: was it an exceptional occurrence, an occasional practice, or a norm? From the evidence of the Wild and Kittel documents, it seems far-fetched to see dual accompaniment as some special, extraordinary practice. Indeed, as demonstrated by the examples of Cantata 109 and Cantata 6, the very occurrence of harpsichord parts in works of the ordinary, weekly cantata cycle weakens the suggestion that dual accompaniment was a special practice. On the other hand, Bach cannot have viewed the harpsichord as indispensable; the absence of significant numbers of parts labeled *Cembalo* must surely be given weight in this regard. It remains to establish what sort of currency—and, more speculatively, what kind of meaning—dual accompaniment had within Bach's Leipzig continuo practice.

The substantial number of figured *Cammerton* continuo parts play a material role in answering this question. As mentioned earlier, the literature has generally slighted these parts, viewing the thorough-bass figures as accretions from later performances of the same work. But this reasoning cannot be detached from the standard viewpoint which has also sought to exclude dual accompaniment from the possible reconstructions of Bach's continuo practice. Although, on their own, the figured parts do not "prove" every time that Bach intended dual accompaniment at the first performance of each cantata, the sheer number of

TABLE 2-5 Other figured *Cammerton* continuo parts

BWV	Cat. number	Date	Autograph figures in movements:	Copyist's figures in movements:	Corresponding organ parts
24	St 19/15	Jun. 20, 1723	1		x
147	St 46/15	Jul. 2, 1723	7–9		x
136	St 20/13, 16	Jul. 18, 1723		complete	x
46	St 78/13	Aug. 1, 1723	1–3		x
199	St 459/15	Aug. 8, 1723	complete		x^a
48	St 53/12	Oct. 3, 1723	2		x
40	St 11/14	Jan. 30, 1724	1–4, 7	1, 4–7	x
81	St 59/13	Jan. 30, 1724	1, 3–7		x
31	St 14/22	Apr. 9, 1724	2–8		x
67	St 40/14	Apr. 16, 1724	complete		x
166	St 108/10	May 7, 1724	1–2		x^a
44	St 86/13	May 21, 1724	1		x
172	Rudrff 172/6	May 28, 1724	complete		x^a
7	Thom 7/12	Jun. 24, 1724	complete		x
10	Thom 10/11	Jul. 2, 1724	complete		x
38	Thom 38/14	Oct. 29, 1724	2–6		x
62	Thom 62/14	Dec. 3, 1724		3, 5	x
124	Thom 124/10	Jan. 2, 1725	1, 2, 4	3, 5	x
42	St 3/13	Apr. 8, 1725	complete		x
183	St 87/16	May 13, 1725		1	x
176	Scheid 176/12	May 27, 1725	complete		x
168	Scheid 168/6	Jul. 29, 1725	complete		x
28	St 37/17	Dec. 30, 1725	4		x
19	St 25a/17	Sep. 29, 1726	complete		x
169	St 38/14	Oct. 20, 1726	complete		
23	St 16/25	1728–1731		4	x
36b	St 15/9	Jul. 28, 1735?		2, 4, 6, 8	
240	St 115/11	1735–1746	complete		x

a. Unfigured organ part.

them supports the view that dual accompaniment was no stranger to conventional cantata performances. Table 2-5 details these parts, each of which includes at least one movement with a more or less complete set of figures. The table notes in addition whether the corresponding organ parts were also figured.

As the table shows, the vast majority of these thirty-seven figured *Cammerton* parts exist side by side with figured *Chorton* organ parts.

FACSIMILE 2-7 Sanctus in G (BWV 240), *Basso Continuo* and *Organo* parts, Deutsche Staatsbibliothek Berlin/DDR, Musikabteilung, Mus. ms. Bach St 115 [St 115/11, St 115/12]

But does the figuring reflect dual accompaniment at the first performance? One cannot easily say. For even if the identities of the copyists and identical watermarks on two parts confirm that the parts were copied for the first performance, a set of figures itself may have been entered at a later performance. The two figured parts for the Sanctus in G (BWV 240), labeled *Basso Continuo* and *Organo,* offer a typical illustration of this problem (see Facsimile 2-7). While the two sets of autograph figures look very much as if Bach entered them with the same pen-nib, the figures themselves strongly suggest, but cannot prove definitively, that organ and harpsichord played simultaneously. The two parts would still reflect a significant participation of the harpsichord in cantata performances but would not necessarily prove any frequency of dual accompaniment itself.

On the other hand, one can sometimes show that two sets of figures were entered before the first performance. Consider Cantata 46, "Schauet doch und sehet," a cantata performed on August 1, 1723. Here the anonymous scribe (Dürr's Anon. Ic) wrote out the transposed *Chorton* continuo part using the autograph figures that Bach had entered into the first three movements of the *Cammerton* part. As the facsimile from the organ part shows (Facsimile 2-8), the accidentals in the thorough bass closely match those in the musical text.[88] Since this copyist stopped working for Bach after April of 1724, before which a second performance of Cantata 46 cannot have taken place, the two sets of figures must date from the first performance.

In five other instances as well (Cantatas 7, 24, 28, 38, 147) Bach figured the *Cammerton* part first, allowing the copyists to transfer his figures into the *Chorton* organ part. And in Cantata 40, as described in the previous chapter, Bach swapped the two continuo parts back and forth, staying one step ahead of the copyist to speed up the figuring process. These cases ensure that the figures in the harpsichord parts were not "emergency" provisions, supplied—if at all—at the last minute. The organ repair hypothesis, moreover, is of no help here. For this would mean that Bach's copyists transposed a *Chorton* part for the organ in vain, even though the organ was not to be played. Surely if the organ was under repair, the transposed part together with its accompanying figures would date from a later performance. These pairs therefore reflect conventional dual accompaniment at the first performance.

Whereas some harpsichord parts contain fewer figures than the corresponding organ part (for example, in Cantatas 24, 31, 38, 101, 124, and elsewhere), others contain even a greater number of figures. In Cantata 7, for example, Bach figured the *Cammerton* part in its entirety, but the scribe who transferred his figures into the organ part copied only those

FACSIMILE 2-8 Cantata 46, organ part, figures in hand of copyist, Berlin, Staatsbibliothek Preussischer Kulturbesitz, Musikabteilung, Mus. ms. Bach St 78 [St 78/14]

from Movements 1 and 7. (Bach took charge of the figures on the second page of Movement 1 and himself figured Movements 3 and 4.) Movements 5 and 6 remain unfigured in this organ part. And in Cantata 166, even more surprisingly, Bach figured the *Cammerton* part in Movements 1 and 2 while leaving the organ part untouched. In Cantata 168 Bach provided complete figures for the *Cammerton* part, while his nephew Johann Heinrich Bach copied figures into the organ part only in the two recitatives.[89]

The unfigured organ part from Cantata 166 raises a crucial question: Does the absence of figures in any one movement mean that a keyboard player did not participate here? Many keyboard continuo parts—both *Cammerton* as well as *Chorton*—lack figures in some and even all movements, yet the assumption that keyboardists could realize thorough bass only from figured parts prevails in much twentieth-century scholarship. The part entitled *Violon e Continuo* for the motet "Der Geist hilft" (BWV 226), mentioned earlier, must be identified as a harpsichord part by a simple process of elimination, although it is unfigured. But is there firmer ground for assuming that continuo players played from unfigured parts?

Consider, first, that the two *Cembalo* parts among the J. L. Bach pieces (JLB 4 and JLB 6) are the only ones among the set of *Cammerton* continuo parts that *lack* figures. According to the traditional view, Bach's intention to have these parts played on the harpsichord therefore remained unfulfilled. But if this reasoning were correct, how would one explain the continuo parts for JLB 15 and JLB 17, in which two *Cammerton* parts are figured while the *Chorton* parts remained unfigured? According to the usual logic, only the harpsichord would have accompanied these cantatas. But then, as I suggested earlier, it is hard to explain why Bach had the copyists go to the trouble of transposing a *Chorton* part in the first place, since such a part could only be used at the organ. Only if the harpsichordist realized the part despite the absence of figures do these parts make any sense. Indeed, lacking figures, this continuo part may have required the *Cembalo* title in order to clarify for whom it was intended.

While figures imply the presence of a keyboard player, the absence of figures (either in one movement of a large-scale work or even in a complete part) does not mean that a keyboardist was not involved. The strongest evidence for this thesis is the presence of fifteen completely unfigured *Chorton* parts prepared for sacred vocal works. For the performances of Cantatas 4, 17, 45, 52, 55, 56, 59, 63(?), 64, 85, 88, 116, 166, 184, and the Sanctus, BWV 232[III], an organ part was prepared but never figured. This can only mean one thing: that the organist realized the continuo despite the absence of figures. Certainly it could have been Bach himself who accompanied from these unfigured parts: after all, he composed the piece. (His habit of figuring parts from memory also suggests that he accompanied from unfigured parts.) But since no verbal testimony suggests that Bach ever played the organ during performances of his Leipzig vocal works, it is more likely that other experienced keyboard players were forced to accompany from unfigured parts.

Eighteenth-century writings testify to this practice. David Kellner's *Treulicher Unterricht im General-Bass* of 1732, for example, states this explicitly: "Without understanding [the preceding discussion], it will be difficult for one to build a solid foundation in music or, as it often happens, to accompany an unfigured bass."[90] To realize an unfigured part was far from ideal. However, to insist, in reconstructions of continuo practice, that figures alone prove the presence of a continuo player is not only dogmatic but historically inaccurate. Never a mere mechanical operation, the continuo realization demanded a superb ear and the ability to formulate a harmonization based on the conventions of the various genres, qualities that Bach's continuo players must have cultivated.

Even when the organ part is the only figured continuo part, it is frequently unfigured in certain movements. In other words, given a "normal" figured organ part, the player must have accompanied some of the movements without the aid of figures. There are revealing patterns to these omissions, although they are not consistent.[91] Most often, if one movement of a cantata lacks figures, it is the final chorale. The explanation is simple: in addition to his part placed in front of him, the continuo player had another critical piece of information at his disposal—a knowledge of the chorale tune in the soprano. Thus, given two parts, the accompanist could guess with some accuracy at the chords comprising the progressions—despite the commonly audacious harmonizations that Bach invented for his chorales. In other instances of incompletely figured parts, recitatives tend to be figured more often than other movements. In Cantata 79, for example, the only movement figured is the one secco recitative (Movement 4). Likewise in Cantata 84 and Cantata 87, the two figured movements (Movements 2 and 4) are a secco and an accompanied recitative. But surely these figures cannot mean that the organist accompanied only the recitatives, for then the very rationale for a regularly transposed organ part would be lost.[92]

Sometimes secondary manuscript sources allude to Bach's use of dual accompaniment. In Cantata 178, for example, Bach figured the *Chorton* part everywhere except the final chorale, while he figured the *Cammerton* part only in the passages of Movement 2 where the arioso is transformed into secco recitative. There is therefore evidence of dual accompaniment at this performance but, curiously, only in the most freely declaimed measures of the piece. Interpreted strictly, this evidence suggests that the harpsichordist participated merely in a few inserted passages of secco recitative within one brief movement. Although the original continuo parts offer no further clues, a secondary source copied in 1755 by C. F. Penzel (1737–1801), then a pupil at the Thomas-Schule, does. The instrumentarium in his score—not textually dependent on Bach's part-set—reads: "Dom. VIII. p. Trinit:/ . . . a/ 4. voci/ 2. Hautb. d'Amour./ 2. Violin/ Viola/ *con*/ *Cembalo* del Signore I. S. Bach/ Poss. CF. Penzel./ 1755" (emphasis mine). Penzel may, of course, have substituted *Cembalo* for the usual *Continuo;* but he just as easily could have reproduced his exemplar. Since the figures in the *Cammerton* part point to the harpsichord, the coincidence is probably not accidental.

On the other hand, in Cantata 89, the organ part is figured in all movements *except* the two secco recitatives. As if compensating for the lack of figures, however, these movements include a textless copy of the vocal line in a "cue stave" placed above the bass part.[93] This means that the keyboardist supplied the continuo realization by inferring the relevant harmony from the two given parts. Given a familiarity with the common conventions of voice-leading in recitatives (even Bach's!), players must have been able to handle such a task. That cue staves can conceptually substitute for figures is shown in the harpsichord part for Cantata 195, Movement 2. Here an accompanied recitative movement was figured and only later found to be lacking four measures of music; the original text in the part was then crossed out and the entire movement recopied from scratch on an insert—this time with a cue stave but with the figures omitted (see Facsimile 2-9). In general, this equivalence between cue staves and figures follows from the observation that a keyboard part—*Cammerton* or *Chorton*—contains either figures or cue staves or a combination of both in secco recitative movements. The rare instances of secco movements that lack both constituents—such as the unfigured organ parts for Cantata 184 or Cantata 64—therefore represent exceptional cases.

As regards dual accompaniment, two parts that contain unequal degrees of figuring can sometimes be considered nearly equivalent: Bach completely figured two continuo parts for Cantata 81 except for a secco recitative (Movement 2) in the *Cammerton* part. But since this part has a cue stave for Movement 2, there is every reason to assume that the harpsichordist accompanied this movement as well. Now consider Cantata 88: here both continuo parts were left entirely unfigured, yet the *Chorton* part has cue staves for the two secco recitatives (Movements 2

FACSIMILE 2-9 Cantata 195, harpsichord part (*above*) and revised insert (*opposite*) for Movement 2, Berlin, Staatsbibliothek Preussischer Kulturbesitz, Musikabteilung, Mus. ms. Bach St 12 [St 12/23]

and 6) while the *Cammerton* part does not. One can therefore guess that the harpsichord probably did not participate in the performance. On the other hand, cues would also have been indicated to help a cellist follow the singer. In Cantata 64, from which two unfigured continuo parts remain, it is the *Cammerton* part—not the organ part—that includes a cue stave to Movement 2. From this sort of evidence, it is difficult to guess who may have accompanied the cantata; all that can be granted is that at least one player realized the continuo. Yet this sort of example is particularly vexing. For if it is conceded that the organist in Cantata 64 played without any figures or even cue staves in the recitatives, then how can the possibility be excluded—given Wild and Kittel—that harpsichordists (or the composer) did not also dispense with figured parts on occa-

sion? Cantata 59, moreover, offers another instance of two unfigured parts without cue staves. But the participation of the harpsichord in this work may be surmised from an eighteenth-century score (dating perhaps from 1731) which labels a figured continuo line *Cemb*[alo].[94]

Details such as these considerably complicate the question of the frequency of dual accompaniment. Although one might restrict any conclusions to those bits of positive evidence pointing directly to the harpsichord, the same standard has not been applied to unfigured organ parts. Then there is the matter of later performances of the same work, for which dual accompaniment cannot be established even if two figured parts remain from the first performance. To err on the side of caution: the figured *Cammerton* parts suggest that harpsichord participation was far more frequent than has been thought, but much less frequent than organ accompaniment alone. Compared with other accounts of Bach's keyboard accompaniments, this is already claiming a great deal.

Tacet-Indications in Organ Parts

In his *Versuch über die wahre Art das Clavier zu spielen,* Carl Philipp Emanuel Bach writes:

> The organ is indispensable in church music because of the fugues, large choruses, and generally because of its binding quality. It provides splendor and maintains order.
>
> But as soon as recitatives and arias appear in church music, particularly those in which the inner voices—comprising a sparse accompaniment—grant the vocal part every opportunity for embellishment, then a harpsichord must be present. One hears unfortunately all too often how empty the performance sounds in such a case when harpsichord accompaniment is missing.[95]

Writing in 1762, Emanuel Bach seems to be prescribing an alternating style of continuo accompaniment for sacred music, in which the organ plays during the large-scale pieces while the harpsichord takes the more lightly scored works. Since there is no simultaneous accompaniment by the harpsichord and the organ, this practice differs fundamentally from the practices thus far described in J. S. Bach's vocal works. By referring to the "empty" (*kahl*) effect of recitatives and arias without harpsichord accompaniment, Emanuel Bach opposes the practice of omitting the continuo realization from lightly scored pieces; it goes without saying that the organ—in addition to the harpsichord—was left out at these occasions. Because of this, and because of those simple inner parts, it is difficult to understand how Emanuel's words might relate to his father's practices. Traditionally, the harpsichord controversy invoked this text on both sides of the dispute: Seiffert (and, paradoxically, Spitta) asserted that it substantiated J. S. Bach's use of the harpsichord, while Schering, Mendel, and others claimed that Emanuel's subscription to a new *galant* aesthetic invalidated any possible applications to J. S. Bach.

Although the musical context for Emanuel Bach's remarks is separated from that of his father both in time and sensibility, there exists a set of Leipzig works by the elder Bach that reflects the differentiated accompaniment advocated by the younger Bach. As Bach scholarship since the publication of the old Bach-Gesellschaft edition has known, organ parts from several cantatas include movements that are marked *tacet.* Facsimile 2-10 shows a page from the organ part for Cantata 97, first performed in 1734. Here the copyist—Friedrich Christian Samuel

FACSIMILE 2-10 Cantata 97, *Organo* part with *tacet*-indications, Deutsche Staatsbibliothek Berlin/DDR, Musikabteilung, Mus. ms. Bach St 64 [St 64/14]

Mohrheim—completed copying the second movement and then wrote *Versus 3 tacet* and *Versus 4 tacet*.[96] There were various explanations advanced in the literature to account for these peculiar markings. Early on, Wilhelm Rust guessed that the *tacet*-markings indicated where Bach took over at the organ, while Arnold Schering attempted to connect them with vesper services on feast-days at which Bach performed abridged versions of cantatas. More plausibly, though, Schering considered that Bach omitted the organ merely to highlight the light orchestration in these particular movements. This explanation seems the most straightforward, since it likens the movements with the organ marked *tacet* to those which include *tasto solo* sections, or to those *bassetto* arias in which the continuo group is excluded altogether.

From the vantage point of the harpsichord controversy, the matter of the *tacet*-indications seemed both puzzling and controversial. Could these markings be signs pointing to the dreaded harpsichord? The answer to this question leads in two directions, for the sixteen pieces in which the *tacet*-indications occur actually fall into two distinct groups. Table 2-6 lists the relevant movements in these works and organizes

TABLE 2-6 Organ parts with *tacet*-indications

BWV	Cat. number	Movements omitted	Movements marked *tacet*	Proposed date of performance[a]
95	St 10/12		5	Sep. 12, 1723
130	Frankfurt/ Chur 130		5	Sep. 29, 1724
26	Thom 26/14	2		Nov. 19, 1724
42	St 3/14	3 (B section)		Apr. 8, 1725
101	Thom 101/18		3	1732–1735(r)
33	Thom 33/11		2, 3, 4	1732–1735(r)
99	Thom 99/12		2, 3, 4, 5	1732–1735(r)
139	Thom 139/12	2, 3, 4		1732–1735(r)
9	Thom 9/11	2, 3, 4		1732–1735
100	St 97/27	2, 3, 4		1732–1735(r)
94	Thom 94/15	2, 4, 7		1732–1735(r)
5	Thom 5/13	2, 3, 4, 6		1732–1735(r)
97	St 64/14	3, 4, 7		1734
14	Fitzwill 14	3, 4		Jan. 30, 1735
177	Thom 177/13	2, 3, 4		1732–1742(r?)
129	Thom 129/16	2, 3, 4		1735–1744(r)

a. (r) = reperformance.

EXAMPLE 2-2 Cantata 130, Movement 5, mm. 1–9

them according to the performance at which Bach curtailed the participation of the organ.[97] As the table shows, in the first group of cantatas—
performed between 1723 and 1725—only one movement was marked
tacet (Cantatas 95 and 130) or was omitted from the part in the first place
(Cantatas 26 and 42).[98] In each instance the movements in question are,
in fact, the most lightly scored arias in the piece. In Cantata 95, for example, Meissner enclosed Movement 5 in brackets with the added note
Aria senza l'Organo, apparently after Bach made explicit his pizzicato
accompaniment in the string parts. Here the organ accompaniment
would only have interfered with the graphic representation of the persistent, ticking clock marking the final hour.[99] Since the harmonies of
the movement are complete, there is no particular loss without a continuo realization. In Cantata 130, on the other hand, the opening ritornello for the aria, "Lass, o Fürst der Cherubinen," is hardly imaginable
without a continuo realization, particularly given the pedal tone which
occurs here and throughout the movement (see Example 2-2). Harpsichord accompaniment appears to be a necessary addition. The *tacet*
organ accompaniment in the second section of Cantata 42, Movement 3
also needs a continuo realization, since the upper strings and two oboes
drop out at this point, leaving only the continuo group. Evidence that
the harpsichord played along with the cello and bassoon, however, is
not difficult to adduce, since the *Cammerton* part was figured by Bach.

Of greater significance for dual accompaniment in general is the fact that the harpsichord part is figured not only in these fifteen measures of Movement 3, but throughout the entire cantata. In withdrawing the organ and lightening up the texture, Bach therefore sought to reduce two continuo realizations to one and not to substitute the harpsichord for the organ.

The later group of pieces with *tacet*-indications in the organ parts—performed starting in 1732—builds on this principle of textural contrast, for here a greater number of movements within a cantata are marked *tacet*. In most of these works, for example, Bach has omitted the organ from as many as three or more movements (Cantatas 33, 99, 139, 9, 100, 94, 5, 97, 177, 129). In addition to numerous instances similar to those in Cantata 130 and Cantata 42 in which another continuo realization becomes necessary, this later group of works includes some ten secco recitatives marked *tacet* in the organ part. Since a secco recitative is unthinkable without punctuated chords, one must conclude that the harpsichord played when the organ stopped. To be sure, of these later works, only Cantatas 33 and 101 have a corresponding figured *Cammerton* part in the *tacet* movement. But even in Cantata 101 the movement in question is not the only one that Bach figured: the other recitative movement (Movement 5) also contains autograph figures. Thus, the manuscript sources show no sign that the harpsichord substituted for the organ merely in its *tacet* movements. One may always suppose, of course, that Bach played the harpsichord in these performances. But in the end, one must explain the accompaniment procedures not based on the "hard" evidence alone but within the context of underlying conventions of performance.

If J. S. Bach's limited experiment in differentiated accompaniment left a residual trace in the original sources, then the practice appears very much intact in Emanuel Bach's *galant* prescription cited earlier. Since Emanuel's last years in Leipzig coincided with performances in which the Thomas-Cantor restricted the organ to the most heavily scored movements, one wonders whether Emanuel's preference for a change in the accompanied texture within the course of a church cantata did not derive from these self-consciously modish experiments that he himself had observed under the elder Bach's tutelage. As it happens, J. S. Bach largely repudiated the stark alternation of continuo textures in his later years within these same pieces, copying out many of the movements earlier marked *tacet* (see, for example, Facsimile 2-10). That Emanuel stuck to the earlier, more stylish method of accompaniment may only indicate that he owed a stronger allegiance to "progress" than to his father's authority. In any event, there was one principle that C. P. E. Bach surely inherited from his father, which he summed up in another important dictum of the *Versuch:* "One cannot perform any piece well without the accompaniment of a keyboard instrument."[100]

Performance of Cantatas with Solo Organ

Near the end of his third annual cycle of church cantatas at Leipzig (1726) Bach composed seven works, all of which include a substantial concerted solo part for the organ (see Table 2-7). These *Organo obligato* parts, in addition to a few others reflecting later instances of the same genre, bring about a qualitatively new situation for the basso continuo. For while the organist is engaged with his concerted part, he can no

TABLE 2-7   Cantatas with organ solos

BWV	Title	Performance	Movement(s) with obbligato organ
71	Gott ist mein König	Feb. 4, 1708	2
161	Komm, du süsse Todesstunde	Oct. 6, 1715	1
70	Wachet, betet, seid bereit allezeit	Nov. 21, 1723	3
172	Erschallet, ihr Lieder	May 28, 1724	5
128	Auf Christi Himmelfahrt allein	May 10, 1725[a]	4
146	Wir müssen durch viel Trübsal	May 12, 1726(?)	1, 2
194	Höchsterwünschtes Freudenfest	Jun. 16, 1726	3, 10
170	Vergnügte Ruh, beliebte Seelenlust	Jul. 28, 1726	3, 5
35	Geist und Seele wird verwirret	Sep. 8, 1726	1, 4, 5
47	Wer sich selbst erhöhet	Oct. 13, 1726	2
169	Gott soll allein mein Herze haben	Oct. 20, 1726	1, 3, 5
49	Ich gehe und suche mit Verlangen	Nov. 3, 1726	1, 2, 6
188	Ich habe meine Zuversicht	ca. 1728	1, 4
120a	Herr Gott, Beherrscher aller Dinge	ca. 1729	4
63	Christen, ätzet diesen Tag	1729(?)	3
29	Wir danken dir, Gott, wir danken dir	Aug. 27, 1731	1, 7
73	Herr, wie du willt, so schicks mit mir	1732–1735	1
27	Wer weiss, wie nahe mir mein Ende	1737(?)	3

a. Although Bach specified "organo solo" in his score, he had the part copied for the oboe d'amore. Apparently, this organ solo was never heard.

longer execute the chordal realization usually entrusted to him. The next question—who plays continuo?—is one that apparently engaged Bach's attention, judging from the manuscript sources. Even though explicit documentary evidence regarding the performance of these pieces is lacking, the original scores and parts reveal that Bach experimented with different methods of substitution, although he never settled on one solution. In turn, the compensatory methods he devised shed further light on the role of the harpsichord in the sacred works.

Although Wilhelm Friedemann is often mentioned in the literature as the intended performer of the organ solos,[101] he cannot, in fact, have participated at their premiere because he was then in Merseburg studying the violin.[102] Since Carl Philipp Emanuel Bach was only 12 years old at the time, it seems at least plausible that J. S. Bach played the solos himself. The sources themselves speak for this claim, since Bach took the trouble in all of the 1726 cantata scores—except in one movement of Cantata 170—to notate the organ part at its playing pitch of *Chorton,* a whole step below the normal *Cammerton* pitch of the orchestra.[103] In all likelihood, then, the transposition in the score indicates that the organist played these pieces from the score and not from a performing part.[104] Considering further the difficulty of realizing the solo part from Bach's composing scores—some are heavily corrected—Bach himself appears to be the most likely soloist.

Consider Facsimile 2-11, which reproduces the first page of Bach's autograph score to Cantata 49: the upper string parts are in E while the organ lines—occupying the lowest two staves of each system—are notated in D. One cannot imagine Bach doing this unless he intended to read from the score, for his copyists now had to transpose the *Cammerton* continuo parts up a whole step from the *Chorton* organ stave in the score—a process quite unfamiliar to them. The opening of Movement 2, seen in Facsimile 2-12, also suggests that the organist played from the score. Here one may observe Bach's own confusion once he decided to keep the continuo line in this composing score at the *Chorton* transposition. Note how he mistakenly copied the continuo part at pitch (mm. 1-3 and in the third and fourth systems) and then had to backtrack and retrace each notehead a step lower. It is therefore fair to conclude that the organist (Bach himself?) remained with the score throughout the cantata and realized the continuo in the movements between his solos.

Other sources reveal different procedures for the keyboard accompaniments. Consider first Cantata 170, in which the organ plays concerted parts in Movements 3 and 5. Movement 3, as a *bassetto* aria dispensing with the continuo, presents no particular problems. Its part in

FACSIMILE 2-11 Cantata 49, first page of autograph score, Deutsche Staatsbibliothek Berlin/DDR, Musikabteilung, Mus. ms. Bach P 111

FACSIMILE 2-12 Cantata 49, autograph score, Movement 2, Deutsche Staatsbibliothek Berlin/DDR, Musikabteilung, Mus. ms. Bach P III

the autograph score was transposed down to *Chorton,* from which it may be concluded that Bach intended to play the solo from the score. The score notates Movement 5, on the other hand, in *Cammerton,* which, in contrast to Movement 3, requires continuo accompaniment. (Of course if Bach were the soloist, the transposition would not pose a problem.) Two continuo parts survive from Cantata 170—an unfigured part in *Cammerton* for the cello and a completely figured, transposed part notated in *Chorton.* If the soloist sat at the main organ, the continuo player must then have played one of the *Positiv* organs brought up to the loft, because two organs are then required for Movement 5. Most likely the continuo player accompanied at the *Positiv* for the entire performance of Cantata 170.

Consider next Cantata 169, performed a few months later. Here Movements 1, 3, and 5 include solo organ parts, all of which Bach transposed down to *Chorton* in his score. Only two continuo parts—both in *Cammerton*—survive from this performance. One contains a complete set of continuo figures and was therefore intended for the harpsichord. (*Tasto solo* markings in Movement 1 also confirm that the harpsichordist was the intended recipient of this part.) The organ and harpsichord therefore played simultaneously during at least three movements, although the sources do not clarify whether the organ also played continuo together with the harpsichord during the remaining movements of the cantata. Given parallel instances elsewhere, it is likely that this was the case.

The performance of Cantata 29 in 1731, on the other hand, offers an instance in which Bach unquestionably planned for dual accompaniment even in the movements where the organist was not playing a concerted part. This is clear from Bach's complete organ part, which includes both solos (Movements 1 and 7) as well as the continuo parts for the remaining movements. Only Movements 2 through 6 are figured here, so that the organist played continuo when he was not occupied with the solos. However, Bach also figured one of the *Cammerton* continuo parts in its entirety. It therefore follows that the harpsichord played not only in the solo movements but throughout the cantata. Consequently, the organ and the harpsichord realized the continuo simultaneously in the inner movements, which include—no longer surprisingly—two secco recitatives. Significantly, the organ repair hypothesis is useless to explain the presence of the harpsichord part, since a functioning organ is the *raison d'être* of the cantata. Furthermore, the two sets of figures cannot reflect two performances, in which the harpsichord accompanied the first but was replaced by the organ in the second. This is evident from an autograph *tasto solo* marking in the organ part in Movement 5 (mm. 7-13), at which the clef change from bass to alto indicates a move from basso continuo to a *bassetto*. Both the marking and the clef change make sense only if the organ had previously been realizing the continuo from the thorough-bass figures. And if one accepts dual accompaniment in this movement, then it follows that the organ and the harpsichord accompanied simultaneously during all the inner movements, with the harpsichord alone playing continuo during the outer movements in which the organ was the soloist.

More perplexing is the unique consolidation of concerted solo and continuo part encountered in a performance of Cantata 73 held sometime between 1732 and 1735. Here the registration markings on the treble line of the solo part—alternately "Rück-Positiv" and "Brust-Positiv"—indicate the manual on which the organist's right hand was occupied in a line alternating between a chorale melody and a concerted obbligato. (They also suggest that someone other than Bach occasionally played the solos: the composer would hardly have noted these markings for himself.) But the bass line in the solo organ part for this opening chorus—which embraces a concerto, a chorale setting, and an accompanied recitative—includes a consistent set of continuo figures. Where are they to be realized? If the player takes the chords in the right hand, beneath the treble obbligato, they protrude uncomfortably, compromising their accompanying function and destroying the distinct "voice" of the solo obbligato. It is likewise difficult to imagine the chords superimposed just over the bass if it is played with the left hand. Not only would this manner of realization be unusual; it would also be quite ungainly, considering how the bass line itself jumps around. Most likely, then, the player took the bass line in the pedal while realizing the continuo in the left hand—a procedure described, for example, in Jakob Adlung's *Anleitung zu der musikalischen Gelahrtheit* (1758).[105] Whatever solution was adopted on this occasion, Bach strove to cast the organ in a solo role without sacrificing its usual ability to accompany.

Dual Accompaniment as Convention

Advanced as a regular alternative to organ continuo in Bach's sacred works at Leipzig, the notion of dual accompaniment rests on a broad array of arguments and evidence. Harpsichords in both main Leipzig churches were maintained throughout Bach's tenure. Documents state not only that student harpsichordists always accompanied at cantata performances (Kittel) and that one, in so doing, was said to "adorn our church music" (Wild), but that Bach himself led a performance from the harpsichord in which the organ was also played (Cantata 198) and that a less prestigious congregation (at Freiberg) purchased harpsichords in order to emulate the practice in Leipzig. Bach's own performance parts, moreover, signal the use of the harpsichord in several ways. First, there are the titled harpsichord parts copied for the same performance as organ parts in works both large and small, some specifying dual accompaniment even in the score (for example, the Kerll Sanctus—BWV 241). Then there are the figured *Cammerton* parts or those with *tasto solo* markings which imply the harpsichord or, more likely, imply a part shared between the harpsichordist and another bassist. In addition, there are known performances when the organist was either absent or occupied with a solo, in which the harpsichordist must have played throughout an entire cantata. Finally, underlying the whole argument is a rejection of the prejudice which—lacking any historical rationale—seeks to exclude the harpsichord from performances of Bach's sacred music.

Nonetheless, many may well persist in the belief that the practice of two keyboard instruments simultaneously realizing Bach's continuo is objectionable on both pragmatic and musical grounds. Schering formulates this distaste well: "How impossible it must have been to continuously maintain the tuning of the harpsichord—which so easily goes out of tune—with the organ pitched a whole step higher! . . . The very thought is unthinkable."[106] No doubt some of this prejudice stems from inexperience with harpsichords. But there is also more than a tinge of distaste at the minor clashes that would have attended two continuo realizations. In this regard, it is well to recall that simultaneous chordal realizations are as old as thorough bass itself. The colorful array of continuo instruments used in early Venetian opera represents a striking example of this traditional practice. But even during Bach's lifetime, the orchestra of the Dresden court—which Bach esteemed so highly—made use of two harpsichords, a fact recorded by both Jean-Jacques Rousseau and Quantz.[107] Emanuel Bach, in fact, discusses the role of two harpsichords in accompanying recitatives,[108] in which clashes between continuo instruments would be particularly noticeable. J. S. Bach, too, made use of dual harpsichord accompaniment in performances of two nonliturgical works (Cantatas 195 and 201), from which two figured *Cammerton* parts survive. And in a similar vein, the sources for the harpsichord concerto in A major (BWV 1055) include a separate harpsichord continuo part. Finally, recall the statement of Mattheson, which, far from seeing anything objectionable, actually recommends blending small *Positiv* organs with one or even two harpsichords in church accompaniments. Given the historical evidence, fears that dual accompaniment endangers some imagined tonal purity in Bach's cantatas prove completely groundless.

Another, more serious objection to dual accompaniment could be put this way: Even if it is agreed that Bach occasionally made use of dual accompaniment, perhaps no one heard the sound of the harpsichord beyond the choir loft. If this is true, then Bach might have employed the harpsichord to help control the ensemble but considered its musical effect, at best, to be marginal. Apart from the fact that this opinion favors the audience over the performers, implying that the essence of what is heard is downstairs where the congregation sits and not upstairs in the ears of the composer, it is probably also inaccurate. For in a large ensemble work such as the Kerll Sanctus (BWV 241), Bach counted the harpsichord, like all the other instruments, as a proper member of the instrumentarium. Would he have listed a participant that no one in the congregation could hear? Kittel's anecdote is likewise hard to explain if the harpsichord were inaudible. Would Bach have intermingled those "masses of harmonies" on the harpsichord if the sounds did not carry beyond those in the immediate vicinity?[109] On the contrary, Emanuel Bach describes the performance of "even heavily scored works, such as operas performed out of doors, where no one would think that the harpsichord could be heard." Even here, he relates, "one misses [the harpsichord] when it is omitted."[110] And if this is the "worst case" he can imagine, how much more he seems to have presumed that the harpsichord, with its inimitably crisp attack, would sound in a resonant church chamber. Invoking the supposedly feeble sound of the harpsichord seems likewise to raise a false issue.

Beyond the terms of the original controversy, what role does dual accompaniment play within the scheme of Bach's music? Clearly, it is far from a major aesthetic concern. And yet the historical evidence is slighted if dual accompaniment is considered a mere practical aid. One problem is our neat division today between artistic intentions and the practicalities of orchestration. But this division itself is probably no older than the Romantic separation between genius and craft. Certainly for a convinced Lutheran of the early eighteenth century, such a thought would have seemed arbitrary, if not downright blasphemous. To be sure, the basso continuo held a special status among the various activities of music making—after all, it was also the site of knowledge about the harmonic system, both its divinely given mysteries as well as the orderly human works it could fashion. The sense of a Bach cantata lay, in any case, in the understanding and application of the divine text that inspired it. The instruments of the orchestra, despite the highly inventive ways in which Bach employs them, are really no more than implements that reinforce the interpretation offered by the musical setting. Viewed in this light, everything that contributes to this goal—whether conceptual or practical—sustains an underlying interpretive idea.

This perspective also clarifies the question of propriety. Did Bach mean for the harpsichord to be played only in those works for which there is evidence of its use? Following the tenets of a strict reconstruction of performance details of a Bach cantata, one arrives at a facile answer: We might not know Bach's intentions, but at least we can be faithful to the evidence.[111] If, on the other hand, the evidence of harpsichord participation merely reflects occasions at which Bach was fortunate enough to have been able to bolster his continuo group, then each individual instance becomes less important. Accordingly, dual accompaniment may just as well have been practiced in the pieces for which there *is* documentation as in others for which there is none. No doubt there is a certain risk in writing the history of music this way; and yet the wide range of evidence supports this view far more compellingly than it does the view that attaches meaning to each individual occurrence of the harpsichord. How else can one explain why Bach intermittently employed dual accompaniment throughout his entire Leipzig career, embracing both the most ordinary cantata of the weekly cycles as well as the vast undertakings of the Passions? It is the historical notion of embellishment—the rhetoric of decoration—that best explains Bach's casual addition of the harpsichord to his church accompaniments. In this regard it is well to recall that Bach, after all, signed a document attesting to the merit of a musician who had "adorned our church music with his . . . accomplishments on the . . . harpsichord."

CHAPTER III

The Accompaniment of Recitatives

The Convention of Short Accompaniment in Secco Recitatives

The genre of recitative, imported into German sacred music from Italian secular sources, represents an aesthetic paradox. On the one hand, recitative is music that avoids "singing" and mimics speech. On the other hand, recitative depends on the harmonic syntax of music in order to sustain the illusion that it is talking. Because of this built-in ambiguity, the performance of recitative is bound to include a sizeable share of curiosities. Perhaps the most pronounced is the discrepancy between notation and execution in the vocal part. As Walther explains in the *Lexikon:* "[Although] one writes down the vocal part in a correct measure, one has . . . the freedom to alter the value of the notes, making them longer or shorter . . . in order to express the affect."[1] That is, even though the recitative is notated as if sung metrically, the singer follows a speechlike declamation of the text rather than the beat. Other practices of the recitative, such as vocal appoggiaturas, were also conventionally "misrepresented" by musical notation. As for the continuo players, they sometimes had to "telescope" cadences—preempting the singer in order to hurry toward a dramatic cadence, which also entailed disregarding the literal notation of their part.[2] Conventions such as these were simply the stock and trade of eighteenth-century musicians.

Another issue of recitative performance—equally fundamental to interpretation—concerns the length of bass notes in secco recitatives. In this kind of recitative, accompanied only by the continuo, composers notated a succession of tied whole and half notes, which, according to several eighteenth-century writers, were not sustained. Instead, the bass players played quarter notes followed by rests until the next change of harmony. Only in the so-called accompagnato recitatives (those with an orchestral complement in addition to the continuo) were the long notes supposed to be played as written. Each long note in the secco recitative was therefore written in shorthand. Consequently, an accompaniment that looks sustained actually sounded highly punctuated, a practice that I call "short accompaniment." A sample of a notated secco recitative bass superimposed over its rendition is given in Example 3-1. The vast majority of Bach's secco recitatives—both in the autograph scores and in the continuo parts—are notated in the usual long values. In this chapter I argue that Bach's bass players knew and used the convention that rendered the long notes short.

Considering the practical differences between two contrasting renditions of a Bach recitative—one applying the convention, the other playing "as written"—it is surprising that the question never commanded a more prominent position in the literature. Arnold Schering mentioned the subject in 1936 only in passing when he noted that "neither the organ nor the cello ever held out the bass notes in secco recitatives."[3] Although he referred to an "old tradition" mandating the convention, Schering based his judgment on the notational inconsistency in Bach's parts for the St. Matthew Passion. While Bach had notated the secco recitatives in his score in long values, he systematically replaced them with quarter notes and rests in the continuo parts. Schering supposed that Bach's parts made explicit a musical practice that was actually implicit in the score. Arthur Mendel supplemented this view in 1950 with further bits of evidence from other manuscript parts and, in addition, cited several eighteenth-century treatises that described the convention. On the other hand, Jack Westrup argued that the quarter-note basses in the Passion intentionally offset the contrasting sustained style that Bach used to accompany Jesus and were therefore not a matter of performance practice, but one of compositional style pertaining specially to the Passion. And in 1955, Friedrich-Heinrich Neumann detailed a comprehen-

EXAMPLE 3-1 The convention of short accompaniment

sive list of documentary sources that mentioned short accompaniment but implied that, as a general practice, it seemed doubtful.[4]

Peter Williams reiterated this skepticism in 1969. Although citing authorities approving of the convention, he questioned whether Bach made any consistent use of it. Asserting that "the fashion for short chords . . . arose or grew during the 1730s, at least in Leipzig," Williams believed that the "organist accompanied according to the ability of the singer, the acoustical conditions, the type of text, any changing fashions, the length of each harmonic unit."[5] In short, there was no convention. Accordingly, he understood the short notation in the secco recitatives in the St. Matthew Passion as an exception underscoring the dramatic contrast between the short style accompanying the Evangelist and the sustained style accompanying Jesus. On the other hand, Ingrid Smit Duyzentkunst took the eighteenth-century writers to mean that the literal rendition of long bass notes in secco recitatives would stand in the way of understanding the words in the vocal part. But on the harpsichord, where the sound diminishes after the attack, short bass notes would not differ noticeably from long held ones. The force of short accompaniment, then, applies more reasonably to the organ and stringed basses, instruments that sustain their tone.[6]

The author treating the subject in the greatest detail is Emil Platen, who argued against a convention of short accompaniment in Bach's sacred recitatives.[7] Encountering contradictory opinions among the eighteenth-century writers, Platen surmised that they only "transmit the subjective opinion of their authors" and decided that the only credible documents germane to Bach's practice are the manuscripts of his works. The thrust of his argument concerns a group of continuo parts in which different secco recitatives in the same work appear to be notated in both short and long notation. For example, from the NBA edition (I/39) of Cantata 30a, it would appear that, of the five secco movements, only Movement 10 has the short notation.[8] If in similar types of recitative, Platen argued, Bach notated one continuo part in quarter notes followed by rests and another in sustained values, then he intended his bass parts to sound as written.[9]

Reconstructing an implicit historical practice, to be sure, presents difficult problems. For some writers, the treatises furnish the most convincing evidence because they verbally attest to a convention. For others, Bach's uniqueness provides an excuse to discount the treatises and to rely solely on the composer's notational habits. Since, on a few occasions, the composer wrote the secco bass lines in quarter notes, one might think that Bach wanted the bass lines played short only when he wrote them that way. But this argument begs the question; the object of the inquiry is whether or not the players took the practice for granted. A convention such as short accompaniment assumes, after all, that a player interprets the signs of duration in one genre differently from the way he does in another. In fact, the most usual mark of a convention is its absence from the musical page. This is why a purely inductive approach will not work: instead of arguing from each bit of evidence, an explanation must account for the origins of a convention, how it was maintained, how people spoke of it, and, finally, why it died out.

In the case of Bach, the most plausible argument runs as follows: Bach's continuo players performed secco recitatives according to the convention because, quite simply, it was the mainstream practice in eighteenth-century Germany. Short accompaniment, having originated in response to an unpleasant drone produced by a sustained organ bass, became the rule for all continuo players, whether in sacred or secular music. While the long bass notes in accompagnato recitatives were played as written, those in secco movements were habitually shortened to quarter notes and rests. Sometimes, in fact, Bach even distinguished between the two subgenres, inserting the direction *accomp[agnato]* in the continuo part or else marking it *piano,* while he left the secco movements unmarked. In the case of a conventional cantata performance, the distinction was useful if also dispensable: it was immediately obvious when the violinists raised their bows that a recitative was accompanied. The composer was also on hand to clear up any confusion. When Bach went to the trouble of writing secco basses in quarter notes and rests— as he did only on a few occasions—he did so to prevent any ambiguity. This was somewhat like the practice of marking a trill or, in later music, a *ritardando,* even when a player knew perfectly well to add it anyway. Bach may have notated explicit parts to help an inexperienced continuo player, such as a bassoonist, or to distinguish secco passages whose presence in the middle of an arioso the players might have missed. In a large-scale work such as the St. Matthew Passion, moreover, the "short" notation would have helped continuo players manage the ever-shifting alternation between secco and accompagnato recitatives. Although this method was more laborious for Bach—it takes far more time to notate quarter notes and rests than tied whole and half notes—it probably improved performances. Finally, the examples of explicit notation all suggest that players did not realize the convention haphazardly but reduced the long values essentially to quarter notes and rests.

To support this interpretation, it is necessary first to establish short accompaniment as a norm. To do this, I attempt to compile a history of the convention in the eighteenth century from the vantage point of the literary sources that refer to it. I then turn to Bach's continuo parts to examine how they not only reflect the mainstream practice described in the treatises but even anticipate specially recommended notational practices mentioned only after Bach's death. In addition, I introduce some fresh evidence for short accompaniment in the form of special cues found in several parts from Bach's Weimar cantatas.

Witnesses to the Convention: 1711–1750

The earliest German source for short accompaniment is Johann David Heinichen's *Neu erfundene und Gründliche Anweisung,* printed in Hamburg in 1711, just two years before Bach began composing recitatives in his vocal works. According to Heinichen, the recitative required special knowledge to interpret it properly. As he puts it: "The recitative is a new and quite special style which, because it is played mostly without instruments, is in all aspects extralegal in the sense that it obeys neither the normal [harmonic] resolutions . . . the meter, nor the other usual rules."[10] Although the recitative was scarcely a novelty in 1711, it was only in 1704 that Erdmann Neumeister had promoted the introduction of Italian arias and recitatives into German sacred cantata texts.[11] It was this new sacred recitative with organ that probably prompted Heinichen to mention short accompaniment:

The way to play the recitative properly, however, varies greatly according to the instruments on which it is played. In church recitatives, since organ pipes that echo and hum are involved, no complications are needed, for one mostly just strikes the notes flat down and the hands remain lying on the keys without further ceremony until another chord follows, which is held out in its turn . . . But if the hands are lifted from the keys immediately after striking a new chord, so that a rest takes the place of the notes, this is done according to the circumstances obtaining, the better to hear and observe either the singer or the instruments that sometimes accompany the recitative. Or else one finds other reasons to lift the hands somewhat; for example, because the bass sometimes remains on one note and chord for three, four or more measures, and consequently one's ear becomes irked by the constant monotony of the humming organ pipes. All these questions must be settled by the taste and judgment of the accompanist.[12]

This text presents something of a puzzle. To be sure, Heinichen sanctions two methods of accompaniment: the sustained and literal as well as the conventional short form. At least, most writers have understood him in this way.[13] Accordingly, he appears to describe short accompaniment as optional, one of two valid practices. But consider Heinichen's first suggestion more closely. As he says, the organist's "hands remain lying on the keys until the next chord," the reason being that "organ pipes that echo and hum are involved." But he seems to have it backwards, for the "humming organ pipes" are precisely what later prompt him to recommend lifting the hands after each chord. Heinichen thus seems to give a contradictory reason for sustaining recitative chords.

Indeed, Heinichen is not at all concerned with the length of bass notes at the beginning of his statement. Given the likelihood that his readers had heard recitative only at the opera, he may have anticipated that continuo players would copy the flourishes and arpeggios observed in the theater in their performances of church recitative.[14] Perhaps this is why the author seems to cater to the novice at the opening of the passage and only later becomes more subtle. Heinichen makes the church organist's first encounter with recitative less daunting with his reassurance that no "ceremony" is required: you just play the chord and wait until the change of harmony. But what ceremony would Heinichen's readers have contemplated? Certainly not the short convention, which he then proceeds to recommend. Rather, the arpeggios previously necessary on the harpsichord to make the accompaniment sound louder become unnecessary on the organ, "since organ pipes that echo and hum are involved." Heinichen's first alternative of playing literally—despite his clear sanction—might therefore be understood less as an endorsement of the *tenuto* style than as a pedagogical tool to distinguish practices of the organ from those of the harpsichord.

This reading also tallies with Heinichen's list of reasons why one should substitute rests for the long notes: one hears the singer better and one can more easily follow the instruments present (that is, in an accompagnato recitative). Or "one finds other reasons" to play short, among which—Heinichen cites only one but implies there are more—is the desire to avoid the monotony of the humming organ pipes. Thus, although the call for "taste and judgment" presumes that short accompaniment is not the obvious choice everywhere, Heinichen seems to prefer it, given the rhetoric with which he describes it. For although he provides no reason at all to sustain the bass lines literally, he furnishes a host of reasons why one should abbreviate them. Perhaps Heinichen's indecision reflects the novelty of the recitative style in German church music.

Unlike Heinichen's treatise, Friedrich Erhard Niedt's *Musicalische Handleitung* (part III), published in Hamburg in 1717, requires short accompaniment in all church recitatives: "To [the organist and the bass players] I must insist that, *nota bene,* when they encounter a recitative with two to three measures set in sustained values, they do no more than play the beginning of each new note that appears and then pause until a new note follows in turn."[15] Although Niedt seems to restrict short accompaniment to bass notes at least two measures in length, the accompanying musical example (Facsimile 3-1) reveals that he consistently reduced all "white" notes to quarter notes and rests. The accompanying text confirms this: "The bass notes should be played as they are notated here in the bass in black; and the same should be observed in all recitatives, if they are to sound properly and not rattle like an old millwheel." Niedt, who died in 1708, is therefore the first to prescribe short accompaniment in all secco recitatives. (He does not discuss recitatives accompanied by melody instruments.) In addition, he makes it clear that the convention applies to the cellos and basses as well as to the organ. While Heinichen had specifically objected to the "humming organ pipes" that became irksome, Niedt's image of the rattling "old mill-wheel" alludes to the obtrusiveness of every bass instrument. Finally, unlike Heinichen, Niedt represents the convention as a reduction of all long values to quarter notes and rests. Although this need not imply that the shortened lengths were exact quarter notes—composers may have considered the reduction itself as only approximate—Niedt suggests that the shortening was uniform rather than arbitrary.

The practice can next be traced to London, where a traveling Frenchman, Pierre Jacques Fougeroux, attended performances of operas by Handel. He wrote to an acquaintance in 1728: "As you are not a devotee of Italian music, I do not mind telling you, Monsieur, that, except for the recitatives and the bad manner of accompanying them, cutting off the sound of each chord, there are some magnificent airs for the winds accompanied by violins which leave nothing to be desired."[16] Thus, to a Frenchman, the objectionable quality of Italianate recitative lies precisely in the application of short accompaniment, according to which the sound of each chord is "cut off." That Fougeroux identifies the convention as Italian is not to say that he knew the practice originated in Italy; perhaps he merely considered indigenous what he heard in an "Italian" opera. In any case, this documented use of the convention in an opera suggests that, its conceivable German origin notwithstanding, short accompaniment was not confined only to church music.

The convention is mentioned next in David Kellner's *Treulicher Unterricht im General-Bass,* a treatise on thorough bass issued in Hamburg in 1732. Kellner was an organist and lutenist from Leipzig who left for

58

Note / die da vor kommt / einen Anschlag oder Anstoß zugeben / und dann so lange einhalten / bis wiedrum eine neue Note erfolge. Ferner / daß sie bey denen Cadentzen die Noten nicht so lange aushalten / als sie geschrieben stehen / sondern gleich zur folgenden schreiten.

16. Wo überm General-Baß in denen Recitativen Ziffern gesetzt sind / so observire der accompagnirende Baßist wohl / ob der Sänger bey denselben und dem Accord feste bleibe / da er dann solche zu exprimiren eben nicht nöthig hat ; Wo aber der Sänger aus dem Thon oder Accord fällt / kan er derselben Ziffern ihre Bedeutung aufm Clavier oder Orgel berühren / damit der Sänger sich wieder auf den rechten Weg helffen könne ; als Z. E. es stünde folgendes Recitativ:

59

Stockholm in 1711. He writes: "The arpeggio is not much used on organs. On the other hand, when the bass has to hold very long notes, one sometimes lifts the hands and rests until the next chord so as to hear the vocalist more clearly and not nauseate anyone with the long drawn-out howling of the organ pipes."[17] It is not coincidental that this passage recalls Heinichen: Kellner's treatise often provides little more than a gloss on Heinichen. This is why it is interesting to note that Kellner omits mention of the literal rendition of recitative as an explicit alternative, suggesting instead that arpeggiated chords are not particularly appropriate to organ accompaniment, something Heinichen had only hinted at. To be sure, Kellner, like Heinichen, states that short accompaniment is an occasional practice. It is possible, therefore, that he wanted organists to play as written in secco movements. But Kellner's objection to such literal renditions is even stronger than Heinichen's: while Heinichen found the blaring organ pipes merely "irksome," Kellner found them even "nauseating."

Georg Philipp Telemann also advocated short accompaniment, but proposed a different method from Niedt's. In his *Singe-, Spiel- und Generalbass-Übungen* of 1733–1734, Telemann notes the following below an example of secular recitative: "About recitative: When a dissonant chord such as at (a) or (c) enters, then only the right hand plays but not, at the same time, the left hand. If such a chord resolves into a consonance, such as at (b), then both hands play" (Example 3-2). Telemann's discussion does not even mention the matter of bass-note length. Nor is he concerned with sacred recitatives played on the organ, or with the practices of the string bass players. And although the musical example shows the bass note sustained and the chords in the right hand shortened, only a second musical example with its accompanying text clarifies his practice: "Here at (c) the bass remains on the keys, because a $\frac{6}{5}$ dissonance is formed above it" (Example 3-3).[18]

Thus, Telemann sustains the bass and shortens the chords in the right hand. The quarter-note reduction in the right hand is something like Niedt's recommendation, except that the bass is not involved. Perhaps Telemann relied on Heinichen's view that the realized organ chords—and not the sustained bass lines—create the disturbance. Echoes of this practice can be found in an anonymous Dutch treatise from around 1750, "Manier om op de clavecimbel te leeren speelen den Generalen Bas of Bassus continuus" ("Method for learning to play thorough bass or basso continuo on the harpsichord"), and in a southern German treatise from 1751, *Der wohlunterwiesene Generalbass-Schüler* by Georg

EXAMPLE 3-2 Telemann, *Singe-, Spiel- und Generalbass-Übungen* (1733–1734)

EXAMPLE 3-3 Telemann, *Singe-, Spiel- und Generalbass-Übungen* (1733–1734)

Joseph Joachim Hahn, who first quotes Telemann nearly verbatim and then specifies that the organist "removes his right hand after striking the chords and pauses until the new chord."[19]

But if Telemann's view was later repeated, it diverged from the mainstream formulation of the convention, judging from the weight of other evidence. Gottfried Heinrich Stölzel, for example, in his "Abhandlung vom Recitativ," recommends that organists play recitative chords for the length of a quarter note followed by a rest.[20] While revealing nothing newsworthy in itself, this formulation led Stölzel to suggest that the composer write no bass note longer than a whole note, since the fundament should not be absent for too long. Obviously this is true only if all bass instruments—not only the organ—systematically shortened their parts in recitatives. A well-traveled musician, Stölzel completed his studies in Leipzig and secured a position in Breslau, after which he journeyed throughout Italy and performed in Prague, Bayreuth, and Gera. In 1719 he became Capellmeister in Gotha (Thuringia). The "Abhandlung," preserved only in manuscript, was submitted to Lorenz Mizler's Society of Musical Sciences around 1740 as Stölzel's scholarly contribution about a year after he joined the organization. His is the first source, then, that documents the convention in a geographic area removed from the influence of Hamburg, and establishes the currency of short accompaniment in Bach's native region.

Another contemporary Thuringian source confirming Stölzel's view is J. S. Voigt's *Gespräch von der Musik,* which appeared in Erfurt in 1742. Voigt includes the following instructions when accompanying recitative: "But I must not remain continually on the keys sounding like a hurdy-gurdy, for this would be no accompaniment at all. No, instead I must lift my hands off properly so that the listener can understand the text."[21] The new metaphor of the hurdy-gurdy reiterates the complaint about the unpleasant drone of the organ pipes and, at the same time, suggests that the rationale for short accompaniment had remained remarkably consistent since Heinichen's treatise of 1711 first raised the subject.

In summary, the reintroduction of Italianate recitative into German sacred music apparently brought with it the practice of playing bass parts in some abbreviated fashion. The most common method—when specified at all—replaced long values with quarter notes and rests. Exactly where the convention was in use or precisely how it was applied is difficult to determine. However, all three writers (including Telemann) who describe any shortening at all specify it in only one form: quarter notes and rests. Short accompaniment—when adopted—seems to have provided a relatively simple method of enhancing the comprehensibility of the text while eliminating an annoying drone in the bass.[22]

Later Witnesses: 1750–1810

Short accompaniment did not always guarantee that bass players would provide a sensitive accompaniment for the singers. In the midst of a review of Johann Adolph Scheibe's opera *Thusnelde,* Christoph Gottfried Krause writes: "Therefore it would not be amiss if the bass instruments would play every note quite softly and always hold them out somewhat, instead, as is usual, of striking them short and loud."[23] Without criticizing the convention per se, Krause takes exception to an exaggerated application of it. This follows from his instructions to "play every note quite softly and always hold them out *somewhat.*" One can easily imagine how a coarse attack on the bass notes, too loud and too short, would interfere with a fluent comprehension of the text, the very effect the convention was designed to achieve. The offending party, moreover, apparently included the entire continuo group, thereby demonstrating that it was not a practice limited to keyboardists.

Another author confirms that short accompaniment had spread to musical centers removed from the German mainstream. Jacob Wilhelm Lustig writes in his *Muzykaale Spraakkonst* (Amsterdam, 1754): "The notes in the continuo, although consisting primarily of tied and whole notes, must only be treated as quarter notes with rests, above all on organs, positive-organs and regals, in order to support the singer and never drown him out."[24] An orthodox advocate of the convention, Lustig continues:

But if certain short emphasized passages appear in the middle or at the end of an Italian recitative, the composer departs from spoken declamation and obliges the performers to play in strict time. He indicates this by the words "Obbligato" or "Arioso." And if such a recitative is to be accompanied by various instruments, such as violins, which either will be heard in long notes, pianissimo, as if floating underneath, or in staccato quarters and eighths, [sometimes] softly and then switching to fortissimo at certain outbursts, this too is played in strict time, for such a [large group] of people cannot otherwise maintain ensemble. It must be done in such a way that each player listens to the singer, while the singer always has the freedom, at least when the violins have only the sustained, long notes, to match the vocal part to spoken declamation. Such pieces, called "accompagnamenti," are eminently suited to arouse and sustain the most powerful and exalted emotions.[25]

Detailing the two types of accompanied recitative—those with sustained chords "floating underneath" and those organized by a repeating motive—Lustig makes clear for the first time that the accompagnato is specially indicated in the parts with a dynamic marking or a term such as "obbligato."[26] When the whole string contingent plays in the sustained style, the accompanying parts play as written and refrain from any shortening. Although not entirely explicit, the distinction drawn between accompagnato and secco styles (with and without dynamic markings) entails a practical advantage for the continuo player. Since, in all other regards, both species of recitative look identical on the page, the player can tell by the dynamic marking whether to exercise the convention: if he sees the "pianissimo" marking, he plays long; if he sees no special marking, he plays short.

Jean-Jacques Rousseau spells this out in his *Dictionnaire de Musique* (1768):

Accompanied recitative is that type to which an accompaniment of violins is added beside the continuo. This accompaniment, which could hardly be syllabic in view of the rapidity of the declamation, ordinarily consists of long notes sustained over entire measures. To denote this, one writes the word "sostenuto" over all parts of the orchestra, but mainly over the bass, who otherwise would only play short and detached strokes at each change of note as in ordinary recitative, whereas in the accompagnato it is necessary to fill and sustain the sounds according to the full value of the notes.[27]

For Rousseau, then, short accompaniment applies automatically in an "ordinary recitative"—that is, in a secco. So powerful is the convention that when one wants the bass players to play as written, the composer must indicate a special marking to dictate that the normal practice be suspended. It is no accident that Rousseau assigns the Italian word *sostenuto* for this purpose. An outspoken partisan of Italian opera in a now well-known dispute, Rousseau discusses the performance of Italianate recitative (which had already made inroads in France) rather than that of the classical French style of Lully and Rameau. This French variety had apparently always been accompanied in sustained notes—recall Monsieur Fougeroux's prejudices—since French opera had never developed a species of a freely declaimed secco. That is, with its emphasis on a formalized "tragic" declamation—the length of bars, not of note values, was altered—native French recitative did not strive for the more "comic" or naturalistic speech rhythms found in Italianate recitative. But whether short accompaniment had anything to do with Italy still remains something of a mystery.

Proposing a divergent method of short accompaniment resembling Telemann's, Johann Samuel Petri—an acquaintance of Wilhelm Friedemann Bach and a cantor in Silesia—marks a departure from the standard method of recitative accompaniment. In 1767 Petri wrote: "In recitatives [the organist] does not always hold the chords, but makes use of dismembered or broken and arpeggiated chords to avoid the howling . . . After playing the chord in the recitative, he often sustains the bass alone, sometimes in the pedal, sometimes in the manual, according to the circumstances obtaining."[28] Evidently dissatisfied with this pronouncement, Petri attached an addendum to it in a later edition of the same work published in 1782: "But I want to note one other thing here. When the organ has a very quiet covered flute stop, one can—in the recitatives without other accompanying instruments—quietly hold out the chords in the left hand with this stop and always tap the new bass notes in the pedal. In this way, you will support the singer satisfactorily without covering him or drowning him out."[29] The earlier statement echoes Telemann's dictum that the harpsichordist sustain the bass notes while shortening the chords; the addendum in the later edition explains how the chords can be sustained while the bass notes are shortened. Petri's first method probably stems from C. P. E. Bach's formulations in the second part to his *Versuch,* published in 1762. Bach, who does not mention the secco convention, notes that in the sustained variety of accompagnato, "the organ holds only the bass, the chords being quitted soon after they are struck."[30] Petri extends this recommendation to all recitatives, apparently to minimize the effect of the droning organ pipes without entirely eliminating the bass. The later formulation then transfers the harmonic burden to the manual, provided that an unobtrusive stop is available. In any case, Petri does not clarify any practices for the other continuo players.

The most exhaustive description of mainstream German practice is found in Christoph Gottlieb Schröter's *Deutliche Anweisung zum General-Bass,* printed in Halberstadt in 1772. Schröter, born in 1699, studied and worked in Leipzig and Dresden, traveled throughout Germany, Holland, and England, and in 1732 assumed the post of organist in Nordhausen (Thuringia), where he remained until his death in 1782. He was one of the first members of Mizler's Society and, moreover, is known to have corresponded with Bach in the late 1740s.[31] His synoptic account reads as follows:

There are three types of recitative. The mark of the first type is when a vocal line appears above the figured bass notes, *nota bene,* without the word "Accompagnement" or "col stromenti." Although the bass here has mostly whole and half notes, the organist must shorten all such boring notes together with their required harmonies into nearly eighth notes . . . In the second type of recitative the bass and the instruments have mostly quarter notes with rests set afterwards. Now and then there are also running sixteenths or thirty-seconds before or at the beginning of a new section. These are played metrically and the organist executes his part as in the first type. By the third type I mean those which are accompanied by violins and where the whole and half notes are sustained sweetly, giving rise to a pleasant humming. In this type of recitative the meter must also be followed exactly. This type must also be designated with the words "accompagnement" or "col violini." Otherwise, the organists and the other accompanying bass players, through no fault of their own, would shorten the notes as in the first type of recitative. I generally shorten every chord on the organ with both hands so that nothing disturbs the humming of the violins. However, I sustain the pedal notes, mainly when the number of accompanying basses is small.[32]

Schröter thus echoes Rousseau in declaring that the absence of any marking on a recitative automatically indicates that it is secco and hence subject to shortening. Schröter also implies that the custom of shortening organ chords in accompagnatos—so as not to "disturb the humming of the violins"—is a secondary matter taken up only after drawing the fundamental distinction in performance between the secco and accompagnato varieties. Only Schröter's stated length of notes under the secco convention is unusual: instead of quarters, he says that bass notes are shortened "nearly into eighths." This was either an idiosyncratic preference or, more probably, an attempt to capture with greater accuracy what he took to be common practice.

Daniel Gottlob Türk, in a treatise of 1787, also mentions the execution of short accompaniment. Here for the first time a writer subjects the notational conventions of the practice to scrutiny, not to attack it but to improve its realization. Türk sets forth an orthodox account of the secco convention, complete with a musical example showing the usual transformation of the long values into quarter notes. He then continues: "Obviously it would be, if not better, at least less misleading if all composers followed the example of some and wrote the notes as they are to be played, such as, for example, Capellmeister Bach did in his Passion and in the *Israelites:* namely, if they wrote quarter notes instead of whole notes, following them with as many rests as necessary until the accompanist is supposed to play a new bass note or another chord. Perhaps then recitatives would be better executed than it now occasionally happens with many an organist and bass player."[33] The Capellmeister Bach is Carl Philipp Emanuel Bach, who, in the printed score of his Hamburg oratorio, "Die Israeliten in der Wüste" ("The Israelites in the Desert"), had notated all secco movements with quarters and rests. Perhaps the fact that he had "spelled out" the convention explains why Emanuel failed to discuss the length of bass notes in his *Versuch* of 1762: if he prescribed the precise lengths of bass notes in his musical works, the issue need never have surfaced in his treatise. In any case, the performance of secco recitative had become something of a problem by the 1780s, as Türk's concluding remark indicates. Writing consistent short values would therefore improve recitative accompaniment. In retrospect, this also explains why composers ever went to the trouble of specifying the quarter notes instead of relying on the convention. Emanuel Bach was apparently not the only composer to attempt this clarification, for his own father had set a notable precedent in this very matter. It can hardly be accidental that the younger Bach notated the recitatives in his *Israelites* with a method identical to that used by J. S. Bach in his parts for the St. Matthew Passion. Although more remains to be said on this matter, it is conceivable that explicit secco notation may even have originated with J. S. Bach.

Authors writing at the end of the eighteenth century and just beyond confirm that short accompaniment in its orthodox form continued to

FACSIMILE 3-2 Short accompaniment disputed in an article from the Leipzig *Allgemeine Musikalische Zeitung* (1810), copy located in Music Library, Yale University

prevail through the turn of the century in such important locales as England, Saxony, and Bavaria. Their treatises include Johann Joseph Klein's *Versuch eines Lehrbuchs des praktischen Musik* (1783), Sebastian Prixner's *Kann man nicht in zwey, oder drey Monaten die Orgel lernen?* (1789), and Augustus Frederic Christopher Kollmann's *Practical Guide to Thorough-Bass* (1801).[34] These writers repeat the familiar formulations of the mainstream convention, often echoing Niedt and Heinichen or even lifting phrases directly from Türk. That the works of Heinichen (1711) and Niedt (1717) continued to be quoted into the nineteenth century says something, surely, about the longevity of practices associated with recitative.

Not until 1810 did the convention become controversial. An unsigned article in the Leipzig *Allgemeine Musikalische Zeitung* entitled "Which is the best and most purposeful manner for the basses to accompany simple recitative?" records an imaginary dialogue between two characters, Altlieb and Neulieb ("Old-fashioned" and "Newfangled"), who argue over a musical example in which a bass line from a secco recitative by Johann Adolph Hasse (1699–1783) is realized in the short values (see Facsimile 3-2):

Neulieb: Wrong, this manner of accompaniment is fundamentally wrong. These whole and half notes must be executed just as the composer prescribed them.

Altlieb: Perhaps a misunderstanding lies at the root of this. The Italian composers, such as Graun and particularly Hasse, made use of this notation as an abbreviation, as it were, to spare themselves and the copyists writing so many rests, and partly to provide the accompanists at the keyboard with an overview by omitting the many signs and by leaving the bass note in clear view. That they never meant these long notes to be sustained is proven even today by the orchestras of Berlin and Dresden, both led by Graun and Hasse for so many years, who still play every change of bass note short, no matter what its written length. Hiller in particular confirmed this: He had trained under Hasse and in so many oratorios and operas in which he led the Leipzig orchestra insisted on the simple short attack of the bass note. And in the cases where the basses were supposed to hold out their notes, why would Hasse especially have written *tenuto* over these parts?

Neulieb: But now this method belongs to the worthless, old junk condemned to the attic. Our conductor, admittedly still a young man but full of artistic knowledge and experience, has heard the orchestras of Italy, Vienna, and Munich, and insists that we sustain the long notes.[35]

The author, who may even have been the editor himself, Johann Friedrich Rochlitz, sides with Altlieb in defending the convention while dramatizing a contemporary dispute.[36] Of particular interest is Altlieb's account of the convention's origins. No longer are the howling organ pipes to blame; rather, the "white" notation better represented the voice-leading and simplified the work for composers and copyists. Despite Altlieb's old-fashioned taste with its eye toward north Germany, the author confirms that short accompaniment was still current in Berlin and Dresden as late as 1810. Just as significant is Neulieb's objection on the grounds that it violates the composer's intentions: modern composers—he seems to say—notate their works as they intend them to sound. Neulieb is therefore the first "author" to state that the bass notes in secco recitatives should be played as written.

The Convention in Historical Perspective

The review of the treatises suggests that, with the assimilation of the Italian recitative into Protestant church music at the beginning of the eighteenth century, musicians in German and German-influenced centers began to shorten long values in the bass parts of simple recitatives. Authors offered various reasons for the convention: it relieved the monotony of sustained organ pipes and droning bass lines, allowed listeners to understand the text better, saved time for the copyist, and represented harmonic progressions with greater clarity for the keyboardists. Writers who mention short accompaniment came from a wide geographic area: Germany, France, England, Holland, and Sweden; and within Germany, they came from both Protestant and Catholic centers including Hamburg, Berlin, Thuringia, Saxony, Silesia, and Bavaria. Nevertheless, the convention was probably not universally known or practiced in the earliest years of the eighteenth century, since some writers prescribe it as a novel corrective to ignorance while others offer it as only one choice—albeit a desirable one. Yet whenever a musical example of the practice accompanies a text's recommendation—as in Niedt, Türk, and others—only quarter notes are supplied. Musical realizations of the convention, in other words, never hint that bass notes of varying lengths were substituted for the long values, although one writer suggests that the reduced notes should be played neither too loud nor too short. Finally, most writers imply that the entire continuo group made use of the convention.

Even the recommendations of Telemann and Petri to detach only the realized chords and not the bass confirm that, in order to understand the text, some form of shortening was required in recitatives. In any case, no eighteenth-century author takes issue with the convention and asserts that one should "play as written." The salient feature of all statements in the literature is that they were founded on essentially the same principles. The polarity between the secco and the accompagnato genres was apparently such that composers marked the accompagnato primarily to distinguish it from the secco. As soon as authors begin to discuss accompanied recitative, they specify that the convention did not apply to it. For if players failed to recognize that a recitative was accompanied, they would be tempted to invoke short accompaniment where it was never intended. This inclination to separate the practice of secco from accompagnato explains why composers ever bothered to write out the short notation and why they often marked accompagnato movements with dynamic signs and provided performance indications directing players to sustain the long values. In so doing, they avoided a potentially annoying notational ambiguity: one musical sign serving two renditions. In fact, Türk praises none other than a son of J. S. Bach for clearing up this unfortunate confusion. Whatever the notational choice made by a particular composer, the convention itself was a standard norm of performance in important German centers through the turn of the century.

Evidence in Bach's Continuo Parts

Weimar Sources

Such were the practices of the eighteenth century. How do the original parts for Bach's vocal works reflect this history? Most striking is the fact that evidence of short accompaniment surfaces in three cantatas from

Bach's Weimar period (ca. 1713–1716), that is, at the very time when descriptions of short accompaniment occur in treatises by Heinichen (1711) and Niedt (1717).

Among the performance materials for two cantatas from the intervening years,[37] Cantatas 18 (1713?) and 185 (1715), are autograph bassoon parts in which Bach notated the only secco recitative in quarter notes and rests. The corresponding movements in the organ, cello, and violone parts are, however, notated in the long values. Confronting this discrepancy, Arthur Mendel suggests that the bassoonist, possibly the most inexperienced member of Bach's ensemble, may have been unfamiliar with the secco convention and that Bach helped him along by notating the part precisely as it was to be played. Although plausible, this explanation does not take into account the circumstances of Cantata 185, in which Bach notated short values for the bassoon in the secco as well as the accompagnato recitative movements. It becomes difficult to argue, then, that the bassoonist realized the continuo part correctly in the secco movements but not in the accompagnato movements, in which the other continuo players played the long notes as written. Indeed, the short notation in both recitative movements in Cantata 185 tends to support Peter Williams's view that Bach intentionally designed the short bassoon notes to articulate a particular timbre against the supposed *tenuto* notes in the organ.[38]

The original parts, however, supply further evidence that had previously escaped notice. Above the long notes in the secco recitatives of all the continuo parts for both Cantatas 18 and 185 is a set of small vertical strokes resembling the staccato marks frequently used by Bach and his contemporaries (see Facsimiles 3-3 and 3-5).[39] Each stroke corresponds to a quarter note in the bassoon part, as can be seen by comparing the corresponding passages in the *Violoncello* and *Fagotto* parts for Cantata 18 (see Facsimiles 3-3 and 3-4). Moreover, since Bach squeezed his continuo figures in the organ part for Cantata 18 around the cues, they are surely original and most likely reminded the continuo players to shorten their bass notes. It is even conceivable that Bach himself gestured at the same moment to bring everyone in together.[40] The cues, of course, might only have directed the player's eye to the next change of chord without indicating anything about short accompaniment. They are not found, however, over the corresponding long notes of the accompagnato movement in Cantata 185. In this case their absence suggests that, despite the bassoon's short quarter notes, the continuo players played the long notes in the accompagnato movement as written.[41]

The continuo parts for Cantata 31, another Weimar cantata from 1715, also contain cues in a secco recitative. In the original *Violoncello*

EXAMPLE 3-4 Cantata 31, Movement 5, placement of cues in *Violoncello* part

part used by the cellist and the organist, Bach must have entered the cues before the thorough-bass figures in Movement 5, a secco recitative. (Example 3-4 represents the placement of the cues.) Since the bassoon is *tacet* in this movement, the cues have nothing to do with a special conflict between two continuo parts. Instead, they apparently helped the player recall that the convention applies in this movement. Arthur Mendel's supposition that Bach wrote a precisely notated part for an inexperienced bassoonist thus proves quite reasonable. However, the cues confirm no less the inexperience of the other continuo players in complying with short accompaniment. Perhaps Bach conceived the staccato marks as a pedagogical device to teach the proper performance of secco recitative. Just a few years earlier, Heinichen had called the recitative a "new and quite special style" that does not "obey the usual rules." But where Heinichen had vacillated about a systematic application of short accompaniment, Bach was consistent. In the bassoon parts, Bach invariably used quarter notes for every "reduction." Moreover, the staccato cues in all three cantatas are likewise distributed consistently across the parts in the designated movements.[42] Except in these three early cantatas, Bach never again employed cues for short accompaniment, probably because—as Lustig, Rousseau, and Schröter state—the convention became an automatic procedure. The presence of the cues thus suggests that Bach's Weimar years saw not only the introduction of the recitative genres into his cantatas but also an awareness that the secco and accompagnato kinds required different manners of execution.

Leipzig Sources

The vast majority of Bach's Leipzig continuo parts do not distinguish between the notation of basses in secco movements and that in accompagnato movements and hence do not constitute evidence pointing to

FACSIMILE 3-3 Cantata 18, *Violoncello* part with staccato cue strokes, Deutsche Staatsbibliothek Berlin/ DDR, Musikabteilung, Mus. ms. Bach St 34 [St 34/12]

FACSIMILE 3-4 Cantata 18, *Fagotto* part with short notation, Deutsche Staatsbibliothek Berlin/DDR, Musikabteilung, Mus. ms. Bach St 34 [St 34/13]

FACSIMILE 3-5 Cantata 185, *Violone* part with staccato cue strokes, Deutsche Staatsbibliothek Berlin/ DDR, Musikabteilung, Mus. ms. Bach St 4 [St 4/10]

short accompaniment. The absence of a marked distinction may, of course, merely indicate that bass players invoked the convention whenever they accompanied the singer alone. Nonetheless, evidence from secco recitatives notated in short values as well as verbal clues found in the parts suggest that, given certain circumstances, Bach found it advantageous to clear up any ambiguity between the intended renditions of the secco and accompagnato genres. Ultimately, it is the strict consistency of method characterizing these exceptional instances which suggests that Bach's orchestra followed the mainstream practice.

Secco recitatives in short values. The normal genres of secco and accompagnato looked identical to the continuo player. Nonetheless, in an ordinary church cantata, with a recitative movement either accompagnato or secco, it could not have been difficult to tell the difference between them: either the violinists (or oboists, or flutists) lifted their instruments to play, or they did not. Yet when secco passages were very brief and led directly into an arioso, players may have failed to note that they should invoke the convention. In Cantatas 69/4 (1723), 58/4 (1727), 94/5 (1732), 30/11 (1738), and 197 (1742), Bach assisted his players by notating secco passages adjoining accompagnato or arioso sections in the short fashion.

This type of shift in genre can be seen, for example, in the two continuo parts for Cantata 69, Movement 4, a recitative that moves from secco to accompagnato. In one part the copyist had copied the long values from the score, but Bach, in the course of his revisions, clarified the necessary change in execution by indicating *accomp.* at the entrance of the violins. But since the composer copied the bassoon part himself, he went even further and specified the short values in the seven measures of secco. In Movement 2, however, a pure secco recitative, Bach retained the long values even in the bassoon part: here there was no confusion.[43] Since Bach must have had some practical purpose in mind when indicating *accomp.*, there is good reason to conclude that, as in the Weimar examples, he intended the short notation in the bassoon part—the one autograph continuo part—to approximate the correct realization of the other bass lines.[44]

In another group of parts, the continuo parts contain regular quarter notes and rests in every secco movement throughout an entire piece, and here again it was Bach as copyist who decided on the explicit short notation. This group includes the conspicuous set of parts for the St. Matthew Passion (1736) as well as parts for the Ascension Oratorio, BWV 11 (1735), and Cantatas 95 (1723), 94 (1732), 97 (1734), and 30a (1737). Consider first the newly rediscovered parts for the Ascension Or-

EXAMPLE 3-5 Ascension Oratorio (BWV 11), Movement 2

atorio.[45] The two *Cammerton* continuo parts were copied by a scribe from Bach's score and hence reflect its readings for the recitatives. Bach, on the other hand, himself prepared the organ part. In each secco movement (Movements 2, 5, 7a, and 7c) Bach spelled out the short notation.[46] The readings in Movements 2 and 7a are particularly revealing because they demonstrate ways in which the secco convention would be applied even to bass lines that include a certain amount of florid writing.[47] In Movement 2 (shown in Example 3-5), after the conventional first two measures, the two roulades are slurred in from the previous note, while in Movement 7a (shown in Example 3-6), the seven sixteenth notes in m. 2 preceding m. 3 evidently require no reiteration of the initial F♯, which sounds only as a quarter note in the first measure.[48]

In Cantata 95, Movement 1 is a choral movement interspersed with a few measures of secco recitative for the tenor. Since the appearance of a recitative in the middle of a choral movement was entirely unexpected—it is also very unusual—Bach took care to notate the secco measures in quarter notes even in the score. He also continued to pre-

EXAMPLE 3-6   Ascension Oratorio (BWV 11), Movement 7a, mm. 1–4

scribe the short values in Movements 2, 4, and 6, all pure secco movements, most likely prompted by his rigor in the opening movement. This type of explicit notation is much like Bach's occasional use of trill signs over cadential dotted figures: they are cautionary if also obligatory.

In a special performance of Cantata 97, a new organ part was prepared that contains the short values. Bach, it seems, wished to foresee uncertain performance conditions on strange turf. Originally performed in Leipzig in 1734 with a normal organ part in *Chorton* (a whole step lower than the *Cammerton* parts of the strings), this cantata was provided with a new organ part transposed down yet another half step to accommodate an orchestra playing at *Tief-Cammerton* ("low chamber-pitch"). Bach may have wished to ensure that the organist would reckon with short accompaniment and therefore notated the one secco recitative (Movement 3) in the short values. As Facsimile 3-6 shows, he decided on the quarter-note values only after first writing out a whole note and nearly reverted to the larger note values in m. 4.

The parts for the St. Matthew Passion present the most impressive

FACSIMILE 3-6 Cantata 97, later organ part with short notation in Movement 3, Deutsche Staatsbiblio-thek Berlin/DDR, Musikabteilung, Mus. ms. Bach St 64 [St 64/15]

evidence regarding Bach's use of short accompaniment. A contemporary copy of Bach's now-lost original score represents the earliest stage of this composition.[49] In this version Bach conceived of only one continuo line, as in the earlier St. John Passion. The secco recitatives, moreover, are notated in their usual long notes. In 1736 Bach prepared a substantially revised version of the work which resulted in a new autograph score incorporating the changes. The most important of these was the division of the continuo into two distinct parts—one for each orchestral choir. Despite some minimally revised recitatives, the score retains the regular notation for the secco movements. In the continuo parts, however, which Bach prepared himself, all secco recitatives were copied with the usual reduction to quarter notes.

The context for this evidence reveals much about its significance. The new score for the St. Matthew Passion is one of Bach's most sumptuous manuscripts, painstakingly copied in the composer's best calligraphic hand. Both the Evangelist's citations of scripture and the chorale text in the opening movement ("O Lamm Gottes") are penned in red ink, a unique practice in Bach's manuscripts. The articulation in the orchestra parts, virtually all autograph, is formulated and revised with utmost care. The special attention that Bach paid to the preparation of these materials, in contrast to the great bulk of the vocal works, is extraordinary and points to the distinctive position occupied by the St. Matthew Passion in Bach's vocal oeuvre.[50] Just as the B-minor Mass was his tribute to Latin figural music, the St. Matthew Passion constituted his magnum opus among sacred works in the vernacular. Because he considered the work so special, the composer concentrated his efforts on revisions that established his text as definitively as possible. The orthographic change from long to short notation in the secco recitatives must be judged in this context.

The resulting clarification of notation also brought with it certain advantages. Whereas the differentiation between the two accompanying styles would have confused the continuo players in a piece of these dimensions, the short notation clears up the ambiguities caused by the continual shifts between secco (the Evangelist) and accompagnato (Jesus). Compositional refinements, otherwise unattainable, now became possible. Thus, one finds a half note accompanying the word *kräht* as in "Before the cock *crows* you will betray me" (BWV 244/38c, m. 29), and a dotted half occurs once beneath the word *schliefen* ("slept") (BWV 244/63a, m. 10). But the most spectacular effect achieved by this literal rendition of the secco parts occurs in Movement 61a, when Bach introduces a *tenuto* style in secco recitative to accompany Jesus' final words, set to the Hebrew text quoting Psalms, "Eli, Eli, lama asab-thani?" ("My God, my God, why have You forsaken me?"). Bach sets Jesus' words over a simple continuo line, dispensing for the first and only time in the Passion with the "hovering" halo effect of the accom-pagnato setting that had previously marked Jesus' statements. Imme-diately thereafter, Bach also sets the Evangelist's poignant translation of this text in the sustained secco style, again referring to the sustained ac-companiment associated with Jesus.

A final example of consistent short notation—in Cantata 30a, "An-genehmes Wiederau"—demonstrates, above all, that the special nota-tion in the St. Matthew Passion was not connected only to its dramatic and theological elements. Here, as in the St. Matthew Passion, Bach no-tated every secco recitative in the short manner.[51] As in the Passion, Bach's score for BWV 30a contained the usual long values in the recita-tives. But the two continuo parts, both autograph, do not reflect their original form because they were later reused for Cantata 30, "Freue dich, erlöste Schar," a sacred parody of Cantata 30a in which the com-poser retained the music to the arias but replaced the recitatives. For this later performance Bach pasted strips of paper with the new recitatives over the old ones, with the result that Movements 2, 4, 6, and 8 are to-tally concealed beneath their replacements. Only Movement 10 is still visible because it was merely crossed out. As Facsimile 3-7 shows, Bach notated this movement in quarters, which is why this version appears in the printed editions.[52] An examination of the ink visible on the other side of the page, which had bled through the paper, made it clear that Bach had written filled-in note heads in the original continuo parts for all three earlier recitatives.[53] By measuring the distance between the note heads, one could see that they were in fact widely separated. Bach's no-tation for the recitatives in Cantata 30a was therefore exactly parallel to his consistent reduction in the St. Matthew Passion.[54]

Yet unlike the St. Matthew Passion—a very special sacred work—Cantata 30a is a rather ordinary dedicatory piece (a so-called *Huldigungs-musik*), written a year later to pay homage to one Johann Christian Hen-nicke. Hennicke, a lackey to the local Count Brühl, had recently been rewarded with a bit of hereditary property just outside Leipzig, an event that prompted Bach's commission to compose a suitable work. The cantata therefore celebrates no more than the fortuitous transformation of a servant into a petty landowner—that is, an occasion conspicuously less lofty than the Good Friday service for which the Passion was de-signed. Yet the notation of the recitatives is identical. Therefore, if Bach

FACSIMILE 3-7 Cantata 30a, *Continuo,* Movement 10 (beneath cross-outs) in short notation, Deutsche Staatsbibliothek Berlin/DDR, Musikabteilung, Mus. ms. Bach St 31 [St 31/19]

had written quarter notes in the Passion only to distinguish the dramatis personae, it becomes difficult to explain why he went to the same trouble here in this ordinary occasional work. One other striking feature held in common by both works points to the answer: the composer himself penned virtually every orchestral part, paying the most scrupulous attention to detail. Bach's notational precision in both the Passion parts and in Cantata 30a thus bears witness to his desire to exercise a high degree of control over the practical circumstances of performance. It is probably not coincidental that Emanuel Bach was cited later in the century as a composer who methodically notated his recitatives as he wanted them played. Considering the similarities, one can speculate that the younger Bach profited from a notational technique he learned from his father.

Verbal instructions. Bach never systematically distinguished between accompagnato and secco movements within most of his vocal works. By and large, accompagnato movements in long values were not specially marked to distinguish them from the seccos. Nonetheless, one detects a hint of differentiation in the occasional use of dynamics and tempo markings found in the parts.[55] Certain accompagnato movements were sometimes denoted by some added instruction, although this was far from the rule. For example, Bach marked several movements *piano* or *a tempo,* indications which, in addition to their conventional meanings, may have helped allude to the *tenuto* style of accompagnato recitative. Other times Bach specifically entitled the movement *Recit. col accomp.* (In these instances his practice corresponded to Schröter's, in which the secco recitative was designated by the absence of the indication *col stromenti.*) Bach's occasional inclination to mark accompagnato rather than secco movements seems therefore in keeping with suggestions made by Lustig and Rousseau to distinguish between the two accompanying styles.

Table 3-1 lists the accompagnato recitatives in original parts which Bach designated with anything other than *Recit.* It is suggestive that each movement (either the sustained type or the motivic variety with a sustained bass line) might have been played in secco style if it were not for the added inscription. Many accompagnato movements notated in long values but unmarked with any special indication might also have been marked *piano* if Bach's scribes had been more astute: since, in his score, the composer often wrote "p" or *piano* only near the uppermost stave, the copyists failed to see that the marking also applied to the continuo line.[56] The St. Matthew Passion parts, exemplary for their ac-

TABLE 3-1 Autograph indications in continuo parts for accompagnato recitatives

BWV	Movement(s)	Indication[a]
8	3	Recit col accomp piano
11	3	col. accomp.
23	2	Rec: col accomp: à tempo é piano
30a	12	Recit: piano
47	3	Recitat pian
55	4	Recit col accomp.
69	4	. . . accomp
78	5	Recit: col'arco e piano
97	5	Recit. col accomp. piano
122	3	Recit pia
128	3	piano Recit
185	2	Recit: pianissimo
199	1, 3, 7	Recit: piano
206	10	. . . accomp
210	1, 9	Recit: à tempo
244	all	. . . piano
248	3, 49	. . . accomp
248	14	. . . Recit tutti
248	38, 40, 56, 61	Rec: accomp

a. Ellipsis dots indicate that the inscription does not begin at the opening of a movement.

curacy, contain consistent indications of *accomp.* at every accompagnato with a sustained bass part, even though the clarified notation did not require it.

In addition to the motivically-based accompagnatos with bass parts in quick notes, there are also accompanied recitatives notated in quarter notes that constitute orchestrated secco movements. The following musical example from Cantata 24 (Example 3-7) illustrates this type of movement.[57] Note that when Bach orchestrates the secco, he never deviates from the quarter-note lengths in the accompanying parts. In other words, the feature that resembles the secco is the uniform abbreviation of the bass notes. None of these movements, moreover, is designated in any special way: the players required no special instructions to perform them. But the absence of a mark such as *piano* supports the notion that special indications in recitatives served a practical purpose in distinguishing between long and short accompaniment.[58]

EXAMPLE 3-7 Cantata 24, Movement 4, mm. 1–7

Bach's Recitatives and Their Performance

In 1737 Johann Adolph Scheibe criticized Bach for "expressing completely in notes everything one thinks of as belonging to the method of playing."[59] Of course Scheibe did not have in mind Bach's notational practices in secco recitatives; rather, he was thinking of Bach's dense melodic style and his failure to distinguish between the essential melodic notes and those embellishments that the performer would ordinarily have supplied. Nonetheless, it is revealing to view Scheibe's complaint in light of Bach's tendency to prescribe in his recitative basses a practice that usually belonged "to the method of playing." Considering Bach's constant preoccupation with musical detail, even in his occasional works, this claim should come as no surprise.

While Bach seems to have presupposed the mainstream secco convention in his vocal works, it is less clear exactly how he wanted short accompaniment to be rendered. For example, did he believe, following Heinichen, that the length of bass notes should be decided by the "taste and judgment" of the accompanist? From the vantage point of Romantic spontaneity, this position is an attractive one. But if it were true, some evidence of altered bass-note lengths in secco recitatives would surely appear somewhere in the Bach sources. On the contrary, the overwhelming consistency of secco bass parts in both the St. Matthew Passion and Cantata 30a suggests that the length of bass notes was not a matter of whim. Given the opportunity in a carefully copied set of autograph continuo parts, Bach relied on a consistent reduction to quarter notes and rests. Moreover, given a continuo group sometimes numbering three or four players, there was scarcely room for the "taste and judgment" of an organist whose variable note lengths conflicted with the other bassists.

Did Bach then follow Telemann (as did Hahn and Petri) in having the organist shorten only the chords in his right hand? If so, Bach would hardly have prescribed every continuo part in quarter notes in those cases of explicit notation. For if he wanted to alleviate the drone of the organ pipes by shortening the continuo realization—leaving the long bass notes intact—Bach would surely have left the bass notes in the continuo parts for the Passion, Cantata 30a, and elsewhere as he had notated them in the score. Or one would be able to point to one instance of conflicting notation, in which the organ played long notes while everyone else played short. But no such example can be produced. Thus, Bach's organists probably followed the dictates of the convention much like everyone else. Whatever reasons were advanced for the short accompaniment convention—to hear the text more clearly, to avoid the droning of the bass line, to spare the labor of writing out the quarter notes and rests, to see the harmonic progressions more clearly—the same practice is documented from 1717 through to the early nineteenth century. Whether one reads Niedt, Stölzel, Voigt, Lustig, Rousseau, Schröter, Türk, Klein, Prixner, or Kollmann, the evidence found in the Bach sources tallies most simply with the most usual description of short accompaniment.

Even with established ground rules for bass notes in secco recitatives, the organist still had to contend with the precise manner of realizing the chords in the right hand, for the figures were not confined to changes of bass note but were placed at each harmonic shift underlying the vocal line. In other words, between two bass notes cut short by the convention, the composer often placed other thorough-bass figures. Were they realized in the right hand alone? Peter Williams suggests that these figures were merely "a guide to the director-accompanist, like the figures Corelli put above notes expressly marked *tasto solo*,"[60] and were therefore only cues to the vocal part. But it is hard to imagine that the composer would regularly have supplied a complete guide to the voice-leading of a recitative without intending the intermittent harmonies to have been reflected in the keyboardist's right hand. Just as Bach did not write *accomp.* merely to name the correct genre, he probably also did not go to the trouble of writing figures that were never meant to be sounded. More likely, the right hand in these instances realized the figure with the bass note still understood, although one cannot conclude this with any great confidence. For neither did the figures always tell the continuo player precisely which notes to include in the realization. The thorough-bass treatises, for example, mention that the accompanist should avoid duplicating the theme in the vocal or instrumental part and should play only one or two notes in the right hand.[61] Niedt, moreover, states explicitly that the accompanist should not duplicate notes in the vocal part except when the singer gets lost, or as he puts it, "falls out of the note or chord." On these occasions the accompanist realizes the exact intervals of the figures to get the singer back on track.[62]

Given a genre such as recitative which, according to Niedt, "more closely resembles speaking than singing," the idea of accompanying the singer in a rigid or mechanical manner was surely inappropriate. This is why the secco convention should not be understood as enforcing a regimen of exact quarter notes, which would forbid expressive leeway. As suggested earlier, the convention may well have approximated the type of shortening procedure employed rather than dictating an absolutely uniform duration. That is, the quarter notes constituted a guide to the punctuated harmonies that highlighted the syntax of the prose delivery and enhanced its comprehensibility. Short accompaniment, therefore, says nothing about the initial attack of the bass note or about its dynamic range, the manner of its release, or the accompanist's interaction with the singer. These were the judgments that demanded that most elusive of eighteenth-century requirements, *le bon goût*. Performed with this requisite "good taste," short accompaniment in Bach's secco recitatives lent a dramatic immediacy to an indispensable genre that personified the spirit of the scriptural message.

CHAPTER IV

The Bassoon

Two Views of the Bassoon

In the Germany of Bach's day, musicians tended to hold one of two opposing attitudes toward the bassoon. The more traditional of these saw the bassoon as an instrument to be tolerated, a crude if sometimes necessary adjunct to the bass contingent, while a more enlightened view welcomed the bassoon as an elegant, even aristocratic companion to the pair of orchestral oboes. A satirical engraving from about 1730 by I. A. Müller (Figure 4-1) captures the older attitude in an emblematic caricature. Entitled "Hanns Krummaul [Hans Crooked-Mouth], municipal fagottist of Krumlingen," the legend reads: "My belly full of air, rapid hand and crooked mouth show the level of my intelligence." The *Kurzgefasstes Musicalisches Lexicon* still reflected this traditional bias as late as 1749 when it termed the "strong sound" of the *Fagot* as "coarse."[1]

This coarseness (often identified with the name *Fagotto*) is allegorized in a humorous tale recounted by Johann Beer: "Two apprentices to the tower-musicians—one a bassoonist, the other a trombonist, having come to verbal blows . . . over the question of whether the bassoon or the trombone were the more important [instrument], once asked me to arrive at a fair ruling [*decisum regulativum*]." Each player, Beer continues, bet two thalers on the outcome, depositing the sum with the author in advance. The trombonist then spoke:

First of all . . . the trombone is an ancient instrument, which, as is known, caused the walls at Jericho to come tumbling down. Moreover . . . the trombone . . . can play all four parts. Thus the trombone . . . and not the bassoon is used for the resurrection of the dead. In addition, the slide technique shows that the trombonist requires more artistry than the bassoonist, who merely has to find the finger holes.

FIGURE 4-1 I. A. Müller, "Hanns Krummaul," Germanisches Nationalmuseum, Nürnberg (engraving, Augsburg, ca. 1730)

The bassoonist (*der Fagottist*) had the next word:

[As for the charge that the trombone can play all four parts], everybody knows
. . . that a jack of all trades is a master of none . . . [The bassoonist], on the
other hand, plays a foundational part—the never praised enough bass—which
is indispensable to the other parts . . . No instrument could thus be more
greatly esteemed, for its resonance projects further than the trombone's; one
heard the bassoon twenty steps before reaching the church door, while with
exacting effort one could hardly hear the trombone inside the church . . . Furthermore, the bassoon is such a sturdy, upright and powerful instrument that,
when an undesirable uproar occurs at church, one can easily use it to quiet
the crowd by vigorously kicking, as it were, the unrestrained ruffians in the
ribs . . . [The trombonist takes up so much room and] sticks his brazen slide
out over the choir-loft like the tall beer-steins people stick out the windows in
Saxony. The bassoonist, on the other hand, can even sit in a narrow corner of
the loft and needs hardly more room than a well twisted tobacco roll . . .

Having heard both sides of the case, Beer promised his decision on
the following day. Taking the four thalers with him, he spent all the
money on provisions for a lavish meal to which he invited several com-
panions who were to help deliver the "fair ruling." The bassoonist and
trombonist were then summoned into their midst and given the following verdict: "Either sit down and help polish off the four thalers's worth
you deposited yesterday or [having had to consider] such vain trifles,
we'll give you a bassoon-sized thrashing on the rump . . . and, after a
well-deserved measure for your useless bickering, throw you down the
stairs."[2] Blinded by his own petty vanity, the bassoonist—an emblem
for the provincial wind player—inflates his role as orchestral "noise-
maker" to comic levels of bathos. Instead of acknowledging his subordinate role within the orchestra, he masks his status by invidious comparisons with an equally foolish rival trombonist.[3]

The young J. S. Bach also held a low opinion of bassoonists. Indeed,
his first recorded difficulty with a musician involved a bassoonist whom
he publicly insulted. According to the protocols of the Arnstadt consis-
tory from 1705, Bach nearly came to blows with a student named
Geyersbach over the very sort of ridicule portrayed by Beer. Whether
Bach actually offended Geyersbach himself (calling him a *Zippelfagott-
ist,* a "nanny-goat bassoonist," according to the document) or merely
reviled his instrument remains unclear.[4] Geyersbach failed, in any event,
to appreciate the difference between the two. As he put it: "Anyone who
insults my bassoon insults me." More interesting is the fact that the 21-
year-old Bach, displaying a scorn for the bassoon typical of his day, had
few qualms about disparaging either the instrument or the puffed-up
pride of the musician attached to it.

During the early years of the eighteenth century, however, there were fundamental changes in the construction of the bassoon. Technical advances in a new multijointed instrument pioneered by makers such as Johann Christoph Denner of Nürnberg eventually eliminated the older dulcian-type instrument prevalent in Germany. Perhaps the success of the newer instrumental types accounts, in part, for the elevation in social status which the bassoon subsequently experienced.[5] This new bassoon, identified more often as "Basson" than "Fagott," overcame its lowly pedigree and, by association with the fashionable practices of Lully's orchestra, even secured a reputable social station.[6] Matheson's modish description of the bassoon in the *Neu-eröffnetes Orchestre* of 1713, with its professed *galant* bias, may well mark a turning point in German attitudes. "The proud bassoon [*der stoltze Basson*]," he writes, "is the ordinary bass, the fundament or accompaniment to the oboes. Because it requires neither the same finesse nor manners (albeit demanding others), it is supposed to be easier to play. But [a bassoonist] who wishes to distinguish himself, particularly playing high and with elegance and speed, will have his work cut out for him."[7]

Interestingly, the same *Kurzgefasstes Musicalisches Lexicon* (1749) cited earlier that identified the *Fagot* as "coarse" quotes Matheson verbatim on the more elegant *Basson*. The rather dapper bassoonist depicted in a drawing by Jean Antoine Watteau (1684-1721) likewise confirms this elevation in social station (Figure 4-2). For some writers, then, the two names evoked two very different associations. The contrasting names also seem to have signified instruments tuned at different pitches: as Martin Heinrich Fuhrmann made clear in 1706, the *Fagotto* played in *Chorton* while the *Bassone* played in *Cammerton*.[8]

It is not clear, however, that German composers of the eighteenth century always conceived of two distinct referents for the terms *Fagotto* and *Basson*. Walther's *Lexikon* (1732), for example, states that "*Fagotto* is just the same as *Basson*" and proceeds to give the common etymology for the former term deriving from two bound pieces of wood.[9] It is under the entry *Fagotto,* moreover, that Walther cites Matheson, who, in his discussion of the *galant* instrument, had called it only by the name *Basson*. Nonetheless, instruments of the older type continued to coexist next to the newer bassoons, especially during the years before Bach arrived in Leipzig. One can therefore expect that a composer such as Bach, in adapting to various church and courtly establishments, would have employed both types of instruments, even if the distinctions in nomenclature are not wholly accurate.

Bach's bassoon parts raise the following practical questions. Which instrumental type does an individual bassoon part signify: the old Ger-

FIGURE 4-2 Jean Antoine Watteau, "Le joueur de basson" ("The Bassoon Player"),
Berlin/DDR, Staatliche Museen, Kupferstichkabinett (drawing in red and black chalk)

man *Fagott* or the more modern French bassoon? At what pitch was the instrument built? Did it play in all movements of a cantata? One can also ask a set of more conceptual questions: To which traditional view of the bassoon can a particular part be assigned? Is the bassoon merely a sturdy prop to the bass section? Or is it a graceful partner, skilled even in *galant* niceties? Although these two sets of questions may overlap considerably, it is important to realize that they are not synonymous. The practical matters alone—which instrument for which performance?—cannot explain how Bach intended his bassoon parts to be understood. Indeed, Bach's writing for the bassoon swung between both poles of contemporary practice at the same time that it remained subordinated to the practical circumstances determining much of his work.

The Original Parts and the Question of Participation

Was the bassoonist a regular member of Bach's orchestra? Did he accompany in every movement? Bach's original bassoon parts offer only incomplete answers to these questions. Table 4-1, which enumerates the extant parts for the vocal works, reveals that autograph bassoon parts are never identical to the main continuo part. In other words, if Bach went to the trouble of copying a bassoon part, it was because he meant to distinguish it in some way. Entirely autograph parts are those for Cantatas 18, 63, 199, 185, 162, 140, and 177, the Missa (BWV 232[1]), the Kerll Sanctus (BWV 241), and a Schmidt motet.[10] In those parts copied by both Bach and a copyist, special circumstances seem to have prevailed. In some pieces the bassoon part was already distinct in Bach's score, so that the scribe simply copied out the single line intact (for example, in Cantata 71). Elsewhere, if Bach wanted to refashion the continuo line for the bassoon in one movement, as in Cantata 172, he would enter the alterations in the part for that movement and then direct his assistant to resume copying from the score. Of the other bassoon parts, the only ones identical to the continuo line in the score are not autograph: all date from Leipzig. These include the parts for Cantatas 70, 44, and 215 and for a work by Johann Ludwig Bach. In two other instances—Cantatas 23 and 140—Bach merely entered the part-title *Bassono,* and, on an older continuo part for the St. John Passion (BWV 245), added the specification *pro Bassono grosso.* Only rarely, then, did copyists write out bassoon parts that represented duplicate continuo parts.

Twentieth-century authorities have interpreted this evidence in contrasting ways. Terry, for example, holds that "the infrequent use of [the

TABLE 4-1 Bassoon parts in original sources for Bach's vocal works

Work	Date	Part-title	Auto-graph part	Score[a]	Identical continuo part	Separate movements	Tacet movements
BWV 71	1708	Bassono	x	x		1, 4, 6, 7	(3), 4
BWV 18	1713	Fagotto	x	–		1, 2, 3	
BWV 63	1713	Bassono	x	–		1, 7	2, 3, 4, 5
BWV 172	1714	Fagotto	x[b]	–		1	2, 4, 5
BWV 199	1714	Fagotto	x	x			2, 5, 6
BWV 132	1714?	(Fagotto)[c]					1
BWV 185	1715	Fagotto	x	x		2, 3, 4	
BWV 31	1715	Bassono	x	–		1, 2, 9	3, 4, 5, 6, 7, 8
BWV 162	1714–1716	Fagotto	x	–		1	2, 3, 4, 5
Schmidt	1713–1716	Fagotto	x	x			2
BWV 21	1718–1723	Fagotto		–		2, 6, 9, 11	
BWV 23	1723	Basson. [e Cembalo]		o	x		
BWV 69a	1723	Bassoni		–		1, 4	
BWV 194	1723	Bassono[c]	x	x		1	
BWV 70	1723	Bassono		–	x		

BWV	Date	Designation					
BWV 44	1724	Bassono		o			
BWV 172	1724	Fagotto		–	x		2, 4, 5
BWV 42	1725	Bassono		x		1	
JLB 16	1726	Violoncello e Bassono		–	x	1, 3	
BWV 52	1726	Fagotto		x		1	
BWV 226	1729	Bassono	x[b]	o		all	
BWV 140	1731	Bassono		–	x		
BWV 177	1732	Bassono obligato	x	x		4	
BWV 232[1]	1733	Basson	x	x		1, 2, 3, 5, 11, 12	
BWV 215	1734	Bassono		o	x		6, 8, 9, 10
BWV 97	1734	Continuo: pro Bassono e Violoncello		x			
BWV 248[1]	1734	Bassono		x		1	
BWV 249	1732–1735	Bassono	x[b]	x		1	
BWV 245	1740–1748	Continuo [pro Bassono Grosso]	x[b]	o			most
BWV 241	1747	Bassono	x	x		all	

a. x: bassoon indicated in score; o: bassoon not indicated in score; –: no original score extant.
b. Part only partially autograph.
c. Bassoon is listed on the original wrapper to the set of parts. The part itself is lost.

TABLE 4-2 Additional vocal works in score indicating the bassoon

Work	Date	Instru-mentarium[a]	Separate stave
BWV 131	1707	x	x
BWV 208	1713	o	x
BWV 12	1714	x	x
BWV 61	1714	x	x
BWV 147a	1716	x	x
BWV 155	1716(?)	o	x
BWV 173a	1717–1722	x	x
BWV 75	1723	–	x
BWV 243a	1723	x	o
BWV 186	1723	–	x
BWV 119	1723	x	o
BWV 243	1728–1731	o	o
BWV 174	1729	x	o
BWV 66	1735(?)	x	x
BWV 173	1735(?)	x	x
BWV 197	1735–1742	o	x

a. x: bassoon listed in instrumentarium; o: bassoon not listed in instrumentarium; –: instrumentarium not listed.

bassoon] in his church music indicates that Bach did not employ [it] as a regular continuo instrument."[11] This position is based on the observation that there are relatively few bassoon parts among the surviving sources. Also in Terry's favor are the parts listed in Table 4-2, which enumerates works that mention the bassoon in an autograph score for which no corresponding part survives. It is striking that, out of sixteen vocal works, the part-sets for fourteen (all except Cantatas 147 and 174) have been lost. In other words, there seems to be a part whenever Bach called for a bassoon; if one is missing, it is generally because the entire set of parts has been lost. If, on the other hand, there were few surviving parts (in complete sets) but frequent listings in Bach's scores, then one would suspect that the bassoonist regularly shared a part with another continuo player.[12] In fact, Cantata 174 is the only work in which Bach included the bassoon in his instrumentarium but did not direct a copyist to prepare a separate part. As a result, it is not clear whether Bach employed a bassoonist unless positive evidence speaks for his participation.

Alfred Dürr and Konrad Brandt, on the other hand, believe that a bassoonist, insofar as one was available, participated at every performance.[13] Their argument rests primarily on documentary rather than musical evidence. For example, the Weimar Chapel supported one bassoonist—the "Fagottiste Bernhard George Ulrich"—for whom Bach virtually always prepared a part. And in Leipzig, according to Bach's Memorandum to the Town Council of 1730, the apprentice to the Town-Pipers and Art-Fiddlers was entrusted with the bassoon part.[14] Moreover, in enumerating the requirements for his orchestra in this memorandum, Bach listed "one, or even two for the *Basson.*" As for the musical sources, Dürr points out the number of bassoon parts that are identical to continuo parts, especially those prepared for Leipzig performances. If the bassoon were merely a doubling instrument, then the player would regularly have shared an unmarked continuo part with a cellist or violonist. Certain parts confirm this practice, such as those for Cantatas 97, 23, and JLB 16. In any event, the appearance of the bassoon in Leipzig works does not seem related to the overall size of the orchestra required for a particular piece: Bach calls for the bassoon in large-scale works with brass and drums, but he also includes it in works with intimate ensembles, such as in Cantatas 42, 44, 66, 70, 97, 173, 177, 186, and 194.

Even with the apprentice assigned to the bassoon, unfilled vacancies elsewhere in the Leipzig orchestra may have forced the composer to assign him to another instrument. He might have been asked, for example, to play oboe when three were required.[15] On the other hand, the apprentice cannot have been the only bassoonist in Leipzig. Arnold Schering, for example, notes that the *cafetier* Zimmermann purchased some seven instruments for the Collegium musicum, including two bassoons.[16] Thus Bach must have been able to call on other players—such as university students—to assist him in cantata performances.[17]

On rare occasions, Bach had two bassoons at his disposal. Although only one cantata (BWV 69a) contains a part labeled *Bassoni,* the plural appears in the scores for Cantatas 75, 119, 194, and 208, as well as in the scores for the Magnificat (BWV 243), the St. John Passion, and the Christmas Oratorio (BWV 248). Indeed, it seems credible that Bach's orchestral ideal included two bassoons. The Missa (BWV 232[1]), that is, the Kyrie and Gloria from the B-minor Mass, offers a certain degree of support here. It was composed for the Dresden court Capelle, an ensemble that Bach held in high esteem, and its Quoniam movement includes an obbligato for two bassoons.[18] Of course this does not mean that Bach would have wanted two bassoons in every cantata performance but rather that, under ideal circumstances, he would have employed two in a large-scale work.

But did the bassoonist, when present, play in all movements of a cantata? Dürr, for example, believes he did, stating that "wherever there is an extant part expressly intended for the bassoon (for example, in the first part of the Christmas Oratorio), it almost always contains all the movements of a cantata."[19] Although this statement tallies with the Leipzig works (except for a repeated performance of Cantata 172 and the Dresden performance of the Missa, BWV 232[1]), it is erroneous with regard to the pieces from Mühlhausen and Weimar (1708–1716), as a glance at Table 4-1 will confirm. The early works, without exception, omit the bassoon from at least one movement of the cantata. Bach seems therefore to have altered his use of the bassoon after he arrived in Leipzig. Whereas he had previously withheld it from some sections of the piece, he later included it in every movement.

To sum up: There is still some doubt as to whether the bassoon participated in performances for which there is no documentation, although it is far from clear that a bassoonist required his own part or that Bach, given an available player, did not simply add him to the continuo ensemble. Although Bach conceived of the bassoon as a regular member of his orchestra, only in Weimar did he demonstrably include the bassoon on a regular basis. In Leipzig, despite an intention to make more or less regular use of a bassoonist, Bach probably found it impossible to write a weekly part for the instrument. When a player was available and could read from a normal continuo part, he may well have played every movement.

The Pitch of Bach's Bassoons

What was the performing pitch of Bach's bassoons? Was the bassoonist ever expected to transpose a part? The original parts shed light on both these questions.

First, though, a review of the relevant terminology will prove useful. Organs of the early eighteenth century were tuned at *Chorton* (Choir-Pitch), a highish pitch which enabled organ builders to conserve on the precious metals used in constructing the pipes. Earlier it was shown how this *Chorton* tuning of the organ necessitated the transposing of continuo parts a whole step lower than the strings and winds. However, the variation in pitch prevalent at Leipzig was by no means a universal standard. For example, woodwind instruments in most musical establishments were invariably constructed at a lower pitch, the so-called *Cammerton* (Chamber-Pitch). In secular music, composers generally used *Cammerton* as the standard, that is, the pitch to which the strings and harpsichord would tune. In sacred music, however, there existed a discrepancy between the woodwinds, on the one hand, and the church organ (and trombones), on the other,[20] a difference that usually amounted to a major second or a minor third. The first pitch was referred to as *(hohe) Cammerton* (high Chamber-Pitch), the second as *Tief-Cammerton* (low Chamber-Pitch). Since pitch did not exist as an absolute acoustic frequency, the tuning of stringed instruments and the harpsichord was considered movable, despite the problems of intonation that resulted from the frequent loosening and tightening of the strings.

When writing a piece of sacred concerted music, then, a composer took into account two different keys, one for the winds and one for the strings. For example, if the winds at a particular church establishment were tuned in normal (high) *Cammerton,* the strings and organ playing in C would have to be complemented by winds playing in D. In other words, the composer would notate the woodwind parts a whole tone *higher* in order to compensate for their actual pitch a whole tone *lower.* One could also see it this way: a composer could conceive a sacred work either in *Chorton* to suit the organ or in *Cammerton* to suit the woodwinds.

A brief account of the performing pitch at Leipzig illustrates some of the practical complications. Sometime around 1701 Bach's predecessor, Johann Kuhnau, changed the performing pitch from *Chorton* to *Cammerton.*[21] That is, instead of taking the high organ pitch as the norm for his church compositions, Kuhnau chose the lower *Cammerton.* As a result, he could compose his concerted works in one key (presuming there were no trombones) and avoid the awkward discrepancy between woodwinds and strings. Under the revised system, the pitch of the oboes and flutes was taken as the standard to which the strings adjusted. The organ thus required a part transposed down a whole step to accommodate its higher *Chorton* to the lower *Cammerton* of the orchestra.

Bach's bassoon parts at Leipzig present no real problems of pitch. All are notated at *Cammerton,* also the performing pitch of the ensemble.[22] The pitch of Bach's bassoons at Mühlhausen and Weimar, however, is somewhat more difficult to determine, because there are parts that exhibit three different pitch relationships.[23] At Mühlhausen, for example, the parts for both Cantata 131 (1707) and Cantata 71 (1708) are pitched a whole step above the strings and organ, that is, at normal *Cammerton.* On the other hand, the majority of bassoon parts at Weimar (1713–1716)—for Cantatas 18, 12, 172, 199, 61, 132, 185, and 162—are notated at pitch with the organ in *Chorton.* Only the parts for Cantata 31, the Schmidt motet, and a now lost part for Cantata 155 were pitched a minor third above the organ, that is, at *Tief-Cammerton*. Finally, the part for Cantata 63 (1713) is pitched in normal *Cammerton* together with the entire ensemble for a Christmas performance that must have taken place outside Weimar.

Despite this stratification of pitches among the various early bassoon parts, Alfred Dürr, citing Mattheson, has argued that Bach's Weimar bassoon was tuned in *Cammerton* and that his bassoonists therefore had to transpose their parts at sight.[24] As Mattheson put it: "But consider the agony when instruments tuned in *Cammerton* such as horns, recorders, bassoons [*Fagotten*] and the like are supposed to accompany others that are in *Chorton,* so that either one group or the other has to be transposed."[25] But since the Weimar *Chorton* parts are mostly entitled *Fagotto,* it seems far more likely that a traditional instrument would have been pitched at *Chorton.* Fuhrmann is explicit on this point: "*Fagotto* or *Dulciano,* an 8-foot dulcian, is in *Chorton. Bassone,* a French *Fagott,* is, however, in *Cammerton.*"[26]

Woodwind instruments, one must realize, could not adjust by even a half step without endangering the intonation. Thus, if oboe parts for different cantatas exist in two distinct *Cammerton* pitches, then Bach must have written for two distinct instruments. Bach's Weimar bassoon parts can be considered analogously, except that they are not separated by a half step but by a minor third. Since one group is at *Chorton* (by far the most common) and the other is at *Tief-Cammerton,* it follows that the Weimar Capelle had at its disposal two bassoons pitched a minor third apart.[27] The Weimar bassoonist would then have always been provided with parts pitched to his instrument. The Weimar norm of a *Chorton* bassoon, moreover, continues the earlier German tradition of the *Chorist-Fagott,* which seems to have resisted the newer French-influenced association to the Lullian trio of "deux hautbois et basson" that Mattheson, for example, considered as one integral group.[28] Indeed, this *Chorton* bassoon may well have been an older dulcian-type instrument, for none of the *Chorton* parts descends below C.[29] On the other hand, it is plausible that these instruments were "modern" bassoons but merely pitched at *Chorton.*

Curiously enough, the only example at Weimar of the French term *Basson* is found in a bassoon part at *Tief-Cammerton* for a motet by Johann Christoph Schmidt, "Auf Gott hoffe ich." Although Bach's part is labeled *Fagotto,* his score reads *Fagotto ô Basson Concert:* (see Facsimile 4-1). Bach's score itself is notated in the key of D (*Chorton*) for all but the brass and winds, which are notated in the key of C. The individual oboe and bassoon parts, on the other hand, all three of them autograph, are pitched in E♭. This must mean that the winds played at

FACSIMILE 4-1 J. C. Schmidt, "Auf Gott Hoffe ich" (in the hand of J. S. Bach), Deutsche Staatsbibliothek Berlin/DDR, Musikabteilung, Mus. ms. 30187

EXAMPLE 4-1 Cantata 31, Movement 9, mm. 1–4

Tief-Cammerton while the strings played in C major (*Chorton.*)[30] None-theless, unusual features in the score reflect Schmidt's more frenchified practices at Dresden rather than Bach's practices at Weimar. As Facsimile 4-1 shows, the motet requires transverse flutes (*Flaut[i] Allem[andi]*), which were not available at Weimar.[31] Neither did Bach have a theorbo, suggested by the figured continuo line *Organo ô Tiorba*. Interestingly, the only other part ever labeled *Basson* is among the parts for the Missa of the B-minor Mass (BWV 232[1]) prepared for Dresden in 1733, where the organ in the Sophien-Kirche was tuned in *Cammerton.*[32] On the other hand, the ambiguous *Fagotto ô Basson* in the Schmidt motet suggests that one cannot reliably distinguish the two types of instruments solely by their names.[33]

In the Easter performance of Cantata 31 in 1715, moreover, the oboes and bassoon (labeled *Bassono*) also played a minor third below the strings. As he also did in Cantata 155, Bach required a low bassoon in *Tief-Cammerton* that dips down to a notated low B♭', corresponding to a low G' at *Chorton* orchestral pitch. This accounts for Bach's use of the bassoon to double the continuo line at the lower octave, as in the final chorale, shown in Example 4-1. Although Bach wrote concertato bassoon parts just as frequently an octave above as below the main continuo line, he took special advantage of the versatility of the modern bassoon at *Tief-Cammerton* by writing in its lowest register.[34] Thus, as far as the pre-Leipzig works are concerned, the following distinctions of nomenclature are suggested: whereas *Fagotto* is ambiguous with respect to pitch, either *Basson* or *Bassono* corresponds to instruments tuned in some sort of *Cammerton*. In Leipzig Bach made predominant, though not exclusive, use of the term *Bassono,* which was generally associated with the new French-influenced bassoon pitched at *Cammerton.*

Weimar Parts

The Weimar parts contain far more varied approaches to orchestration than later parts because Bach himself undertook most of the copying. The only exceptions are the parts for Cantatas 21 and 172. In Cantata 21, the bassoon part was copied from a now-lost part dating from an earlier performance. And in Cantata 172 the Weimar scribe began with the continuo line, while Bach notated both the diverging passages and the *tacet* indications.[35]

Only the composer could have designed the sort of arrangement that occasionally appears in the composing score. Bach's practice in Cantata 172, for example, is clarified by the parts for Cantatas 199 and 185. In

BWV 199, Bach selected three movements in which the bassoon was excluded: Movement 2, an aria with oboe obbligato, but not the accompanied recitative that precedes it; Movement 5, a secco recitative; and Movement 6, a chorale arrangement with obbligato viola. In BWV 185, Bach decided on a reduced bassoon part in four of the movements. In Movement 1, he marked the bassoon *tacet;* in Movement 2, he specified quarter-note values for the accompagnato recitative and omitted the bassoon from the adjacent arioso passage; in Movement 3, he included it in the instrumental tutti sections; and in Movement 4, he wrote out the short values for the secco recitative. In all these plans a copyist could never have arrived at these revisions (really orchestral decorations): they are dependent on an autograph part. Where Bach's scores have not survived, it is likely that the extant bassoon parts contain similar arrangements that postdate the completion of the respective score. To be sure, there are later instances in which an obbligato part appears in the first movement of the score; but even here Bach's score usually ignores the bassoon in the subsequent movements. It is therefore useful to consider the "deviations" in the Weimar parts more as refinements of performance practice than as conscious alterations in the original conception.

The bassoon part for BWV 63 exemplifies another method of reduction. The bassoon part for Movement 1 was probably found in the autograph score, which no longer survives. Here the bassoon, properly called *Bassono,* functions as the bass member of the oboe group. Its part represents a diminution of the continuo line at the same time that it plays a quasi-obbligato role by sounding an octave above the other continuo instruments.[36] Bach then marked Movements 2, 3, 4, and 5 *tacet;* these include an accompanied recitative, a duet with oboe obbligato, a secco recitative with fiery scale passages, and a duet accompanied by the strings. The bassoon then joins the continuo line for the following accompanied recitative and plays a reduced *ripieno* role in the final choral movement with brass and drums. Most likely, this part resulted from Bach's inclination to elaborate the disposition of his orchestra after he had completed the formal invention of the work in his score. If he did not extend this decorative "trim" to the Leipzig bassoon parts, perhaps his increased responsibilities as Thomas-Cantor are to blame: whereas at Weimar he wrote a church cantata every four weeks, at Leipzig he was responsible for weekly concerted works. In general, it is striking how clean and careful the Weimar orchestral parts appear vis-à-vis their Leipzig counterparts. Thus the contrast in the bassoon parts may reflect the varied working conditions between the two locales.

Yet even at Weimar there is no precise pattern to Bach's omissions and reductions. The only standard rule is that the bassoon participates in the framing outer movements of the cantata. Both arias and recitatives, on the other hand, are treated ambiguously. This ambiguity might reflect the absence of a standard pattern of genres which later determine a more or less regular internal sequence of recitative and aria pairs. In Cantata 18, for example, set to a text by Neumeister, a Vivaldi-inspired sinfonia for four violas (two *concertino* and two *ripieno*) opens the work. Here the bassoon certifies the concerto-like credentials of the movement by pausing in all the solo episodes, playing only in the peculiar *ritornelli* based on a haunting unison bass ostinato. (The autograph *Fagotto* part is reproduced in Facsimile 3-4; see also Example 5-7.) The bassoon next joins in the secco recitative but is *tacet* in the expansive third movement except to play *colla parte* from time to time with the vocal basses. It is also *tacet* in the soprano aria and rejoins the continuo only for the final chorale. The idiosyncratic design of the work therefore militates against any conventional scheme specifying where the bassoon should or should not participate.

Leipzig Parts

Compared to the number of part-sets surviving from Leipzig, there are few distinct bassoon parts. A great many of these parts, moreover, result directly from a separate bassoon line that Bach placed in the score to the opening movement. Since there was frequently no further mention of the bassoon in the score, the scribes copied out the continuo line intact beginning with the second movement. This evidence suggests that the bassoonist regularly played in all notated movements, which marks a striking change from Bach's practice at Weimar.

The only sources that furnish any information comparable to the Weimar bassoon parts are those belonging to the B-minor Mass (BWV 232[1]) and the St. John Passion (BWV 245), both of which reduce the bassoon's involvement much like the Weimar cases. Admittedly, both are special: the materials to the Missa were intended for a performance in Dresden, and the part for the Passion calls for a *Bassono grosso,* a somewhat larger instrument than usual, although probably not a true contra-bassoon.[37]

Table 4-3 shows the scheme of the bassoon part for the Mass, indicating the instrument's functions in the various movements of this work. Except for the Quoniam, where the bassoons and horn play obbligato, the part is marked *tacet* in all arias and duets. It is also significant that the

TABLE 4-3 Bassoon parts in the Missa (BWV 232[I])

Movement	Section	Genre	Scheme[a]
1	Kyrie	Chorus	seguente/continuo/seguente/continuo
2	Christe	Duet	*tacet*
3	Kyrie	Chorus	seguente
4	Gloria	Chorus	continuo/seguente/continuo/*tacet*/ continuo
5	Et in terra	Chorus	seguente/continuo/*tacet*/continuo/ seguente/continuo
6	Laudamus te	Aria	*tacet*
7	Gratias	Chorus	seguente
8	Domine deus	Duet	*tacet*
9	Qui tollis	Chorus	*tacet*
10	Qui sedes	Aria	*tacet*
11	Quoniam	Aria	obbligato *a 2*
12	Cum sancto	Chorus	continuo/*tacet*/continuo

a. seguente: basso seguente, follows vocal bass line; continuo: normal continuo part; *tacet:* rests for full movement or partial section; obbligato: duet for two bassoons.

bassoon part for the second Kyrie and the Gratias doubles the vocal bass line in the two movements of the Mass composed in the *alla breve* notation of the *stile antico*. The corresponding continuo part for these movements is mostly independent of the vocal bass line, frequently descending below it. As the instrumental support for the vocal basses, the bassoon is additive rather than continuous, a detail confirmed in many other earlier autograph parts. Two other examples of this type of bass support include the parts for the motet "Der Geist hilft unsrer Schwachheit auf" (BWV 226) and the reworked Sanctus (BWV 241) by Johann Caspar Kerll.

Another type of distinctive role occurs in the choral movements composed in the concertato manner of the *stile moderno*. In the Cum Sancto the bassoon is a reduced continuo part and is omitted from the middle section of the movement. In the other concertato movements the bassoon takes on a more complex function, doubling the vocal basses in fugal passages and jumping to the continuo line for ritornello material and other tuttis, and even dropping out of the texture when the vocal basses are still singing. As a whole, this inventive scheme mediates in a highly sophisticated fashion between the two historical roles of the bassoon—that of the choral bassist and that of modern continuo player. Because of this chameleon-like character, the bassoon part in the Mass is able to highlight contrasting features in the musical texture.

The continuo part *pro Bassono Grosso* for the St. John Passion dates from sometime in the 1740s and applies the principles of the Weimar bassoon arrangements to a part for a large instrument.[38] In the main, the *bassono grosso* plays only in choruses and in simple choral settings. Otherwise, Bach excludes it from all arias and recitatives with the exception of four movements: In the tenor aria "Ach, mein Sinn" (Movement 13), the bassoon plays the continuo part in the opening ritornello accompanied by the strings, withdrawing as soon as the voice enters and rejoining only for the last three measures of the movement. In the bass arioso "Betrachte, meine Seel'" (Movement 19), accompanied by harpsichord obbligato and two violins, the bassoon plays with the continuo throughout, but unlike the continuo is marked *pianissimo*. In the bass aria "Eilt, ihr angefochten Seelen" (Movement 24), accompanied by the upper vocal parts and the full string contingent, the *bassono grosso* plays whenever the solo bass is not singing. And finally, in the alto aria "Es ist vollbracht" (Movement 30), it plays only during the contrasting *vivace* section. Bach's disposition of the *bassono grosso* in this work, therefore, represents the most severe limitation of activity he ever imposed on a bassoon continuo part.[39]

The Bassoonist as Adjunct Continuo Player

Although the bassoon in Leipzig was destined to play a generally undistinguished role, Bach's occasional bassoon obbligatos include some remarkable music. Consider the first movement of Cantata 42, a full-fledged concerto movement hiding behind the name of a sinfonia. Here Bach transforms the Lullian trio of two oboes and a bassoon into a bona fide concertino within the Italian concerto grosso. This is no mere Corellian concertino, with its echo effects and reinforcing functions, but a true Vivaldian solo grouping disposed according to Bach's own rules for the concerto genre. Thus the bassoon is primarily active as a third solo voice in the solo episodes premised on the absence of the ritornello, as in mm. 9-10 (see Example 4-2). However, as elsewhere in Bach's inventive concerto genre, the empirical grouping of players into *concertino* and *ripieno* does not distinguish ritornello from episode. The rich interplay of surface orchestration already becomes apparent at mm. 20-23, where the *Fortspinnung,* heard in the dominant, is divided between two opposing groups, oblivious to the solo–tutti distinction. Following another episodic diversion in mm. 24-25, the second ritornello segment from the *Epilog* (m. 26) is overtaken by the trio of soloists. As a result, the following solo episode in mm. 27-28, posing as ritornello material

EXAMPLE 4-2 Cantata 42, Movement 1, mm. 1–11

EXAMPLE 4-2 *(continued)*

EXAMPLE 4-3 Cantata 42, Movement 1, mm. 20–28

EXAMPLE 4-3 *(continued)*

by the usual device of motivic resemblance, feigns an identity that further elaborates the concerto's broad array of guises (see Example 4-3). The bassoon exemplifies not only its identity as a *galant* partner but also a stylish virtuosity brandished in the envious struggle.[40]

Ultimately, the changing historical position of the bassoon complicates the recovery of its orchestral practice. The bassoon and its forebears, it should be recalled, had an extended history of accompanying sacred music long before concerted church cantatas came into vogue. Within this tradition, the omnipresent bassoonist played *colla parte* with the choral basses. The new *galant* bassoonist, on the other hand, seems to have been prized for his special, elegant timbre, and thus was featured only on special occasions. It was perhaps in reconciling these two traditions, and at the same time subordinating them to the requirements of contemporary basso continuo practice, that Bach arrived at the solutions governing the bassoon's participation in his vocal works.

CHAPTER V

The String Instruments in the Continuo Group

The Violoncello

Until recently a central doctrine of the twentieth-century performance of Baroque music held that, in ensemble works of any dimension, the keyboard continuo required a doubling instrument to sustain the bass line. The most recommended candidate was the cello. A passage often cited in support of this position is found in C. P. E. Bach's *Versuch* (1762): "The most complete accompaniment to a solo, against which no one will object, is a keyboard instrument joined by a violoncello."[1] But this cornerstone of belief requires some qualification. First, Emanuel Bach is not speaking about continuo doubling in general but only about the accompaniment of solos.[2] In fact, the passage is a reply to an anonymous "Italian master" who had published duets accompanied by a violin or viola. Cautioning against *bassetto* accompaniments on a soprano or alto instrument without keyboard realization, Emanuel Bach recommends the combination of harpsichord and cello as the most complete accompaniment to a solo. In his study of seventeenth-century Italian accompaniments, moreover, Tharald Borgir found that the accompanying bass instruments varied greatly from one genre to another. The conventional notion that J. S. Bach used the cello in every ensemble work cannot therefore be taken merely as an article of faith but must be based on an examination of the original parts.

In Bach's earliest ensemble works, the participation of the cello as a regular partner to the keyboard cannot be taken for granted. Cantata 71 demonstrates this clearly. In this work of 1708 composed for the inauguration of the Mühlhausen town council, Bach arranges the instrumental forces in four choirs: (1) three trumpets and timpani, (2) two recorders and cello, (3) two oboes and bassoon, and (4) two violins, viola, and violone. The "fifth" choir consists of a four-part chorus of singers (concertists and ripienists) accompanied by the organ. Each choir has its own bass instrument. The doubling instruments, interestingly, do not duplicate the organ part but are *tacet* for much of the piece. The participation of the doubling instruments seems to depend on the genre of a particular movement. For example, the organ continuo accompanies alone in the following sections: Movement 2, a continuo aria for tenor with an embellished chorale in the soprano; Movement 3, a choral motet for concerted soloists with *basso seguente;* the middle section of Movement 4, a continuo aria for solo bass; the arioso inserts in Movement 5 for solo alto; and in Movement 7 during the polychoral vocal sections in the Andante and in the fugal motet for solo choir above a walking bass. In other words, as long as a movement avoids the concerted *stile moderno,* Bach intends the organ to be the sole—and evidently sufficient—accompanying continuo instrument. The cello in Cantata 71—*tacet* in Movements 2, 3, and 5 and in the concertists' sections of Movements 1 and 7—plays as restricted a role as the bassoon or violone.[3]

This practice is not peculiar to Cantata 71 but replicates a common tradition of performing sacred music in the seventeenth century. For example, as Tharald Borgir has amply demonstrated, the sources to Italian "works for solo voice, or voices, whether printed or in MS, have only one single basso continuo part. Works with obbligato instruments or orchestral accompaniment, on the other hand, more frequently have the basso continuo line doubled."[4] In sacred solos, therefore, doubling instruments were optional, while in choral genres a progressively more complete contingent of bass instruments could be added.

In pieces composed before Weimar, therefore, the cello probably did not join the continuo group unless Bach explicitly required it. In Cantata 131, for example, the score mentions only a "Fagotto" and a "Fundamento." In the opening section the bassoon, the nominal bass to the instrumental choir, drops out whenever the obbligato instruments stop playing. It also pauses during two lengthy continuo arias and during a fugal motet section without *colla parte* instruments, returning only during the choral settings with full instrumental ensemble. If the bassoonist was therefore merely a *ripieno* player who participated only during accompanied choral movements, it follows that the organ was the sole continuo instrument for much of the piece. Nothing argues for the additional participation of a cello.

Cantata 106, the Actus Tragicus ("Gotteszeit ist die allerbeste Zeit"), also suggests a staffing of the continuo without cello. The work is scored for two recorders, two gambas, and continuo, and there is no reason to imagine any additional doubling bass instruments. The internal evidence is particularly persuasive here because in the tenor aria, "Ach, Herr! lehre uns bedenken," the second viola da gamba doubles the organ continuo line. That is, since Bach has written out the doubling in an aria in which the full complement of instruments participates, the doubled part makes little sense if a cello has been playing all along.[5] Following the same dictates of genre implied by Cantata 71, much of the Actus Tragicus—in addition to several other early cantatas—would likely have been accompanied by organ continuo alone.

These earlier principles are still manifested in three Weimar cantatas from 1714–1715. In Cantata 182, the cello is *tacet* in certain passages of Movements 2 and 7, when the violin "choir" interrupts its fugal interplay with the vocal chorus. In Cantata 199, the autograph part is entitled *Violoncello e Hautbois,* and the cellist plays continuo only in Movements 1, 3, 4, and 7, in which the upper strings accompany recitatives and an aria. In Movement 2 the cellist—somewhat surprisingly—plays an obbligato on the oboe and then in Movement 6 seems to have turned to a viola for an ornamented chorale obbligato. Only the violone doubled the organ throughout the cantata at this first performance of Cantata 199. Bach treats the cello similarly in Cantata 31, where it serves as a *ripieno* string instrument, playing *basso seguente* in the choral movements and serving as the doubling bassist in one heavily scored tenor aria (Movement 6). Since the cello part is marked *tacet* in Movements 3–5 and 7–8, it follows that the organ accompanied alone for much of the cantata. These Weimar cello parts therefore demonstrate that, even as late as 1715, Bach did not consider the cello a necessary doubling instrument throughout an entire vocal work. Significantly, in Leipzig performances of these very three works, Bach had new cello parts copied, which eliminated the anachronism by filling in passages or movements previously marked *tacet.* Continuous doubling by the cello became the rule in Leipzig ensemble works.

Nonetheless, at the time Bach began composing cantatas in Weimar, the cello made an appearance at every performance. In sources surviving from Weimar and Cöthen works, the cello is specified in ten parts (Cantatas 18, 21, 172, 182, 199, 31, 185, 162, 184a, and 23).[6] Nearly all parts within this group bear the title *Violoncello* written in Bach's own hand. And in several of these compositions (Cantatas 172, 162, 182, 184a, and 23), the cello doubles the organ throughout the cantata, anticipating a practice that became standard only at Leipzig.

Bach's cello was almost certainly the Italianate four-string variety

P 45 (version in score)

St 377/22 (version in part)

EXAMPLE 5-1   Cantata 71, Movement 6, comparison of two versions of cello part

tuned in fifths above low C, the lowest pitch of which shows up frequently in titled cello parts from all periods. Only in the Mühlhausen cantata, "Gott ist mein König" (BWV 71), is there evidence that Bach used another instrument, probably the five-string variety mentioned by Mattheson and Walther. In Movement 6 of this work, the ornamental figures in the cello part reach as high as b♭'. Thereafter, in the version preserved in Bach's score, the cello soars to an extraordinary high f″ in bar 18. Whether Bach's imagination got the better of him is unclear, but a certain degree of restraint overcame him when he prepared the orchestral part, in which the nine measures were transposed down an octave. Example 5-1 compares samples of the two versions. The corrected version rises to c″, probably too high for a normal four-string cello of that time—Walther sets a' as the upper limit of the cello's playable range—and likely indicates a five-string instrument. Since the part does not require the low C-string, perhaps Bach used a four-string violoncello piccolo.

Unlike the Weimar continuo parts with their often explicit instrumental designations, the Leipzig parts are most often merely entitled *Continuo,* and therefore the case for the conventional participation of the cello at Leipzig must be somewhat more indirect. There is, of course, Bach's statement in the 1730 Memorandum to the Town Council that the "instrumental music" requires "2 for the Violoncello." But most persuasive are the Leipzig bass lines themselves. Which other instrument could have negotiated the challenging (unfigured) continuo parts copied each week? Sometimes the title *Violoncello* appears on a Leipzig part; but of the four specified cello parts among cantatas of the first *Jahrgang* performed at Leipzig (Cantatas 147, 162, 172, 182), all were copied from Weimar exemplars. Thereafter, parts labeled *Violoncello* from any original cantata among the cantata cycles of the 1720s are rare.[7] But this absence is no more troubling than the infrequent occurrence of the label *Organo* on *Chorton* continuo parts. Wherever Bach listed the complete instrumentarium—such as on the title page to his score for the Kerll Sanctus (BWV 241), or in the autograph parts for a late version of Cantata 100—the cello invariably appears. The cello is also occasionally listed on the original wrappers enclosing sets of parts. The wrapper for Cantata 7, for example, mentions *violoncel e Continuo,* while the (figured) *Cammerton* part itself is merely labeled *Continuo.* Explicit cello parts were therefore rare because the Leipzig copyists labeled virtually all instrumental bass parts *Continuo* (see Appendix A). As suggested in Chapter 2, there were several good reasons for this lack of specificity: the cellist may have shared a figured part with the harpsichordist, as in Cantata 7, or he could have shared an unfigured part with the bassoonist, as demonstrated by the autograph part from Cantata 97 labeled *Continuo pro Bassono e Violoncello.* Certain parts, moreover, confirm that Bach sometimes employed two cellos at one performance. The part for the Christmas Oratorio (Part I) specifies a *divisi* in the first movement between *Violoncelli* on the one hand and *Bassoni e Continuo* on the other, and the plural can hardly have been written in error.[8] Clearly, during the period when Bach composed and performed the bulk of his vocal works (1724–1729), the cello had not disappeared. Because of its regularity, it merely became superfluous to mention it.

The Problematic Identity of the Violone

While the term *violoncello* refers almost always to one sort of instrument, the term *violone* is far more ambiguous. What kind of instrument did Bach have in mind when he called for a violone? The question, it turns out, is complicated. The standard accompanying pitch of basso continuo instruments in the seventeenth century sounded in the 8-foot octave. Derived from organ terminology, this 8-foot octave refers to the relative length of pipe necessary to produce pitches in the normal bass register. To signify pitches an octave below this notated norm, musicians referred to pipes or instruments in the 16-foot range. Although actual instruments—including, of course, the German organ itself—existed that sounded at an extremely low range, it remains to be clarified exactly when instruments at the 16-foot pitch came into general use. In Italy, contrabasses at the low pitch were rare during the seventeenth century and became prevalent only in the larger orchestras when prompted by operatic practice in urban centers around the 1670s. The term designating the lower instrument, according to Borgir, was consistently *Contrabasso,* while *Violone*—meaning bass viol—could indicate a generic term for the lowest string bass, or the instrument slightly larger than the cello; the latter began to replace the violone as the favored bass accompanying instrument during the last third of the century.[9] In France, dominated by the pervasive influence of Lully's *Petite Bande,* the lowest string instrument in use was the *Basse de violon* or bass violin, an instrument only slightly larger than a cello but tuned a whole tone lower.[10] Only after the turn of the century did true double basses begin to make inroads in the French orchestra. In addition to the obvious influence of both these national practices, German bass practice had to contend with local traditions that were far from uniform. Bach's violone, in sum, might mean many things.

It is also far from certain that the designation *Violone* in Bach's works refers only to one type of instrument; the only incontrovertible fact is that the violone always indicates the lowest instrument in the German continuo group. As a composer tied to court and church establishments, Bach was obviously constrained by the availability of certain instruments. In order to determine the conventions governing Bach's use of the violone, therefore, it is necessary to reconstruct the local traditions. To be sure, these traditions fluctuated during Bach's lifetime. But if the orchestral parts are situated in the context of demonstrable local practices, an outline of the changing nature and use of the various instruments Bach called the "violone" begins to take shape.

Definitions of the German Violone: 1697–1752

The seventeenth-century German violone, referring to the lowest bass instrument in the viol family, seems generally to have been tuned an octave below the tenor viol and a fifth lower than the conventional six-string (bass) viola da gamba. When Daniel Speer (1636–1707), for example, wrote about the violone in the 1697 edition of his *Grundrichtiger Unterricht der musicalischen Kunst,* he put forth a traditional German idea of the instrument: "A *Bass-Violon* has six strings and is tuned in the following manner . . ." (see Facsimile 5-1).[11] Speer also took for granted that the violone did not transpose its parts an octave lower than written. The actual notated pitches given by him indicate this, as do the letter names assigned to them, which replicate the same octave as those given in his preceding entry for the viola da gamba. Most revealing of all is that Speer, in a complete account of contemporary instruments, nowhere described the violoncello. In a sample sonata for two violas, for example, he titled the figured continuo line simply "Violon."[12]

Johann Beer (1655–1700), Konzertmeister at Weissenfels, also attests

FACSIMILE 5-1 Daniel Speer, *Grundrichtiger Unterricht der musicalischen Kunst* (1697), reproduced in facsimile (Leipzig: Edition Peters, 1974)

to this German tradition. In his *Musicalische Discurse* (Nürnberg, 1719), probably written in the 1690s, Beer names the personnel required for a complete "Music" (that is, ensemble). As string "ripienists," he lists the violists followed by the violonist, whom "one must not forget. Since the bass is the fundament upon which all parts rest as on a foundation, this player in particular must be given a discreet upper hand [*eine discrete Faust angeordnet werden*]." [13]

Georg Muffat, on the other hand, displays a more cosmopolitan outlook on the violone when he considers it in the context of the two great national music traditions, France and Italy. Having lived in Paris in the 1660s and in Rome in the 1680s, he was unusually well qualified to interpret the French and Italian styles. In the introduction to his *Florilegium secundum* of 1698, for example, Muffat makes the following statement about bass practice: "To play the bass well, it is best to use a little *Basse à la Françoise* that the Italians call a *violoncino,* which cannot be omitted without spoiling the true harmonic proportion. This can be doubled, according to the number of players, and if that is large, mixing among them the *double basse* (to the Italians, *contrabasso;* to the Germans, *violone*) can only make the concert more majestic, despite the fact that the French still do not use it in their *airs de ballets.*" [14] Muffat documents the fact that French orchestras made use of the *basse de violons* at the bottom of their ensemble. The instruments were tuned B♭-F-C-G, that is, a whole step below the cello. In adapting French practices to different performance conditions, moreover, Muffat pragmatically equates the *basse de violon* with its smaller Italian cousin, the violoncello (or *vio-*

loncino, as he calls it). Then, in an admitted departure from French practice, he suggests the addition of a larger bass instrument to more substantial ensembles. From the Italian and French names for this instrument, it appears that this formidable double bass played considerably lower than the cello, perhaps by as much as an octave. Muffat gives the name for this larger instrument—the violone.[15]

Muffat's view is echoed in Sébastien de Brossard's *Dictionaire de Musique* of 1705, which was devoted in large measure to the explication of foreign terms. Defining "Violoncello" as the *Petite Basse de Violon* (with five or six strings), Brossard proceeds to the "Violone": "This is our *Basse de Violon,* or rather, more correctly it is a *Double Basse* of which the body and neck are nearly twice as large as those of the ordinary *Basse de Violon* . . . and the sound is consequently an octave lower than the ordinary *Basse de Violon.* This makes quite a charming effect in accompaniments and in large choruses and I am rather surprised that its use is not more frequent in France."[16] Although Brossard intends to define the violone as a 16-foot instrument, it is curious that he begins by calling it "our *Basse de Violon*" before furnishing a more precise explanation. Perhaps in seeking a nominal equivalent, Brossard supplied the term ordinarily indicating the lowest string instrument type in France— the *basse de violon.* Strictly speaking, he is not in error: a contrabass is indeed a bass-fiddle if the term is treated literally. Nonetheless, if only because of Brossard's prestige, his terminological slip caused a degree of confusion when later German writers came to write about the violone.

Johann Mattheson, for example, adopts Brossard's French translation in the *Neu-eröffnetes Orchestre* of 1713. "The excellent Violoncello," he writes, is a "small Bass-Fiddle . . . with five or also six strings upon which one can play all types of fast pieces, variations and ornaments more easily than on the large instruments." The "rumbling Violone [*der brummende Violone*]," on the other hand, "*Basse de Violon* in French, large Bass-Fiddle in German, is fully twice as large or often even larger than the aforementioned. Consequently the thickness and length of its strings are proportionally greater. It sounds in the 16-foot register and is an important and cohesive fundament to polyphonic pieces such as choruses and the like, and is also very necessary for arias and even recitatives in the theater because its heavy sound projects and is heard farther than the harpsichord and the other bass instruments."[17] Although Mattheson does not supply tunings for the violone, his reference to its imposing size clearly indicates some sort of contrabass instrument. This is true even though he follows Brossard and mistakenly equates his "contrabass" violone with the *basse de violon.* By his use of the term

"16-foot," he undoubtedly meant that his violone sounded an octave below the cello in practice.

Johann Gottfried Walther, who in his *Lexikon* of 1732 drew on a variety of sources, voices a different opinion by his intentional selection of references. His entry for "Violoncello" follows Mattheson almost verbatim except that he names the four-string variety of cello as the most common and gives its tuning as C-G-D-A.[18] Under "Violone" he first cites Mattheson's (and Brossard's) French "equivalent," *Basse de Violon*, calls it a "Grosse Bass-Geige," but specifies the same six-string G-tuning cited earlier in Speer, that is, a fourth below the cello. Thus, despite his familiarity with Mattheson, Walther continues to indicate the traditional violone that falls short of the contrabass octave. This can be substantiated through an earlier entry in the *Lexikon,* in which Walther defines *Basse double* or *double Basse* as "a double *Bass-Violon,* so called because it is almost twice as large as an ordinary French *Bass-Violon* and accordingly sounds an octave lower." Walther borrows this definition from Brossard and not from Mattheson, but clarifies what he believed was Brossard's confusion in designating the violone as a *Basse de Violon*. But only if the violone meant something else for Walther could he have made a point of adding a special foreign name for the larger 16-foot instrument. In other words, Walther insisted on the word "Double" in order to denote the 16-foot contrabass because for him the term "Violone" signified the smaller 8-foot instrument. As a distant cousin of Bach who lived and worked in Weimar as town organist from 1707 until his death in 1748, Walther must have reflected local practice in defining the violone as the lowest bass instrument. Considering that Bach worked in Weimar from 1708 until 1717, it is likely, at least during the Weimar years, that he too followed the same usage.

A Swabian treatise on instruments published the same year as Walther's *Lexikon,* J. F. B. C. Majer's *Museum musicum,* confirms further that Walther and Mattheson were of two minds about the violone. Majer's definition of "Violoncello" copies Mattheson word for word except that he names only the four-string variety, specifying the conventional C-tuning. Under "Violone" Majer quotes virtually all of Mattheson's entry, but adds that the violone has six strings and is tuned in G.[19] He has therefore conflated his two sources: he quotes Mattheson in calling the violone a 16-foot instrument but follows Walther in prescribing a G-tuning. Moreover, Majer's violone is also smaller than Mattheson's; instead of describing the instrument as "*fully* twice as large or even larger" than the cello, he writes "*almost* twice as large" (emphasis added). This shift in meaning also tallies with his G-tuning (indicating an instrument midway between a cello and double bass) but does not explain why Majer retained the term "16-foot," which conventionally implies a doubling at the lower octave. For with an instrument tuned in G, the violone could only reproduce the notes on the cello's C-string at the unison. Perhaps by this octave designation, Majer did not wish to signify a regular practice of octave transposition but rather that a composer could prescribe certain notated passages in the 16-foot register. Majer gives some hint of this view when he writes out in musical notation the actual notes his violone can play without any reference to an octave transposition. By specifying these, Majer must have meant to describe an instrument at pitch.

A treatise printed in Erfurt in 1738, J. P. Eisel's *Musicus autodidaktos,* sums up various trends in violone practice, at least as they emerge in central Germany. Eisel also copies Mattheson's definitions for the violoncello and the violone, with small variations. He calls the Bass-Violon the largest string instrument, "sometimes even twice as large as the Violoncello." Like Majer and Walther, Eisel primarily cites the six-string tuning in G for his "Bass-Violon" but improves on Majer's text by omitting the misleading reference to the 16-foot range. He continues by enumerating two other types of violone. The first, he says "has a far larger and wider Corpus and goes a fourth lower than the Bass-Violon." That is, this instrument also has six strings but is tuned a full octave below the bass viola da gamba, with a low D′ as its bottom tone. The second subtype of "Violon" has just as large a body but is even wider than this first subtype and "has only four strings among which, the 16-foot contra-C. It is tuned by many like a Violoncello (an octave lower) but most tune it in fourths. [This violone] cuts through better in the orchestra than the six-string one and also requires more force to play it than the other two. The Italians call it the *Violone grosso.*"[20] Thus there are two varieties of contrabass violone, a six-string type that descends to a low D′ and a four-string type with a low C′. That this *violone grosso* was the only instrument to survive through the mid-eighteenth century is attested to by J. J. Quantz, who notes in 1752 that "the so-called German Violon with five or six strings has been justly abandoned."[21]

In this discussion I have intentionally ignored the intricate issues of organology that also played a role in the development and use of the violone. Many questions remain unanswered—the exact tuning of the instruments, whether they were built with straight or curved backs, with F-holes or C-holes, with sloped or perpendicular ribs, with or without frets.[22] Yet there is no compelling reason to believe that the physical construction of the various types of instruments ever commanded a composer's special attention. For only the question of pitch— and, to a lesser extent, that of volume—could have materially influenced usage. There are, then, three instrument types: the small six-string violone in G that played at pitch, the larger six-string transposing contrabass violone in D, and the four-string violone grosso that descended to the low C. Although the scholarly literature has generally assumed that Bach used only one sort of violone and that it was a 16-foot instrument, an examination of the original sources discloses that, at different stages in his career, the composer made use of all three varieties.

Case Study: The Brandenburg Concertos

The violone parts for the Brandenburg Concertos (BWV 1046-1051) furnish a useful perspective from which to view the instrumental parts for Bach's vocal works. In the dedication score that Bach sent to the Margrave of Brandenburg in 1721 (Berlin, Am. B. 78), the violone is specified in all six works. This permits a detailed examination of the peculiarities of a small but self-contained sample. The issues of names, pitch, and usage emerge clearly here and help to place the more ambiguous sources for the vocal works in context.

Nearly every scholar who has studied the Brandenburg parts—or, indeed, any other source for Bach's violone—has concluded that his instrument was consistently a large double bass sounding an octave below notated pitch.[23] The Brandenburg parts in particular seemed to substantiate this claim because the violone parts for Concertos 4 and 5 avoid the low notated C (below the bass staff), which would indicate a large violone with a gamba tuning starting on D.[24] The parts for three concertos—Nos. 1, 3, and 6—are more difficult to assess because the violone is not given a separate system in the score but instead shares a line with the harpsichord. The only puzzling evidence is found in No. 2, where Bach allocates the violone its own line but frequently calls for the low C. Some have concluded that the composer was merely in error here. However, the careful preparation of the Margrave's dedicatory score suggests that this judgment is too hasty. If one considers the accumulating evidence that Bach may have composed the six concertos at different times over the eight-year period preceding 1721, it is plausible that the set of violone parts does not conform to a uniform standard.[25] Judging from internal evidence, all three varieties of violone cited in the historical sources seem to have made an appearance here.

It is striking that Bach names the participants in the continuo section differently in each instrumentarium listing found in the Brandenburg manuscript. Further complicating the assortment is a separate and often

TABLE 5-1 Continuo designations in the Brandenburg Concertos[a]

Number[b]	Instrumentarium	System[c]	Label[d]
1	Violoncello col Basso Continuo	S 11 S 12	Violoncello Continuo (e Violono Grosso)
2	Violone in Ripieno col Violoncello e Basso per il Cembalo	S 8 S 9	Violone ripieno Violoncello e Cembalo al unisono
3	tre Violoncelli col Basso per il Cembalo	S 7 S 8 S 9 S 10	Violoncello 1 Violoncello 2 Violoncello 3 Violone e Cembalo
4	Violone in Ripieno Violoncello e Continuo	S 7 S 8 S 9	Violoncello Violone Continuo
5	Violoncello, Violone e Cembalo concertato	S 5 S 6 S 7 } S 8 }	Violoncello Violon Cembalo Concertato
6	Violoncello, Violone e Cembalo	S 5 S 6	Violoncello Violone e Cembalo

a. The concertos are preserved in a manuscript in Berlin, DStB, Am.B. 78.
b. The numbers 1 through 6 refer to BWV 1064–1051.
c. System numbers are counted from top to bottom in the opening brace of the first movement.
d. Bach's instrument labels placed adjacent to each stave; parentheses indicate a later autograph addition.

conflicting enumeration of the instruments given adjacent to each stave in the score. Table 5-1 provides a comparison of these two designations. Only Concerto No. 1, as the table shows, calls for a *violono grosso,* and even this was a later addition to the score that Bach indicated in darker ink only adjacent to the continuo stave. Undoubtedly Bach meant a large instrument in the 16-foot range. Since, moreover, the part requires a low C, the instrument is probably identical to the four-string contra-bass described by Eisel. In all the other pieces the violone is listed either as *violone* or *violone in ripieno* except in Concerto No. 3, where Bach again omits it from the instrumentarium.

Concerto No. 4 furnishes a lucid example of a distinct violone part meant to sound an octave below pitch. Since the part steers conspicu-

FACSIMILE 5-2 Brandenburg Concerto No. 4, Movement 2 (BWV 1049), autograph score, mm. 27–43, Deutsche Staatsbibliothek Berlin/DDR, Musikabteilung, Am.B. 78

ously clear of the low C, Bach surely intended the large violone in D; that is, as an instrument tuned a minor seventh below the cello, the violone must avoid the one note which it cannot double at the lower octave. The first movement of this concerto contains repeated examples of intentional transpositions away from the low C. Perhaps the most palpable is in Movement 2, where the violone doubles both the cello and harpsichord lines note for note except in the one spot (at m. 31) where they descend to C (see Facsimile 5-2). Bach referred to this instrument in Concerto No. 4 as a violone—not as a *violone grosso*—a nomenclature consistent with Eisel, who used the term "Violon" to signify the larger six-string intrument in D as well as the smaller instrument in G.[26] Although six-string bass gambas in the English and German traditions occasionally tuned down the lowest string from D to C, Bach appears not to have copied this practice on the violone, perhaps because it would have been too ungainly to negotiate the resulting jumps in the bottom of the register. In any case, the inconsistency in the two names for the three instruments seems to account for the different nomenclature between Concertos 1 and 4, which both require distinct contrabass instruments.

The violone part in Concerto No. 4 suggests certain characteristic features that allude to a double bass part. First, as part of the *ripieno,* the violone never plays an independent role but always some sort of reduced continuo part. This entails frequent rests and simplifications of the cello part such as those illustrated in Example 5-2. Bach also attempted to lessen the bass "load" by occasionally writing violone parts an octave higher. These passages place the violone and the cello at the unison and do not occur, significantly, merely when the violone part jumps in order to avoid the low C (see Example 5-3). Although Bach does not completely avoid a two-octave gap between cello and violone by actually notating the contrabass at the lower octave, these occurrences are never extended for very long. (One such example is shown in Facsimile 5-3.) A violone was most likely tuned at the low double-bass pitch when the composer conspicuously avoided the low C, since only on an instrument pitched almost an octave below the cello would this note be unplayable. That is, the use of the (double-bass) violone in D can be demonstrated whenever the composer conspicuously avoided a notated C (sounding C′). Furthermore, a violone part that ascends a written octave above the cello for an extended passage likewise suggests a transposing contrabass sounding occasionally at the unison.

EXAMPLE 5-2 Brandenburg Concerto No. 4, Movement I (BWV 1049/1), mm. 52–56

EXAMPLE 5-3 Brandenburg Concerto No. 4, Movement I (BWV 1049/1), mm. 24–28

FACSIMILE 5-3 Brandenburg Concerto No. 4, Movement 1 (BWV 1049), autograph score, mm. 361–378, Deutsche Staatsbibliothek Berlin/DDR, Musikabteilung, Am.B. 78

By these criteria, Concerto No. 5—as represented in the dedication score—must also have been written for the same instrument as Concerto No. 4. Consider the following copying error in Bach's score. In the second statement of the complete ritornello, the composer began by mechanically duplicating the cello line, but then realized his error in m. 124 and placed the part up an octave (see Facsimile 5-4). The correction only makes sense if seen as an effort to avoid the low C♯. Elsewhere the violone stays clear of this note and, as in the part for Concerto No. 4, is sometimes notated at the upper octave. Finally, this violone part resembles that of No. 4 in its simplifications and reductions of the continuo line, in which the player participates in the *ripieno*. The intended instrument can be none other than the violone in D.

Yet in an earlier version of Concerto No. 5 (BWV 1050a), Bach could not have intended a violone in the 16-foot register. From a set of parts copied (ca. 1748–1759) mostly by Bach's son-in-law, Johann Christoph Altnikol, BWV 1050a required only two continuo parts: *Cembalo concertato* and *Violone*. Bearing no relation to its successor, this violone part represented a reduced harpsichord part that made no attempt to avoid the low pitches.[27] Moreover, it was consistently notated in the same octave as the harpsichord and probably shared the lowest stave with the Cembalo in the lost score. Dürr, for one, believed that the continuo in

FACSIMILE 5-4 Brandenburg Concerto No. 5, Movement 1 (BWV 1050), autograph score, mm. 117–125, Deutsche Staatsbibliothek Berlin/DDR, Musikabteilung, Am.B. 78

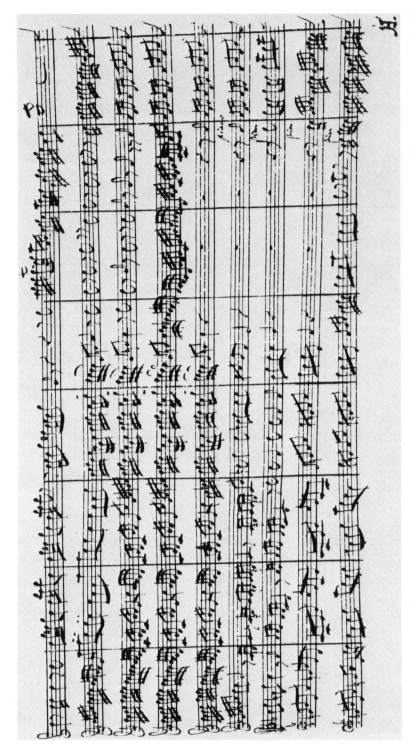

FACSIMILE 5-5 Brandenburg Concerto No. 2, Movement 1 (BWV 1046), autograph score, mm. 24–31, Deutsche Staatsbibliothek Berlin/DDR, Musikabteilung, Am.B. 78

this version consisted of a 16-foot contrabass and the harpsichord, but this seems a bit odd. Quantz, for example, even warns the cellist not to play his parts an octave below notated pitch, for then "the distance from the violins would be too great, and the notes would . . . lose the sharpness and animation which the composer had in mind."[28] Indeed, the instrumentarium listed on Altnikol's violone part notes a *Cembalo concertato* and *violone* but no cello. Moreover, the word "Violoncello" is squeezed onto the title wrapper of Bach's Cöthen part for No. 5, a part-set that corresponds to an intervening stage in the history of Concerto No. 5.[29] But would Bach have scored a concerto with harpsichord and a doubling instrument an octave lower? Another explanation is far more likely: the original violone in BWV 1050a was the traditional doubling violone in G. Here, a six-string instrument tuned a fourth below the cello would easily negotiate the required notes at pitch. (Walther writes that the upward ambitus extended to d' or e'.) This use of the violone (without cello) would correspond to an older seventeenth-century German and Italian tradition which called for a violone at 8-foot range as the only doubling string instrument in the continuo.[30]

The suspicion that Bach subscribed to Walther's and not Mattheson's definition of the violone when he composed BWV 1050a is further confirmed by internal evidence found in Concerto No. 2. Here the part is notated on its own stave above the cello's, but it does not correspond to any criteria noted for the larger instrument exhibited in No. 4. In No. 2, the violone is the actual bass member of the ripieno section; its part does not ascend above the cello's and makes no attempt to avoid the low C. Moreover, on several occasions, it goes out of its way to emphasize both the lower octave and the low C, as Facsimile 5-5 illustrates. In fact, an earlier version of No. 2 survives in both a score and set of parts copied by C. F. Penzel in the 1750s. Here too, as in BWV 1050a, the sources require a violone as the sole string instrument in the continuo.[31] The violone part is likewise undifferentiated from the harpsichord continuo part and must have been intended for the smaller instrument. However, when Bach came to design a new version of No. 2 for the Margrave's score with differentiated bass parts (presumably in 1721), he assigned the cello to the part that the violone had previously played (alluding, again, to the identity in pitch) but designed a reduced violone part that was much busier than the part in No. 5 and, moreover, stressed the low C. For this reason, the instrument that survived the revisions in Concerto No. 2 must have been the violone in G.[32] In his update of Concerto No. 2, in other words, Bach apparently felt no need to revise the violone part for a 16-foot instrument.

Although the violone does not occupy its own stave in Concerto No. 6, two striking passages hint that Bach used an instrument in the 8-foot range. In Movement 1, the violone (together with the harpsichord) is either notated at pitch with the concerted cello part or at the lower octave. There are no examples, moreover, in which the violone ever ascends above the cello. At mm. 56-58, two octaves briefly separate the cello and violone, which, with a double bass, would have created an unlikely three-octave gap. Second, the last movement of No. 6 ends with a low B♭′, as shown in Example 5-4, a pitch that no transposing violone—including the *violono grosso*—could have played, but one easily negotiated on the smaller violone in G. A telltale sign of the smaller instrument also makes an appearance here: a passage notated at the octave which is intended to sound as written. In the second movement, it seems likely that the violone was *tacet* and that only the harpsichord continued to accompany, following the example of the slow movement to Concerto No. 2. (In both instances Bach's score is unclear.) This omission makes sense not only because the two bass lines would interfere with each other if played by two string instruments, but also because, together with the gambas, the violone is a ripienist who returns only in the concluding concerted movement. At the same time, the decorative principle of orchestration underlying the use of the 8-foot violone remains the same. Whereas much of the bass movement in the two parts hovers around the unison, the extended "solo" passage at mm. 44-52 splits into a real octave, as shown in Example 5-5, and then at m. 33 even moves to a gap of two notated octaves.[33]

The violone part in Concerto No. 3, also shared with the harpsichord, is more ambiguous. For one thing, a heavily orchestrated bass section already consists of three concertato cellos. The violone functions generally as a reduced cello part, although occasionally it plays an independent role when the cellos are resting. Nonetheless, one encounters no signs of the small violone. On the contrary, a secondary source suggests that a large instrument was intended. A set of parts

EXAMPLE 5-4 Brandenburg Concerto No. 6, Movement 3 (BWV 1051/3), mm. 109–110

EXAMPLE 5-5 Brandenburg Concerto No. 6, Movement 2 (BWV 1051/2), mm. 44–52

copied by Penzel in 1755 reflected a version of No. 3 that no longer survives.[34] One part in this set is labeled "Violono grosso," even though it resembles the later Violoncello 3 part. Despite the confused transmission of the sources, it seems that an exemplar for a violone grosso may have existed in an earlier version. This would explain the frequent low notes in the later violone part, as in Concerto No. 1.

To summarize: Bach's "Violone" in the Brandenburg concertos implies three differently pitched instruments. The first, the so-called *Violono grosso,* a 16-foot instrument with a low C-string, was used in Concertos 1 and 3. The second, a contrabass instrument with a low D string that falls a whole step short of the larger instrument, was required in Concertos 4 and 5. Finally, the third instrument is the violone in G traceable in Concertos 2 and 6 and in the early version of No. 5 (BWV 1050a).

Violone Parts from Mühlhausen, Weimar, and Cöthen

Considering the sketchy transmission of sources for the early Bach vocal works (ca. 1707–1721), the sum of extant violone parts is substantial. In addition to the six parts listed in Table 5-2, references to the violone are also found in the sources for six other works (Cantatas 196, 208, 147a, 165, 134a, and 173a). Three locales—Mühlhausen, Weimar, and Cöthen—are represented in these pieces.

Mühlhausen. The works from Mühlhausen exemplify the most old-fashioned trends in continuo practice. As discussed in the case of Cantata 71, each of the four instrumental choirs retained its own bass player,

TABLE 5-2 Violone parts from Mühlhausen and Weimar

Work	Date	Cat. number	Part-title	Identical continuo part	Separate movements	*Tacet* movements
BWV 71	1708	St 377/16	Violon.		1, 7	2, 3, 4, (7)
BWV 18	1713?	St 34/1	Violono [o Organo]		1	
BWV 199	1714	St 459/13	Violono	x		
BWV 132	1714?	St 5/1	Violone		1, 3	
BWV 162	1714–1716	St 1/1	Violono	x		
BWV 185	1715	St 4/10	Violono	x		

Violoncello St 377/22

Violono St 377/16

EXAMPLE 5-6   Cantata 71, Movement 7, mm. 38–39

and the organ functioned as the sole continuo support for much of the piece.[35] Moreover, as indicated, the high cello part suggests a five-string instrument. The violone part, which accompanies the upper strings without the cello (recalling the later Brandenburg Concerto No. 2) was often notated at the octave below the cello, as shown in Example 5-6; this part also calls for the low C. From the range, the frequent octave spacing, and the fact that the violone serves as the only bass to the violins and violas, it seems certain that the required instrument in Cantata 71 was the small instrument in G.

In the other Mühlhausen cantatas, the evidence for this smaller violone is only indirect. In Cantata 196, the only source—a score copied after Bach's death by J. P. Kirnberger—contains two bass lines. The first is labeled "Violoncello" and the second "Organo e Continuo," so a violone might have been included, although a lute or a theorbo should be considered equally plausible candidates. As for the notated pitch of the two parts, the cello and continuo are virtually always separated by the octave, as in Cantata 71. It is also possible that Bach used the violone in Mühlhausen only for the large-scale occasion of Cantata 71, which celebrated the election of the Town Council.[36]

Weimar. One traceable performance in Weissenfels of Cantata 208, the *Jagdkantate* ("The Hunt"), on February 23, 1713, preceded the main set of Weimar cantatas that followed Bach's appointment in 1714 as *Concert-Meister.*[37] In the extant autograph score Bach does not specify any continuo instruments until Movement 11, where he labels the two bass staves *Violons e Bassons* and *Cont. e Violono grosso.* This juxtaposition is especially revealing in that the "Violono grosso" is distinguished from the "Violons," which must probably be understood to indicate cellos, as is clear from the idiomatic passages in Movement 13. The part for the larger instrument, moreover, requires the low C, which is consistent with Eisel's largest violone. It also makes sense that this instrument is a

EXAMPLE 5-7 Cantata 18, Movement 1, mm. 64–72

EXAMPLE 5-7 *(continued)*

true contrabass, since Bach writes for it more or less in the same octave as the bassoon and cello. When it deviates, as in the fugal entries in Movement 11, its part is generally not a full octave lower. The only unusual treatment is in Movement 15, where, with the harpsichord, the large violone is occasionally the only continuo support. Perhaps when he subsequently copied the parts, Bach omitted the violone here. At the very least, one may observe that this curious sort of orchestration did not survive in Bach's later works and is, for example, strictly avoided in the Brandenburg concertos.[38]

Thus there is no substance to the view that Bach's lowest string instrument in Weimar was a double bass. On the contrary, all signs point to the smaller violone in G as the lowest member of Bach's continuo ensemble. Walther, after all, had chosen only the six-string instrument in G to illustrate the term "Violone" in his *Lexikon* of 1732. Most likely he reflected a local practice to which Bach also subscribed.[39]

Virtually all the Weimar violone parts, most of which were copied by Bach himself, include notes below low D, that is, C's and C♯'s. In addition, they occasionally point to the smaller violone by notations at the lower octave. A passage from Cantata 18, Movement 1, illustrates this (see Example 5-7); here the ritornello is reiterated by the continuo in octaves (the cello above the bassoon and violone) beneath the motivic decoration of the violas. This mirrors the opening and closing statements of the ritornello, which are stated in octaves between the violas and the continuo (mm. 68-72). When the violas play the ritornello, the violone is notated at the same pitch as the cello; when the violas are otherwise occupied, the violone plays at the lower octave. This change in notated octave, however, only makes sense for a violone at pitch.[40]

Bach never marked a Weimar violone part *tacet* in any movement. Indeed, the violone parts for Cantatas 199, 185, and 162 duplicate the corresponding cello parts. This may seem paradoxical given that just at this time the composer went out of his way to arrange bassoon parts so that this instrument's part was reduced within a cantata. The Weimar parts therefore suggest that the violone played in an ordinary range that did not require special attention.

Cöthen. From Bach's Cöthen years (1717–1723), no violone parts survive from any of the composer's vocal works,[41] but references to the violone in the scores for Cantatas 134a and 173a in addition to the parts for the Brandenburg concertos ensure that the violone played a role here. In Bach's autograph score for Cantata 134a the word "Violoni" is found in Movement 8, but this term most likely designates a generic plural for string basses of any size, including cellos.[42] The case of Cantata 173a is more clear-cut: in Movement 7 the continuo line is entitled "Cembalo e Violone" because the bassoon and cello play an obbligato. But whether this violone was a "violone grosso"—the part descends to a low C♯—or a smaller instrument in G remains ambiguous.

Leipzig Violone Parts

The regular participation of the violone at Leipzig is especially difficult to determine because the violone was probably one of the first instruments to be omitted when Bach's orchestral forces were depleted as a result of illnesses or unfilled vacancies. Although the 1730 Memorandum had stated Bach's requirements—one or even two bassoons, two cellos, and "1 for the Violon," this is not to say that the composer had these forces available to him. Of the Town Pipers and Fiddlers he lists by name, both spots for cello and violone are noted as vacant. Although students from the university filled these positions, this emptied the choir of the necessary singers. On certain occasions, though, the staffing of the continuo was particularly problematic and the violone may not have participated in every performance, even when one was clearly desirable. The wrapper enclosing the set of parts for Cantata 7, for example, names only *violoncel e Continuo,* which seems conspicuously to omit the violone. Perhaps, then, Bach's requirement for a violone stated in the 1730 Memorandum reflected an often unfulfilled request.

Two violone parts from cantatas performed in the early Leipzig years, Cantatas 78 and 137, also suggest that a regular violone player was not always available. Each includes only one movement for the violone, and these parts are located on the reverse sides of brass parts: the special violone obbligato to Cantata 78/2 is on the back of the horn part, while the continuo part for Cantata 137/4 is on the back of the third trumpet part.[43] It follows that in each case the violonist and the brass player were the same person. This conclusion is not all that surprising: the Town Pipers were in fact required to pass auditions (though without remarkably high standards) on all the brass instruments and violone, among several others.[44] Thus, in Cantata 78, the player would take up the horn for the first movement, move over to the violone in Movement 2, and return to the horn for the final movement.[45] On other occasions, one can easily imagine that Bach had to dispense with the violone altogether.

The Leipzig performances of Cantata 182 offer further hints that the violone did not always participate at performances. In the Weimar version of this work, the cello and organ constituted the continuo section without any trace of a (subsequently lost) violone part.[46] The cello, however, was not a ubiquitous doubling instrument but functioned—as described earlier—as a quasi-independent bass of the instrumental choir. In this earliest version of Cantata 182 the organ often accompanies the choir without the cello, and the two bass instruments are even notated at occasional octaves. By 1724 Bach must have found this manner inappropriate, for at the Leipzig performance—evidently prepared in greater haste than usual[47]—he charged his chief copyist, J. A. Kuhnau, with the preparation of a cello part that consolidated the two former bass lines. Although Kuhnau's new cello part was somewhat ungainly, Bach now had a doubling part that included the necessary concertato sections.[48] This rearrangement—still lacking a 16-foot doubling instrument— seemed to be sufficient, since a violone part was not copied until a later performance sometime around 1728. With this part, the sound of the continuo contingent was radically changed from the original conception: Bach evidently told the scribe merely to copy Kuhnau's consolidated part for the violone, so that both cello and violone now doubled consistently throughout all movements of the piece. The most reasonable explanation here is that Bach lacked a violone player for the 1724 performance, and when one became available later, he merely included him in the ensemble.

On the other hand, given a full complement of players and a large-scale work, Bach would certainly have wanted the violone in the continuo group. The complete set of autograph parts for Cantata 100, for example, contains a separate *Continuo pro violone*. Likewise, the Kerll Sanctus (BWV 241) includes a violone part. But more usually, the player probably shared a continuo part with another bassist. The Kerll parts, in fact, allude to this practice: while the violone part is entitled *Violone Grosso,* the cello part is entitled *Violoncello senza Violone,* suggesting that the violonist and cellist normally read from the same part (see Facsimile 5-6). The part for BWV 226 labeled *Violon e Continuo* suggests that two cellists shared a part, while the violonist looked over the shoulder of the harpsichordist.[49]

Bach's Leipzig violone seems to have been pitched in the 16-foot range. When Bach first arrived in 1723, he probably had two instruments at his disposal, one in each main church. One violone was quite old and had belonged to the churches before Johann Kuhnau became Thomas-Cantor in 1701;[50] the other was acquired by Kuhnau himself in 1711. A third instrument was purchased at auction in 1735–1736. The records refer to it as a "large" violone, presumably in contrast to the other instruments. On the other hand, the church inventory thereafter referred to each surviving instrument merely as a "violon."[51] No further information sheds light on these instruments, except that Bach called for a "violono grosso" in the instrumentarium of Cantata 205, a secular work performed in 1725. Whether an instrument belonging to one of the churches was used is not known.

One document that may bear on the matter of pitch is a statement by Carl Philipp Emanuel Bach in a preface to the Birnstiel edition of his father's chorales (1765), intended either for instruments or singers. Emanuel Bach notes that "in those passages where the bass descends so much lower than the other parts that it cannot be played without a pedal, one transposes the line to the upper octave. One then returns to the lower octave as soon as the bass crosses above the tenor. The author (of blessed memory) took care of this latter circumstance with a sixteen-foot bass instrument [*ein sechzehnfüssiges bassirendes Instrument*], which had always played along with these chorales."[52] It is possible that the 16-foot instrument mentioned here was the violone, although Emanuel Bach may merely be referring to an organ. In any event it is clear that, in four-part writing from Leipzig, a doubled fundament in octaves was conventional, indeed necessary, for proper part-writing. In ten simple four-part chorales from Weimar cantatas,[53] for example, the tenor crosses the bass only once—in Cantata 12, Movement 7 (m. 9). And even here, the composer correctly prepared the resulting dissonance of the fourth. Al-

FACSIMILE 5-6 Kerll, Sanctus (BWV 241), *Violoncello senza Violone* and *Violone Grosso* parts, Kunst-sammlungen der Veste Coburg, V, 1109, 1b

TABLE 5-3   Violone parts from Leipzig

Work	Date	Cat. number	Part-title	Autograph part	Identical continuo part	Separate movements	Tacet movements
BWV 147	1723	St 46/15	—			7	
BWV 78	1724	Thom 78/12	Violone	x		2	
BWV 62	1724	Thom 62/14	Continuo			1	
BWV 137	1725	Thom 137/16	—			4	
BWV 49	1726	St 55/15	Violono		x		
BWV 182	1728–1731	St 47/14	Violono		x		20
BWV 245	1728–1731	St 111/22	Continuo			(1, 27b)	
BWV 226	1729	St 121/11	Violon e Continuo	x		seguente	
BWV 42	1732–1735	St 3/15	Violon.	x		2, 3, 4	
BWV 62	1732–1735	Thom 62/13	Violone			1	
BWV 214	1733	St 91/6	Violono			1	
BWV 91	1734	St 64/13	Continuo			1	
BWV 248[1]	1734	St 112[1]/19	Continuo			1	
BWV 100	1735?	St 97/14	Continuo pro Violone		x		
BWV 210	1742–1748	St 76/7	Violone	x		2, 8, 10	3, 4, 5, 6, 7
Palestrina[a]	1742–1748	—	Violone	x	x		
Pergolesi[b]	1744–1748	—	Violone	x	x		
Goldberg[c]	1744–1748	—	Violon	x	x		
BWV 241[d]	1747	—	Violono grosso	x		all	some sections
J. C. Bach[e]	1745–1749	—	Violone	x		seguente	
BWV 195	1748?	St 12/21	Violone	x		seguente	

a. Palestrina, *Missa sine nomine*, Berlin, DStB, Mus. ms. 16714.
b. Pergolesi, *Stabat Mater*, Berlin, DStB, Mus. ms. 17155/16.
c. Johann Gottlieb Goldberg, "Durch die herzliche Barmherzlichkeit," Berlin, SPK, Mus. ms. 7918.
d. Kerll, *Sanctus* (BWV 241), Kunstsammlungen der Veste Coburg.
e. Johann Christoph Bach, "Lieber Herr Gott, wecke uns auf," Berlin, DStB, Musikabteilung, Fot. Bü 42/3.

though this occurrence constitutes only weak negative evidence, it suggests that no technical features of the part-writing in Weimar necessitated a 16-foot doubling instrument. On the other hand, it is conceivable that Bach regularly instructed the organist to add a 16-foot stop to accompany chorales even in Weimar. It is rather in the Leipzig chorales that tenor parts frequently descend below the vocal bass, requiring, according to Emanuel Bach's account, a 16-foot accompaniment. Although this cannot confirm that Bach's Leipzig violone was a double bass instrument, it alludes to 16-foot accompaniment as a new aesthetic desideratum.

The musical sources help to demonstrate that the violone played at the lower octave at Leipzig. The list of extant parts is given in Table 5-3.[54] The earliest trace of the violone at Leipzig is found in a continuo part for Cantata 147, performed in 1723, which contains a *divisi* in Movement 7, reminiscent of simplifications elsewhere. Although the violone generally follows a strict reduction of the cello part without a change of octave, Example 5-8 shows a passage in which the violone rises an octave above the cello. As in Brandenburg Concertos 4 and 5, this alludes to the 16-foot octave sounding here at the unison.[55] The special violone part for Cantata 78, Movement 2, mentioned earlier, furnishes another example alluding to the low pitch of the violone. Here

EXAMPLE 5-8 Cantata 147, Movement 7, mm. 40–43

EXAMPLE 5-9 Cantata 78, Movement 2, mm. 1–10

Bach reduces the cello part's steady eighth notes to quarter notes in the violone, marking them "staccato e pizzicato" (see Example 5-9). Considering how relatively high this part is notated in relation to the cello, a 16-foot instrument seems the most appropriate candidate. Perhaps the low C's in this part (as well as in other Leipzig parts) even indicate a four-string "violone grosso," although, in a simple part such as this, perhaps a player of the six-string violone in D tuned down his lowest string to C.

Cantata 62 provides even stronger evidence that the Leipzig violone was a transposing instrument. As Facsimile 5-7 shows, Bach notates the continuo line in octaves (sounding the cantus firmus) and reverses the stems. The composer evidently wished to set off the chorale quotation in the bass from the answer several bars later in the oboe part. Since the

FACSIMILE 5-7 Cantata 62, first page of autograph score, Berlin, Staatsbibliothek, Preussischer Kulturbesitz, Musikabteilung, Mus. ms. Bach P 877

oboes play the tune in unison, the continuo likely followed suit. The notation—replicated in the continuo part—therefore meant that the violone should play the notes on top while the cello should play the notes on the bottom, resulting in a unison. One might think that the notation could have signified an octave *divisi* that could have been rendered by two cellists (the reversal of stems is not maintained consistently); a violonist might then have doubled at the lower octave. Nonetheless, the implied violone must have been in the 16-foot range. For when Anna Magdalena Bach came to copy a later violone part for a performance of Cantata 62 in the 1730s, she chose the upper line of the chorale melody for the violone. That is, she clearly understood the notation as an intended unison—a unison that depended on a violone in the 16-foot range.

Regarding the group of violone parts copied on paper dating from 1732 to 1735 (see Table 5-3), it is likely that Bach had performed these works without a violone at previous performances. In addition, the parts for Cantatas 62, 42, 214, 97, and 10 and the Sanctus (BWV 240) may have resulted from the purchase of a new violone around 1735–1736. If so, these performances might be datable somewhat later than his hitherto been suspected.

But did the Leipzig violone—when it finally entered the picture—play in every movement of a vocal work? This question is difficult to answer. The Weimar bassoon parts, for example, were largely in Bach's hand and commonly contained several *tacet*-indications, whereas the autograph Weimar violone parts did not. The Weimar violone, to the extent that it was present, was therefore a regular participant in the continuo group. Yet with the change in size and pitch—from 8-foot to 16-foot— Bach may have wanted to restrict the Leipzig violone to a greater extent, at least in some concerted works. But so few Leipzig violone parts are in Bach's own hand that it is difficult to confirm this view. If motets, mass movements, and works in *stile antico* are excluded, the *tacet*-indications in several Leipzig violone parts provide some revealing, if contradictory, clues.

In a performance of Cantata 100 that reinstated an organ part previously marked *tacet,* Bach copied a violone part that excluded the instrument from Movement 3 (an aria with *traverso* obbligato) and confined its participation in Movement 5 to ritornello passages marked *forte*. The violone part to a cantata for solo soprano, BWV 210, seems to extend these principles further. Here the violone takes part fully only in Movements 1 and 9, both accompagnato recitatives; otherwise, Bach drastically curtailed its role in three arias, Movements 2, 8, and 10, and omitted it entirely from the remaining arias and recitatives. In Movement 2, moreover, the composer designed a rather sophisticated reduction for the violone in which it primarily plays the ritornellos—pausing when the singer enters—but joins the strings for certain ritornello fragments when the singer sustains a long note (mm. 56-60). Although these parts constitute exceptions to the rule of undifferentiated violone parts, one suspects that, given the time and inclination, Bach might have reduced more violone parts accordingly.

On the other hand, the autograph part for Cantata 195 includes all movements of the piece, suggesting that Bach thought it perfectly acceptable for the violone to play throughout a complete vocal work, particularly one such as this large wedding cantata which excluded arias with delicate scorings.[56] Nonetheless, the evidence is simply too slim to arrive at a meaningful conclusion. Most likely, the Leipzig violone was a welcome member of the continuo group to the extent that Bach could find someone to play it.

Bach's Violone Types

For Bach, the term "violone" stood as an identifying label for three different instrumental types. The small violone in G that played at pitch is the oldest instrument; it appears in early works from Mühlhausen and Weimar and can last be detected in Cöthen, where it figures in the earliest layer of the Brandenburg Concertos. No trace of the small violone can be found in Leipzig. There, it seems, the church establishments had already expressed a preference for the 16-foot transposing instrument, as had many courts and chapels throughout Germany, France, and Italy. The principles underlying Bach's use of the smaller instrument are as interesting as they are unfamiliar. Originally, before composers had adopted the idea of a ubiquitous doubling bass instrument, the violone served as a fundament reinforcing the continuo in large-scale concerted movements and descended occasionally to outline the 16-foot register by playing an octave below the cello or organ. These forms of reinforcement were exceptional only in that they required parts notated at the lower octave, since the player of this small violone in G did not transpose his parts. Later, in a normal concerted work, the violone in G seems to have functioned in a capacity nearly equal to that of the cello. Since both instruments were located in the same octave, the only real difference was timbre, a matter that Bach and his contemporaries could not have taken very seriously.

Bach also used the small violone to support the continuo while the cello took on a quasi-concertato role. This resembles later practice chiefly because, with both cello and violone functioning in the same octave, the result is a reinforced bass section, but one that lacks the added weight of the 16-foot register. On the other hand, the new sonority mixing the 8-foot and 16-foot sonorities, which Brossard termed "tout charmant," was less a standard feature of a large ensemble than a device creating a special textural effect. One might even say that the Leipzig orchestra, with its constant octave doublings, took a historical turn that covered up a far more inventive and variegated approach to the orchestration of the continuo group.

The introduction of the larger types of violone—the instrument in D, a fretted, six-string double-bass gamba, and the *violone grosso* in C, a four-string instrument twice as large as the cello—gave rise to a new possibility of orchestral decoration: the reduced continuo part for contrabass. Here the composer could conceive the doubled 16-foot register as a sonority to *exclude* from the aggregate sound of the orchestra. As an elaborative tool in the service of concerted principles of alternation, the contrabass served to highlight the surface tensions between tutti and solo, for its presence immediately denoted something powerful and commanding. As Mattheson put it, the violone provided "an important and cohesive fundament." At the same time, the evidence shows that in a work of consistently massive proportions, the violone sometimes participated consistently from beginning to end.

The Viola da gamba

In Bach's Germany, the viola da gamba was no longer an ordinary accompanying instrument in any large ensemble. In fact, by the time Bach had begun to compose, it was already considered something unusual and had taken on a special set of meanings. In one of his earliest works—the Actus Tragicus (Cantata 106)—Bach employed the traditional "quiet instruments" (*stille Instrumenta*), gambas and recorders, to signify the remote realm of the pastoral. In this cantata written for a funeral service, the solace of otherworldly instruments offers comfort to the mourners. In other works, because of its special cultivation by the French court composers, Bach's gamba also became an icon of royalty. It is no mere coincidence that all three solos in the two Passions are comprised of regal dotted figures, which elevate the reference to the French monarch (via his royal overture) into the Christian allegory.

Similarly, the same mixture of pastoral and royal references characterizes Bach's gamba parts in the *Trauer-Ode* for Queen Christiane Eberhardine (BWV 198). In the opening *tombeau,* the gambas help allude to the French overture, just as they lend a pastoral complexion to the *siciliano* settings of Movements 5 and 11. This is not to say that Bach could not detach the gamba from its traditional identities. Consider, for example, the three sonatas with obbligato harpsichord (BWV 1027-1029). In these stylish pieces Bach invents a new guise for the gamba, which he treats much like the nearly interchangeable *galant* instruments that occupy the musical world of Telemann's *Getreuer Music-Meister.*[57]

When Bach calls for a gamba to play continuo, he virtually always does so in conjunction with an adjacent solo gamba part. Indeed, only one example of a gamba continuo exists where the player is not also engaged as a soloist.[58] One reason must be practical: with its underhand bowing and reversed bow strokes (up-bow is the strong stroke), the gamba cannot articulate short bass notes as easily as the cello. In addition, the gamba is not properly a bass instrument: although its range with six strings is only a whole step short of the cello (D on its lowest string) and with seven strings a third lower than the cello (descending to low A'), its repertoire historically favored the distinctive alto and tenor registers. (In fact, Bach sets the gamba parts in the Brandenburg Concerto No. 6 in the alto and tenor clefs.) Though the gamba never avoided its lowest strings, it rarely remained there for an extended passage. Bach, like his contemporaries, knew that the gamba was far from an ideal accompanist in large-scale concerted works.[59]

Nonetheless, the gamba either joins or supplants the continuo in several instances in Bach's vocal works. The second gamba part in Cantata 106 (discussed earlier) reveals how the organ, following an earlier practice, accompanies alone for much of the cantata. The gamba's move to the continuo line in Movements 2b and 2d fortifies an organ bass which elsewhere manages well without any other doubling instruments. In several passages this second gamba plays at the upper octave to the continuo (for example, in Movement 2, mm. 152, 156, and 165-167), thereby adding to the depth of the accompaniment by the mixture of the 8-foot and 16-foot registers. This same principle underlies the use of the gamba in Cantata 152, a Weimar work for the Sunday after Christmas, in which the gamba appears together with a recorder, an oboe, and a viola d'amore. The opening Sinfonia weds an embellished Corellian Andante (expanded in texture from a trio to a quartet) to a fugal reprise from a French overture. In the slow introduction the gamba reproduces the continuo line exactly at the upper octave, and then, in the fugue, plays the subject either doubling the continuo or diverging in diminutions at the upper octave. Particularly the intensified passage at the upper octave beginning at m. 93 seems to indicate, again, that no other doubling continuo instrument was present. It is unclear whether in the subsequent movements the gamba doubled the continuo at all.[60] (Only Bach's score survives, and the gamba is not mentioned after the opening movement.) The final movement offers a hint that it did not: next to the single obbligato line to this dialogue duet between Jesus and the Soul, Bach notes *Gli Stromenti all'unisono*. Presumably the gamba, as one of "the instruments," played the obbligato (at the lower octave) rather than the continuo part.

Both in a Cöthen performance of Cantata 199 and in a second performance of Cantata 76, the viola da gamba appears as soloist at the moment when the text turns to notions of consolation, comfort, and reconciliation, and then remains as continuo player for subsequent movements. In Cantata 199 the gamba (replacing a viola in the Weimar version) first plays in Movement 6, an elaborated chorale movement. Thereafter, for the remaining two movements, it joins the continuo, perhaps supplementing another doubling instrument such as the cello. In the first performance of Cantata 76 in 1723, the gamba appeared only as soloist in Movement 8 (an instrumental sinfonia that opens the second half of the cantata following the sermon) and Movement 12 (an alto aria). The copyist, J. A. Kuhnau, marked the intervening movements *tacet*. The second performance of the work took place on Reformation Day of 1724 and included only the second part of the cantata. Bach himself prepared a new part for the gamba, revising selected details in the process, and included the continuo part for Movement 9 (an accompanied recitative), Movement 10 (a tenor aria), and Movement 11 (a secco recitative with arioso). But the part ends shortly thereafter, so that the gambist either joined the other continuo players for the final two movements, or, just as likely, withdrew after his last solo.

In the original version of the famous gamba obbligato in the St. John Passion, "Es ist vollbracht," Bach merely added the gamba to the continuo during the heroic *vivace* section. Later, in the final version preserved in Bach's autograph part, the gamba duplicates the vocal line (at the lower octave) during this middle section. As a result, Bach more forcefully identifies the gamba with both of the contrasting poses struck by the text: the grief of mourning as well as the heroic dream of victory over evil. At the second performance of the Passion in 1725, moreover, the gamba also apparently played continuo in Movement 20, the tenor aria "Erwäge." (Another continuo part is marked *tacet,* and the movement is actually labeled *Aria Viola da Gamba.*) Most likely Bach's use of the two violas d'amore occasioned the use of a similarly "remote" instrument to double the continuo. However, little would have been gained had Bach merely added the gamba to the other group of doubling instruments. It makes sense to assume that the *tacet*-indication in one part was duplicated in others that have not survived, and that the gamba functioned soloistically as the only string accompaniment in the aria "Erwäge."

The St. Matthew Passion presents a parallel situation. In a late performance of the piece, probably in the 1740s, Bach added a chordal accompaniment for the gamba to a tenor recitative (Movement 34), "Mein Jesus schweigt zu falschen Lügen stille." The autograph gamba part proceeds with the continuo line for the following aria, "Geduld." There are no corresponding *tacet*-indications in any of the other continuo parts, so it is conceivable that the gamba played along with the cellos and the violone. However, given the dotted figures and the associations with the French style, Bach more likely intended the gamba to accompany alone and instructed the doubling continuo players in the second orchestra to omit this movement.[61]

The continuo movements allocated to the gambas in Bach's *Trauer-Ode* (Cantata 198) are also far from typical. In Movement 7, a choral motet in fugal style, the two gambas do not double the bass line but play *colla parte* with the altos and tenors. Only in an intervening instrumental episode do both gambas play a unison bass to the two transverse flutes. However, even this section is special in that it points to the *galant* trio *senza continuo*. The passage is scored without continuo realization so that the gambas allude to the stylish *bassetto* accompaniments in contemporary chamber music that dispense with chordal filler. In the next aria, a subtle play on a French chaconne coupled with the falling tetrachord of the *lamento,* the obbligato line of the gambas is an old-fashioned diminution (perhaps even "division") of the continuo realized by the two lutes. The broken gamba lines even include the typical *style luthé* common in French gamba repertoire, with its leaps to the bottom strings rearticulating the bass harmonies.[62]

In sum, there are exceptionally few movements among Bach's Leipzig vocal works in which the viola da gamba acts anything like a normal bassist. It took some extraordinary occasion to usher it into the ensemble in the first place and another good reason to include it in the continuo group. Although Bach did not shy away from adding the gamba to the usual complement of cellos and violone on those rare occasions when it was expedient, he used the instrument chiefly to signal a symbolic referent, something ordinary members of the continuo group could not do.

The Lute

The lute in Bach's concerted works presents something of a mystery. Although both lutenists and luthiers are associated with the Bach circle, the name "lute" scarcely ever appears in the surviving sources for his ensemble music. In contrast to the practices of many European ensembles, in which the lute's regular participation was taken for granted, in Bach's works the lute makes an appearance only in two pieces: the St. John Passion and the *Trauer-Ode,* both works of special dimensions.

For both of these works a score constitutes the only source, since no individual lute part survives. Because the part for the Arioso "Betrachte, meine Seel'" in the Passion, while representing a continuo realization in diminution, is an obbligato,[63] the only lute continuo parts are found in the *Trauer-Ode.* In the choral movements of this work (Movements 1, 7, and 10) Bach has both lutes double the continuo line. (They play obbligato in Movement 4, an accompanied recitative.) In the alto aria, Movement 5, the lutes alone play continuo to the two gambas; in the tenor aria, Movement 8, they join the other members of the continuo group. Presumably Bach provided them with a figured continuo part. The complete record of references to the lute in extant sources for Bach's ensemble music is therefore a brief one.[64]

Johann Kuhnau, Bach's predecessor at Leipzig, had apparently made much greater use of the lute and referred to it on several occasions. In his Memorandum of 1704 to the Mayor, for example, Kuhnau made known his requests: "For our concerted sacred music we always have to borrow the so-called *Colochons* [*Colochonen*], a type of lute [whose sound], however, penetrates and is necessary for all contemporary concerted music. Since we do not always manage to have them lent to us, [I request the purchase of] at least one of these (with a case) for both churches."[65] Although most writers confuse the *colochon* with the *colascione,* describing both of them as exotic "Turkish" instruments,[66] Johann Mattheson seems to have understood the nomenclature precisely in Kuhnau's sense. Writing in 1713, Mattheson states: "Finally we would like now and then to permit the punctual *colochon* [*den prompten Calichon*]—which is a small, lute-like instrument . . . and tuned almost like the viola da gamba (D.G.c.f.a.d.)—to accompany some little part [*ein Stimmchen*] even in the company of the ruling keyboard instrument."[67]

Continuo playing was precisely what Kuhnau had in mind. In a later memorandum decrying the inadequate number of musicians and singers allotted to him, he enumerates the instruments, listing among the basses "violones, cellos, calichons, bassoons," which, he notes, cannot be managed by the *Kunst-Pfeiffer* [*sic*] because they are occupied with the other wind instruments, such as the trumpet, trombone, oboe, and the like.[68] Kuhnau's *colochon* can also be documented in an engraving depicting the performance of a sacred work at the Thomas-Kirche from about 1710.[69] Mattheson, although in Hamburg, clarifies this use further under his entry for the lute proper: "In churches and operas the accompaniment demanded of the lute is far too paltry [*lausicht*] and serves more to put on airs than to help the singer. For this [purpose] the *colochon* is better suited [*geschickter*]. What the lute can accomplish in chamber music playing thorough-bass might be well and good, if only one could [manage to] hear it."[70]

It is important to realize that in Bach's day the lute was no stranger to Leipzig. On the contrary, its presence can be felt in the immediate Bach circle. For example, one of Bach's closest friends, Johann Christian Hoffmann, was known as one of the leading luthiers in Europe, his lutes said to be prized even in Holland, England, and France.[71] A pupil of Bach's, Johann Christian Weyrauch (1694–1771), had studied the lute in the immediate environs of Leipzig with Adam Falckenhagen (1697–1761), and both men were located in Leipzig from about 1720 to 1726.[72] Johann Caspar Gleditsch, still mentioned as Bach's first oboist in the 1730 Memorandum, evidently composed for the instrument.[73] Other Leipzig lutenists include three alumni of the Thomas-Schule, Johann Ludwig Krebs (1713–1780), Maximilian Nagel (1712–1748), and Rudolph Straube (1717?–1740).[74] Finally, a rather expensive lute is listed among the possessions in Bach's estate, although it is quite possible that his estate received this instrument as a bequest from Johann Christian Hoffmann, who had died in February 1750 and whose estate was settled in August of that year, a few days after Bach's own death.[75]

Because of this extensive set of connections between Bach and the lute, it is plausible that it occasionally played in Bach's continuo section, perhaps even playing from the figured *Cammerton* parts discussed at length in Chapter 2. On the other hand, it is also important to consider the documents from which the lute is absent. No mention of the instrument appears, for example, in the 1730 Memorandum to the Town Council, or in any corresponding protocol listing the instruments in Bach's ensemble.[76] Nor does any hint of the lute surface when Bach goes to the trouble of enumerating all his bass instruments, such as in his score for the Kerll Sanctus. Moreover (as Appendix A makes clear), even though a number of part-sets include continuo parts with precise instrumental designations, not one refers even obliquely to the lute. Perhaps Bach found that the sound of the lute (or *colochon*) never penetrated well enough to warrant its use in church as a continuo instrument. In the *Trauer-Ode,* for example, Bach has the two lutes doubling each other in every movement where they play continuo. Considering the probable frequency with which Bach used the harpsichord continuo, moreover, it is likely that augmented support by the lute would not have added measurably to the ensemble. Although a continuo part realized by the lute cannot by any means have been considered inappropriate by Bach, the evidence—apart from the score for the *Trauer-Ode*—suggests that he made little use of it in his sacred vocal works.

The Violoncello piccolo and the Viola pomposa

From October 1724 through November 1726, Bach wrote eight (or possibly nine) cantatas that called for a violoncello piccolo as a solo obbligato instrument in certain arias.[77] Since none of these solos are even attached to a continuo part, a consideration of the violoncello piccolo would be irrelevant here were it not for one curious autograph part belonging to Bach's Lutheran Mass in A major (BWV 234). The part-title reads (in the composer's hand): *Continuo pro Violincello piccolo* [*sic*] (see Facsimile 5-8).[78] The part, which constitutes the entire continuo line to the Mass, is a transposed *Chorton* part and contains complete autograph figures for a thorough-bass realization. The part was therefore shared between the organist and a player on the violoncello piccolo who had tuned his instrument up a whole step. This part remains utterly mysterious. Why Bach designed a continuo part for the violoncello piccolo, why he had the instrument tune differently from the other bassists, why the player would have played from the same part as the organist, why Bach omitted the one movement accompanied by a *bassetto* of violins and violas—all these questions remain unanswered. Nonetheless, the existence of such an odd part warrants asking about the violoncello piccolo itself.

For years the identity of this instrument was hotly debated in the literature. Was it the same instrument as the viola pomposa, an instrument that Bach is said to have invented? The labyrinthine arguments regarding this question are detailed in an excellent account by Winfried Schrammek, who has provided the most informed explanation of the matter.[79] As far as organology is concerned, Schrammek maintains, there can be no doubt that the two instruments, although related to each other, are wholly distinct.[80] While both are tuned like a cello with an added fifth string ascending to e′, the height of the ribs of the viola

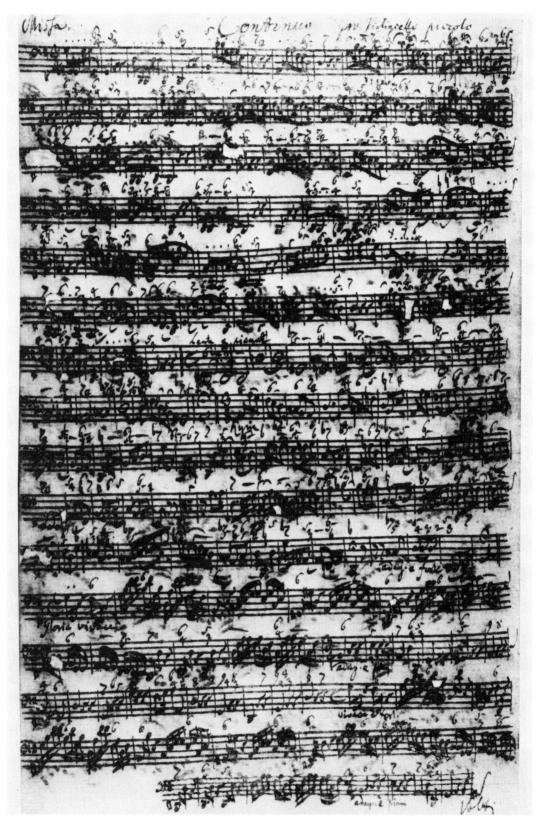

FACSIMILE 5-8 Mass in A major (BWV 234), *Continuo pro Violincello piccolo,* Darmstadt, Hessische Landes- und Hochschulbibliothek, Mus. ms. 971 [Darmstadt 234]

pomposa must be considerably less (around 3 to 4 cm.) so that it can be held on the arm.[81] Assuming that Bach indeed invented this viola pomposa, his achievement was to have added a fifth string to an instrument of this type that was already known: the so-called *viola da spalla* or shoulder-viola, which was also tuned like a cello.[82] The violoncello piccolo, on the other hand, can be distinguished by its greater rib height (approximately 7.5 to 9 cm.), which enabled the player to hold it comfortably between the legs.

Although the two instrumental types can be clearly differentiated in their construction, it makes most sense to conclude that Bach actually intended his solo parts labeled *violoncello piccolo* to be played on the viola pomposa. Consider the following points. According to an account by Ernst Ludwig Gerber in 1790, Bach is said to have invented the pomposa around 1724, precisely at the time when the solos for the violoncello piccolo appear in the cantatas.[83] Furthermore, not one part among any of Bach's works makes reference to the viola pomposa.[84] Nor are any of these obbligatos notated in a continuo part: on the contrary, when not copied on separate sheets of paper, the obbligatos are included in the first violin part (as in Cantatas 41 and 6).[85] Moreover, two parts— for Cantatas 6 and 175—had to be renotated from the alto clef into a treble clef to be read at the lower octave. In this way Bach seems to have accommodated a violinist who could orient his left hand to violinistic fingerings (based on a high e' string) to find the right notes.[86] The *raison d'être* of the instrument, as described by Gerber, also accords perfectly with the solos: "The stiff manner with which cellos were handled in his time compelled [Bach] to invent the so-called viola pomposa for the lively basses in his works . . . This comfortable instrument enabled the player to more easily manage those high and fast passages."[87] If Gerber heard the story correctly—his father was a pupil of Bach's in the 1720s and hence a credible witness—then Bach did not invent the pomposa merely for the purposes of domestic music making, as some have suggested.[88] Most likely, he did so for his experimental set of demanding solos in the cantatas. As several of the preceding chapters have suggested, names are often an unreliable guide to things.

The anomalous continuo part for violoncello piccolo dating from Bach's later Leipzig period—the final puzzle of this study—may therefore have been played by the viola pomposa. The part could then have been shared with an organist, since the viola pomposa player could stand next to him and still see the music. A violoncello piccolo player, on the other hand, would have been seated at some distance from the music. No matter how one reconstructs the situation, a continuo part for a small cello falls outside of any pattern established for doubling bass instruments. Accordingly, the sort of occasion that prompted Bach to specify a doubling part for the violoncello piccolo remains a subject for pure speculation.

The Bass Players in Perspective

What may surprise us about Bach's continuo group is how utterly unlike a modern ensemble it is—no assigned seats, no hierarchical positions, a fluctuating number of personnel, occasional visits from itinerant horn players and passing lutenists, unlimited permissible absences, few rational principles of governance, and, above all, no guarantee of orderly conduct. When one considers that the church organist could not even see his colleagues collaborating on the same bass part, it is a wonder that these performances met any standards of acceptability. Yet the continuo group was the vital nerve center of the larger ensemble, for it was the only group that remained anchored throughout the constantly shifting genres of a multimovement work. At the same time, it provided the fundamental harmonic orientation that guided expression and set the tone. Johann Joachim Quantz's remarks are worth quoting in this regard. Commenting on the role of the accompanying cellist in terms that apply equally well to any bass player, Quantz writes that

[He] is in an advantageous position to help the other parts in the expression of light and shadow, and can give vigor to the whole piece. In preserving the correct tempo in a piece, and the proper degree of liveliness, in expressing the Piano and Forte at the appropriate time, in distinguishing and making recognizable the different passions that should be aroused, and hence in facilitating the performance of the concertante part, the violoncellist is very important. He must therefore neither rush nor drag, and must direct his thought with constant attentiveness both to the rests and to the notes, so that it is unnecessary to remind him to begin again after a rest, or to play loudly or softly. It is very disagreeable in an ensemble if all parts do not begin together in earnest at a new entrance after a rest, or if the Piano or Forte is not observed where it is written, especially if the bass is remiss, since the precision of the execution depends largely upon it on these occasions.[89]

As a kind of autonomous institution within the early eighteenth-century orchestra, the continuo group thus played a role of strategic importance in the execution of a piece of music. It is not so much that there existed some ideal formula in combining various instruments that necessarily produced a good performance; rather, as Quantz makes clear, it was the qualities of vigilance and musicality among members of the continuo group that influenced the entire ensemble and gave "vigor to the whole piece." This is why one must resist the temptation to treat historical findings on how Bach employed his continuo instruments as holy relics. There is nothing magical in discovering what happened at one or another performance of a particular church cantata; after all, these were occasional works in which Bach gave little thought to posterity. In the case of almost any vocal work, one can easily imagine minor changes in the staffing of the continuo group with no significant alteration of effect. Far more important is the sense behind the conventions, which, though an interpretive matter, is what motivates historians and musicians alike.

An overview of Bach's doubling bassists suggests the image of a spectrum encompassing both the instruments and the conventions governing their use. At one end are the occasional instruments, such as the viola da gamba and the lute, whose exceptional appearances had more to do with a special symbolic intent than with continuo practice per se. At the other end is the cello, whose regular appearance in every movement of a vocal work was taken for granted by the time the composer arrived at Leipzig. And occupying points midway are the violone and the bassoon, which, though not indispensable, lent both substance and cohesion to the ensemble. This spectrum not only captures the main outlines of Bach's mature Leipzig practice but also embodies a covert historical progression, recounting, as it were, a narrative of Bach's continuo practice itself. For the story begins with a genial blend of creativity and chaos in the Mühlhausen works and culminates in the rationality of the well-oiled Leipzig machinery. On the one hand, the special instruments stand as remnants of the arbitrary but inspired experimentation of Bach's early years. Each work, it seemed, presented a fresh opportunity for novel combinations of genres and an unpredictable division of labor within the continuo group. The later works, on the other hand, celebrate the free play of speculative reason exercised in a highly formal environment. In many ways far more creative, the Leipzig vocal works accept the genres as axiomatic and then proceed to excavate an astonishing amalgam of new meanings. As compensation, perhaps, Bach no longer felt so compelled to tinker with the Leipzig continuo group. Instead, he came to view it as one of his most reliable tools, a trusty instrument that helped enable the practice of his daily craft.

Guide to the Appendixes

Appendix A · *Appendix B*

Guide to the Appendixes

The following appendixes constitute an informal catalog of the extant original manuscript parts (both vocal and instrumental) for Bach's vocal works (Appendix A) and a list of the basso continuo parts sorted by date of performance (Appendix B). Works are numbered throughout according to the *Bach-Werke-Verzeichnis* (BWV): pieces called "Cantata" in the main text have an identical BWV number. Appendix A enumerates the dates of performance at which Bach is known to have used a particular set of parts, the present location of the original parts (and extant autograph scores), and the designated part-titles. The entries for *Continuo* parts distinguish between parts at orchestral pitch (*Cammerton*) and parts transposed for the Leipzig organs (*Chorton*). They also detail the extent of thorough-bass figuring and identify the figures as Bach's or a copyist's. Appendix B sorts the continuo parts by chronological layer, identifying which continuo parts were copied for a particular performance and—when a work is known to have been performed more than once—which parts were used at the same performance. Because the listings distinguish between figured and unfigured *Cammerton* parts, Appendix B gives an overview of the evidence for dual accompaniment of harpsichord and organ.

The general format of a catalog listing in Appendix A is as follows:

BWV number — Title of work
    Liturgical occasion — Date(s) of Performance
    Score: Location of source
    Parts: Location of source(s)
    Catalog numbers   Part titles

Date(s) of Performance

A single date indicates the date of the first performance; the parts can be assumed to have been copied just shortly before this time. Multiple performances revealed by subsequently copied parts (identified through later datable watermarks or new scribal hands) are also shown: the listing "2:April 9, 1724;"

under the entry for Cantata 4 denotes a second performance on that date, while "2:1732-35;" under the entry for Cantata 5 means that a second performance is known to have taken place between 1732 and 1735, although the precise day cannot be identified. (Each listing by dated performance generally corresponds to the chronological entries in Appendix B.) A parenthetical date indicates a performance for which extant parts no longer survive.

Scores and Parts: Location of Sources

The locations of original autograph scores and original sets of parts follow the traceable dates of performance. The largest collection of original materials belonged to the former Berlin State Library, presently divided between libraries in the two Berlins: the Staatsbibliothek Preussischer Kulturbesitz in West Berlin—"SPK"—and the Deutsche Staatsbibliothek in Berlin (DDR)—"DStB." The collection bears the signature "Mus. ms. Bach" and distinguishes between scores (*Partituren*), "P", and parts (*Stimmen*), "St." Prewar call numbers have been retained. The location of the score for Cantata 6 is therefore listed as "Berlin, SPK, Mus. ms. Bach P 44," while its parts are found in "Berlin, DStB, Mus. ms. Bach St 7." The locations of other scores and parts are given as a city followed by a library or institution. (A call number is included when this would facilitate access.) Original sources in private hands are so designated.

Catalog Numbers

The catalog assigns a number to each individual part following the order of sources listed under "Parts." Before World War II librarians in the Berlin collection numbered individual parts in pencil, often just above the part-title. Since these numbers are often visible even on microfilm, the catalog generally attempts to match the penciled numerals on the Berlin parts. A slash separates the call number of the part-set from the number of the individual part. Thus, the *Violoncello* part for BWV 18 is called "St 34/12" because it has been numbered as "12" on the Berlin original, as can be seen in Facsimile 3-3. (The critical reports of the NBA, by contrast, sometimes number the parts systematically and place the Berlin library numbers within parentheses.) Other sets of parts are designated by abbreviations followed by a BWV number before the slash. "Thom 1" refers to the set of parts for BWV 1 in the Thomana Collection, Leipzig. Within sets such as these a conventional order prevails, beginning with vocal parts, winds, and strings and ending with continuo parts. The *Tromba* part for BWV 5, found in the Thomana collection, is therefore cataloged as "Thom 5/5". Single parts detached from a part-set are cataloged without a slash; an abbreviation followed by the BWV number serves to designate them. Throughout the catalog, listings are consolidated by placing groups of parts together: "Thom 5/6-7" designates Oboe 1 and Oboe 2 as parts 6 and 7 within the Thomana set for BWV 5. Likewise, the tenor part in this set, Thom 5/3, is listed on one line with the other three vocal parts so that the entry for all four reads "Thom 5/1-4." Continuo parts are always cataloged separately.

Part-Titles

Since variations in spelling the names of instruments or vocal ranges are of no practical significance, they have been neglected unless they seem of special interest. The following abbreviations are used:

A	Alto
B	Basso (vocal)
Bc	(Basso) Continuo
Bctr	(Basso) Continuo—transposed part
Cno	Corno
Cto	Cornetto
Fl	Flauto (recorder)
Ob	Oboe, Hautbois
Ob d'Am	Oboe d'Amore
Ob da Ca	Oboe da Caccia
S	Soprano, Canto
T	Tenore
Tamb	Tamburi
Tbe	Trombona
Tr	Tromba, Clarino
Trav	(Flauto) traverso
V	Violino
Va	Viola
Vc	Violoncello
(2x)	two parts

Continuo part-titles, moreover, are given whenever any name but *Continuo* appears. In any event, either "Bc" or "Bctr" follows the part-title, indicating whether a part is untransposed or transposed. The abbreviation "fig" designates a completely figured continuo part; if the figures are autograph, then Bach's initials appear, as in "(fig: JSB)." Figured movements in an incompletely figured part are also enumerated, as in "(fig Mvt 3,5,7: JSB)." Partly figured movements are noted as follows: "(pt fig Mvt 1)." In addition, a set of figures textually dependent on another set (such as a copyist's figures on Bach's) is noted whenever possible. For example, the entry for a continuo part from BWV 24, St 19/13, reads: "Bctr (fig Mvt 1: copied from Bc, Mvt 2-6: JSB)." This means that a transposed part labeled *Continuo* was figured in Movement 1 by a scribe who copied the figures from the untransposed continuo part. Thereafter, Bach completed the figuring himself in Movements 2 through 6. Where no identification is given, then the authorship of the figures and their provenance are unclear.

Appendix B lists continuo parts copied for a single performance. For the first performance of BWV 24 on June 20, 1723, for example, Appendix B shows that Bach had three continuo parts copied: an unfigured *Cammerton* part, a figured *Cammerton* part, and a *Chorton* part. Referring to Appendix A under BWV 24, one sees that Bach figured the first movement of the *Cammerton* part, had his figures transferred to the organ part, and himself figured Movements 2 through 6. Boldface catalog numbers indicate that a part survives from an earlier performance of the work and was still compatible with the new part. When all available continuo parts are in boldface, there is evidence independent of the continuo parts that confirms a repeat performance. From such instances one learns, for example, that unfigured organ parts remained unfigured at later performances. Identical catalog numbers for one part-set are assumed when two or more continuo parts of the same type are listed above one another. Since transposed continuo parts for the organ are a feature of Bach's Leipzig works, pre-Leipzig works are not distinguished in the same manner. Moreover, several figured autograph scores seem to have been used in performance (see Chapter 2, n. 69), and these have also been included. Works labeled "JLB" in Appendix B refer to J. S. Bach's performances of cantatas composed by his Meiningen cousin, Johann Ludwig Bach (see Chapter 2). The sources for these cantatas, prepared by J. S. Bach and his copyists, are listed in Table 2-4.

Catalog of Original Performance Parts for Bach's Vocal Works

BWV 1 — Wie schön leuchtet der Morgenstern
    Annunciation — March 25, 1725
    Parts: Leipzig, Thomana Collection

Thom 1/1–4	S,A,T,B
5–6	Cno 1–2
7–8	Ob da Ca 1–2
9–10	Violino Concert: 1–2
11–13	V 1, V 2, Va
14	Bc
15	Bctr (fig Mvt 1, pt fig 2: JSB)

BWV 2 — Ach Gott, vom Himmel sieh darein
    2nd Sunday after Trinity — June 18, 1724
    Score: London, Private collection
    Parts: Leipzig, Thomana Collection

Thom 2/1–4	S,A,T,B
5–8	Tbe 1–4
9–10	Ob 1–2
11–13	V 1, V 2, Va
14	Bc
15	Bctr (fig Mvt 1–4, pt fig Mvt 5: JSB)

BWV 3 — Ach Gott, wie manches Herzeleid
    2nd Sunday after Epiphany — January 14, 1725
    Score: Private collection
    Parts: Leipzig, Thomana Collection
           Berlin, SPK, Mus. ms. Bach St 157

Thom 3/1–4	S,A,T,B
5	Tbe, Cno
6–7	Ob d'Am 1–2
8–10	V 1, V 2, Va
11	Bc (pt fig Mvt 1: copied from Bctr)
St 157/5–6	V 1, V 2
11	Bctr (fig: JSB)

BWV 4 — Christ lag in Todes Banden
    First day of Easter — (1:1707?); 2:April 9, 1724; 3:April 1, 1725
    Parts: Leipzig, Thomana Collection

Thom 4/1–4	S,A,T,B
5	Cto
6–8	Tbe 1–3
9–12	V 1, V 2, Va 1, Va 2
13	Bc
14	Bctr

BWV 5 — Wo soll ich fliehen hin
    19th Sunday after Trinity — 1:October 15, 1724; 2:1732–35
    Score: Private collection
    Parts: Leipzig, Thomana Collection

Thom 5/1–4	S,A,T,B
5	Tromba (da Tirarsi)
6–7	Ob 1–2
8–10	V 1, V 2, Va
11	Bc
12	Continuo pro Organo: Bctr (fig Mvt 1,2,4, 6–8, pt fig Mvt 5: JSB)
13	Organo: Bctr (fig: JSB)

BWV 6 — Bleib bei uns, denn es will Abend werden
 2nd day of Easter — April 2, 1725
 Score: Berlin, SPK, Mus. ms. Bach P 44
 Parts: Berlin, DStB, Mus. ms. Bach St 7

St 7/1–4	S,A,T,B
5–8	V 1 (2x), V 2 (2x)
9	(Violoncello piccolo)
10	Va
11–13	Ob 1–2, Ob da Ca
14	Cembalo: Bc (fig: JSB)
15	Bc
16	Bctr (fig: JSB)

BWV 7 — Christ unser Herr zum Jordan kam
 St. John — June 24, 1724
 Parts: Leipzig, Thomana Collection
  Private collection (Teri Noel Towe, New York City)

Thom 7/1–4	S,A,T,B
5–6	Ob d'Am 1–2
7–8	Violino Concertino
9–11	V 1, V 2, Va
12	Bc (fig: JSB)
Towe 7	Bctr (fig Mvt 1,7: copied from Bc, Mvt 1,3,4: JSB)

BWV 8 — Liebster Gott, wann werd ich sterben
 16th Sunday after Trinity — 1: September 24, 1724; 2: 1735–50
 Parts: Brussels, Bibliothèque Royale, Ms. II 3905
  Leipzig, Thomana Collection

Brus 8/1–4	S,A,T,B
5–9	V 1 (2x), V 2 (2x), Va
10	Bc
11	Bc
12	(Fiauto piccolo) Trav
13–14	Ob d'Am 1–2
15	Cno
Thom 8/1–4	S,A,T,B
5	Trav
6–8	Ob d'Am 1–2, Taille
9–10	Violino 1,2 Concertato
11–13	V 1, V 2, Va
14	Continuo pro Violoncello
15	Organo: Bctr (fig: JSB)

BWV 9 — Es ist das Heil uns kommen her
 6th Sunday after Trinity — 1732–35

Score: Washington, Library of Congress
Parts: Vienna, Gesellschaft der Musikfreunde
 New York, Pierpont Morgan Library,
  Mary Flagler Cary Music Collection, ML 96 B 186
 New York, Private collection

Thom 9/1–4	S,A,T,B
5	Trav
6	Ob d'Am
7–9	V 1, V 2, Va
10	Bc
11	Bctr (fig except pt fig Mvt 5: JSB)
Vienna 9/1–2	V 1, Trav
Cary 9/1	V 2
2	Bc
Priv 9	Trav

BWV 10 — Meine Seel erhebt den Herren
 Visitation of the Virgin — 1: July 2, 1724; 2: 1744–50
 Score: Washington, Library of Congress
 Parts: Leipzig, Thomana Collection

Thom 10/1–4	S,A,T,B
5	Tr
6–7	Ob 1–2
8–10	V 1, V 2, Va
11	Bc (fig: JSB)
12	Bctr (fig: JSB)

BWV 11 — Lobet Gott in seinen Reichen (Ascension Oratorio)
 Ascension — 1735
 Score: Berlin, SPK, Mus. ms. Bach P 44
 Parts: Cracow, Biblioteka Jagiellońska (formerly Berlin, Mus. ms. Bach St 356)

St 356/1–4	S,A,T,B
5–9	V 1 (2x), V 2 (2x), Va
10–11	Trav 1–2
12–13	Ob 1–2
14–17	Tr 1–3, Tamb
18	Bc
19	Organo: Bctr (fig: JSB)
20	Bc

BWV 12 — Weinen, Klagen, Sorgen, Zagen
 Jubilate — 1: April 22, 1714; 2: April 30, 1724
 Score: Berlin, SPK, Mus. ms. Bach P 44
 Parts: Berlin, SPK, Mus. ms. Bach St 109

St 109/1–4	S,A,T,B
5	Bc

BWV 13 — Meine Seufzer, meine Tränen
    2nd Sunday after Epiphany — January 20,
      1726
    Score: Berlin, DStB, Mus. ms. Bach P 45
    Parts: Berlin, DStB, Mus. ms. Bach St 69

St 69/1–4	S,A,T,B
5–9	V 1 (2x), V 2 (2x), Va
10–11	Fiauto 1–2
12	Ob da Ca
13	Bc
14	Bc
15	Organo: Bctr (fig: JSB)

BWV 14 — Wär Gott mit uns dieser Zeit
    4th Sunday after Epiphany — January 30,
      1735
    Score: Berlin, DStB, Mus. ms. Bach P 879
    Parts: Leipzig, Thomana Collection
      Berlin, DStB, Mus. ms. Bach St 398
      Cambridge (England), Fitzwilliam
        Museum, Ms. Box 53c

Thom 14/1–4	S,A,T,B
5	Corne par force
6–7	Ob 1–2
8–10	V 1, V 2, Va
11	Bc
St 398/1–2	V 1, V 2
3	Bc
Fitzwill 14	Organo: Bctr (fig Mvt 5, pt fig Mvt 1,2: JSB)

BWV 16 — Herr Gott, dich loben wir
    New Year's Day — 1: January 1, 1726;
      2: 1728–31; 3: 1735–50
    Score: Berlin, DStB, Mus. ms. Bach P 45
    Parts: Berlin, DStB, Mus. ms. Bach St 44

St 44/1–4	S,A,T,B
5–8	V 1 (2x), V 2 (2x)
9	Violetta
10	Va
11–12	Ob 1–2
13	Corno da Caccia
14	Bctr (fig Mvt 1–4, pt fig Mvt 5: JSB)

BWV 17 — Wer Dank opfert, der preiset mich
    14th Sunday after Trinity — September 22,
      1726

Score: Berlin, DStB, Mus. ms. Bach P 45
Parts: Berlin, SPK, Mus. ms. Bach St 101

St 101/1–4	S,A,T,B
5–6	Ob 1–2
7–11	V 1 (2x), V 2 (2x), Va
12	Bctr
13	Bc

BWV 18 — Gleichwie der Regen und Schnee vom
    Himmel fällt
    Sexagesima — 1: February 19, 1713?; 2: Feb-
      ruary 13, 1724
    Parts: Berlin, DStB, Mus. ms. Bach St 34

St 34/1	Violono o Organo: Bctr (fig: JSB)
2–5	S,A,T,B
6–7	Fl 1–2
8–11	Va 1–4
12	Violoncello
13	Fagotto
14	Bc (pt fig Mvt 2,3: copied from Bctr)

BWV 19 — Es erhub sich ein Streit
    Michaelmas — September 29, 1726
    Score: Berlin, DStB, Mus. ms. Bach P 45
    Parts: Berlin, SPK, Mus. ms. Bach St 25a

St 25a/1–4	S,A,T,B
5–8	Tr 1–3, Tamb
9–11	Ob 1–2, Taille
12–16	V 1 (2x), V 2 (2x), Va
17	Bc (fig: JSB?)
18	Bc
19	Bctr (fig: Mvt 1–3,6–7: JSB)

BWV 20 — O Ewigkeit, du Donnerwort
    1st Sunday after Trinity — June 11, 1724
    Score: Private collection
    Parts: Leipzig, Thomana Collection

Thom 20/1–4	S,A,T,B
5	Tromba da tirarsi
6–8	Ob 1–3
9–11	V 1, V 2, Va
12	Bc (pt fig Mvt 2,4: copied from score, some JSB)
13	Bctr (fig: JSB)

BWV 21 — Ich hatte viel Bekümmernis
   3rd Sunday after Trinity — 1: June 17, 1714;
     2: 1717–22; 3: June 13, 1723
   Parts: Berlin, DStB, Mus. ms. Bach St 354

St 354/1–6,8	S,S,A,A,T,B
7,9	T in rip, B in rip
10–15	V 1 (2x), V 2 (2x), Va (2x)
16–18	Ob (3x)
19–21	Tr 2–4
22	Fagotto
23	Violoncello
24	Violoncello
25	Organo (fig: JSB)
26	Bctr (fig: copied from Organo)
27–29	Tr 1–3

BWV 23 — Du wahrer Gott und Davids Sohn
   Estomihi — 1: February 7, 1723; 2: February
     20, 1724; 3: 1728–31
   Score: Berlin, SPK, Mus. ms. Bach P 69
   Parts: Berlin, DStB, Mus. ms. Bach St 16

St 16/1–4	S,A,T,B
5–8	Cto, Tbe 1–3
9–12	S,A,T,B inserts
13–14	Ob 1–2
15–16	Ob d'Am 1–2
17–21	V 1 (2x), V 2 (2x), Va
22	Violoncello
23	Violoncello
(24)	Basson. é Cembalo (fig Mvt 1–3: copied from Bctr, fig Mvt 4: JSB)
(25)	Violoncello (fig Mvt 4: copied from Cembalo)
(26)	Bctr (fig: JSB)

BWV 24 — Ein ungefärbt Gemüte
   4th Sunday after Trinity — June 20, 1723
   Score: Berlin, SPK, Mus. ms. Bach P 44
   Parts: Berlin, SPK, Mus. ms. Bach St 19

St 19/1–4	S,A,T,B
5–9	V 1 (2x), V 2 (2x), Va
10–11	Ob 1–2
12	Tr
13	Bctr (fig Mvt 1: copied from Bc, Mvt 2–6: JSB)
14	Bc
15	Bc (fig Mvt 1: JSB)

BWV 25 — Es ist nichts gesundes an meinem Leibe
   14th Sunday after Trinity — August 29, 1723
   Parts: Berlin, SPK, Mus. ms. Bach St 376

St 376/1–4	S,A,T,B
5–8	Cto, Tbe 1–3
9–11	Fl 1–3
12–13	Ob 1–2
14–16	V 1, V 2, Va
17	Bc
18	Bctr (pt fig: JSB)

BWV 26 — Ach wie flüchtig, ach wie nichtig
   24th Sunday after Trinity — November 19,
     1724
   Score: Berlin, DStB, Mus. ms. Bach P 47
   Parts: Leipzig, Thomana Collection

Thom 26/1–4	S,A,T,B
5	Cno
6	Trav
7–9	Ob 1–3
10–12	V 1, V 2, Va
13	Bc
14	Organo: Bctr (fig: JSB)

BWV 27 — Wer weiss, wie nahe mir mein Ende
   16th Sunday after Trinity — 1: October 6,
     1726; 2: 1735–50
   Score: Berlin, SPK, Mus. ms. Bach P 164
   Parts: Berlin, SPK, Mus. ms. Bach St 105

St 105/1–4	S,A,T,B
5	Cno
6–7	Ob 1–2
8–12	V 1 (2x), V 2 (2x), Va
14	Bc
15	Bctr (fig Mvt 1,2,4: JSB)
16	[Cembalo] (Organo) obligato

BWV 28 — Gottlob! nun geht das Jahr zu Ende
   Sunday after Christmas — December 30, 1725
   Score: Berlin, DStB, Mus. ms. Bach P 92
   Parts: Berlin, SPK, Mus. ms. Bach St 37

St 37/1–4	S,A,T,B
5–7	Ob 1–2. Taille
8–12	V 1 (2x), V 2 (2x), Va
13–16	Cto, Tbe 1–3
17	Bc (fig Mvt 4: JSB)
18	Bctr (fig Mvt 4: copied from Bc)
19	Bc

BWV 29 — Wir danken dir, Gott, wir danken dir
    Town Council Inauguration — August 27,
    1731
       Score: Berlin, DStB, Mus. ms. Bach P 166
       Parts: Berlin, SPK, Mus. ms. Bach St 106

St 106/1–4	S,A,T,B
5–8	S,A,T,B in ripieno
9–10	Ob 1–2
11–14	Tr 1–3, Tamb
15–19	V 1 (2x), V 2 (2x), Va
20–21	Organo: Bctr (fig Mvt 2–6: JSB)
22	Bc (fig: JSB)
23	Bc

BWV 30a — Angenehmes Wiesderau, freue dich in
deinen Auen!
    (Freue dich, erlöste Schar — BWV 30)
       Homage cantata — September 28, 1737 (St.
       John — 1738–42)
       Score: Berlin, SPK, Mus. ms. Bach P 44
       Parts: Berlin, DStB, Mus. ms. Bach St 31

St 31/1–5	S,A,T,B (4–5)
6	Trav 2
7–8	Ob 1–2
9	Trav 1 (Violino Concert.)
10–14	V 1 (2x), V 2 (2x), Va
18	Organo: Bctr (fig: JSB)
19	Bc
20	Bc (fig Mvt 2,4,7,9,11: copied from Bctr)

BWV 31 — Der Himmel lacht! die Erde jubilieret
    1st Day of Easter — 1: April 21, 1715; 2:
    April 9, 1724; 3: March 25, 1731
       Parts: Cracow, Biblioteka Jagiellońska (for-
       merly Berlin, Mus. ms. Bach St 14)

St 14/1–5	S (2x),A,T,B
6–9	Tb 1–3, Tamb
10	Ob 1
11	Ob 1
11a	Ob 2
12	Ob 3
13	Taille
14	Bassono
15–20	V 1 (2x), V 2 (2x), Va (2x)
21	Violoncello (tacet Mvt 3–5, 7–8)
22	Violoncello (fig Mvt 2–7, pt fig Mvt 8)
23	Bctr (fig: JSB)

BWV 32 — Liebster Jesu, mein Verlangen
    1st Sunday after Epiphany — January 13, 1726
       Score: Berlin, DStB, Mus. ms. Bach P 126
       Parts: Berlin, DStB, Mus. ms. Bach St 67

St 67/1–4	S,A,T,B
5	Ob
6–10	V 1 (2x), V 2 (2x), Va
11	Bctr (fig Mvt 2,4: JSB)
12	Bc

BWV 33 — Allein zu dir, Herr Jesu Christ
    13th Sunday after Trinity — September 3,
    1724
       Score: Scheide Library, Princeton University
       Library
       Parts: Leipzig, Thomana Collection

Thom 33/1–4	S,A,T,B
5–7	V 1, V 2, Va
8–9	Ob 1–2
10	Bc (fig: copied from Bctr except in Mvt 5)
11	Bctr (fig: JSB)

BWV 34a — O ewiges Feuer, O Ursprung der
Liebe
    Wedding cantata — March 6, 1726
       Parts: Berlin, DStB, Mus. ms. Bach St 73

St 73/1–4	S,A,T,B
5–6	V 1, Va
7	Bc (pt fig Mvt 2)

BWV 35 — Geist und Seele wird verwirret
    12th Sunday after Trinity — September 8,
    1726
       Score: Berlin, SPK, Mus. ms. Bach P 86
       Parts: Berlin, DStB, Mus. ms. Bach St 32

St 32/1	A
2–4	Ob 1–2, Taille
5–9	V 1 (2x), V 2 (2x), Va
10	Bc
11	Bc

BWV 36 — Die Freude reget sich
    1st Sunday in Advent — December 2, 1731
       Score: Berlin, DStB, Mus. ms. Bach P 45
       Parts: Berlin, SPK, Mus. ms. Bach St 82

St 82/1–4	S,A,T,B
5–6	Ob d'Am 1–2
7–11	V 1 (2x), V 2 (2x), Va
12	Bc
13	Bc

BWV 36b — Die Freude reget sich
Congratulatory cantata — July 28, 1735?
Parts: Berlin, DStB, Mus. ms. Bach St 15
St 15/1–4   S, A, T, B
       5   Trav
       6–8   V 2 (2x), Va
       9   Bc (fig Mvt 2,4,6,8)

BWV 37 — Wer da gläubet und getauft wird
Ascension — 1: May 18, 1724; 2: May 3, 1731
Parts: Berlin, SPK, Mus. ms. Bach St 100
St 100/1–4   S, A, T, B
       5–6   Ob 1–2
       7–9   V 1, V 2, Va
       10   Bctr (fig: JSB)
       11   Bc

BWV 38 — Aus tiefer Not schrei ich zu dir
21st Sunday after Trinity — October 29, 1724
Parts: Leipzig, Thomana Collection
Thom 38/1–4   S, A, T, B
       5–8   Tbe 1–4
       9–10   Ob 1–2
       11–13 V 1, V 2, Va
       14   Bc (fig 2–4,6, pt fig Mvt
              5: JSB)
       15   Bctr (fig Mvt 2–4,6:
              copied from Bc, Mvt
              1–4: JSB)

BWV 39 — Brich dem Hungrigen dein Brot
1st Sunday after Trinity — June 23, 1726
Score: Berlin, DStB, Mus. ms. Bach P 62
Parts: Berlin, SPK, Mus. ms. Bach St 8
St 8/1–4   S, A, T, B
       5–6   Fl 1–2
       7–8   Ob 1–2
       9–11   V 1, V 2, Va
       12   Bctr (fig Mvt 1–4: JSB)
       13   Bc

BWV 40 — Dazu ist erschienen der Sohn Gottes
2nd Day of Christmas — December 26, 1723
Score: Berlin, DStB, Mus. ms. Bach P 63
Parts: Berlin, SPK, Mus. ms. Bach St 11
St 11/1–4   S, A, T, B
       5–6   Cno 1–2
       7–8   Ob 1–2
       9–13   V 1 (2x), V 2 (2x), Va
       14   Bc (fig Mvt 1,4–7: copied from

Bctr; pt fig Mvt 2, fig Mvt
              1,3,4,7: JSB)
       15   Bctr (fig Mvt 1,4–7: JSB; fig
              Mvt 1,4, pt fig Mvt 2,3:
              copied from Bc)
       16   Bc

BWV 41 — Jesu, nun sei gepreiset
New Year's Day — 1: January 1, 1725; 2:
1732–35
Score: Berlin, SPK, Mus. ms. Bach P 874
       Saalfeld, Heimatmuseum
Parts: Leipzig, Thomana Collection
       Berlin, SPK, Mus. ms. Bach St 394
Thom 41/1–4   S, A, T, B
       5–7   Tr 1–3
       8–10   Ob 1–3
       11–14 V 1 (2x), V 2 (2x), Va
       15   Bc
       16   Organo: Bctr (fig Mvt
              3,5: JSB)
St 394/19–20 V 1, V 2
       21   Bc

BWV 42 — Am Abend aber desselbigen Sabbats
Quasimodogeniti — 1: April 8, 1725; 2: April
1, 1731; 3: 1735–50
Score: Berlin, DStB, Mus. ms. Bach P 55
Parts: Berlin, DStB, Mus. ms. Bach St 3
St 3/1–3b   S, A, T, B
       4–5   Ob 1–2
       6–10   V 1 (2x), V 2 (2x), Va
       11   Bassono
       12   Bctr [frag] (fig Mvt 1–6: JSB)
       13   Bc (fig: JSB)
       14   Organo: Bctr (fig: JSB)
       15   Violon(e)

BWV 43 — Gott fähret auf mit Jauchzen
Ascension — May 30, 1726
Score: Berlin, SPK, Mus. ms. Bach P 44
Parts: Berlin, DStB, Mus. ms. Bach St 36
St 36/1–4   S, A, T, B
       5–8   Tr 1–3, Tamb
       9–10   Ob 1–2
       11–15 V 1 (2x), V 2 (2x), Va
       16   Bc
       17   Bc
       18   Bctr (fig except Mvt 2,4,8:
              JSB)

BWV 44 — Sie werden euch in den Bann tun
    Exaudi — May 21, 1724
    Score: Berlin, DStB, Mus. ms. Bach P 148
    Parts: Berlin, SPK, Mus. ms. Bach St 86

St 86/1–4	S, A, T, B
5–6	Ob 1–2
7–11	V 1 (2x), V 2 (2x), Va
12	Bassono
13	Bc (fig Mvt 1: JSB)
14	Bctr (fig Mvt 1: JSB)

BWV 45 — Es ist dir gesagt, Mensch, was gut ist
    8th Sunday after Trinity — August 11, 1726
    Score: Berlin, DStB, Mus. ms. Bach P 80
    Parts: Berlin, SPK, Mus. ms. Bach St 26

St 26/1–4	S, A, T, B
5–6	Trav 1–2
7–8	Ob 1–2
9–11	V 1, V 2, Va
12	Bctr

BWV 46 — Schauet doch und sehet
    10th Sunday after Trinity — August 1, 1723
    Parts: Berlin, SPK, Mus. ms. Bach St 78

St 78/1–4	S, A, T, B
5–6	Fl 1–2
7	Tromba o Corno da Tirarsi
8–9	Ob da Ca 1–2
10–12	V 1, V 2, Va
13	Bc (fig Mvt 1–3: JSB)
14	Bctr (fig Mvt 1–3: copied from Bc)

BWV 47 — Wer sich selbst erhöhet
    17th Sunday after Trinity — 1: October 13, 1726; 2: 1734
    Score: Berlin, DStB, Mus. ms. Bach P 163
    Parts: Berlin, DStB, Mus. ms. Bach St 104

St 104/1	(Violin solo: Mvt 2)
2–3	Ob 1–2
4–5	V 1 (2x)
6	(Violin 1: Mvt 4)
7–9	V 2 (2x), Va
10	Bc
11	Bc
12	Bctr (fig except pt fig Mvt 2: JSB)
13–16	S, A, T, B

BWV 48 — Ich elender Mensch
    19th Sunday after Trinity — October 30, 1723
    Score: Berlin, DStB, Mus. ms. Bach P 109
    Parts: Berlin, DStB, Mus. ms. Bach St 53

St 53/1–4	S, A, T, B
5	Tr
6	Hautbois all'unisono
7–11	V 1 (2x), V 2 (2x), Va
12	Bc (fig Mvt 2: JSB)
13	Bc
14	Bctr (fig Mvt 2: JSB)

BWV 49 — Ich geh und suche mit Verlangen
    20th Sunday after Trinity — November 3, 1726
    Score: Berlin, DStB, Mus. ms. Bach P 111
    Parts: Berlin, DStB, Mus. ms. Bach St 55

St 55/1–2	S, B
3	Ob d'Am
4–13	V 1 (2x), V 2 (2x), Va [sic]
14	Violoncello piccolo
15	Violono
16	Bc

BWV 51 — Jauchzet Gott in allen Landen
    15th Sunday after Trinity — September 17, 1730
    Score: Berlin, DStB, Mus. ms. Bach P 104
    Parts: Berlin, SPK, Mus. ms. Bach St 49

St 49/1	S
2–6	V 1 (2x), V 2 (2x), Va
7	Tr
10	Bc
11	Bc
12	Bctr (fig: JSB)

BWV 52 — Falsche Welt, dir trau ich nicht
    23rd Sunday after Trinity — November 26, 1726
    Score: Berlin, SPK, Mus. ms. Bach P 85
    Parts: Berlin, SPK, Mus. ms. Bach St 30

St 30/1–4	S, A, T, B
5–9	V 1 (2x), V 2 (2x), Va
10–12	Ob 1–3
13–14	Cno 1–2
15	Fagotto
16	Bc
17	Bctr

BWV 55 — Ich armer Mensch
 22nd Sunday after Trinity — November
  17, 1726
 Score: Berlin, SPK, Mus. ms. Bach P 105
 Parts: Berlin, SPK, Mus. ms. Bach St 50
 St 50/1–4   S,A,T,B
       5   Trav
       6   Ob
      7–11   V 1, V 2, V 1, V 2, Va
      12   Bc
      13   Bc
      14   Bctr

BWV 56 — Ich will den Kreuzstab gerne tragen
 19th Sunday after Trinity — October 27, 1726
 Score: Berlin, SPK, Mus. ms. Bach P 118
 Parts: Berlin, SPK, Mus. ms. Bach St 58
 St 58/1–4   S,A,T,B
      5–7   Ob 1–2, Taille
      8–12   V 1 (2x), V 2 (2x), Va
      13   Bc
      14   Bctr

BWV 57 — Selig ist der Mann
 2nd Day of Christmas — December 26, 1725
 Score: Berlin, DStB, Mus. ms. Bach P 144
 Parts: Berlin, SPK, Mus. ms. Bach St 83
 St 83/1–4   S,A,T,B
      5–7   Ob 1–2, Taille
      8–12   V 1 (2x), V 2 (2x), Va
      13   Bc
      14   Bc
      15   Continuo pro Organo: Bctr
              (fig: JSB)

BWV 58 — Ach Gott, wie manches Herzeleid
 Sunday after New Year's Day — 1:January 5,
  1727; 2:1733
 Score: Berlin, SPK, Mus. ms. Bach P 866
 Parts: Leipzig, Thomana Collection
     Berlin, SPK, Mus. ms. Bach St 389
 Thom 58/1–2   S,B
      3–5   Ob 1–2, Taille
      6–8   V 1, V 2, Va
      9   Bc
      10   Bctr (fig Mvt 1–4: JSB)
 St 389/1–2   V 1, V 2
      3   Bc

BWV 59 — Wer mich liebet, der wird mein Wort
 halten
 Whitsunday — May 28, 1724
 Score: Berlin, SPK, Mus. ms. Bach P 161
 Parts: Berlin, SPK, Mus. ms. Bach St 102
 St 102/1–3   B,A,T
      4–6   V 1, V 2, Va
      7   Bc
      8–10   Tr 1–2, Tamb
      11   Bctr

BWV 60 — O Ewigkeit, du Donnerwort
 24th Sunday after Trinity — November 7,
  1723
 Parts: Berlin, SPK, Mus. ms. Bach St 74
 St 74/1–3a   S,A,T,B
      4–5   Ob d'Am 1–2
      6–9   V 1 (2x), V 2 (2x), Va [sic]
      10   Cno
      11   Bc
      12   Bctr (fig Mvt 1–4)

BWV 62 — Nun komm, der Heiden Heiland
 1st Sunday in Advent — 1:December 3, 1724;
  2:1732–1735
 Score: Berlin, SPK, Mus. ms. Bach P 877
 Parts: Leipzig, Thomana Collection
 Thom 62/1–4   S,A,T,B
      5   Cno
      6–7   Ob 1–2
      8–12   V 1 (2x), V 2 (2x), Va
      13   Violone: Bc (fig Mvt 3,5:
              copied from Bc)
      14   Bc (fig Mvt 3,5: copied
              from Bctr)
      15   Bctr (fig: JSB)

BWV 63 — Christen, ätzet diesen Tag
 Christmas — 1:December 25, 1713; 2:De-
  cember 25, 1723; 3:1729?
 Parts: Berlin, SPK, Mus. ms. Bach St 9
 St 9/1–6   S, A (2x), T (2x), B
      7–11   Tr 1–4, Tamb
      12–14 Ob 1–3
      15–17 V 1, V 2, Va
      18   Bassono
      19   Violono: Bctr (fig: JSB)
      20   Organo: Bctr
      21   Organo: Bc [sic]

BWV 64 — Sehet, welch eine Liebe hat uns der
   Vater erzeiget
      3rd Day of Christmas — 1: December 27,
         1723; 2: 1735–50
      Score: Berlin, SPK, Mus. ms. Bach St 84
      St 84/9–12   S, A, T, B
         13   Cornettino
         14–16   Tbe 1–3
         17   Ob d'Am
         18–20   V 1, V 2, Va
         21   Bc
         22   Organo: Bctr

BWV 67 — Halt im Gedächtnis Jesum Christ
   Quasimodogeniti — April 16, 1724
   Score: Berlin, DStB, Mus. ms. Bach P 95
   Parts: Berlin, SPK, Mus. ms. Bach St 40
   St 40/1–4   S, A, T, B
      5   Trav
      6–7   Ob d'Am 1–2
      8–12   V 1 (2x), V 2 (2x), Va
      13   Corno da Tirarsi
      14   Bc (fig: JSB)
      15   Bctr (fig: JSB)
      16   Bc

BWV 68 — Also hat Gott die Welt geliebt
   2nd Day of Whitsuntide — May 21, 1725
   Parts: Leipzig, Thomana Collection
   Thom 68/1–4   S, A, T, B
      5–7   Ob 1–2, Taille
      8–10   V 1, V 2, Va
      11   Violoncello piccolo
      12   Cno
      13–15   Tbe 1–3
      16   Bc
      17   Bctr (fig: JSB)

BWV 69a — Lobe den Herrn, meine Seele
   12th Sunday after Trinity — 1: August 15, 1723;
      2: August 31, 1727?; 3: 1743–50 (BWV 69)
   Parts: Berlin, DStB, Mus. ms. Bach St 68
   St 68/1–4   S, A, T, B
      5–8   Tr 1–3, Tamb
      9–11   Ob 1–3
      12   Bassoni
      13–15   V 1, V 2, Va
      16   Bc

BWV 70 — Wachet! betet! betet! wachet!
   2nd Sunday in Advent — 1: December 6, 1716
      (BWV 70a);
   26th Sunday after Trinity — 2: November 21,
      1723; 3: November 18, 1731
   Parts: Berlin, SPK, Mus. ms. Bach St 95
   St 95/1–4   S, A, T, B
      5   Tr
      6   Ob
      7–11   V 1 (2x), V 2 (2x), Va
      12   Violoncello obligato
      13   Bc
      14   Bassono
      15   Bctr (fig Mvt 1,2,5,6, pt fig
                   Mvt 3: JSB)
      16   Bctr (fig: JSB)

BWV 71 — Gott ist mein König
   Town Council Inauguration — February 4,
      1708
   Score: Berlin, DStB, Mus. ms. Bach P 45
   Parts: Berlin, DStB, Mus. ms. Bach St 377
   St 377/1–4   S, A, T, B
      5–8   S, A, T, B in ripieno
      9   Tr
      10–13   Tr 1–3, Tamb
      14–15   V 1, Va
      16   Violon(o)
      17–18   Fl 1–2
      19–20   Ob 1–2
      21   Bassono
      22   Violoncello
      23   Organo: Bc (fig: JSB)

BWV 72 — Alles nur nach Gottes Willen
   3rd Sunday after Epiphany — January 27,
      1726
   Score: Berlin, DStB, Mus. ms. Bach P 54
   Parts: Berlin, DStB, Mus. ms. Bach St 2
      Berlin, Hochschule der Künste Ms.
         47211
      Eisenach, Bachhaus
   St 2/1–4   S, A, T, B
      5–6   Ob 1–2
      7–9   V 1, V 2, Va
      10   Bc
   Berlin 72/1–2   V 1, V 2
   Eisen 72   Bc

BWV 73 — Herr, wie du willt, so schicks mit mir
3rd Sunday after Epiphany — 1: January 23, 1724; 2: 1732–35
Parts: Berlin, SPK, Mus. ms. Bach St 45

St 45/1–4	S,A,T,B
5–6	Ob 1–2
7–9	V 1, V 2, Va
10	Bc
11	Organo: Bctr (fig: JSB)
12	Cno
13	Bctr (fig: JSB)

BWV 74 — Wer mich liebet, der wird mein Wort halten
Whitsunday — May 20, 1725
Parts: Berlin, SPK, Mus. ms. Bach St 103

St 103/1–4	B,T,A,S
5–7	Ob 1–2, Ob da Ca
8–11	Tr 1–3, Tamb
12–16	V 1 (2x), V 2 (2x), Va
17	Bc
18	Bc
19	Bctr (fig: JSB)

BWV 76 — Die Himmel erzählen die Ehre Gottes
2nd Sunday after Trinity — 1: June 6, 1723; 2: October 31, 1724?
Score: Berlin, DStB, Mus. ms. Bach P 67
Parts: Berlin, SPK, Mus. ms. Bach St 13b

St 13b/1–4	S,A,T,B
5–7	S (2x), A in ripieno
8–9	V 2, Va
10	Viola da gamba
11	Viola da gamba (JSB)

BWV 78 — Jesu, der du meine Seele
14th Sunday after Trinity — September 10, 1724
Parts: Leipzig, Thomana Collection

Thom 78/1–4	S,A,T,B
5	Cno (Thom 78/12 on verso)
6	Trav
7–8	Ob 1–2
9–11	V 1, V 2, Va
12	Violone (Mvt 2)
13	Bc
14	Bctr (fig: JSB)

BWV 79 — Gott der Herr ist Sonn und Schild
Reformation — October 31, 1725; 2: 1728–31

Score: Berlin, DStB, Mus. ms. Bach P 89
Parts: Berlin, SPK, Mus. ms. Bach St 35

St 35/1,5,9,13	S,A,T,B
17–21	V 1 (2x), V 2 (2x), Va
22–23	(Ob 1) Trav 1–2
24–25	Ob 1–2
26–27	Cno 1–2
28	Tamb
29	Bc
30	Bc
31	Organo: Bctr (fig Mvt 4: JSB)

BWV 81 — Jesus schläft, was soll ich hoffen
4th Sunday after Epiphany — January 30, 1724
Score: Berlin, DStB, Mus. ms. Bach P 120
Parts: Berlin, DStB, Mus. ms. Bach St 59

St 59/1–4	S,A,T,B
5–6	Fl 1–2
7–11	V 1 (2x), V 2 (2x), Va
12	Bc
13	Bc (fig except Mvt 2: JSB)
14	Bctr (fig: JSB)

BWV 82 — Ich habe genug
Purification — 1: February 2, 1727; 2: February 2, 1731?; 3: February 2, 1735; 4: 1745–48
Score: Berlin, SPK, Mus. ms. Bach P 114
Parts: Berlin, DStB, Mus. ms. Bach St 54

St 54/1	B
2–3	Ob da Ca
4	Organo: Bctr (fig: JSB)
5	S
6	Trav
7–12	V 1 (3x), V 2 (3x)
13	Bc
14	Bc
15	Va

BWV 83 — Erfreute Zeit im neuen Bunde
Purification — 1: February 2, 1724; 2: February 2, 1727
Parts: Berlin, SPK, Mus. ms. Bach St 21

St 21/1–4	S,A,T,B
5–6	Cno 1–2
7–8	Ob 1–2
9	Violino concertato
10–12	V 1, V 2, Va
13	Bc
14	Bctr (fig: JSB)

BWV 84 — Ich bin vergnügt mit meinem Glücke
    Septuagesima — February 9, 1727
    Score: Berlin, DStB, Mus. ms. Bach P 108
    Parts: Berlin, SPK, Mus. ms. Bach St 52
    St 52/1–4   S, A, T, B
          5   Ob
          6–10   V 1 (2x), V 2 (2x), Va
          11   Bc
          12   Bctr (fig Mvt 2,4: JSB)

BWV 85 — Ich bin ein guter Hirt
    Misericordia Domini — April 15, 1725
    Score: Berlin, DStB, Mus. ms. Bach P 106
    Parts: Berlin, DStB, Mus. ms. Bach St 51
    St 51/1–4   S, A, T, B
          5–6   Ob 1–2
          7–11   V 1 (2x), V 2 (2x), Va
          12   Violoncello piccolo
          13   Bc
          14   Bctr

BWV 87 — Bisher habt ihr nichts getan in meinem
    Namen
    Rogate — May 6, 1725
    Score: Berlin, DStB, Mus. ms. Bach P 61
    Parts: Berlin, DStB, Mus. ms. Bach St 6
    St 6/1–4   S, A, T, B
          5–7   Ob 1–2, Ob da Ca
          8–12   V 1 (2x), V 2 (2x), Va
          13   Bc
          14   Bctr (fig Mvt 2,4: JSB)

BWV 88 — Siehe, ich will viel Fischer aussenden
    5th Sunday after Trinity — July 21, 1726
    Score: Berlin, SPK, Mus. ms. Bach P 145
    Parts: Berlin, SPK, Mus. ms. Bach St 85
    St 85/1–3   Ob d'Am 1–2, Taille
          4–5   Cno 1–2
          6–10   V 1 (2x), V 2 (2x), Va
          11   Bctr
          12   Bc
          13–16   S, A, T, B

BWV 89 — Was soll ich aus dir machen, Ephraim
    22nd Sunday after Trinity — October 24,
    1723
    Parts: Berlin, SPK, Mus. ms. Bach St 99
    St 99/1–4   S, A, T, B
          5–6   Ob 1–2
          7   Corne du Chasse
          8–10   V 1, V 2, Va

          11   Bc
          12   Bctr (fig Mvt 1,3,5,6: JSB)

BWV 91 — Gelobet seist du, Jesu Christ
    Christmas — December 25, 1724; 2:1732–33
    Score: Berlin, SPK, Mus. ms. Bach P 869
    Parts: Leipzig, Thomana Collection
        Berlin, SPK, Mus. ms. Bach St 392
    Thom 91/1–4   S, A, T, B
          5–6   Cno 1–2
          7   Tamb
          8–10   Ob 1–3
          11–13   V 1, V 2, Va
          14   Bc
          15   Bctr (fig: JSB)
    St   392/1–2   V 1, V 2
          3   Bc

BWV 92 — Ich hab in Gottes Herz und Sinn
    Septuagesima — January 28, 1725
    Score: Berlin, SPK, Mus. ms. Bach P 873
    Parts: Leipzig, Thomana Collection
    Thom 92/1–4   S, A, T, B
          5–6   Ob 1–2
          7–9   V 1, V 2, Va
          10   Bc
          11   Bctr (fig Mvt 1–5,7: JSB)

BWV 93 — Wer nur den lieben Gott lässt walten
    5th Sunday after Trinity — 1:July 9, 1724;
        2:July 13, 1732
    Parts: Leipzig, Thomana Collection
    Thom 93/1–4   S, A, T, B
          5–6   Ob 1–2
          7,9,11   V 1, V 2, Va
          12   Bc
          13   Bctr (fig: JSB)

BWV 94 — Was frag ich nach der Welt
    9th Sunday after Trinity — 1:August 6, 1724;
        2:1732–35
    Score: Berlin, DStB, Mus. ms. Bach P 47
    Parts: Leipzig, Thomana Collection
    Thom 94/1–4   S, A, T, B
          6–7   Ob 1–2
          8,10,12 V 1, V 2, Va
          13   Bc
          15   Organo: Bctr (fig: JSB)

BWV 95 — Christus, der ist mein Leben
   16th Sunday after Trinity — September 12, 1723
   Score: Berlin, SPK, Mus. ms. Bach St 10

St 10/1–4	S, A, T, B
5	Cno
6–7	Ob d'Am 1–2
8–10	V 1, V 2, Va
11	Bc
12	Bctr (fig Mvt 1,3, pt fig Mvt 2: JSB)

BWV 96 — Herr Christ, der einge Gottessohn
   18th Sunday after Trinity — 1: October 8, 1724; 2: October 24, 1734?; 3: 1744–48
   Score: Berlin, DStB, Mus. ms. Bach P 179
   Parts: Leipzig, Thomana Collection
      Berlin, DStB, Mus. ms. Bach P 179

Thom 96/1–4	S, A, T, B
5	Cno, Tbe
6	Fiauto piccolo
7–8	Ob 1–2
9	Violino Piccolo
10–12	V 1, V 2, Va
13	Bc
14	Bc (fig Mvt 1,3–6: copied from lost Bctr?; Mvt 2: JSB)
P 179	Bctr [frag] (fig Mvt 5–6: copied from Bc)

BWV 97 — In allen meinen Taten
   Without liturgical designation — 1: 1734; 2: 1735–50 (two performances)
   Score: New York Public Library
   Parts: Berlin, DStB, Mus. ms. Bach St 64

St 64/1–4	S, A, T, B
5–6	Ob 1–2
7–11	V 1 (2x), V 2 (2x), Va
12	Continuo pro Bassono e Violoncello
13	Bc
14	Organo: Bctr–g (fig until Mvt 7: JSB)
15	Organo: Bctr–a♭ (fig: JSB)

BWV 98 — Was Gott tut, das ist wohlgetan
   21st Sunday after Trinity — November 10, 1726
   Score: Berlin, SPK, Mus. ms. Bach P 160
   Parts: Berlin, SPK, Mus. ms. Bach St 98

St 98/1–4	S, A, T, B
5–7	Ob 1–2, Taille
8–12	V 1 (2x), V 2 (2x), Va
13	Bc
14	Bctr (fig Mvt 1: JSB)
15	Bc

BWV 99 — Was Gott tut, das ist wohlgetan
   15th Sunday after Trinity — September 17, 1724
   Score: Cracow, Biblioteka Jagiellońska (formerly Berlin, Mus. ms. Bach P 647)
   Parts: Leipzig, Thomana Collection

Thom 99/1–4	S, A, T, B
5	Cno
6	Trav
7	Ob d'Am
8–10	V 1, V 2, Va
11	Bc
12	Bctr (fig Mvt 1: JSB)

BWV 100 — Was Gott tut, das ist wohlgetan
   Without liturgical designation — 1: 1732–35; 2: 1735–50 (two performances)
   Score: Berlin, DStB, Mus. ms. Bach P 159
   Parts: Berlin, SPK, Mus. ms. Bach St 97

St 97/1–4	S, A, T, B
5	Trav
6	Ob d'Am
7–8	Cno 1–2
9	Tamb
10–12	V 1, V 2, Va
13	Continuo pro Violoncello
14	Continuo pro Violone
15	Organo: Bctr (fig: JSB)
16	Trav
17	Ob d'Am
18–19	Cno 1–2
20	Tymb:
21–25	V 1 (2x), V 2 (2x), Va
26	Bc
27	Organo: Bctr (fig: JSB)
28	Organo: Bctr (fig: JSB)

BWV 101 — Nimm von uns, Herr, du treuer
  Gott
    10th Sunday after Trinity — 1: August 13,
      1724; 2: 1735–50
    Parts: Leipzig, Thomana Collection
    Thom 101/1–4   S, A, T, B
           5–8   Cto, Tbe 1–3
           9   Trav
           10–12   Ob 1–2, Taille
           13   Violino Solo
           14–16   V 1, V 2, Va
           17   Bc (fig Mvt 3,5: JSB)
           18   Bctr (fig Mvt 1,3,5:
                        JSB)

BWV 102 — Herr, deine Augen sehen nach dem
  Glauben
    10th Sunday after Trinity — August 25, 1726;
      2: 1737?
    Score: Berlin, DStB, Mus. ms. Bach P 97
    Parts: Berlin, DStB, Mus. ms. Bach St 41
           Berlin, DStB, Mus. ms. Bach P 97
    St 41/1   S
    P 97   Bctr (fig: JSB)

BWV 103 — Ihr werdet weinen und heulen
    Jubilate — 1: April 22, 1725; 2: April 15, 1731
    Score: Berlin, DStB, Mus. ms. Bach P 122
    Parts: Berlin, SPK, Mus. ms. Bach St 63
    St 63/1–4   S, A, T, B
           5   Tr
           6   Flauto piccolo
           7–8   Ob d'Am 1–2
           9   Violino Conc: ov Trav
           10–14   V 1 (2x), V 2 (2x), Va
           15   Bc
           16   Bc

BWV 104 — Du Hirte Israel, höre
    Misericordia Domini — April 23, 1724
    Parts: Berlin, SPK, Mus. ms. Bach St 17
    St 17/1–4   S, A, T, B
           5–7   Ob 1–2, Taille
           8–10   V 1, V 2, Va
           11   Bc
           12   Bctr (fig: JSB)

BWV 107 — Was willst du dich betrüben
    7th Sunday after Trinity — July 23, 1724

Parts: Leipzig, Thomana Collection
Thom 107/1–4   S, A, T, B
       5   Corne da Caccia
       6–7   Trav 1–2
       8–9   Ob d'Am 1–2
       10–12   V 1, V 2, Va
       13   Bc
       14   Bctr (pt fig Mvt 1, fig
                    Mvt 2: JSB)

BWV 108 — Es ist gut, dass ich hingehe
    Cantate — April 29, 1725
    Score: Berlin, DStB, Mus. ms. Bach P 82
    Parts: Berlin, SPK, Mus. ms. Bach St 28
    St 28/1–4   S, A, T, B
           5–6   Ob d'Am 1–2
           7–11   V 1 (2x), V 2 (2x), Va
           12   Bc
           13   Bc
           14   Bctr (fig: JSB)

BWV 109 — Ich glaube, lieber Herr
    21st Sunday after Trinity — October 17, 1723
    Score: Berlin, DStB, Mus. ms. Bach P 112
    Parts: Berlin, DStB, Mus. ms. Bach St 56
    St 56/1   Corne du Chasse (V 2 on verso)
           2–5   S, A, T, B
           6–7   Ob 1–2
           8–12 V 1 (2x), V 2 (2x), Va
           13   Bc
           14   Bctr (fig: JSB)
           15   Continuo pro Cembalo (fig Mvt
                   1,6: JSB, Mvt 1–6: copied
                   from Bctr)

BWV 110 — Unser Mund sei voll Lachens
    Christmas — 1: December 25, 1725; 2:
      1728–31
    Score: Berlin, DStB, Mus. ms. Bach P 153
    Parts: Berlin, DStB, Mus. ms. Bach St 92
    St 92/1,3,5,7   S, A, T, B
          2,4,6   S, A, T in ripieno
          8–11   Tr 1–3, Tamb
          12–13   Trav 1–2
          14–16   Ob 1–3
          17–21   V 1 (2x), V 2 (2x), Va
          22   Bassono
          23   Bc
          24   Organo: Bctr (fig Mvt 1,3:
                      JSB)

BWV 111 — Was mein Gott will, das gscheh
   allzeit
     3rd Sunday after Epiphany — January 21,
      1725
     Score: Cracow, Biblioteka Jagiellońska (for-
      merly Berlin, Mus. ms. Bach P 880)
     Parts: Berlin, SPK, Mus. ms. Bach St 399

St 399/1–2	V 1, V 2
3	Bc

BWV 112 — Der Herr ist mein getreuer Hirt
   Misericordia Domini — April 8, 1731
   Score: New York, Pierpont Morgan Library
   Parts: Leipzig, Thomana Collection

Thom 112/1–4	S,A,T,B
5–6	Cno 1–2
7–8	Ob d'Am 1–2
9,11,13	V 1, V 2, Va
14	Bc (pt fig Mvt 1: copied from Bctr)
15	Bctr (fig: JSB)

BWV 114 — Ach lieben Christen, seid getrost
   17th Sunday after Trinity — October 1, 1724
   Score: Switzerland, Private collection
   Parts: Leipzig, Thomana Collection

Thom 114/1–4	S,A,T,B
5	Cno
6	Trav
7–8	Ob 1–2
9–11	V 1, V 2, Va
12	Bc (fig Mvt 1,5: copied from Bctr)
13	Bctr (fig: JSB)

BWV 116 — Du Friedenfürst, Herr Jesu Christ
   25th Sunday after Trinity — November 26,
    1724
   Score: Paris, Bibliothèque nationale, Con-
    servatoire collection
   Parts: Leipzig, Thomana Collection
     Morlanwelz (Belgium), Bibliothèque
     du Chateau, Sig 1084/3

Thom 116/1–4	S,A,T,B
5	Cno
6–7	Ob d'Am 1–2
8–10	V 1, V 2, Va
11	Bc
Morlanwelz 116	Bctr

BWV 120a — Herr Gott, Beherrscher aller Dinge
   Wedding cantata — 1729?
   Score: Berlin, SPK, Mus. ms. Bach P 670
   Parts: Berlin, DStB, Mus. ms. Bach St 43

St 43/1–4	S,A,T,B
5	Va
6	Bc
7	Bc
8	Bctr (fig Mvt 1,2,5: JSB)

BWV 121 — Christum wir sollen loben schon
   2nd Day of Christmas — December 26, 1724
   Score: Cracow, Biblioteka Jagiellońska (for-
    merly Berlin, Mus. ms. Bach P 867)
   Parts: Leipzig, Thomana Collection
     Berlin, SPK, Mus. ms. Bach St 390

Thom 121/1–4	S,A,T,B
5–8	Cto, Tbe 1–3
9	Ob d'Am
10–12	V 1, V 2, Va
13	Bc
14	Bctr (fig: JSB)
St 390/1	S
2–3	V 1, V 2
4	Bc

BWV 122 — Das neugeborne Kindelein
   Sunday after Christmas — December 31, 1724
   Score: Berlin, SPK, Mus. ms. Bach P 868
   Parts: Leipzig, Thomana Collection
     Berlin, SPK, Mus. ms. Bach St 391

Thom 122/1–4	S,A,T,B
5–7	Ob 1–2, Taille
8–10	V 1, V 2, Va
11	Bc
12	Bctr (fig Mvt 3,5: JSB)
St 391/1–2	V 1, V 2
3	Bc

BWV 123 — Liebster Immanuel, Herzog der
   Frommen
     Epiphany — January 6, 1725
     Parts: Leipzig, Thomana Collection
        Berlin, SPK, Mus. ms. Bach St 395

Thom 123/1–4	S,A,T,B
5–6	Trav 1–2
7–8	Ob d'Am 1–2
9–11	V 1, V 2, Va
12	Bc
13	Bctr (fig Mvt 1–4: JSB)
St 395/11–12	V 1, V 2
13	Bc

BWV 124 — Meinen Jesum lass ich nicht
     1st Sunday after Epiphany — January 7, 1725
     Score: Berlin, SPK, Mus. ms. Bach P 876
     Parts: Leipzig, Thomana Collection
        Berlin, SPK, Mus. ms. Bach St 396

Thom 124/1–4	S,A,T,B
5	Cno
6	Ob d'Am
7–9	V 1, V 2, Va
10	Bc (fig Mvt 1,2,4: JSB, Mvt 3,5: copied from Bctr)
11	Organo: Bctr (fig: JSB)
St 396/1–2	V 1, V 2
3	Bc

BWV 125 — Mit Fried und Freud ich fahr dahin
     Purification — February 2, 1725
     Parts: Leipzig, Thomana Collection
        Berlin, SPK, Mus. ms. Bach St 384

Thom 125/1–4	S,A,T,B
5	Cno
6	Trav
7	Ob, Ob d'Am
8–10	V 1, V 2, Va
11	Bc
12	Bc
13	Organo: Bctr (fig: JSB)
St 384/1–2	V 1, V 2
3	Bc

BWV 126 — Erhalt und Herr bei deinem Wort
     Sexagesima — February 4, 1725
     Parts: Leipzig, Thomana Collection

Thom 126/1–4	S,A,T,B
5	Tr
6–7	Ob 1–2
8–10	V 1, V 2, Va
11	Bc
13	Bctr (fig: JSB)

BWV 127 — Herr Jesu Christ, wahr' Mensch
   und Gott
     Estomihi — February 11, 1725
     Score: Berlin, SPK, Mus. ms. Bach P 872
     Parts: Leipzig, Thomana Collection
        Berlin, SPK, Mus. ms. Bach St 393

Thom 127/1–4	S,A,T,B
5–6	Fl 1–2
7–8	Ob 1–2
9–11	V 1, V 2, Va
12	Bc
13	Bctr (fig Mvt 2, pt fig Mvt 4: JSB)
St 393/1–2	V 1, V 2
3	Bc

BWV 128 — Auf Christi Himmelfahrt allein
     Ascension — May 10, 1725
     Score: Private collection
     Parts: Berlin, SPK, Mus. ms. Bach St 158

St 158/1–4	S,A,T,B
5–6	Cno 1–2
7–9	Ob 1–2, Ob da Ca
10–12	V 1, V 2, Va
13	Bc
14	Bctr (fig: JSB)

BWV 129 — Gelobet sei der Herr, mein Gott
     Trinity — 1: June 8, 1727; 2: 1732–35; 3:
       1735–50

Thom 129/1–4	S,A,T,B
5–8	Tr 1–3, Tamb
9	Trav
10–11	Ob 1–2
12–14	V 1, V 2, Va
15	Bc
16	Organo: Bctr (fig: JSB)
17	Bc

BWV 130 — Herr Gott, dich loben wir alle
  Michaelmas — 1: September 29, 1724; 2:
    1732–35
  Score: Private collection
  Parts: Edinburgh, Scottish Record Office,
    GD. 205 Portfolio 17
    Cambridge, Harvard University,
      Houghton Library
    Berlin, DStB, Mus. ms. Bach P 895
    Paris, Royaumont Cloister
    Brussels, Archives Royales, Papiers
      Reine Elisabeth no. 161
    Coburg, Kunstsammlungen der Veste,
      V. 1109.3
    London, British Museum, Add. MS.
      41629
    Austria, Private collection
    Vienna Gesellschaft der Musikfreunde,
      A 92
    Eisenach, Bachhaus, A A.4
    Frankfurt (M), Stadt- und Univer-
      sitätsbibliothek, Mus. Hs. 1537
    Chur, Private collection

Edinburgh 130	S
Harvard 130	A
P 895	T
Paris 130	Tr 1
Brussels 130	Tr 2
Coburg 130	Tr 3
Brit Mus 130	Ob 1
Austria 130	V2
Vienna 130	V2 (insert)
Private 130	Va
Eisenach 130	Bc
Frankfurt/	
Chur 130	Bctr [frag] (pt fig: JSB)

BWV 132 — Bereitet die Wege, bereitet die Bahn
  4th Sunday in Advent — 1714?
  Score: Berlin, SPK, Mus. ms. Bach P 60
  Parts: Berlin, SPK, Mus. ms. Bach St 5

St 5/1	Violone

BWV 133 — Ich freue mich in dir
  3rd Day of Christmas — 1: December 27,
    1724; 2: 1735–50
  Score: Berlin, DStB, Mus. ms. Bach P 1215

Parts: Leipzig, Thomana Collection
  Berlin, SPK, Mus. ms. Bach St 387

Thom 133/1–4	S, A, T, B
5	Cto
6–7	Ob d'Am 1–2
8, 10, 12	V 1, V 2, Va
13	Bc
15	Bctr (fig: JSB)
St 387/1–2	V 1, V 2
3	Bc

BWV 134 — Ein Herz, das seinen Jesum lebend
weiss
  3rd Day of Easter — 1: April 11, 1724; 2:
    March 27, 1731
  Score: Berlin, SPK, Mus. ms. Bach P 44
  Parts: Berlin, DStB, Mus. ms. Bach St 18

St 18/1–5	S (2x), A, T, B
9–11	V 1, V 2
15	Bctr (fig Mvt 1, 3, 5: JSB)
15a	Continuo pro Organo: Bctr [for recits] (fig: JSB)

BWV 134a — Die Zeit, die Tag und Jahre macht
  Congratulatory cantata for New Year's Day —
    January 1, 1719
  Score: Paris
  Parts: Berlin, DStB, Mus. ms. Bach St 18

St 18/6–7	Ob 1–2
8, 10, 12	V 1, V 2, Va
13	Bc
14	Bc (fig Mvt 1, 3, 5: JSB)

BWV 136 — Erforsche mich, Gott, und erfahre
mein Herz
  8th Sunday after Trinity — July 18, 1723
  Score: Berlin, SPK, Mus. ms. Bach St 20
  Parts: Berlin, SPK, Mus. ms. Bach St 20

St 20/1–4	S, A, T, B
5	Cno
6–7	Ob 1, Ob 2 d'Am
8–12	V 1 (2x), V 2 (2x), Va
13	Bc (fig: copied from Bctr)
14	Bctr (fig: JSB)
15	Bc

BWV 137 — Lobe den Herren, den mächtigen
König der Ehren
12th Sunday after Trinity — 1: August 19,
1725; 2: 1744–50
Parts: Leipzig, Thomana Collection
Thom 137/1–4   S, A, T, B
      5–8   Tr 1–3, Tamb
      9–10   Ob 1–2
      11–13   V 1, V 2, Va
      14   Bc
      15   Bctr (fig: JSB)
      16   (Bc for Mvt 4): Thom
              137/7 (Tr 3) on verso

BWV 139 — Wohl dem, der sich auf seinen Gott
23rd Sunday after Trinity — 1: November 12,
1724; 2: 1732–35; 3: 1744–48
Parts: Leipzig, Thomana Collection
Thom 139/1–4   S, A, T, B
      5–6   Ob d'Am
      7   V 1
      8   V (Mvt 4)
      9–10   V 2, Va
      11   Bc
      12   Bctr (fig: JSB)

BWV 140 — Wachet auf, ruft uns die Stimme
27th Sunday after Trinity — November 25,
1731
Thom 140/1–4   S, A, T, B
      5   Cno
      6–8   Ob 1–2, Taille
      9   Violino piccolo
      10–12   V 1, V 2, Va
      13   Bc
      14   Bassono
      15   Bctr (fig: JSB)

BWV 147 — Herz und Mund und Tat und Leben
Visitation — 2: July 2, 1723 (no parts from
1716 performance)
Score: Berlin, SPK, Mus. ms. Bach P 102
Parts: Berlin, SPK, Mus. ms. Bach St 46
St 46/1–4   S, A, T, B
      5–6   Ob 1–2
      7–11   V 1 (2x), V 2 (2x), Va
      12   Tr

      13   Violoncello
      14   Bctr (fig Mvt 3–5,7: JSB, fig
              Mvt 1–3, Mvt 7–9: copied
              from Bc)
      15   (Bc for Mvt 7–9) [frag] (fig:
              JSB)

BWV 151 — Süsser Trost, mein Jesus kommt
3rd Day of Christmas — 1: December 27,
1725; 2: 1728–31
Score: Coburg, Kunstsammlungen der Veste
Parts: Berlin, DStB, Mus. ms. Bach St 89
    Coburg, Kunstsammlungen der Veste,
      V. 1109, K. 121
St 89/1–4   S, A, T, B
      5   Trav
      6   Ob d'Am
      7–9   V 1, V 2, Va
      10   Bctr (fig Mvt 2,4: JSB)
Coburg 151/1   V 1
      2   (V or Trav? Mvt 1)
      3   V 2
      4   Bc

BWV 153 — Schau, lieber Gott, wie meine Feind
Sunday after New Year's Day — January 2,
1724
Parts: Berlin, SPK, Mus. ms. Bach St 79
St 79/1–4   S, A, T, B
      5–7   V 1, V 2, Va
      8   Bc
      9   Bctr (fig Mvt 1,3,5–8, pt fig
              Mvt 2,4: JSB)

BWV 154 — Mein liebster Jesus ist verloren
1st Sunday after Epiphany — 1: January 9,
1724; 2: 1736–37
Score: Berlin, DStB, Mus. ms. Bach P 130
Parts: Berlin, DStB, Mus. ms. Bach St 70
St 70/1–4   S, A, T, B
      5–7   V 1, V 2, Va
      8–9   Ob 1–2
      10   Bc
      11   Bctr (fig: JSB)
      11a   Cembalo zur Alt Aria: Mvt 4
              (fig: JSB)

BWV 162 — Ach, ich sehe itzt, da ich zur Hochzeit
  gehe
  20th Sunday after Trinity — 1:1714–16; 2:
    October 10, 1723
  Parts: Berlin, SPK, Mus. ms. Bach St 1
  St 1/1   Violono
      2–5   S,A,T,B with inserts
      6a   Corno da Tirarsi: St 1/6 (V 1) on
              verso
      6–9   V 1 (2x), V 2, Va (2x): new parts
              on verso
      10   Violoncello
      11   Fagotto
      12   Violoncello e l'organo (fig: JSB)

BWV 164 — Ihr, die ihr euch von Christo nennet
  13th Sunday after Trinity — August 16, 1725
  Score: Berlin, SPK, Mus. ms. Bach P 121
  Parts: Berlin, DStB, Mus. ms. Bach St 60
  St 60/1–4   S,A,T,B
      5–9   V 1 (2x), V 2 (2x), Va
      10–11   Trav 1–2
      12–13   Ob 1–2
      14   Bctr (fig Mvt 2,4: JSB)
      15   Bc

BWV 166 — Wo gehest du hin
  Cantate — May 7, 1724
  Parts: Berlin, SPK, Mus. ms. Bach St 108
  St 108/1–4 S,A,T,B
      5   Ob
      6–8   V 1, V 2, Va
      9   Bctr
      10   Bc (fig Mvt 1–2: JSB)

BWV 167 — Ihr Menschen rühmet Gottes Liebe
  St John — June 24, 1723
  Parts: Berlin, SPK, Mus. ms. Bach St 61
  St 61/1–4   S,A,T,B
      5   Tr
      6   Ob
      7–9   V 1, V 2, Va
      10   Bctr (fig: JSB)
      11   Bc

BWV 168 — Tue Rechnung! Donnerwort!
  9th Sunday after Trinity — July 29, 1725
  Score: Berlin, DStB, Mus. ms. Bach P 152
  Parts: Paris, Private collection
    Cambridge (England), Fitzwilliam
      Museum
    Berlin, SPK, Mus. ms. Bach St 457
    Scheide Collection, Princeton Univer-
      sity Library
    Princeton University Library
  Paris 168   S
  Fitzwill 168   A
  St 457   T
  Scheid 168/1–2   Ob d'Am 1–2
        3–5   V 1, V 2, Va
        6   Bc (fig: JSB)
        7   Bc
        8   Bctr (fig Mvt 2,4: copied
                   from Bc)
  Princeton 168   V 2

BWV 169 — Gott soll allein mein Herze haben
  18th Sunday after Trinity — October 20, 1726
  Score: Berlin, SPK, Mus. ms. Bach P 93
  Parts: Berlin, SPK, Mus. ms. Bach St 38
  St 38/1–4   A,S,T,B
      5–7   Ob 1–2, Taille
      8–12   V 1 (2x), V 2 (2x), Va
      13   Bc
      14   Bc (fig: JSB)

BWV 170 — Vergnügte Ruh, beliebte Seelenlust
  6th Sunday after Trinity — 1:July 28, 1726;
    2:1744–50
  Score: Berlin, SPK, Mus. ms. Bach P 154
  Parts: Berlin, SPK, Mus. ms. Bach St 94
  St 94/1   Trav
      2   Ob d'Am
      3   A
      4–6   V 1, V 2, Va
      7   Bc
      8   Bctr (fig: JSB)

BWV 172 — Erschallet, ihr Lieder, erklingt, ihr
Saiten
    Whitsunday — 1:May 20, 1714; 2:May 28,
       1724; 3:May 13, 1731
    Parts: Berlin, DStB, Mus. ms. Bach St 23
       Leipzig, Rudorff Collection Ms. 1

St 23/1–4	S, A, T, B
5–7	V 1, V 2, Va
8	(Ob insert)
9	V 2
10–13	Tr 1–2, Prencipale, Tamb
14	Violoncello
15	Fagotto
16	(Organ obbligato)
17	Organo: Bctr (fig: JSB)
Rudrff 172/1–2	V 1, V 2
3	Trav
4	Ob
5	Fagotto
6	Violoncello: Bc (fig: JSB)

BWV 174 — Ich liebe den Höchsten von ganzem
Gemüte
    2nd Day of Whitsuntide — June 6, 1729
    Score: Berlin, SPK, Mus. ms. Bach P 115
    Parts: Berlin, SPK, Mus. ms. Bach St 57, St
       456
       London, Private collection
       Washington, Library of Congress, ML
       96 .B 186 (case)
       Stanford University, Memorial Library
       of Music
       Berea (Ohio), Riemenschneider Bach
       Institute

St 57/1–3	V 1, V 2, Va ripieno
4	Organo: Bctr (fig: JSB)
St 456	Vc 1 concertato
London 174	Taille
Washington 174	Va 2 concertato
Stanford 174	B
Riemen 174/1–4	S, A, T, B
5	Cno 2
6–7	Ob 1–2
8–10	V 1, V 2, V 3 con-certato
11–12	Va 2, Va 3 concertato
13–14	Vc 2, Vc 3 concertato
15	Bc

BWV 175 — Er rufet seinen Schafen mit Namen
    3rd Day of Whitsuntide — 1:May 22, 1725;
       2:1735–50
    Score: Berlin, DStB, Mus. ms. Bach P 75
    Parts: Berlin, SPK, Mus. ms. Bach St 22

St 22/1–4	S, A, T, B
5–7	V 1, V 2, Va
8–10	Fl 1–3
11–12	Tr 1–2
13	Violoncello piccolo
14	Bctr (fig Mvt 1,3,5: JSB)
15	Bc
16–17	V 1, V 2
18	Violoncello picolo [sic]

BWV 176 — Es ist ein trotzig und verzagt Ding
    Trinity — May 27, 1725
    Score: Berlin, DStB, Mus. ms. Bach P 81
    Parts: Scheide Collection, Princeton Univer-
       sity Library
       England, Private collection [lost since
       1934]

Scheid 176/1–4	S, A, T, B
5–7	Ob 1–2, Taille
8–11	V 1 (2x), V 2, Va
12	Bc (fig: JSB)
13	Bc
England 176	Bctr (fig)

BWV 177 — Ich ruf zu dir, Herr Jesus Christ
    4th Sunday after Trinity — 1:July 5, 1732;
       2:1735–50
    Score: Berlin, DStB, Mus. ms. Bach P 116
    Parts: Leipzig, Thomana Collection

Thom 177/1–4	S, A, T, B
5–6	Ob 1–2
7	Bassono obligato
8	Violino Concertino
9–11	V 1, V 2, Va
12	Bc
13	Organo: Bctr (fig: JSB)

BWV 178 — Wo Gott der Herr nicht bei uns hält
8th Sunday after Trinity — July 30, 1724
Parts: Leipzig, Thomana Collection
    Leipzig, Rudorff Collection Ms. 6
Thom 178/1–4   S,A,T,B
          5–6   Ob 1–2
          7–9   V 1, V 2, Va
          10   Bc (pt fig Mvt 2 [recits]: JSB)
          12   Bctr (fig Mvt 1–5: JSB)
Rudrff 178/1–2 V 1, V 2
          3   Cno
          4   Bc

BWV 179 — Siehe zu, dass deine Gottesfurcht
nicht Heuchelei sei
11th Sunday after Trinity — August 8, 1723
Score: Berlin, SPK, Mus. ms. Bach P 146
Parts: Berlin, SPK, Mus. ms. Bach St 348
St 348/1–2   Ob 1–2

BWV 181 — Leichtgesinnte Flattergeister
Sexagesima — 1: February 13, 1724; 2:
    1735–50
Parts: Berlin, SPK, Mus. ms. Bach St 66
St 66/1–4   S,A,T,B
          5–7   V 1, V 2, Va
          8   Trav
          9   Ob
          10   Tr
          11   Bc
          12   Bctr (fig Mvt 1–4,6: JSB)

BWV 182 — Himmelskönig, sei willkommen
Palm Sunday (Annunciation) — 1: March 25,
    1714; 2: March 25, 1724; 3: 1728?
Score: Berlin, SPK, Mus. ms. Bach P 103
Parts: Berlin, DStB, Mus. ms. Bach St 47, St
    47a
St 47/1–4   S,A,T,B
          5   Fl
          6–8   V (3x)
          9   V 1
          10   V 2 in ripieno
          11–12 Va 1, Va 2
          13   Violoncello
          14   Violono

St 47a/1–4 S,A,T,B
          5   Fl
          6   V
          7–8   Va 1, Va 2
          9   Violoncello

BWV 183 — Sie werden euch in den Bann tun
Exaudi — May 13, 1725
Score: Berlin, DStB, Mus. ms. Bach P 149
Parts: Berlin, SPK, Mus. ms. Bach St 87
St 87/1–4   S,A,T,B
          5–6   Ob d'Am 1–2
          7–8   Ob da Ca 1–2
          9–13 V 1 (2x), V 2 (2x), Va
          14   Violoncello piccolo
          15   Bctr (fig Mvt 1)
          16   Bc (fig Mvt 1)

BWV 184 — Erwünschtes Freudenlicht
3rd Day of Whitsuntide — 1: 1719? (BWV
    184a); 2: May 30, 1724; 3: May 15, 1731
Score: Berlin, SPK, Mus. ms. Bach P 77
Parts: Berlin, SPK, Mus. ms. Bach St 24
St 24/1–4   S,A,T,B
          5–6   Trav 1–2
          7–8   V 1, V 2
          9   Violoncello
          10   Bctr

BWV 185 — Barmherziges Herze der ewigen Liebe
4th Sunday after Trinity — 1: July 14, 1715;
    2: 1715–1717?; 3: June 20, 1723
Score: Berlin, SPK, Mus. ms. Bach P 59
Parts: Berlin, DStB, Mus. ms. Bach St 4
St 4/1–4   S,A,T,B
          5–7   V 1, V 2, Va
          8   Ob
          9   Fagotto
          10   Violone
          11   Bctr (fig: JSB)
          13–17 V 1, V 2, V 1, V 2, Va
          18   Violoncello
          19   Violoncello
          20   Violone (fig: JSB)
          21   Ob
          22   Tr

BWV 186 — Ärgre dich, o Seele, nicht
  7th Sunday after Trinity — July 11, 1723
  Score: Berlin, SPK, Mus. ms. Bach P 53
  Parts: Leipzig, Musikbibliothek der Stadt Leipzig, Gorke Collection 5
  Leipzig 186   Bc

BWV 187 — Es wartet alles auf dich
  7th Sunday after Trinity — 1: August 4, 1726; 2: 1735–50
  Score: Berlin, DStB, Mus. ms. Bach P 84
  Parts: Berlin, SPK, Mus. ms. Bach St 29
    Scheide Collection, Princeton University Library

St 29/1,3,5,8	S,A,T,B
Scheid 187/1–2	Ob 1–2
3–7	V 1 (2x), V 2 (2x), Va
8	Bc
9	Bc
10	Continuo pro Organo: Bctr (fig: JSB)

BWV 190 — Singet dem Herrn ein neues Lied
  New Year's Day — 1: January 1, 1724; 2: 1735–50
  Score: Berlin, SPK, Mus. ms. Bach P 127
  Parts: Berlin, SPK, Mus. ms. Bach St 88

St 88/1–4	S,A,T,B
5–6	V 1, V 2

BWV 192 — Nun danket alle Gott
  Without liturgical designation — 1730
  Parts: Berlin, SPK, Mus. ms. Bach St 71

St 71/1–3	S,A,B
4–8	V 1 (2x), V 2 (2x), Va
9–10	Ob 1–2
11–12	Trav 1–2
13	Bc
14	Bc
15	Bctr (fig: JSB)

BWV 193 — Ihr Tore zu Zion
  Town Council Inauguration — 1727?
  Parts: Berlin, SPK, Mus. ms. Bach St 62

St 62/1–2	S,A
3–7	V 1 (2x), V 2 (2x), Va
8–9	Ob 1–2

BWV 194 — Höchsterwünschtes Freudenfest
  Organ Dedication (Trinity) — 1: 1719? (BWV 194a); 2: November 2, 1723; 3: June 4, 1724; 4: June 16, 1726
  Score: Berlin, DStB, Mus. ms. Bach P 43
  Parts: Berlin, SPK, Mus. ms. Bach St 48, St 346

St 48/1–4	S,A,T,B
5–7	Ob 1–3
8–12	V 1 (2x), V 2 (2x), Va
13	Bc
14	Bc
St 346/1–3	Ob 1–3
4–6	V 1, V 2, Va
7	Bctr – g (fig Mvt 3–8: JSB)
8	Bctr – a♭ (fig Mvt 3,5,7,10: JSB)

BWV 195 — Dem Gerechten muss das Licht
  Wedding cantata — 1748
  Score: Berlin, DStB, Mus. ms. Bach P 65
  Parts: Berlin, SPK, Mus. ms. Bach St 12

St 12/1–4	S,A,T,B
5–8	S,A,T,B in ripieno
9–12	Tr 1–2, Principal, Tympana
13–14	Trav 1–2
15–16	Ob 1–2
17–20	V 1 (2x), V 2, Va
21	Violone
22	Violoncello (fig Mvt 1: JSB)
23	Bc (fig Mvt 1: copied from Violoncello, Mvt 4: JSB)

BWV 199 — Mein Herze schwimmt im Blute
  11th Sunday after Trinity — 1: August 12, 1714; 2: 1720–21; 3: August 8, 1723
  Score: Copenhagen, Royal Library
    Berlin, DStB, Mus. ms. Bach P 1162
  Parts: Berlin, SPK, Mus. ms. Bach St 459
    Berlin, DStB, Mus. ms. Bach P 1162
    Vienna, Gesellschaft der Musikfreunde

St 459/1	Ob
2–10	V 1 (4x), V 2 (3x), Va (2x)
3a,9a	V, Va inserts (Mvt 8)
11	(Violoncello piccolo)
12	Violoncello e Hautbois
13	Violono
14	Fagotto
15	Bc (fig: JSB)
16	Bc (fig: copied from Bc)
P 1162	Va obbligato (Mvt 6)
Vienna 199	Viola da gamba

BWV 201 — Geschwinde, ihr wirbelnden Winde
1729?
Score: Berlin, SPK, Mus. ms. Bach P 175
Parts: Berlin, SPK, Mus. ms. Bach St 33a

St 33a/1–8	S (2x), A (2x), T (2x), B (2x)
9–12	Tr 1–3, Tamb
13–14	Trav 1–2
15–16	Ob 1–2
17–21	V 1 (2x), V 2 (2x), Va
22	Bc (fig: JSB)
23	Bc (fig: JSB)
24	Bc

BWV 206 — Schleicht, spielende Wellen
Congratulatory cantata — October 7, 1736
Score: Berlin, DStB, Mus. ms. Bach P 42
Parts: Berlin, SPK, Mus. ms. Bach St 80

St 80/1–2	Ob 1–2
3	Va
4	Bc (fig: JSB)
5–6	Bc (fig: JSB)
1a,4a	S,A
5a,6a	T,B
7,10	V 1, V 2
11–13	Trav 1–3
14–17	Tr 1–3, Tamb

BWV 207 — Vereinigte Zwietracht der wechseln-
den Saiten
Congratulatory cantata — 1:December 11,
1726; 2:August 3, 1735 (BWV 207a)
Score: Berlin, SPK, Mus. ms. Bach P 174, St
347/1
Parts: Berlin, SPK, Mus. ms. Bach St 93,
St 347

St 93/1–4	S,A,T,B
5–8	Tr 1–3, Tamb
9–10	Trav 1–2
11–14	Ob 1, Ob d'Am 1, Ob 2, Taille
15–22	V 1 (3x), V 2 (3x), Va (2x)
23	Bc
24	Bc
25	Bc
26	Bc [frag]
St 347/2–5	S,A,T,B

BWV 210 — O holder Tag, erwünschte Zeit
Wedding cantata — April 3, 1742

Parts: Berlin, DStB, Mus. ms. Bach St 76

St 76/1	la Voce e Basso per il Cembalo (fig Mvt 2,4,6,8,10, pt fig Mvt 3,5,7: JSB)
2–4	V 1, V 2, Va
5	Trav
6	Ob d'Am
7	Violone

BWV 210a — O angenehme Melodei!
Homage cantata — 1738–40
Parts: Cracow, Biblioteka Jagiellońska (for-
merly Berlin, Mus. ms. Bach St 72)

| St 72/1 | S |

BWV 211 — Schweigt stille, plaudert nicht
Coffee Cantata — 1734?
Score: Berlin, DStB, Mus. ms. Bach P 141
Parts: Vienna, Österreichische National-
bibliothek, SA.67.B.32

Vienna 211/1–3	S,T,B
4	Trav
5–7	V 1, V 2, Va
8	Bc
9	Cembalo: Bc (fig Mvt 2,4,6,8,10, pt fig Mvt 1,3,5,7,9: JSB)

BWV 213 — Lasst uns sorgen, lasst uns wachen
Congratulatory cantata — September 5, 1733
Score: Berlin, DStB, Mus. ms. Bach P 125
Parts: Berlin, DStB, Mus. ms. Bach St 65

St 65/1–5	S,A, Echo, T,B
6–10	V 1 (2x), V 2 (2x), Va
11–12	Viola certata 1–2
13–14	Ob 1–2
15–16	Cno 1–2
17	Bc

BWV 214 — Tönet, ihr Pauken! Erschallet,
Trompeten!
Congratulatory cantata — December 8, 1733
Score: Berlin, DStB, Mus. ms. Bach P 41
Parts: Berlin, DStB, Mus. ms. Bach St 91

St 91/1–4	S,A,T,B
5	Va
6	Violono

BWV 215 — Preise dein Glücke, gesegnetes
Sachsen
    Congratulatory cantata — October 5, 1734
    Score: Berlin, DStB, Mus. ms. Bach P 139
    Parts: Berlin, DStB, Mus. ms. Bach St 77

St 77/1–4	S, A, T, B 1
5–8	S, A, T, B 2
9–12	Tr 1–3, Tamb
13–14	Trav 1–2
15–16	Ob 1–2
17–21	V 1 (2x), V 2 (2x), Va
22	Bassono
23	Bc
24	Bc

BWV 226 — Der Geist hilft unsrer Schwachheit
auf
    Burial service — October 20, 1729
    Score: Berlin, SPK, Mus. ms. Bach P 36
    Parts: Berlin, SPK, Mus. ms. Bach St 121

St 121/1–6	S 1, S 2, A, T, B 1, B 2
7–9	V 1, V 2, Va
10	Violoncello
11	Violon e Continuo: Bc
12	Organo: Bctr (fig: JSB)
13–15	Ob 1–2, Taille
16	Bassono

BWV 232^I — B-minor Mass (Missa)
    May 21, 1733
    Score: Berlin, SPK, Mus. ms. Bach P 180
    Parts: Dresden, Sächsische Landesbibliothek,
      Mus 2405 D 21 Aut. 2⁴

Dresd 232/1–5	S 1, S 2, A, T, B
6–9	Tr 1–2, Principale, Tamb
10	Cornu du Caccia
11–12	Trav 1–2
13–14	Ob d'Am 1–2
15–18	V 1 (2x), V 2, Va
19	Basson
20	Violoncello
21	Bc (fig: JSB)

BWV 232^{III} — Sanctus in D
    1: December 25, 1724; 2: April 11, 1727;
      3: 1748–49
    Score: Berlin, DStB, Mus. ms. Bach P 13
    Parts: Berlin, SPK, Mus. ms. Bach St 117

St 117/1–6	S 1, 2, 3, A, T, B
7–10	Tr 1–3, Tamb
11–13	Ob 1–3
14–18	V 1 (2x), V 2 (2x), Va
19	Bctr
20	Bc
21	Bc
22	Bc

BWV 234 — Mass in A
    1742–50
    Score: Darmstadt, Hessische Landes-
      bibliothek
    Parts: Berlin, SPK, Mus. ms. Bach St 400
      Darmstadt, Hessische Landesbiblio-
      thek, Mus. ms. 971

St 400/1–3	S, A, T
4–6	V 1, V 2, Va
7–8	Trav 1–2
9	Bc
10	Bc
Darmstadt 234	Continuo pro Violincello piccolo [sic]: Bctr (fig: JSB)

BWV 237 — Sanctus in C
    1723
    Score: Berlin, DStB, Mus. ms. Bach P 13
    Parts: Berlin, SPK, Mus. ms. Bach St 114

St 114/1	Bc
2–5	S, A, T, B
6–9	Tr 1–2, Principale, Tamb
10–11	Ob 1–2
12–16	V 1 (2x), V 2 (2x), Va
17	Bc
18	Bctr (fig: JSB)

BWV 240 — Sanctus in G
    1735–46
    Score: Berlin, DStB, Mus. ms. Bach P 13
    Parts: Berlin, DStB, Mus. ms. Bach St 115

St 115/1–2	Ob 1–2
3–6	S, A, T, B
7–9	V 1, V 2, Va
10	Violono
11	Bc (fig: JSB)
12	Organo: Bctr (fig: JSB)

BWV 244 — St. Matthew Passion
(1:1727); 2:March 30, 1736; 3:1742–44
Score: Berlin, DStB, Mus. ms. Bach P 25
Parts: Berlin, SPK, Mus. ms. Bach St 110
St 110/1–2　　S in ripieno (numbering fol-
　　　　　　　　lows NBA)
　　　　　Chorus I
　　3–9　　S (2x), A, T, B
　　10–11　Trav 1–2
　　12–13　Ob 1–2
　　14–18　V 1 (2x), V 2 (2x), Va
　　19　　　Viola da gamba
　　20　　　Bc
　　21　　　Bc
　　22　　　Organo: Bctr (fig: JSB)
　　　　　Chorus II
　　23–26　S, A, T, B
　　27–28　Trav 1–2
　　29–30　Ob 1–2
　　31–35　V 1 (2x), V 2 (2x), Va
　　36　　　Viola da gamba
　　37　　　Bc
　　38　　　Bc
　　39　　　Organo: Bctr (fig: JSB)
　　40　　　Cembalo: Bc (fig: JSB)

BWV 245 — St. John Passion
1:April 7, 1724; 2:March 30, 1725; 3:1728–
31; 4:1746–49
Score: Berlin, SPK, Mus. ms. Bach P 28
Parts: Berlin, DStB, Mus. ms. Bach St 111
St 111/1–2　　Trav 1–2
　　3–4　　Ob 1–2
　　5–11　　V 1 (3x), V 2 (2x), Va (3x)
　　12　　　Viola da Gamba
　　13,15　S, A in ripieno
　　17,19　TB in ripieno
　　14,16　S, A
　　18,20　T, B
　　21　　　Bc (pro Bassono grosso)
　　22　　　Bc (pt fig: copied from
　　　　　　　Cembalo?)
　　23　　　Cembalo: Bc (fig)
　　24　　　Cembalo: Bc
　　25　　　Organo (Mvt 19)
　　26　　　Cembalo (Mvt 19)

BWV 248[I] — Christmas Oratorio: Part 1
December 25, 1734
Score: Berlin, SPK, Mus. ms. Bach P 32

Parts: Berlin, SPK, Mus. ms. Bach St 112[I]
St 112[I]/1–4　　S, A, T, B
　　5–8　　Tr 1–3, Tamb
　　9–10　Trav 1–2
　　11–12　Ob 1–2
　　13–17　V 1 (2x), V 2 (2x), Va
　　18　　　Violoncello
　　19　　　Bc
　　20　　　Bassono
　　21　　　Organo: Bctr (fig: JSB)

BWV 248[II] — Christmas Oratorio: Part 2
December 26, 1734
Score: Berlin, SPK, Mus. ms. Bach P 32
Parts: Berlin, SPK, Mus. ms. Bach St 112[II]
St 112[II]/1–4　　S, A, T, B
　　5–6　　Trav 1–2
　　7–8　　Ob d'Am 1–2
　　9–10　Ob da Ca 1–2
　　11–15　V 1 (2x), V 2 (2x), Va
　　16　　　Bc
　　17　　　Bc
　　18　　　Organo: Bctr (fig: JSB)

BWV 248[III] — Christmas Oratorio: Part 3
December 27, 1734
Score: Berlin, SPK, Mus. ms. Bach P 32
Parts: Berlin, SPK, Mus. ms. Bach St 112[III]
St 112[III]/1–4　　S, A, T, B
　　5–8　　Tr 1–3, Tamb
　　9–10　Trav 1–2
　　11–12　Ob 1–2
　　13–17　V 1 (2x), V 2 (2x), Va
　　18　　　Bc
　　19　　　Bc
　　20　　　Organo: Bctr (fig: JSB)

BWV 248[IV] — Christmas Oratorio: Part 4
January 1, 1735
Score: Berlin, SPK, Mus. ms. Bach P 32
Parts: Berlin, SPK, Mus. ms. Bach St 112[IV]
St 112[IV]/1–5　　S (2x), A, T, B
　　6–7　　Cornu da Caccia 1–2
　　8–9　　Ob 1–2
　　10–14　V 1 (2x), V 2 (2x), Va
　　15　　　Bc (fig Mvt 36,39,40: partly
　　　　　　　copied from Bctr, fig
　　　　　　　Mvt 36–42: JSB)
　　16　　　Bc
　　17　　　Organo: Bctr (fig: JSB)

BWV 248^V — Christmas Oratorio: Part 5
    January 2, 1735
    Score: Berlin, SPK, Mus. ms. Bach P 32
    Parts: Berlin, SPK, Mus. ms. Bach St 112^V

St 112^V/1–4	S, A, T, B
5–6	Ob d'Am 1–2
7	V 1
8	Violino solo (Mvt 51)
9–12	V 1, V 2 (2x), Va
13	Bc
14	Bc
15	Organo: Bctr (fig: JSB)

BWV 248^{VI} — Christmas Oratorio: Part 6
    January 6, 1735
    Score: Berlin, SPK, Mus. ms. Bach P 32
    Parts: Berlin, SPK, Mus. ms. Bach St 112^{VI}

St 112^{VI}/1–4	S, A, T, B
5–8	Tr 1–3, Tamb
9–10	Ob 1–2
11–15	V 1 (2x), V 2 (2x), Va
16	Bc
17	Bc
18	Organo: Bctr (fig: JSB)

BWV 249 — Easter Oratorio
    April 1, 1725; 2:1735?; 3:1740–50
    Score: Berlin, SPK, Mus. ms. Bach P 34
    Parts: Berlin, SPK, Mus. ms. Bach St 355

St 355/1–4	S, A, T, B
5–8	S, A, T, B
9–13	V 1 (2x), V 2 (2x), Va
14	Bassono
15–18	Tr 1–2, Principal, Tamb
19	Trav
20–21	Ob 1–2
22	Bctr (fig: JSB)

BWV 250–252 — Three Wedding Chorales
    1729?
    Parts: Berlin, DStB, Mus. ms. Bach St 123

St 123/1–4	S, A, T, B
5–6	Cno 1–2
7–8	Violino e Hautbois 1–2
9	Va
10	Bc
11	Organo: Bctr (fig: JSB)

APPENDIX B

Bach's Continuo Parts Arranged by Date of Performance

Pre-Leipzig Performances

BWV	Date	Continuo (unfigured)	Continuo (figured)	Score (figured)
71	2/7/08	St 377/16 21 22	St 377/23	
18	2/19/13?	St 34/12 13	St 34/1	
63	12/25/13	St 9/18		
182	3/25/14	St 47/13		P 103
21	6/17/14	St 354/23	St 354/25	
172	5/20/14	St 23/14 15		
199	8/12/14	St 459/12 13 14		Copenhagen
132	1714?	St 5/1		P 60
31	4/21/15	St 14/14 21		
185	7/14/15	St 4/9 10 14		
162	1714–16	St 1/1 11	St 1/12	
185	1715–1717?	St 4/19	St 4/20	
21	1717–22	St 354/22 24		
134a	1/1/19	St 18/13	St 18/14	Paris

BWV	Date	Continuo (unfigured)	Continuo (figured)	Score (figured)
184a	1719?	St 24/9		
199	1720–21	Vienna 199 St 459/16		

Leipzig Performances

BWV	Date	Cammerton (unfigured)	Cammerton (figured)	Chorton
23	2/7/23	St 16/22 23 25	St 16/24	St 16/26
237	1723	St 114/1 17		St 114/18
76	6/6/23	St 13b/10		
21	6/13/23	**St 354/23**	**St 354/25**	St 354/26
24	6/20/23	St 19/14	St 19/15	St 19/13
185	6/20/23	**St 4/19**	**St 4/20?**	St 4/11
167	6/24/23	St 61/11		St 61/10
147	7/2/23	St 46/13	St 46/15	St 46/14
186	7/11/23	Leipzig 186		
136	7/18/23	St 20/15	St 20/13	St 20/14
46	8/1/23		St 78/13	St 78/14
199	8/8/23		St 459/15	
69a	8/15/23	St 68/12 16		
25	8/29/23	St 376/17		St 376/18
95	9/12/23	St 10/11		St 10/12
48	10/3/23	St 53/13	St 53/12	St 53/14
162	10/10/23	St 1/10		**St 1/12**
109	10/17/23	St 56/13	St 56/15	St 56/14
89	10/24/23	St 99/11		St 99/12
194	11/2/23	St 48/14		
60	11/7/23	St 74/11		St 74/12
70	11/21/23	St 95/13 14		St 95/15
238	12/25/23	St 116/10 11		
63	12/25/23	**St 9/18**		

BWV	Date	Cammerton (unfigured)	Cammerton (figured)	Chorton
40	12/26/23	St 11/16	St 11/14	St 11/15
64	12/27/23	St 84/21		
153	1/2/24	St 79/8		St 79/9
154	1/9/24	St 70/10	[St 70/11a]	St 70/11
73	1/23/24	St 45/10		St 45/13
81	1/30/24	St 59/12	St 59/13	St 59/14
83	2/2/24	St 21/13		
181	2/13/24	St 66/11		St 66/12
18	2/13/24	**St 34/12**	St 34/14	**St 34/1**
23	2/20/24	**St 16/22**	**St 16/24**	**St 16/26**
		23		
		25		
182	3/25/24	St 47a/9		
245	4/7/24	St 111/21		
4	4/9/24	Thom 4/13		
31	4/9/24	**St 14/21**	St 14/22	
134	4/11/24			St 18/15
67	4/16/24	St 40/16	St 40/14	St 40/15
104	4/23/24	St 17/11		St 17/12
12	4/30/24	St 109/5		
166	5/4/24		St 108/10	St 108/9
37	5/18/24			St 100/10
44	5/21/24	St 86/12	St 86/13	St 86/14
172	5/28/24	Rudrff 172/5	Rudrff 172/6	**St 23/14**
59	5/28/24	St 102/7		
184	5/30/24	**St 24/9**		St 24/10
194	6/4/24	**St 48/14**		St 346/7
		13		
Anh. 24	6/24?			St 327/3
20	6/11/24		Thom 20/12	Thom 20/13
2	6/18/24	Thom 2/14		Thom 2/15
7	6/24/24		Thom 7/12	Towe 7
10	7/2/24		Thom 10/11	Thom 10/13
93	7/9/24			Thom 93/13
107	7/23/24	Thom 107/13		Thom 107/14
178	7/30/24	Rudrff 178/4	Thom 178/10	Thom 178/12
94	8/6/24	Thom 94/13		
101	8/13/24		Thom 101/17	Thom 101/18
33	9/3/24		Thom 33/10	Thom 33/11

BWV	Date	Cammerton (unfigured)	Cammerton (figured)	Chorton
78	9/10/24	Thom 78/12 13		Thom 78/14
99	9/17/24	Thom 99/11		Thom 99/12
8	9/24/24	Brus 8/10 11		
130	9/29/24	Eisenach 130		Frankfurt/Chur 130
114	10/1/24		Thom 114/12	Thom 114/13
96	10/8/24	Thom 96/13	Thom 96/14	
5	10/15/24	Thom 5/11		Thom 5/12
38	10/29/24		Thom 38/14	Thom 38/15
76	10/31/24?	St 13b/11		
139	11/12/24	Thom 138/11		
26	11/19/24	Thom 26/13		Thom 26/14
116	11/26/24	Thom 116/11		Morlanwelz 116
62	12/3/24		Thom 62/14	Thom 62/15
91	12/25/24	Thom 91/14		Thom 91/15
232III	12/25/24	St 117/21		
121	12/26/24	Thom 121/13 St 390/4		Thom 121/14
133	12/27/24	Thom 133/13 St 387/3		Thom 133/15
122	12/31/24	Thom 122/11 St 391/3		Thom 122/12
41	1/1/25	Thom 41/15 St 394/21		Thom 41/16
123	1/6/25	Thom 123/12 St 395/13		Thom 123/13
124	1/7/25	St 396/3	Thom 124/10	Thom 124/11
3	1/14/25	Thom 3/12	Thom 3/11	St 157/11
111	1/12/25	St 399/3		
92	1/28/25	Thom 92/10		Thom 92/11
125	2/1/25	Thom 125/11 12 St 384/3		Thom 125/13
126	2/4/25	Thom 126/11		Thom 126/13
127	2/11/25	Thom 127/12 St 393/3		Thom 127/13
1	3/25/25	Thom 1/14		Thom 1/15
245	3/30/25	**St 111/21** 22		

BWV	Date	Cammerton (unfigured)	Cammerton (figured)	Chorton
249	4/1/25			St 355/22
4	4/1/25	**Thom 4/13**		Thom 4/14
6	4/2/25	St 7/15	St 7/14	St 7/16
42	4/8/25	St 3/11	St 3/13	St 3/14 12?
85	4/15/25	St 51/13		
103	4/22/25	St 63/15 16		
108	4/29/25	St 28/12 13		St 28/14
87	5/6/25	St 6/13		St 6/14
128	5/10/25	St 158/13		St 158/14
183	5/13/25		St 87/16	St 87/15
74	5/20/25	St 103/17 18		St 103/19
68	5/21/25	Thom 68/16		Thom 68/17
175	5/22/25	St 22/15		St 22/14
176	5/27/25	Scheid 176/13	Scheid 176/12	England 176
168	7/29/25	Scheid 168/7	Scheid 168/6	Scheid 168/8
137	8/19/25	Thom 137/14 16		Thom 137/15
163	8/26/25	St 60/15		St 60/14
79	10/31/25	St 35/29 30		St 35/31
110	12/25/25	St 92/22 23		St 92/24
57	12/26/25	St 82/13 14		St 82/15
151	12/27/25			St 89/10
28	12/30/25	St 37/19	St 37/17	St 37/18
16	1/1/26			St 44/14
32	1/13/26	St 67/12		St 67/11
13	1/20/26	St 69/13 14		St 69/15
72	1/27/26	St 2/10 Eisen 72		
JLB 9	2/2/26		St 314/12 14	St 314/13
JLB 1	2/3/26		St 310/10 11	St 319/12

BWV	Date	Cammerton (unfigured)	Cammerton (figured)	Chorton
JLB 2	2/10/26		St 303/10 12	St 303/11
JLB 3	2/17/26	St 302/12	St 302/11	St 302/10
JLB 4	2/24/26	St 301/10 11		St 301/12
JLB 5	3/3/26	St 311/10 11		St 311/12
34a	3/6/26	St 73/7		
15 (JLB)	4/21/26	St 13a/16	St 13a/14	St 13a/15
JLB 11	4/23/26	St 309/10 11		St 309/12
JLB 6	4/28/26	St 317/11 12		St 317/13
JLB 12	5/5/26		St 316/11 12	
JLB 14	5/19/26	St 306/12	St 306/13	St 306/14
43	5/30/26	St 36/12 17		St 36/18
194	6/16/26	**St 48/13 14**		St 346/8
39	6/23/26	St 8/13		St 8/12
JLB 17	6/24/26	St 315/14	St 315/12	St 315/13
JLB 13	7/2/26	St 304/13	St 304/15	St 304/14
88	7/21/26	St 85/12		St 85/11
170	7/28/26	St 94/7		St 94/8
JLB 7	7/28/26	St 313/17	St 313/15	St 313/16
187	8/4/26	Scheid 187/8 9		Scheid 187/10
45	8/11/26			St 26/12
102	8/25/26			P 97
JLB 15	9/1/26		St 307/13 14	St 307/12
35	9/8/26	St 33/10 11		
JLB 16	9/15/26	St 312/12	St 312/14	St 312/13
17	9/22/26	St 101/13		St 101/12
19	9/29/26	St 25a/18	St 25a/17	St 25a/19
27	10/6/26	St 105/14	St 105/16	St 105/15
47	10/13/26	St 104/10 11		St 104/12

BWV	Date	Cammerton (unfigured)	Cammerton (figured)	Chorton
169	10/20/26	St 38/13	St 38/14	
56	10/27/26	St 58/13		St 58/14
49	11/3/26	St 55/15 16		
98	11/10/26	St 98/13 55		St 98/14
55	11/17/26	St 50/12 13		St 50/14
52	11/24/26	St 30/15 16		St 30/17
207	12/11/26	St 93/23 24 25 26		
58	1/5/27	Thom 58/9 St 389/3		Thom 58/10
82	2/2/27	St 54/13		
83	2/2/27	**St 21/13**		St 21/14
84	2/9/27	St 52/11		St 52/12
232[III]	4/11/27	**St 117/21** 20		St 117/19
129	6/8/27	Thom 129/15		
69a	8/31/27?	**St 68/12** 16		
182	1728?	**St 47a/9** St 47/14		
23	1728–31	**St 16/22** 23	**St 16/25**	St 16/24
79	1728–31	**St 35/29** 30	**St 35/31**	
110	1728–31	**St 92/22** 23		**St 92/24**
151	1728–31	Coburg 151/4		**St 89/10**
245	1728–31	**St 111/21** 22		
174	6/6/29	St 456 Riemen 174/13 14 15		St 57/4
226	10/29/29	St 121/10 11 16		St 121/12

BWV	Date	Cammerton (unfigured)	Cammerton (figured)	Chorton
63	1729?	**St 9/18** 21		St 9/19 20
120a	1729?	St 43/7	St 43/6	St 43/8
250–252	1729?	St 123/10		St 123/11
201	1729?	St 33a/24	St 33a/22 23	
51	9/17/30	St 49/10 11		St 49/12
192	1730?	St 71/13 14		St 71/15
82	2/2/31?	**St 54/13**		
31	3/25/31	**St 14/21**	**St 14/22**	St 14/23
134	3/27/31			**St 18/15** 15a
42	4/1/31	**St 3/11**	**St 3/13**	**St 3/14**
112	4/1/31		Thom 112/14	
103	4/15/31	**St 63/15** **16**		
37	5/3/31	St 100/11		St 100/10
172	5/13/31	**St 23/14** **15**		St 23/17
184	5/15/31	**St 24/9**		**St 24/10**
29	8/27/31	St 106/23	St 106/22	St 106/20
70	9/18/31	**St 95/13** **14** 12		St 95/16
140	9/25/31	Thom 140/13 14		Thom 140/15
36	12/2/31	St 82/12 14		
177	7/6/32	Thom 177/7 12		
93	7/13/32	Thom 93/12		**Thom 93/13**
91	1732–33	**Thom 91/14** St 392/3		**Thom 91/15**
5	1732–35	**Thom 5/11**		Thom 5/13
9	1732–35	Thom 9/10 Cary 9/2		Thom 9/11
41	1732–35	**Thom 41/15** **St 394/21**		**Thom 41/16**
62	1732–35		**Thom 62/14** 13	**Thom 62/15**

BWV	Date	Cammerton (unfigured)	Cammerton (figured)	Chorton
73	1732–35	**St 45/10**		St 45/11
94	1732–35	**Thom 94/13**		Thom 94/15
100	1732–35	St 97/26		St 97/27
129	1732–35	**Thom 129/15**		
139	1732–35	**Thom 138/11**		Thom 139/12
232^{I}	7/26/33	Dresd 232/19 20	Dresd 232/21	
213	9/5/33	St 65/17		
214	12/8/33	St 91/6		
215	10/5/34	St 77/22 23 24		
96	10/24/34?	**Thom 96/13**	**Thom 96/14**	
97	1734	St 64/13 12		St 64/14
211	1734?	Vienna 211/8	Vienna 211/9	
248^{I}	12/25/34	St 112^{I}/18 19 20		St 112^{I}/21
248^{II}	12/26/34	St 112^{II}/16 17		St 112^{II}/18
248^{III}	12/27/34	St 112^{III}/18 19		St 112^{III}/20
248^{IV}	1/1/35	St 112^{IV}/16	St 112^{IV}/15	St 112^{IV}/17
248^{V}	1/2/35	St 112^{V}/13 14		St 112^{V}/15
248^{VI}	1/6/35	St 112^{VI}/16 17		St 112^{VI}/18
14	1/30/35	Thom 14/11 St 398/3		Fitzwill 14
82	2/2/35?	**St 54/13**		
36b	7/28/35?		St 15/9	
207a	8/3/35	**St 93/23 24 25 26**		
249	1735?	St 355/14		**St 355/22**
244	3/30/36	St 110/20 21 37 38		St 110/22 39
238	1736?	**St 116/10 11**		St 116/12

BWV	Date	Cammerton (unfigured)	Cammerton (figured)	Chorton
154	1736–37	St 70/10	[St 70/11a]	St 70/11
102	1737?			P 97
240	1735–46	St 115/10	St 115/11	St 115/12
8	1735–50	Thom 8/14		Thom 8/16
27	1735–50	St 105/14	St 105/16	St 105/15
42	1735–50	St 3/11 15	St 3/13	St 3/14
64	1735–50	St 84/21		St 84/22
100	1735–50	St 97/13 14		St 97/15
100	1735–50	St 97/13 14		St 97/28
101	1735–50		Thom 101/17	Thom 101/18
129	1735–50	Thom 129/15 17?		Thom 129/16
133	1735–50	Thom 133/13 St 387/3		Thom 133/15
177	1735–50	Thom 177/7 12		Thom 177/13
181	1735–50	St 66/11		St 66/12
187	1735–50	Scheid 187/8 9		Scheid 187/10
JLB 8	1735–50	St 305/11	St 305/12	
30	1738–42	St 31/19 20		St 31/18
249	1740–50	St 355/14		St 355/22
244	1742–44	St 110/20 21 37 38	St 110/40	St 110/22
234	1742–50	St 400/9 10		Darmstadt 234
69a	1743–50	St 68/12 16		
97	1743–50	St 64/13 12		St 64/15
210	1743–50	St 76/7	St 76/1	
96	1744–48	Thom 96/13	Thom 96/14	P 179
139	1744–48	Thom 138/11		Thom 139/12
137	1744–50	Thom 137/14 16		Thom 137/15
170	1744–50	St 94/7		St 94/8

BWV	Date	Cammerton (unfigured)	Cammerton (figured)	Chorton
82	1745–48	St 54/13 14		St 54/4
245	1746–49	St 111/21 24 26	St 111/23 22	
195	1748	St 12/21	St 12/22 23	
232III	1748–49	St 117/21 20 22		St 117/19

Abbreviations

Notes

Index to Cited Works of Bach

General Index

Abbreviations

BDok   *Bach-Dokumente,* ed. Werner Neumann and Hans-Joachim Schulze, 4
         vols. (Leipzig, 1963, 1969, 1972, 1978)

BG   Bach-Gesellschaft, *Johann Sebastian Bachs Werke* (1850–99)

BJ   *Bach-Jahrbuch*

BR   *Bach Reader,* ed. Hans. T. David and Arthur Mendel, 2nd ed. (1945;
         New York: W. W. Norton, 1966)

BWV   *Bach-Werke Verzeichnis.* Wolfgang Schmieder, *Thematisch-systematisches
         Verzeichnis der musikalischen Werke von Johann Sebastian Bach* (1950;
         Wiesbaden: Breitkopf & Härtel, 1969)

JAMS   *Journal of the American Musicological Society*

KB   Kritischer Bericht (Critical report of the NBA)

LKM   Arnold Schering, *Johann Sebastian Bachs Leipziger Kirchenmusik* (1936;
         Leipzig: Breitkopf & Härtel Musikverlag, 1954)

MQ   *The Musical Quarterly*

NBA   Neue Bach-Ausgabe. Johann Sebastian Bach, *Neue Ausgabe sämtlicher
         Werke* (since 1954)

Notes

Throughout this book, the notes give the original language of quoted passages only when a translation is problematic or when the source is not easily accessible. Unless otherwise indicated, translations are my own.

I. Introduction

1. Johann Gottfried Walther, *Musikalisches Lexikon* (Leipzig, 1732; facsim. Kassel: Bärenreiter, 1953), p. 79.

2. Ibid.

3. Bach's text, transmitted by two anonymous pupils in a manuscript dated 1738, is a free paraphrase of Friedrich Erhard Niedt's *Musicalische Handleitung . . . Erster-Teil* (Hamburg, 1700), chap. 2. See *BDok,* II, 333–334.

4. *BDok,* I, 127; Eng. trans. in *BR,* p. 111.

5. See Arnold Schering, *LKM,* p. 118, who reproduces an example of this scoring on pp. 205–206.

6. Philipp Spitta, *Johann Sebastian Bach,* 2 vols. (1873, 1880; Wiesbaden: Breitkopf & Härtel, 1970); translations adapted from Philipp Spitta, *Johann Sebastian Bach,* trans. Clara Bell and J. A. Fuller-Maitland, 3 vols. (London, 1889; New York: Dover, 1951), II, 996; I, xxviii; I, 710; II, 102; I, 711.

7. Charles Sanford Terry, *Bach's Orchestra* (London: Oxford University Press, 1932; rpt. 1972), p. 11.

8. Dart's foreword (1958) to Terry, *Bach's Orchestra,* pp. vii–viii.

9. Alfred Dürr, "Zur Chronologie der Leipziger Vokalwerke Johann Sebastian Bachs," *BJ,* 1957, pp. 5–162; revised and reissued as *Zur Chronologie der Leipziger Vokalwerke Johann Sebastian Bachs* (Kassel: Bärenreiter, 1976) and Georg von Dadelsen, *Beiträge zur Chronologie der Werke Johann Sebastian Bachs,* Tübinger Bach-Studien, vols. 4–5 (Trossingen: Hohner-Verlag, 1958).

10. The initial research led to my doctoral dissertation, "Basso Continuo Practice in the Vocal Works of J. S. Bach: A Study of the Original Performance Parts" (Columbia University, 1980). Beginning in 1976, I compiled a handlist

of manuscript sources for Bach's vocal works. Works that survive only in score received somewhat less attention. I sorted sets of parts and corresponding autograph scores into chronological layers, separating them by the watermarks on the various papers and by identifiable scribal hands. The critical notes to volumes of the NBA as well as Alfred Dürr's *Chronologie* and his *Studien über die frühen Kantaten Johann Sebastian Bachs* (1951; rev. ed. Wiesbaden: Breitkopf & Härtel, 1977) were my principal guides. In cases where the relevant volumes of the NBA had not yet appeared, I was fortunate to work with the unpublished notes of Hans-Joachim Schulze at the Bach-Archiv Leipzig. I also carried out my own informal investigations. Concerned chiefly with continuo parts, I became accustomed to recognizing Bach's hand in the thorough-bass figures. My dissertation also asserted the identity of the continuo figures written by Bach's chief copyists (Kuhnau and Meissner); I have since abandoned these claims and am now content to sort out Bach's hand from his copyists in the continuo figures. With few exceptions, I was able to examine the original sources, especially those housed in the two major Berlin collections. In addition, I inspected original sources in the Royal Library, Copenhagen, and in the Scheide Library at Princeton University. The remaining sources I have studied in photocopies or on microfilm, with the exception of three sets of parts from the Thomana collection, which were accessible in 1977 at the Bach-Archiv Leipzig. Appendix A represents a simplified version of this handlist that omits the identification of watermarks and copyists, for which the critical reports of the NBA are better suited.

11. I have only rarely been able to consider manuscript evidence from the works of other composers, the study of which naturally presents a fertile area for future research.

12. The cantatas are listed by their familiar numbering in Wolfgang Schmieder's *Thematisch-systematisches Verzeichnis der musikalischen Werke von Johann Sebastian Bach: Bach-Werke Verzeichnis* (1950; Wiesbaden: Breitkopf & Härtel, 1969; hereafter cited as BWV). Schmieder orders the works by genre and not by date of composition. The numbering of the cantatas follows the order in which they appeared in the Bach-Gesellschaft edition. Here, as elsewhere, a "Cantata" number is equivalent to a "BWV" number: Cantata 40 is the same as BWV 40.

13. I have relied on Robert Marshall, *The Compositional Process of J. S. Bach,* 2 vols. (Princeton, N.J.: Princeton University Press, 1972), pp. 4, 9, for a characterization of the various types of scores.

14. Throughout his life Bach collected and arranged the scores and parts for his more than 200 vocal works. At his death the manuscripts, which evidently had been kept under lock and key, were divided among his heirs. Scores were often separated from their accompanying parts in order to enable at least two sons working in different locales to perform one composition.

15. See Dürr, *Chronologie,* pp. 123, 64.

16. Appendix A generally follows this numbering whenever possible in order to simplify further research.

17. It is useful to distinguish two groups here: a core part-set, copied by the principal copyist directly from the score, and the duplicate parts copied by the auxiliary copyists from the core set.

18. I do not accept the view of Joshua Rifkin, who asserts that singers, unlike instrumentalists, only read one to a part. See a sample of this debate in his "Bach's 'Choruses'—Less than they seem?" *High Fidelity,* 32 (September 1982), pp. 42–45 and Robert L. Marshall's response in "Bach's 'Choruses' Reconstituted," *High Fidelity,* 32 (October 1982), pp. 64–66, 94.

19. The scribe referred to as "Anonymous Ic" (see Dürr, *Chronologie,* p. 150) must have been a somewhat older and more responsible copyist, for he had participated as a copyist since the tenure of the previous Thomas-Cantor, Johann Kuhnau. See Hans-Joachim Schulze, *Studien zur Bach-Überlieferung im 18. Jahrhundert* (Leipzig: Edition Peters, 1984), p. 122. Perhaps he was also a continuo organist, since he copied the transposed parts not only for Cantata 40 but also (in order of performance) for Cantatas 25, 48, 89, 60, 70, 154, 73, and 81. That is, from September 1723 through January 1724, this copyist was the one most often charged with the transposed part, perhaps because he himself played it.

II. The Organ and the Harpsichord

1. Schering, *LKM.*

2. Johann Philipp Kirnberger, *Grundsätze des Generalbasses* (Berlin, 1781), p. 64. The passage is translated in Arthur Mendel, "On the Keyboard Accompaniments to Bach's Leipzig Church Music," *MQ,* 36 (1950), p. 342.

3. J. S. Bach, *Actus Tragicus. Cantate: "Gottes Zeit ist die allerbeste Zeit,"* arranged by Robert Franz (Breslau: Leuckart, n.d.).

4. Franz refers to the disappointing criticisms of his efforts in *Offener Brief an Eduard Hanslick über Bearbeitungen älterer Tonwerke* (Leipzig, 1871), p. 9.

5. His open letter was reprinted in 1910 in Robert Franz, *Gesammelte Schriften über die Wiederbelebung Bach'scher und Händel'scher Werke,* ed. Robert Bethge (Leipzig, 1910) together with a number of Franz's important prefaces and examples of his arrangements. A preface by Otto Reubke, Franz's successor at Halle, indicates that even at this late date, some fifty years after Franz published his first arrangements, his point of view was still worth defending. Albert Schweitzer, *J. S. Bach* (Leipzig, 1908), p. 808, remarks, moreover, that Franz's "'practical arrangements,' and those that followed his lead, became the standard among lovers of Bach, and to some extent still remain the standard."

6. Heinrich Bellermann, "Robert Franz' Bearbeitungen älterer Tonwerke," *Allgemeine musikalische Zeitung,* 31–33 (Leipzig, 1872), pp. 489–495, 505–510, and 521–526, esp. p. 508; Friedrich Chrysander, "Händels Orgelbegleitung zu Saul und die neueste englische Ausgabe dieses Oratoriums," *Jahrbücher für musikalische Wissenschaft,* 1 (1863), pp. 408–428.

7. Spitta, I, 827–828.

8. These terms stem from the papal encyclical of 1864, *Quanta cura,* which

Bismarck exploited for German nationalist purposes. See J. A. S. Grenville, *Europe Reshaped, 1848–1878* (Ithaca, N.Y.: Cornell University Press, 1976), pp. 366–367.

9. Spitta, *Johann Sebastian Bach,* I, xxvii–xxviii.

10. Ibid., I, 717.

11. Ibid., I, 829, 830.

12. Ibid., I, 828, 830.

13. Ibid., I, 828, 830.

14. Ibid., II, 156–159.

15. Ibid., II, 773, 161. Spitta's earlier notion (I, 828) that Bach could have used the harpsichord at "rehearsals which did not take place in church" conflicts with a later statement (II, 774) that the Thomas-Schule never owned a harpsichord. Yet the Thomas-Schule is precisely where Spitta says the rehearsals must have taken place (II, 774). According to Spitta, then, Kittel must have been wrong on two counts: not only did he mean rehearsals instead of performances, but he intended the term "harpsichord" to be understood loosely. How Kittel could have so misled his readers remains unexplained.

16. Max Seiffert, "Praktische Bearbeitungen Bachscher Kompositionen," *BJ,* 1904, pp. 51–76, esp. p. 58.

17. Ibid., pp. 64–65.

18. In fact, the sources for these two cantatas are exceptional in that the organ parts contain *tacet*-markings. Curiously, there are no corresponding harpsichord parts for the movements in which the organ is silent. See the section on *tacet*-indications later in the chapter.

19. See the discussion that followed Seiffert's paper at the 1904 Bach-Fest as well as an article by W. Voigt in *BJ,* 1906, pp. 11–13.

20. In 1908 Bernhard Friedrich Richter, in an examination of the cantatas with concerted organ solos, argued with Seiffert that Bach must have conducted from the harpsichord in order to have the singers and players in full view. See Richter, "Über Seb. Bachs Kantaten mit obligater Orgel," *BJ,* 1908, pp. 50, 62. Albert Schweitzer, on the other hand, a progenitor of the "Orgel-Bewegung," attempted to summarize Spitta in the German version of his popular Bach study in 1908, asserting that "the only original instrument that can be considered in connection with the thorough-bass realization is the organ." Albert Schweitzer, *J. S. Bach* (1908; Leipzig: Breitkopf & Härtel, 1920), p. 808. While recognizing that a harpsichord existed in the organ gallery, he agrees that "it may have been used for rehearsals." But then echoing Spitta's qualifications that Bach may have directed performances from the harpsichord, Schweitzer quickly adjures: "But whatever may be thought of this hypothesis, we can be certain of the unshakable fact that the cantata was accompanied throughout by the organ." Stopping here, he fails to draw the inference of dual accompaniment.

21. Max Schneider, "Der Generalbass Johann Sebastian Bachs," *Jahrbuch der Musikbibliothek Peters,* 21–22 (1914–1915), pp. 28–30. But it is puzzling that Schneider writes that Bach "entrusted the [thorough-bass] accompaniment to *a* pupil," (emphasis added), which suggests that there was only one pupil for

the two instruments. One suspects that Schneider assumed some form of alternation between organ and harpsichord.

22. Ibid., pp. 27, 31–32.

23. Charles Sanford Terry, *Bach's Orchestra* (London: Oxford University Press, 1932; rpt. 1972), pp. 164–165.

24. Except possibly "when both chorus and orchestra were simultaneously in action." Ibid., p. 165.

25. Schering, *LKM,* p. 49.

26. Schering, "Über Bachs Parodieverfahren," *BJ,* 1921, pp. 49–95, esp. p. 52. In a footnote he states: "I might mention that in the course of my studies in recent years I have become more and more convinced that in the Leipzig church practice the harpsichord played a rare and subordinate role as an accompanying instrument and never seriously competed with the organ."

27. Schering, *LKM,* pp. 49–52.

28. Spitta, *Johann Sebastian Bach,* II, 857. Kuhnau used the term "Music," which clearly indicates the main concerted work performed during the service, that is, the cantata, oratorio, or passion. In jotting down notes on the order of the Leipzig church service on the 1st of Advent in 1723, Bach himself refers to the cantata as the "Hauptmusic" or "Music." The Custos at the Thomas-Kirche, Johann Christoph Rost, likewise uses the term, as in: "When, on the 1st Sunday in Advent, there is the 'Music,' then the Credo is not intoned." *BDok,* I, 248–249.

29. Schering (*LKM,* p. 84) does not share Spitta's view that they functioned as rehearsal parts.

30. Arthur Mendel, "Pitch in Western Music since 1500: A re-examination," *Acta Musicologica,* 50 (1978), pp. 13, 73.

31. Schering, *LKM,* p. 71. Spitta (II, 771) relates how an organ in Zittau built by Gottfried Silbermann in 1741 and pitched at *Cammerton* was still viewed as a curiosity in 1757.

32. Schering, *LKM,* pp. 121–123.

33. In the Bach scholarship since World War II, a compensatory source-critical spirit has prevailed, which, if anything, has tended to slight the seemingly subjective evidence of verbal testimony in favor of the hard evidence of manuscripts. In the literature, scholars generally cites Schering's study as the most complete treatment of the harpsichord question, even if they express reservations about certain of his conclusions. Nearly everyone reveals some blind spot toward the documents. (A notable exception is Werner Neumann, who called for a fresh reexamination in the course of his editorial work for the NBA. See NBA I/38, KB, pp. 128–129).

Arthur Mendel, for example, asserts that "[although] . . . some data have come to light since Spitta's time they mostly confirm his conclusions." Arthur Mendel, "On the Keyboard Accompaniments to Bach's Leipzig Church Music," *MQ,* 36 (1950), p. 340. Significantly, Mendel ignores Wild, Kittel, and Sicul, sources that bear directly on Bach's use of the harpsichord. He maintained this position at least until 1974 when, in the critical notes to his edition of the St. John Passion for the NBA, he tries to account for the extant harpsichord part, either connecting it with an organ repair or questioning whether it was even used. He cites a private communication from Alfred Dürr regarding previously unknown harpsichord parts for works performed in the 1740s and wonders if dual accompaniment "might therefore be a characteristic of Bach's late practice," again neglecting the well-known documents from the 1720s. See NBA II/4, KB, p. 98, n. 52.

Alfred Dürr deals with the controversy tangentially in the context of his work on Bach's performance of the *Trauer-Ode* (Cantata 198), in which the composer is reported to have directed this piece from the harpsichord while someone else played the organ. Alfred Dürr, "Bachs Trauer-Ode und Markus-Passion," *Neue Zeitschrift für Music,* Jg. 124, vol. 12 (1963), pp. 462–463. Given this unambiguous reference to dual accompaniment, Dürr allows that Bach may have used it elsewhere but only if he directed from his score at the harpsichord. But arguing against this possibility, he points out Emanuel Bach's statement that his father "from his youth until his . . . old age" directed his ensemble from the violin, not the keyboard. Thus, for Dürr, the question of regular dual accompaniment remains open. Yet if he had quoted the familiar documents about the student harpsichordists (Wild and Kittel), one can imagine a different conclusion. Dürr reiterates his skepticism in the introduction to his two-volume set, *Die Kantaten von Johann Sebastian Bach* (Kassel: Bärenreiter, 1971), p. 69. Most recently (*BJ,* 1982, pp. 160–161), he considers my theory of dual accompaniment as proposed in "Zur Frage der Cembalo-Mitwirkung in den geistlichen Werken Bachs," *Bachforschung und Bachinterpretation heute,* ed. Reinhold Brinkmann (Kassel, 1981), pp. 178–184. He asks how two *Cammerton* continuo parts could have been shared among the already large number of bass players Bach cites as desirable in his Memorandum to the Town Council of 1730 and questions, moreover, whether contemporary documents will ever clearly answer the question, since they may reflect practices that change with time.

In his "Basso Continuo on the Organ," *Music and Letters,* 50 (1969), p. 230, Peter Williams repeats Schering's claim that the *Trauungspositiv* may have been pitched at *Cammerton* but does not accept that it accompanied the introit motets, terming this thesis "a little too ingenious." He doubts, however, that figured *Cammerton* parts point to any regular harpsichord participation. (Like Mendel and Dürr, Williams neglects the testimony concerning the student harpsichordists.) Instead, the figured *Cammerton* parts might be "the source for the transposing copyist, a practice part, a bass part for the string-player used to ignoring figures or a bass part for a cellist who might play chords" (p. 231). By referring to the prices paid for certain Leipzig harpsichords, Williams also implies that the church instruments were probably smallish and were probably not heard anyway by the congregation (pp. 233–234). (Against this, Bach's predecessor, Johann Kuhnau, called the harpsichords "die grossen Clavicimbeln," a description he would not have used if they were merely small spinets.) More recently, in his article on "Continuo" for *The New Grove Dictionary* (1980), vol. 4, p. 696, Williams speculates that the unfigured continuo parts might have been "used by harpsichordists in rehearsal, to save the bellows-blower." Although plausible at first glance, this suggestion would mean that, at the performance, the keyboardist would have been confronted with an organ part a whole tone lower—a strangely cruel task for Bach to impose on his organist. Conceding that "the matter cannot be irrefutably solved," Williams still concludes that "the use of the harpsichord, however discreetly played, can be regarded as unjustifiable in Bach cantatas if they are to be performed as in their original liturgical setting."

It is also of interest that many twentieth-century performers—particularly those hostile to "Early Music"—continue to subscribe to an alternation between organ and harpsichord in Bach's sacred vocal works despite the lack of any scholarly support in the Bach literature. Julius Rietz's preface to the Bach-Gesellschaft edition of the St. Matthew Passion (from the 1850s) is the likely source for this still influential practice (BG, vol. 4). According to Rietz, the harpsichord "with certainty accompanied the recitatives" alone. In fact, the only surviving harpsichord part from the Passion belonged to the second choir and did not include any recitatives.

34. Thomas-Cantor Sebastian Knüpfer (d. 1677) had purchased the instrument for the Thomas-Kirche in 1672. It is not known when an instrument came into the Nikolai-Kirche, but it must have arrived sometime before 1709. Schering, *LKM,* pp. 61–64.

35. Spitta, II, 857. Concerning the 300 Thalers' "interest," one imagines some fund of capital willed from an estate, from which the accrued interest was earmarked for a specific purpose. See *BDok,* II, 113 for one such example. Remarks in the church records from 1722–1723 indicate harpsichord repairs, less frequent tunings, and finally a repair with new strings "since [the harpsichord] was completely broken down and unusable." Williams ("Basso Continuo on the Organ," p. 234) may be right that Kuhnau used the harpsichord in his later years only for special occasions. But Williams also confuses quarterly payments with tunings, for the tuners were remunerated at set intervals (such as annually or quarterly) rather than being paid for each tuning.

36. "Weil er 'ein *apartes Accompagnement* mit einem Clavecimbel,' wie es in Leipzig und andern vornehmen Orten gebräuchlich sei, auch für seine Passions-, Auferstehungs- und die meisten solennen Musiken 'höchst nötig' erachtete." The instrument was subsequently purchased for the church. See Ernst Müller, "Musikgeschichte von Freiberg," in *Mitteilungen des Freiberger Altertumsverein,* ed. Walther Herrman, vol. 68 (Freiberg, 1939), p. 37. My thanks to Christoph Wolff for pointing out this reference. Further support is offered by Johann Samuel Petri (1738–1808) in his discussion of sacred performance practice in the *Anleitung zur practischen Musik* (Lauban, 1767). An acquaintance of Wilhelm Friedemann Bach's, Petri states that "the harpsichordist (if one is there) should accompany and, especially at *piano* markings play as short as possible" (p. 42). Again, this should not be taken as proof of Bach's practice but as another indication of the casual—that is, uncontroversial—manner in which mentions of the harpsichord in sacred accompaniments occur. In

the later, much expanded edition of his book (Leipzig, 1782), Petri implies that the harpsichord *or* the organ might accompany sacred music, thereby refraining from endorsing dual accompaniment proper (p. 169).

37. "Das Clavicymbel mit seiner Université gibt ein accompagnirendes, fast unentbehrliches Fundament zu Kirchen- Theatral- und Cammer-Music ab, und ist recht Wunder, dass man hiesiges Ortes die schnarrenden höchst eckelhaften Regalen in den Kirchen noch beybehält, da doch die säuselnde und lispende Harmonie des Clavicymbels, wo man deren sonderlich 2. haben kan, eine weit schönere Würckung auff dem Chor hat." Johann Mattheson, *Das neueröffnete Orchestre* (Hamburg, 1713), p. 263. English trans. adapted from Williams, "Basso Continuo on the Organ," p. 234.

38. Johann Mattheson, *Der vollkommene Capellmeister* (Hamburg, 1739; facsim. Kassel: Bärenreiter, 1954), p. 484. English trans. in Ernest C. Harriss, *Johann Mattheson's 'Der vollkommene Capellmeister'* (Ann Arbor, Mich.: UMI Research Press, 1981), p. 870.

39. Spitta, I, 828; Mendel, "Keyboard Accompaniments," p. 343; Williams, "Basso Continuo on the Organ," pp. 234–235.

40. "Acta Den verledigten Cantorat Dienst Betr: alhier in Weissenfels 1724," Stadtarchiv Weissenfels, A I 1974, pp. 21–22, cited in Hans-Joachim Schulze, "Zur Frage des Doppelaccompagnements (Orgel und Cembalo) in Kirchenmusikaufführungen der Bach-Zeit," *BJ*, 1987, pp. 173–174. I am grateful to Hans-Joachim Schulze for sending me his article in advance of publication.

41. *BDok*, II, 121–122 and Schering, *LKM*, pp. 62–65.

42. *BDok*, II, 122–123.

43. English trans. from *BR*, pp. 96–97; *BDok*, II, 140.

44. Neither a harpsichord nor an organ part survives from the first performance of the St. John Passion. There is, however, a part labeled *Cembalo* (St 111/23) that dates from the third or fourth traceable performance of the work near the end of Bach's career, which may well have been copied from an earlier harpsichord part. By that time the Passion had undergone considerable revisions, and Bach had either overloaded the earlier parts with inserts or, as he probably did here, discarded the old part after ordering a new part copied which incorporated the latest revisions. Further evidence for an earlier harpsichord part can be adduced from *tasto solo* markings mistakenly copied into St 111/21, a continuo part originally from the first performance. (The marking *tasto solo* instructs a keyboardist to play the bass line without continuo realization.) The exemplar for this part (used also to transfer dynamic markings) can only have been a keyboard part. Since organ parts had to be transposed, they did not generally serve as exemplars for other continuo parts. It follows that the earlier *tasto solo* markings stem from a harpsichord part.

45. Terry, *Bach's Orchestra*, p. 165; Schering, *LKM*, pp. 84, 89–96; Dürr, NBA I/10, KB, p. 46; Dürr, *Die Kantaten von Johann Sebastian Bach*, I, 69.

46. Schering, *LKM*, pp. 89–96: ". . . man hat doch continuirlich darauf gespielt, ohngeacht fortgebaut worden . . ." (p. 91).

47. Schering, *LKM*, p. 92; *BDok*, II, 439.

48. *BR*, pp. 111–112. *BDok*, I, 127.

49. It was actually Wild who penned the recommendation and Bach who affixed his signature. See the commentary in *BDok*, I, 128. Perhaps Bach dictated the contents to Wild to spare himself the chore. Whatever the reason, Wild would hardly have had the audacity to invent the text himself, nor could he conceivably have written anything false that Bach was to read and sign. It is also hard to imagine why Wild might lie about his harpsichord playing.

50. Schering suspiciously withheld any mention of Wild until after he had associated the harpsichord with Italian opera and had arrived at his belated hypothesis of the *Motettencembalo*. His reference to the Wild recommendation occurs only in a footnote, and then as "evidence" that Wild accompanied only the German motets (*LKM*, p. 135).

51. Adapted from *BR*, p. 266: "Wenn Seb. Bach eine Kirchenmusik aufführte, so musste allemal einer von seiner fähigsten Schülern auf dem Flügel accompagnieren. Man kann wohl vermuten, dass man sich da mit einem magern Generalbassbegleitung ohnehin nicht vor wagen durfte. Demohnerachtet musste man sich immer darauf gefasst halten, dass sich oft plötzlich Bachs Hände und Finger unter die Hände und Finger des Spielers mischten und, ohne diesen weiter zu geniren, das Accompagnement mit Massen von Harmonien ausstaffierten, die noch mehr imponierten, als die unvermuthete nahe Gegenwart des strengen Lehrers." Johann Christian Kittel, *Der angehende praktische Organist, Dritte Abtheilung* (Erfurt, 1808), p. 33.

52. Kittel's anecdote is so damning to the standard view excluding the harpsichord that nearly everyone discounts his testimony. Spitta doubts Kittel's memory and contends that, if he is at all credible, then he must be referring to rehearsals, since the scene invoked by the recollection is too fantastic to have occurred at a performance. (Spitta, I, 712, 830; II, 612, 773–774.) In the main text (I, 712), moreover, Spitta omits the crucial phrase—"When Sebastian Bach performed a cantata"—relegating this only to the endnote (I, 830). Later (II, 773) he goes out of his way to discount Kittel, claiming that in Bach's final years, the harpsichord in the Thomas-Kirche had been removed. But, as was shown, it was the church records detailing the allocated payments that were missing: the instrument itself remained in the Thomas-Kirche until it became unplayable in 1756. The verb *aufführen* (to perform) is, moreover, entirely unambiguous. Terry (*Bach's Orchestra*, p. 164) gives the text in its entirety but follows Spitta's view: Since Kittel "was nearly eighty when he published the statement . . . it is obvious that such incidents . . . occurred at general rehearsals in the gallery of one or other of the churches, and not at a public performance." Schering (p. 134) uses Kittel to support his notion of the *Motettencembalo* and claims that he refers to the performance of the introit motets. Like Spitta, Schering suppresses Kittel's explicit language in the opening phrase. As Schering well knew, "eine Kirchenmusik" only refers to a concerted piece of sacred music. In any event, the elementary chordal realization required by the old-fashioned motets could scarcely have occasioned the dramatic intervention of the composer. Finally, Arthur Mendel and Hans David unaccountably contribute to this suspicious cover-up in the *Bach Reader* when they too fail to translate the same opening clause (p. 266). It is difficult to excuse this omission as an

accident; for even if Mendel and David had never read Kittel's own text, their source for the translation can be none other than Spitta's footnote, which renders the passage intact. Kittel makes no mention of the organ, but no one doubts that it was a regular participant. This is why the anecdote constitutes one of the strongest pieces of evidence in favor of dual accompaniment.

53. *BR*, p. 231; *BDok*, II, 331–332.

54. Yet Gesner's flattering remarks probably stemmed from real situations that he observed. A collection of reminiscences passed down from pupils of the Thomas-Schule and compiled by Johann Friedrich Köhler around 1775 still recalled that Gesner had been "very affable and kind in his relations with the pupils, visited them even in their singing rehearsals (where Rectors otherwise did not often come), and listened with pleasure to their performances of cantatas [*die aufgeführten Kirchenstücke*]." *BDok*, III, 315.

55. Schering, *LKM*, p. 138. He also ridicules the example in order to discard the possibility that Bach directed from the harpsichord.

56. The terms *symphonicis,* translated here as "musicians," does not exclude vocalists, as in *puer symphonicus,* a choir boy.

57. Translation adapted from *BR,* p. 113: "Also liess auch darauf die Trauer-Music, so diessmal der Herrn Capellmeister Johann Sebastian Bach nach Italiänischer Art componieret hatte, mit Clave di Cembalo, welches Herr Bach selbst spielete, Orgel, Violes di Gamba, Lauten, Violinen, Fleutes douces und Fleutes traverse &c." *BDok,* II, 176.

58. NBA I/38, KB, p. 126.

59. The views of Gottsched's influential *Deutsche Gesellschaft* were propagated by the chief instigator for the celebration, Carl von Kirchbach, a student at the University of Leipzig, who belonged to the "German Society."

60. Gottsched set great store by distinct and nonoverlapping genres. The "euphony of the ode," according to a contemporary description, "consists chiefly in the equal length of its sections." Even Bach's pupil Lorenz Mizler, commenting on Gottsched's *Versuch einer kritischen Dichtkunst* ten years later, agreed that confusing ode and cantata "is very unnatural." See Werner Neumann in NBA I/38, KB, p. 125.

61. Although Bach nowhere else treats the lute as a continuo instrument, it is inconceivable, given the traditions of the instrument, that a lutenist would not have realized chords when confronted with a bass line. See Chapter 5.

62. NBA I/38, KB, p. 128.

63. Schering, *LKM,* p. 72.

64. See the engraving of Johann Kuhnau directing at the Thomas-Kirche, paper-roll(s) in hand, in Schering, *LKM,* Tafel II and Tafel III. The latter is the frontispiece to J. G. Walther's *Musikalisches Lexikon* (1732; Kassel: Bärenreiter, 1953).

65. *BR,* p. 222; *BDok,* III, 87.

66. *BR,* p. 277; *BDok,* III, 285.

67. C. P. E. Bach, *Essay on the True Art of Playing Keyboard Instruments,* trans. William J. Mitchell (New York: W. W. Norton, 1949), p. 35; C. P. E. Bach, *Versuch über die wahre Art das Clavier zu spielen* (Berlin, 1753; facsim. Leipzig: VEB

Breitkopf & Härtel, 1976), p. 8. Moreover, it is Emanuel's experience that the keyboard will always remain the visual signal of the beat ("das Clavier allezeit das Augenmerck des Tactes seyn und bleiben wird") (p. 6). It is J. J. Quantz who prefers that a violinist lead the ensemble. See *On Playing the Flute,* trans. Edward R. Reilly (London: Faber, 1966), p. 208; *Versuch einer Anweisung die Flöte traversiere zu spielen* (Berlin, 1752).

68. This methodological position differs from an inductivist approach—common in Bach studies—which supposes that an explanation (such as dual accompaniment) must emerge independently and conclusively from the source evidence, while affecting, as it were, an amnesia toward the written documents. But this strategy fails even as satisfactory empiricism, since the "objective" starting point for judging the source evidence maintains that the organ alone accompanies Bach sacred works "until otherwise notified." This assumption, however, has been controlled by the controversy and stacks the deck. An imagined demand for an inductive argument from the sources "proving" dual accompaniment therefore conceals its own prejudices against the harpsichord.

69. Although many of Bach's autograph scores contain a smattering of assorted figures, they apparently represent the composer's shorthand notation during the compositional process and are not relevant to performance. Ordinarily, the copyists did not expect to find figures when they wrote out the continuo parts, although they often unthinkingly transmitted whatever figures they happened to encounter adjacent to the continuo line in the score. Therefore, when Bach went to the trouble of entering a consistent set of figures in one of his scores, he probably intended a keyboardist to play directly from it. Of course in Leipzig, should Bach himself have played from a score at the harpsichord, the figures would have been unnecessary. In five Weimar cantatas (BWV 182, BWV 12, BWV 199, BWV 132, BWV 155), Bach's autograph scores contain a significant number of figures, a fact which suggests that they were used at the organ. See NBA I/5, p. xii, for a facsimile of one page of the score for BWV 155. Unlike at Leipzig, *Chorton* was the performing pitch at Weimar, so that transposition was unnecessary. The absence of corresponding organ parts in these Weimar part-sets supports this interpretation. (See Appendix B.) Moreover, in the score for BWV 182, one finds an indication *volti presto,* meaning "turn the page quickly," a meaningless directive unless someone besides Bach played from the score. On the other hand, the marking *volti* occurs too frequently in Bach's scores for it to be significant; it is the extra adverb and the figures that signal a special situation.

70. For example, an autograph *forte* marking (Movement 3, m. 25) is placed rather high to avoid the continuo figures that were already present. Another figure (Movement 5, m. 81) is noticeably squeezed in at an angle to accommodate the scribe's continuo figures on the line below.

71. See the seventh eighth note in m. 57. In Facsimile 2-2, this measure is located on the penultimate line in the next to last bar, while in Facsimile 2-3 it is located in the second bar of the last line. Note that the copyist in the harpsichord part has transferred Bach's natural sign from the organ part, whereas, in fact, to denote a raised third above d (that is, an f♯), he should have written a sharp. In

general, copyists faithfully copy their exemplars, thereby making either errors of omission—skipping a figure or one numeral in a configuration—or errors of commission—misreading a figure, such as substituting a flat for the number 6. Errors of transposition occur when the copyist—not necessarily conversant in thorough bass—fails to make necessary changes allowing for the difference in key between a *Cammerton* and a *Chorton* part. More experienced copyists, such as J. A. Kuhnau or C. G. Meissner, tried to make the necessary adjustments, although these mistakes occur easily, given the mechanical nature of copying. When Bach figured a part, he seems most often to have figured the part from memory without referring to the score. Mendel voices this opinion in NBA, KB II/4, p. 183, and cites several interesting examples. Bach's mistakes are therefore of a different order; they scarcely ever involve transposition errors or ungrammatical figures. Instead, they result from a less than perfect memory. When Bach figured a second continuo part, he must have thought it less tedious to figure it from scratch than to laboriously duplicate his first set of figures. In this way one can best account for two sets of figures that differ significantly in orthography but are comparable in substance. No copyist could have presumed to "reformulate" the spelling to the extent that Bach did when he figured two parts separately. The last page of the *Cammerton* part for BWV 109 is exceptional in this regard: here, Bach apparently found it more convenient to copy the somewhat sparse figures from the organ part into the harpsichord part.

72. Quantz, *On Playing the Flute* (p. 211), remarks that the cellist and violonist can sit at the right and left of the harpsichordist.

73. My reading of the sources for Cantata 6 runs counter to the opinion of Alfred Dürr, who believes that the figures in the transposed part are copied from the *Cammerton* exemplar. Dürr also believes that the title page inscription—*Cembalo*—is in the hand of W. F. Bach or the later J. S. Bach. (NBA I/10, KB, p. 39.) One wonders if Dürr's dating of Bach's hand may have been motivated by his justifiable discomfort caused by two extant keyboard parts. As he puts it (KB, p. 46): "The surviving performance materials for the basso continuo might have stemmed from two different performances, for nothing forces us to assume that harpsichord and organ were used simultaneously. Instead, the [*Cammerton*] part bearing the title *Continuo* could have first been prepared for a string instrument and the figures and *Cembalo* inscription could derive from a later time, when, for some reason, the organ did not play continuo. The *pizzicato* marking in Movement 2, which cannot of course apply to the harpsichord, alludes to this. While this assumption is by no means compelling, it simply will not do to cite the present set of parts as proof for a simultaneous use of organ and harpsichord at the performance of this cantata." Dürr may therefore have interpreted the philological evidence in a way that served the dichotomy of the harpsichord controversy.

74. See Hans-Joachim Schulze, "Zur Rückkehr einiger autographer Kantatenfragmente in die Bach-Sammlung der Deutschen Staatsbibliothek Berlin," *BJ,* 1977, pp. 132–134; see also Christoph Wolff, "Bachs Leipziger Kantoratsprobe und die Aufführungsgeschichte der Kantate 'Du wahrer Gott und Davids Sohn,' BWV 23," *BJ,* 1978, pp. 78–94.

75. Wolff, "Kantoratsprobe," pp. 86–87. Wolff notes that another applicant

for the cantorate, Christoph Graupner, had also made use of two keyboard instruments in his audition pieces. Two figured *Chorton* parts survive from both cantatas he performed at Leipzig, which means that Graupner's secondary keyboard instrument, unlike Bach's, must have been a small *Positiv* organ.

76. The following observations are proof of this. The figures in the *Cembalo* part originally contained sharps in mm. 4, 7, and 8 designating major thirds built above c♯ and b♮. In transforming this part into an organ part one half-step lower, Bach altered the sharps to natural signs, which was necessary in order to realize the same thirds above c♮ and b♭. It was this set of *post-correcturam* figures with natural signs that was mindlessly copied into the cello part. Over the continuo notes d and c (with a key signature of two flats), the figures ought to contain sharps and not natural signs. Moreover, one can identify a copyist's hand rather than Bach's from the square tails on the natural signs and the sharp corners of the sevens and fours uncharacteristic of the composer.

77. But why did the copyist enter figures only in the final movement of the cantata? As Christoph Wolff points out ("Kantoratsprobe," pp. 90–91), if the harpsichordist accompanied from the autograph score, he would only have been able to accompany three movements of the piece, since the score did not contain the fourth and final movement.

78. See NBA II/4, KB, esp. pp. 181–185, which includes a facsimile of the harpsichord part. Mendel claims that, because of the errors, the "player could not have made much use of it."

79. Winfried Schrammek, "Fragen des Orgelgebrauchs in Bachs Aufführrungen der Matthäus-Passion," *BJ*, 1975, pp. 114–123; *BDok*, II, 141.

80. In making this claim, I assume that all other keyboard instruments— such as the School *Positiv* or the portable *Trauungspositiv*—were pitched in *Chorton*.

81. Walther, *Lexikon,* p. 595.

82. Dürr bases his opinion on an autograph *pizzicato* marking in Movement 57, which clearly indicates that the part was used by a string player. See NBA II/6, KB, p. 172. But this does not preclude the participation of the harpsichord at the first performance, as shown by shared parts such as *Bassono e Cembalo*.

83. The abbreviation JLB is commonly used to refer to these works. See Dürr, *Zur Chronologie der Leipziger Vokalwerke Johann Sebastian Bachs* (Kassel: Bärenreiter, 1975), p. 161.

84. Andreas Glöckner, "Johann Sebastian Bachs Aufführungen zeitgenössischer Passionsmusiken," *BJ*, 1977, pp. 76–78. The presence of a harpsichord in the Weimar Schlosskirche is documented by a payment for a repair in March of 1717. See Reinhold Jauernig, "Johann Sebastian Bach in Weimar," in *Johann Sebastian Bach in Thüringen* (Weimar, 1950), p. 70. In general, however, no evidence speaks for its regular use in cantata accompaniments there.

85. This set of parts together with the autograph score first surfaced in 1931. See Hans T. David, "A Lesser Secret of J. S. Bach Uncovered," *JAMS,* 14 (1961), pp. 199–223. See also the preface to the edition of the Sanctus, ed. Hermann Harrassowitz, *Die Kantate,* vol. 187 (Stuttgart-Hohenheim: Hänssler-Verlag, 1963).

86. Schering, *LKM,* pp. 52, 88.

87. See Christoph Wolff, *Der stile antico in der Musik Johann Sebastian Bachs* (Wiesbaden, 1968), p. 171, where Wolff supposed that the harpsichord part either was designed as a rehearsal part or was used at another church.

88. Robert L. Marshall identified the copyist in preparing his critical notes to NBA I/19 and kindly shared this information in advance of publication.

89. The *Cammerton* part from Cantata 19 also contains better and more complete figures than the corresponding autograph figures in the organ part, if the figures in the *Cammerton* part are indeed autograph.

90. "Weil nun aber, ohne solches zu verstehen, es einem schwer ankommt, einen festen Grund in der Music, und insonderheit im General-Bass, zu legen, oder auch, wie es offt vorfällt, einen unbezifferten Bass zu accompagniren." David Kellner, *Treulicher Unterricht im General-Bass* (1732; Hamburg, 1737), p. 29. Similar statements alluding to unfigured parts populate the literature. C. P. E. Bach, for example, writes: "Every composer who really wants his work well accompanied is required to figure the bass part correctly and completely. Any possible rules for realizing unfigured basses are inadequate and often wrong." *Versuch* (Berlin, 1762), II, 11.

91. Appendix A details which movements are figured in works with incompletely figured continuo parts.

92. The parts with figures only in the recitatives inspired Schering's theory of the accompanied violoncello recitatives. See Schering, *LKM,* pp. 106–110. Believing figures absolutely necessary to any thorough-bass realization, he could not fathom why the organ would only play in recitatives, even though these were *Chorton* continuo parts. He thus imagined that the cellists accompanied these recitatives chordally, assuming mistakenly that chordal technique on the cello was as developed as on the viola da gamba. He buttressed his argument with a description from 1774 of "cello recitative" by Johann Baumgärtner, which, however, renders only the most simple and idiomatic chords on the cello—a far cry from the chromatic vocabulary of Bach's recitatives. But it is unlikely that the Leipzig cellists—members of the Kunst-Geiger whose mediocre qualities Bach found so irksome—would have had any knowledge of thorough bass, much less the technique to manage such a difficult task. Furthermore, Schering cannot explain why the cellists would play from a *Chorton* part nor how they would retune their instruments for the recitative movements. Already in 1956, Alfred Dürr suggested that a continuo part with figures present only in the recitatives was doubtless a simplification for an experienced organ player. NBA I/10, KB, p. 92. Consider, in this connection, Cantata 48. Here Bach figured both the *Cammerton* and *Chorton* continuo parts, but only in Movement 2, an accompanied recitative containing somewhat complex harmonic progressions. The opening chorus, two four-part chorales, two solo arias, and a secco recitative all remain unfigured. Can one really imagine a performance of these movements without continuo? After all, Bach went to the trouble of having the organ part transposed and even himself figured the same movement in two parts. Most likely he was pressed for time because of the hectic preparations for a performance and made a quick decision to figure the most problematic sections in both parts, leaving the continuo players to fend for

themselves in the remaining movements. If such emergency measures seem unlikely, consider further that, in later performances of this same work, the composer never returned to the continuo parts to remedy the obvious deficiencies.

93. Cue staves are found regularly in Bach's continuo parts but are by no means indicated in every recitative.

94. NBA I/13, KB, pp. 67–68, 73, 81–83.

95. C. P. E. Bach, *Versuch*, II, 1–2.

96. Movement 7 was also marked *tacet*. The *tacet*-indications were subsequently crossed out for a later performance that took place after 1742.

97. Arguments for a proposed dating of these pieces are advanced in my article "J. S. Bach's Experiment in Differentiated Accompaniment: Tacet Indications in the Organ Parts to the Vocal Works," *JAMS,* 32 (1979), pp. 323–332. See also Alfred Dürr's remarks in NBA I/15, KB, pp. 87–88. Wilhelm Rust's remarks on the *tacet*-indications are found in the preface to BG, 22 (Leipzig, 1872 [1875]), p. xv; Schering's discussion is found in *LKM*, pp. 102–106.

98. NBA I/30, p. ix, reproduces a page of the organ part for Cantata 130 in which the *tacet*-indication occurs.

99. Alfred Dürr and others hear the pizzicato strings as the chiming of funeral bells. Dürr, *Kantaten*, II, 452.

100. C. P. E. Bach, *Versuch*, II, 2.

101. This view originated with Bernhard Friedrich Richter, "Über Seb. Bachs Kantaten mit obligater Orgel" in BJ, 1908, p. 58, but his guess presumed Spitta's now disproved dating of 1731 for the cantatas in question. In his *Beiträge zur Chronologie der Werke Johann Sebastian Bachs,* Tübinger Bach-Studien, vols. 4–5 (Trossingen: Hohner-Verlag, 1958), p. 32, Georg von Dadelsen corrects Spitta's dating but maintains Richter's claim that Bach composed the obbligatos for Wilhelm Friedemann. Alfred Dürr mentions the possibility most recently in *Kantaten*, I, p. 54.

102. See my article "The Metaphorical Soloist: Concerted Organ parts in Bach's Cantatas," *Early Music*, 13 (1985), p. 238; also printed in *J. S. Bach as Organist,* ed. George Stauffer and Ernest May (Bloomington, Ind.: Indiana University Press, 1986).

103. The organ part for Cantata 194 in A♭ *Chorton* takes over parts previously assigned to the Oboe 1 (in Movement 3) and Oboe 2 (in Movement 10) and is not included in this tabulation.

104. Separate transposed obbligato parts survive only from the later pieces (composed after 1731). It is also possible, although unlikely, that original obbligato parts have been lost.

105. Jakob Adlung, *Anleitung zu der musikalischen Gelahrtheit* (Erfurt, 1758), pp. 489–490. I am grateful to Philip Swanton for pointing out to me that this practice was not unconventional, and, additionally, that the use of the pedal in continuo accompaniment is documented from Viadana and Praetorius through to Adlung, Türk, Schröter, and their contemporaries.

106. Schering, *LKM,* pp. 88–89.

107. Jean-Jacques Rousseau, *Dictionnaire de musique* (Paris, 1768), Planche G, fig. I, and J. J. Quantz, *Versuch,* chap. 17, sec. I, par. 13.

108. C. P. E. Bach, *Versuch,* II, 315.

109. Commenting on Emanuel Bach's recommendations regarding harpsichords in church is one dissenting observer from the latter half of the eighteenth century. In his *Neue Wahrnehmungen zur Aufnahme und weiterer Ausbreitung der Music* (Berlin, 1784), p. 8, Christian Carl Rolle writes: "To be sure, introducing the harpsichord into church music is most advisable. But whereas in theater music the sound rises [from the orchestra pit], the sound must descend from the organ loft in church music. The participation of the harpsichord therefore gives no special, emphatic support." See Spitta, II, 161. Spitta also remarks (II, 771) that Rolle's treatise received harshly negative reviews from his contemporaries "and was soon forgotten." Nevertheless, it is important to note that Rolle favors the harpsichord in church: his objection to it is an acoustic one.

110. C. P. E. Bach, *Versuch,* II, 2.

111. For an interpretation of this attitude in the Early Music movement, see my article "Early Music Defended against Its Devotees: A Theory of Historical Performance in the Twentieth Century," *MQ,* 69 (1983), pp. 297–322, esp. pp. 299–306.

III. The Accompaniment of Recitatives

1. Johann Gottfried Walther, *Musikalisches Lexicon* (Leipzig, 1732; facsim. Kassel: Bärenreiter, 1953), p. 515.

2. On telescoping cadences, see Robert Donington, *The Interpretation of Early Music* (1963; rev. ed. London: Faber and Faber, 1975), pp. 210–211; Jack A. Westrup, "The Cadence in Baroque Recitative," *Natalica Musicologica Knud Jeppesen* (Copenhagen, 1962), pp. 243–252; Sven Hansell, "The Cadence in 18th-Century Recitative," *MQ,* 54 (1968), p. 228.

3. Schering, *LKM,* p. 110.

4. Schering, *LKM,* p. 111; Arthur Mendel, "On the Keyboard Accompaniments to Bach's Leipzig Church Music," *MQ,* 36 (1950), pp. 339–362; also Mendel, ed., J. S. Bach, *The Passion according to St. John* (New York: Schirmer, 1951), pp. xvi–xx; Jack A. Westrup, "The Continuo in the 'St. Matthew Passion,'" *Bach-Gedenkschrift 1950* (Zürich: Atlantis Verlag, 1950), pp. 103–117, esp. pp. 115–116; Friedrich-Heinrich Neumann, "Die Theorie des Rezitativs im 17. und 18. Jahrhundert" (diss., Göttingen, 1955), pp. 360–372.

5. Peter Williams, "Basso Continuo on the Organ," *Music and Letters,* 50 (1969), p. 240.

6. Ingrid Smit Duyzenkunst, *De Uitvoeringspraktijk van het Recitatief in de 17e en 18e Eeuw,* Scripta Musicologica Ultrajectina IV (Utrecht, 1973), pp. 52–54.

7. Emil Platen, "Aufgehoben oder ausgehalten? Zur Ausführung der Rezitativ-Continuopartien in J. S. Bachs Kirchenmusik," *Bachforschung und Bachinterpretation heute. Bericht über das Bachfest-Symposium 1978 der Philipps-Universität Marburg* (Kassel: Bärenreiter, 1981), pp. 167–177.

8. In fact, each secco movement in the continuo parts for BWV 30a is consistently notated in short values. The NBA does not follow this reading be-

cause of pasted strips that concealed these movements after Bach reused the parts for his sacred parody, BWV 30. See the discussion that follows in the text. Of the two other examples in Platen's group, BWV 197 survives only in score, while BWV 246 (the St. Luke Passion) is a work by another composer.

9. Platen ("Aufgehoben," p. 177) allows one exception to a literal rendition. Citing a treatise—not a preferred method elsewhere in his argument—he suggests that the organist may have shortened the chords in the right hand in order to mitigate the raw, sustained quality of the sound.

10. "Das Recitative ist ein neuer und gantz a parter Stylus, welcher, weil er ohne dis meist ohne Instrumenta gehet, in allen zu sagen Ex Lex bleibet, indem er weder die ordentlichen Resolutiones . . . weder Tact noch andere gewöhnliche Legalitäten in acht nimmt." Johann David Heinichen, *Neu erfundene und Gründliche Anweisung . . . zu vollkommener Erlernung des General-Basses* (Hamburg, 1711), p. 214.

11. The recitative originated a century before in Italy. Heinrich Schütz, as early as 1619 in the *Psalmen Davids* and in 1623 in his *Historia der Auferstehung Jesu Christi,* had introduced elements of the recitative to Germany. In Schütz's principal early usage, the reciting voice freely intones over one held chord, a scheme that lacks the inflected harmonic vocabulary of the later style. The Evangelist's recitatives in Schütz's *Die sieben Worte* (ca. 1645) occasionally approach the later genre of secco, but they are notated in much slower note values. The three Passions that Schütz composed from about 1653 to 1666 extend the evangelist's recitatives in an entirely new direction, setting the texts in neo-Gregorian chant and dispensing with all continuo accompaniment. The genre that was known in the eighteenth century as *recitativo semplice* only coalesced in the early 1700s after the recitative became distinct from the arioso. That is, the rapidly declaimed recitative, imitating prose speech rhythms, ceded all lyrical functions to the aria and arioso. Comparing this development with the earlier *stylus recitativus* of Schütz, it is difficult to establish a direct lineage to the newer Italianate type adopted in Germany around 1700. Simple recitative was first termed "secco" or "dry" recitative by nonprofessional writers on music in the late eighteenth century. For the early history of this terminological shift, see Thomas Baumann, "Benda, the Germans, and Simple Recitative," *JAMS,* 34 (1981), pp. 119–131, esp. pp. 126–129.

12. "Die Manier und Weise aber, das Recitativ wohl zu tractiren, ist denen Instrumenten nach, worauf es tractiret wird, auch sehr unterschieden. In Kirchen-Recitativ, da man mit nachklingenden und summenden Pfeiff-Werck zu thun hat, braucht es eben keiner Weitläuffigkeiten, denn man schläget die Noten meist nur platt nieder, und die Hände bleiben hierbey ohne weiteres Ceremoniel so lange liegen, bis ein anderer Accord folgt, mit welchem es wiederum, wie zuvor, gehalten wird . . . Hebet man aber ja die Hände so gleich auf, nach Anschlagung eines neuen Accordes, und machet statt der Noten gleichsam eine Pause; so geschiehet solches nach Gelegenheit der Umstände, entweder den Sänger, oder die bissweilen zum Recitativ accompagnirende Instrumenta besser zu hören, und zu observiren. Oder man findet auch wohl andere Raison, die Hände Z. E. deswegen in etwas aufzuheben, weil et-

wan jezuweilen im Basse 3, 4 und mehr Tacte stetig summende Pfeiff-Werck kan verdriesslich gemachet werden. Welches alles dem Judicio und Gefallen eines Accompagnisten heimgestellt bleiben." Heinichen, *Neu erfundene und Gründliche Anweisung,* p. 226; English translation adapted from Mendel, "Accompaniments," pp. 357–358.

13. Mendel, "Accompaniments," p. 358; Williams, "Basso Continuo," p. 237; Platen, "Aufgehoben," pp. 169–170.

14. According to the *Kurzgefasstes Musicalisches Lexicon* (Chemnitz, 1749; facsim. Leipzig: Zentralantiquariat der DDR, 1975), p. 48, the arpeggio was "the basis of a good theatrical accompaniment and rests more on practice than on its own theory."

15. "Von [den Herren Organisten und Bassisten] bitte ich mir aus, dass NB. wenn ein Recitativ vorkommt, und zwey bis drey gantzer Tacte haltend gesetzt ist, sie nicht mehr thun, als bey jeder neuen Note, die da vor kommt, einen Anschlag oder Anstoss zugeben, und dann so lange einhalten, bis wiederum eine neue Note erfolge." Friedrich Erhard Niedt, *Musicalische Handleitung,* part III (Hamburg, 1717; facsim. Buren, The Netherlands: F. Knuf, 1976), pp. 57–58. Mattheson published this third part of the *Handleitung* posthumously. In the foreword, he mentions that this was Niedt's last work, completed shortly before his death in 1708 (p. 2). The phrase in brackets is the antecedent from the previous paragraph.

16. "Comme vous n'estes pas sectateur de la musique italienne, je n'ose vous dire, Monsieur, qu'excepté le recitatif et la mauvaise manière d'accompagner en coupant le son de chaque accord, il y a des ariettes magnifiques pour l'harmonie avec des accompagnements de violons qui ne laissent rien la souhaiter." Quoted in Winton Dean, "A French Traveller's View of Handel's Operas," *Music and Letters,* 55 (1974), p. 178.

17. "Auf Orgeln braucht man zwar das Harpeggio nicht so sehr, hingegen aber, wann der Bass sehr lange Noten zu halten hat, so nimmt man wohl zuweilen die Hände auf und pausirt bis zum nächsten Accord um den Vocalisten desto deutlicher zu hören, und niemanden mit dem lang ausgehaltenden Geheule des Pfeiffwerks einen Eckel zu machen." David Kellner, *Treulicher Unterricht im General-Bass* (Hamburg, 1732), p. 20.

18. Georg Philipp Telemann, *Singe-, Spiel- und Generalbass-Übungen* (Hamburg, 1733–1734; mod. ed., Max Seiffert, Berlin, 1914), pp. 39–40.

19. "Manier om op de clavecimbel te leeren speelen den Generalen Bas of Bassus continuus," Royal Library, the Hague, Ms. 72 F 36, cited in Smit Duyzentkunst, *Uitvoeringspraktijk,* p. 54; Georg Joseph Joachim Hahn, *Der wohlunterwiesene Generalbass-Schüler* (1751; Augsburg, 1768), p. 82. Perhaps this practice was the more authentic Italian manner of accompanying operatic recitative on the harpsichord. Francesco Gasparini, although not entirely clear on this point, seems to imply as much in his *L'armonico pratico al cimbalo* (Venice, 1708), p. 61, when he refers to "una nota ferma del fondamento."

20. Gottfried Heinrich Stölzel, "Abhandlung vom Recitativ," Ms. Vienna (1739), cited in Werner Steger, "G. H. Stölzels 'Abhandlung vom Recitativ'" (diss., Heidelberg, 1962), p. 130.

21. "Ich muss aber nicht beständig dabey liegen bleiben, und eine Leyer daraus machen, sonst wäre es kein Accomp. Nein, sondern, ich muss die Hände fein aufheben, damit die Zuhörer den Text wohl verstehen können." J. S. Voigt, *Gespräch von der Musik* (Erfurt, 1742), p. 29. The exemplar of Voigt that I consulted at the Deutsche Staatsbibliothek (Berlin, DDR) had belonged to Lorenz Mizler.

22. One misses any explicit reference to the accompagnato recitative until the second half of the century, despite the fact that the genre was cultivated everywhere. Theory probably lagged behind practice here. Later sources nonetheless clarify differences that were already palpable in the first half of the eighteenth century.

23. "Es würde also nicht übel gethan seyn, wenn die Bassinstrumente, anstatt, wie gewöhnlich, kurz und stark anzuschlagen, jeden Ton sachte angäben, und immer etwas aushielten." "Thusnelde vom Herrn Scheiben," in F. W. Marpurg's *Historisch-kritische Beyträge* (Berlin, 1754), I, 116.

24. "De generaalbas-nooten, schoon enkelyk uit gebondene en geheele bestaande, moeten hier, vooral op orgelen, positiven en regaalen, om den zanger te ondersteunen, maar hem geenzins te overstemmen, slegts als vierendeelen met pausen behandeld worden." Jacob Wilhelm Lustig, *Muzykaale Spraakkonst* (Amsterdam, 1754), p. 137. Of German parentage, Lustig was the son of a Reinken pupil who was organist at St. Michael's in Hamburg. About 1722, Jacob Lustig began his studies in theory and composition with Mattheson and Telemann. Even though a pupil of Telemann, Lustig did not follow his teacher's method of short accompaniment.

25. "Doch, komt er eens in 't midden of op 't einde van italiaansche recitativen, zeker nadrukkelyk spreukje voor, de Componist wykt van den spreektrant af, verpligt de uitvoerders tot stipte maat, en duidt zulks aan door de woorden *Obligato* of *Arioso*. En zal zulk een recitatyf verzeld worden door verscheiden instrumente, neem eens, vioolen, die of enkelyk in lange nooten, *pianissimo,* als er onder zweeven, of in vieren en achtendeelen, kort afgestooten (staccato) zig zagjes, en vervolgens, by zekere uitbarstingen, tot aflossing, alleen, *fortissimo,* hooren laaten zullen, het komt insgelyks aan op stipte maat, voor so verre verscheiden persoonen anders niet wel in balance konnen blyven, zo echter, dat ieder speeler naar den zanger luistere, en deeze, ten minsten wanneer de vioolen slegts gebondene lange nooten hebben, de vryheid behoude, den zang altoos nog iets naar spreektrant te doen gelyken. Dusdanige stukke, *accompagnamenti* genoemd, zyn by uitneemendheid bekwaam tot het verwekken en onderhouden der allersterkste, verhevenste gemoedsbeweegingen." Ibid., pp. 137–138.

26. Quantz also mentioned these two types of accompanied recitative, noting that the long sustained style requires an attentiveness to the declamatory freedom of the singer whereas the accompagnato with motivically contrived fast notes necessitates a strictly metric reading. Although Quantz never discusses the length of the bass notes in plain recitative, he gives a musical example illustrating how the accompanist can anticipate the singer's line with his right hand that inadvertently realizes the left-hand chords with filled note heads.

Considering the quarter rest in the penultimate measure, it seems plausible that Quantz presumes short accompaniment. See Johann Joachim Quantz, *Versuch* (Berlin, 1752; 2nd ed. Breslau, 1780), p. 272.

27. "Récitatif accompagné est celui auquel, outre la Basse-continue, on ajoûte un Accompagnement de Violons. Cet Accompagnement qui ne peut guère être syllabique, vu la rapidité du débit, est ordinairement formé de longues Notes soutenues sur des Mesures entières, & l'on écrit pour cela sur toute les Parties de Symphonie le mot Sostenuto, principalement à la Basse, qui, sans cela, ne frapperoit que des coups secs & détachés à chaque changement de Note, comme dans le Récitatif ordinaire; au lieu qu'il faut alors filer & soutenir les sons selon toute la valeur des Notes." Jean-Jacques Rousseau, *Dictionnaire de Musique* (Paris, 1768), pp. 410–411.

28. "In Recitativen bleibe er nicht mit den Accorden stets liegen, sondern gebrauche sich, um das Geheule zu vermeiden, der zergliederten oder gebrochenen und arpeggierten Accorde . . . Oft lasse er im Recitative nach angeschlagenen Accorden den Bass allein, bald im Pedale bald im Manuale stehen, je nachdem es die Umstände mit sich bringen." Johann Samuel Petri, *Anleitung zur Practischen Musik* (Lauban, 1767), p. 44.

29. "Eins aber will ich hier noch mit anmerken, dass wenn man in der Orgel eine recht sehr still gedeckte Flöte hat, dass man mit derselben in Recitativen ohne weitere Begleitung von Instrumenten die Accorde mit der linken Hand still liegend aushalten könne, und die neuen Noten nur immer mit dem Pedalbasse kurz abstossen. Der Sänger wird dadurch ungemein unterstützt, und doch nicht verdunkelt oder überstimmt." Petri, *Anleitung* (Leipzig, 1782), p. 311.

30. C. P. E. Bach, *Versuch,* II, 315–316. English trans. from C. P. E. Bach, *Essay on the True Art of Playing Keyboard Instruments,* trans. William J. Mitchell (New York: W. W. Norton, 1949), pp. 422–423.

31. *Die Musik in Geschichte und Gegenwart (MGG),* vol. 12, pp. 83–84. Schröter joined the Society in 1739 and contributed many articles to Mizler's *Musicalische Bibliothek.* Bach's letter to Schröter, which does not survive, is described in *BDok,* I, 121.

32. "Es giebt dreyerley Arten des Recitativs. Das Kennzeichen der ersten Art ist, wenn man über den Bassnoten mit Signaturen auch eine Singstimme, N.B. ohne Beywort: *Accompagnement* oder *col stromenti* erblicket. Obgleich der Bass hier meistenteils ganze und halbe Tacte Noten hat; so muss doch der Organist jegliche solche langweiligen Noten nebst denen erforderten harmonischen Griffen fast wie ein 8tel kurz abstossen . . . Bey der zweyten Art des Recitativs hat der Bass und die Instrumente meistenteils 4tel Noten mit nachgesetzten Pausen. Bisweilen findet man auch vor oder bey Eintretung einer neuen Periode etliche laufende 16tel oder 32tel. Es muss also der Tact dabey gehalten werden, und der Organist verhält sich übrigens wie bey der ersten Art. Unter der dritten Art des Recitativs verstehe ich, wenn selbiges mit Violinen also begleitet wird, dass die ganzen oder halben Tactnoten durchgehends sanft ausgehalten werden, wodurch ein angenehmes Säuseln entsteht. Bey dieser Art des Recitativs wird der Tact billig auch gegeben, und muss selbiges mit dem

Worte: *Accompagnement,* oder *col Violini* angedeutet seyn: Widrigenfalls würde der Organist und die andern begleitenden Bassisten, wie bey der ersten Art, die Töne wider ihr Verschulden abstossen. Damit aber bey dieser dritten Art des Recitativs dem angenehmen Säuseln der Violinen nichts benommen werde, so pflege ich auf der Orgel jeglichen harmonischen Satz mit beyden Händen kurz abzustossen; hingegen halte ich im Pedale die Töne völlig aus: zumahl wenn die Anzahl der andern begleitenden Bässe klein ist." Christoph Gottlieb Schröter, *Deutliche Anweisung zum General-Bass* (Halberstadt, 1772), pp. 185–186.

33. "Freylich wär' es, wo nicht besser, doch wenigstens nicht so verführerisch, wenn die Komponisten alle, wie es Einige thun, z.B. der Herr Kapellmeister Bach, in seiner Passion und den Israeliten u. die Noten so hinschrieben, wie sie vorgetragen werden müssen; wenn sie nehmlich, anstatt der ganzen Taktnoten, blosse Viertel, und alsdenn so viele Pausen setzten, bis der Begleiter einen neuen Grundton oder eine andere Harmonie anschlagen soll. Vielleicht würden alsdenn die Rezitative besser aufgeführt, als es jetzt von manchem Organisten, und von denen, welche die Bässe spielen, hin und wieder geschiet." Daniel Gottlob Türk, *Von den wichtigsten Pflichten eines Organisten* (Halle, 1787), pp. 162–164.

34. Johann Joseph Klein, *Versuch eines Lehrbuchs des praktischen Musik* (Gera, 1783), p. 256; Sebastian Prixner, *Kann man nicht in zwey, oder drey Monaten die Orgel lernen?* (Landshut, 1789), p. 79; Augustus Frederic Christopher Kollmann, *Practical Guide to Thorough-Bass* (London, 1801), pp. 27–29.

35. *Allgemeine Musikalische Zeitung,* 61 (Leipzig, 1810), pp. 969–974.

36. Nculicb may have been intended to portray Johann Philipp Christian Schulz (1773–1827), who in 1810 had just become director of the Gewandhaus at the age of 36.

37. The first piece in which Bach composed recitatives was the so-called "Hunt" cantata (*Jagdkantate*), BWV 208, probably written in 1713. It survives only in score.

38. Mendel, "Accompaniments," p. 358; Williams, "Basso Continuo," p. 239. Mendel and Williams were only aware of the bassoon part for Cantata 18.

39. In all editions of BWV 18, including the NBA I/7 and its accompanying critical notes, the cues have been ignored, although they are virtually identical to Bach's staccato marks in the continuo parts for BWV 185/5.

40. Such a practice was particularly useful because the continuo players could not see the vocal part, which was always to be sung in free, proselike declamation. This may account for the cues over certain quarter notes, indicating that they would also be conducted and might well be played detached. Consider the cues over the two quarter notes in m. 11 of BWV 18/2 (see Facsimile 3-4); here the cues help the players coordinate the transition from the secco to the linked arioso. The arioso thus begins only after the second quarter and not at the beginning of the bar.

41. The short notation in BWV 185/2 will be discussed further in the context of other Weimar bassoon parts in Chapter 4, where it is shown that this reduction tallies with other parts in which Bach omits the bassoon entirely in recitatives. In BWV 185/2, in fact, the bassoon drops out in the arioso section.

42. Only one long note in BWV 185/4 (m. 5) is missing a cue stroke, probably the result of an oversight.

43. If it was the bassoon's timbre that induced Bach to specify the short notation in Movement 4 while everyone else played *tenuto,* then it is hard to explain why he did not similarly "orchestrate" the bassoon's part in Movement 2, completely in secco. Moreover, one loses a reason for the autograph marking "accomp." Certainly Bach had no need to give his cellists lessons in the classification of genres.

44. Cantatas 58, 30, and 197 also contain one movement that begins in secco style and moves after a few measures to arioso. Bach again seems to have notated these secco passages in short notation in order to ensure that the players would not be confused. In Cantata 58, Bach placed the quarter notes into the two continuo parts he copied while the continuo part written by the copyist retained the long notation. Why the conflict between the parts? While the copyist merely copied directly from the score, Bach took the opportunity to clarify a mildly ambiguous situation. In Cantatas 58 and 30, moreover, this is the only occurrence of a secco succeeded by an arioso. Platen ("Aufgehoben," pp. 173–174) misses this point when he asserts that if Bach used two notational forms within one set of parts for secco recitatives, each must correspond to a distinct musical execution. Cantata 197, however, has two such movements, and only the second was notated in short values. However, the anomaly exists only in Bach's score; the parts from this cantata do not survive. Why Bach did not notate both mixed genres in short notation is not known; perhaps he later clarified the notation in the parts. In any event, since the explicit notation was a convenience in the first place and never a necessity, the parts would not have proved confusing to the players.

45. Now located in the Biblioteka Jagiellońska, Cracow, the manuscript bears the signature Mus. ms. Bach St 356. Before 1945 it belonged to the main Bach collection in Berlin. Because the NBA edition of BWV 11 (1978) appeared before the parts were available for study—they were presumed missing since World War II—the edition does not reflect the readings in the parts. Thanks to Alfred Dürr, I was able to examine photocopies of St 356 at the Johann-Sebastian-Bach-Institut in Göttingen.

46. Bach's own greater attention to detail also explains an autograph organ part from a second performance of Cantata 94 in 1732. Here Bach provided a new organ part in conjunction with his plan to exclude the organ from certain movements. (See Chapter 2.) In Movement 5, which shifts quickly back and forth between arioso and secco, he notated consistent quarter notes. The fact that he left the other continuo parts intact with the long values is further evidence that short accompaniment was a foregone conclusion.

47. Exceptional here were the final notes to each secco movement (Movements 2, 5, 7a, and 7c), where Bach retained whole or half notes with fermatas. These seem to constitute an unusual but essentially unproblematic "mixed mode" of the convention. One encounters a further irregularity in the penultimate bar of Movement 5, which includes a half note over B (*Chorton*). Evi-

dently this half note was intended to be played as such, since it coincided with two quarter notes that jump the octave in the other continuo parts from c♯ to C♯ (*Cammerton*), the latter of which was unplayable on Bach's organ. (See Examples 3-5 and 3-6.)

48. Citing a similar passage in long notation from Cantata 14, Movement 3, Platen argues against any general validity for short accompaniment. (See Example 3-5.) If the short convention were invoked here, he continues ("Aufgehoben," p. 176), "the characteristic voice-leading of some secco continuo parts would lose its musical sense." On the contrary, the organ part for the Ascension Oratorio suggests that custom and logic dictated when the player should invoke the convention. All of Platen's three examples are identified incorrectly. They should read: (a) BWV 43/8, (b) BWV 155/3, (c) BWV 14/3.

49. See NBA II/5a for a facsimile of this manuscript.

50. See Alfred Dürr, "Beobachtungen am Autograph des Matthäus-Passion," *BJ*, 1963–1964, pp. 47–52. Dürr shows nonetheless how many errors still crept into the score and parts, particularly with regard to articulation. He concludes that musicians and listeners alike were both accustomed to living "cum imperfectis." On errors in Bach's manuscript sources, see Dürr, "De vita cum imperfectis," *Studies in Renaissance and Baroque Music in Honor of Arthur Mendel* (Kassel: Bärenreiter, 1974), pp. 243–253.

51. The NBA edition of Cantata 30a appears to suggest that Bach employed short notation only in Movement 10, retaining the long values in the other recitative movements; see NBA I/39 (Werner Neumann) as well as the edition of the BG, 5. Indeed, Platen ("Aufgehoben," p. 173, n. 14) enumerates the sources for this cantata as evidence of conflicting (and hence unintelligible) differentiation of notation within one set of parts. In fact, he is mistaken about Movement 12. As an accompagnato—not a secco—movement (p. 172), its long notation is perfectly ordinary.

52. Neumann surmised correctly that the other secco movements were probably rendered short as in Movement 10 but did not let his edition reflect this guess. NBA I/39, KB, pp. 81–82.

53. "White notes" would not have bled through the paper, nor was there enough room for quarter notes and rests, which take up more space.

54. This find confirms that short accompaniment was not only a practice of sacred music but prevailed in Bach's secular works as well.

55. Bach usually denoted his secco recitatives with the word *Recit.*, or else gave no indication at all. Rarely did he attach any dynamic or tempo markings to secco movements, and when he did, they may well have signified a temporary *tenuto*. There are three instances of seccos marked *piano*: BWV 78/3, BWV 99/2, and BWV 249/6, the latter a bassoon part. Bach may well have marked the first two to ensure a special *tenuto* rendition. Compare these with the sustained secco passage in the St. Matthew Passion discussed earlier in the text.

56. Instances of accompagnato recitatives in which the *piano* designation was not transmitted to the continuo parts include BWV 28/4, BWV 32/4, BWV 37/4, BWV 39/7, BWV 62/5, BWV 84/4, BWV 111/5, BWV 164/4, and BWV

201/8. Likewise, in BWV 213/12, Bach had labeled the movement *Recit: con accomp.*, which the copyist ignored when copying the continuo parts. In some instances, such as BWV 87/4 and BWV 91/4, it was Bach himself who marked the upper string parts *piano* but neglected to do so when he revised the continuo parts. In five other cases (BWV 19/4, BWV 27/4, BWV 30/7, BWV 36b/4, and BWV 39/7), the accompagnato is conspicuously the only recitative movement without a cue stave. Other accompagnato movements in long values that include no special designations of any kind include BWV 34a/3, BWV 48/2, BWV 49/3, BWV 51/2, BWV 56/4, BWV 59/2, BWV 63/2, BWV 70/2, BWV 70/9, BWV 73/1, BWV 74/6, BWV 85/4, BWV 107/2, BWV 110/3, BWV 116/5, BWV 122/5, BWV 125/3, BWV 139/5, BWV 140/5, BWV 147/2, BWV 170/4, BWV 174/3, BWV 175/1, BWV 175/5, BWV 195/4, BWV 214/6, BWV 215/2, BWV 215/6, BWV 215/8, BWV 248/18, BWV 248/27, and BWV 248/32.

57. Other examples from works with extant sets of parts include passages from BWV 40/5, BWV 46/2, BWV 63/6, BWV 94/3, BWV 102/5, BWV 127/4, BWV 183/3, BWV 207/8, BWV 214/8, BWV 248/7, and BWV 248/14. Werner Neumann, in his *Handbuch der Kantaten Johann Sebastian Bachs,* 4th rev. ed. (1947; Leipzig: VEB Breitkopf & Härtel, 1971), adopts the term *ausinstrumentiertes Secco* (orchestrated secco) to denote not only the accompagnato in short values but also those with the usual sustained notation. He erroneously classifies on the basis of appearance rather than of execution. That is, the conventional accompagnato in long values only *appears* to resemble a secco; in practice, it sounds very different. Only the abbreviated kind of accompanied recitative—a mixed genre—can be thought of as an orchestrated secco.

58. Platen cites a passage from the Christmas Oratorio (BWV 248^1/7) that seems to confound any clear-cut differentiation between secco and accompagnato ("Aufgehoben," pp. 174–175). In the four passages of recitative interspersed between chorale statements, each segment is similar in structure. The oboes d'amore conclude their arioso phrase on the first beat, and, in the first three passages, merely append an exclamatory flourish in the second bar. In the final recitative segment the oboes are more active. What variety of recitative has Bach written in these four interpolations—secco or accompagnato? A more important question is, what kind of recitative do the continuo players believe they are playing? After emerging from the arioso as the only surviving instrumental part (the oboes are resting at this point), the continuo would most likely have played short. This probably explains why Bach went to the trouble of notating the continuo line in quarters by the time he reached the third segment: in this way, he confirmed that the proper recitative style was in fact secco, even though the oboes were also permitted a brief say.

59. *BDok,* II, 286; English trans. in *BR,* p. 238.

60. Williams, "Basso Continuo," p. 238.

61. See, for example, the compendium published by the brothers Stötzel called *Kurzgefasstes Musicalisches Lexicon* (Chemnitz, 1749; facsim. Leipzig: Zentralantiquariat der DDR, 1975), pp. 155–156.

62. Niedt, *Handleitung,* III, 58.

IV. The Bassoon

1. *Kurzgefasstes Musicalisches Lexicon* (Chemnitz, 1749; facsim. Leipzig: Zentralantiquariat der DDR, 1975), p. 135.

2. Johann Beer, *Musicalische Discurse* (Nürnberg, 1719; facsim. Leipzig: VEB Deutscher Verlag für Musik, 1982), pp. 85–90.

3. Bach's trombone was not actually a member of his continuo group. Whenever it appears in a Bach vocal work, the trombone is always associated with a chorale melody or a motet movement. In addition, it is virtually always a member of an old-fashioned choir comprised of either four trombones or a cornetto and three trombones. The opening movement of Cantata 135 offers the single instance of the trombone doubling the continuo line (rather than playing *colla parte* with the choir), but here a chorale tune in the continuo line prompts the addition of a trombone. In the final movement, a simple chorale, the player apparently played the cornetto so as to double the chorale tune conventionally in the soprano.

4. *BDok,* II, 15–18.

5. See Ulrich Prinz, "Zur Bezeichnung 'Bassono' und 'Fagotto' bei J. S. Bach," *BJ,* 1981, pp. 111–114 for a useful summary of the developments in the construction of the bassoon. See also *New Grove Dictionary,* vol. 2, pp. 270–273.

6. Lully first used his influential trio of two oboes and bassoon as an alternating texture in *Psyché* (1674).

7. Johann Mattheson, *Neu-eröffnetes Orchestre* (Hamburg, 1713), p. 269. Mattheson distinguishes the bassoons from what he calls the "bombards," probably bass dulcians (although usually translated as "shawms"), "which previously served instead of bassoons [*Bassons*] [and] are now no longer in fashion."

8. Martin Heinrich Fuhrmann, *Musicalischer Trichter* (Berlin, 1706), p. 92, cited in Prinz, "'Bassono' und 'Fagotto'," p. 110.

9. The ambitus—from C to f′ or g′, also descending to B♭′ or A′—is the same as that cited for the entry *Basson*.

10. The motet is a work by Johann Christoph Schmidt, "Auf Gott hoffe ich." The score, Mus. ms. 30187, found in the Deutsche Staatsbibliothek (Berlin, DDR), was previously known to specialists. In 1977 Barbara Brewer discovered three parts (Oboe 1, Oboe 2, and Bassoon) in the Staatsbibliothek Preussischer Kulturbesitz (Berlin) and identified them as Bach autographs. They are catalogued as Mus. ms. 19921/1.

11. Charles Sanford Terry, *Bach's Orchestra* (London: Oxford University Press, 1932; rpt. 1972), p. 115.

12. The bassoon part for Cantata 147 is most probably lost, since the separate stave in the score would automatically have prompted the copyist to prepare a separate part.

13. Alfred Dürr, *Die Kantaten von Johann Sebastian Bach,* 2 vols. (1971; Kassel: Bärenreiter, 1975), I, p. 69 and Konrad Brandt, "Fragen zur Fagottbesetzung in den kirchen-musikalischen Werken Johann Sebastian Bachs," *BJ,* 1968, p. 66.

14. *BDok,* II, 62; I, 61. Yet Bach made known his dissatisfaction with the

musicianship of the Town-Pipers and Art-Fiddlers. As he put it in the Memorandum: "Discretion forbids me to speak at all truthfully of their qualities and musical knowledge." And if this was his evaluation of the professionals, he must have found the abilities of their apprentice bassoon player less than formidable. Thus it is conceivable that, if Bach was not especially pleased with the apprentice player, he may have refrained from writing a regular bassoon part for his weekly cantata performances.

15. As Konrad Brandt points out ("Fragen zur Fagottbesetzung," p. 66), the position of 3rd Oboe became vacant around 1730, so that the bassoonist probably played oboe when three were required. This would explain why, in 1728 or 1729, Bach could write for three oboes and a bassoon in Cantata 149 but in 1732, for example, composed Cantata 177 for only two oboes and a bassoon. This shift of personnel also makes sense of the 1736 performance of the St. Matthew Passion, from which the bassoon is inexplicably absent: because of the number of players required to staff the two sets of winds, the bassoonist must have been needed elsewhere in the orchestra. On the other hand, Brandt's explanation cannot account for the 1731 performance of Cantata 140, with its two oboes, *taille*, and bassoon.

16. Arnold Schering, *Musikgeschichte Leipzigs*, II (Leipzig: Fr. Kistner & C. F. W. Siegel, 1926), p. 135, n. 5, cited in Prinz, "'Bassono' und 'Fagotto,'" p. 113.

17. See Hans-Joachim Schulze, "Studenten als Bachs Helfer bei der Leipziger Kirchenmusik," *BJ*, 1984, pp. 45–52. Early in the tenure of Johann Kuhnau, most so-called *studiosi* lost the compensation they had previously received for these extra duties, a budget cut that Bach greatly regretted. See the Memorandum, *BDok*, I, 62 and also Herbert R. Pankratz, "J. S. Bach and his Leipzig Collegium Musicum," *MQ*, 69 (1983), pp. 327–328. But, as Schulze puts it: "There is no reason to assume that the documented circle of persons comprises the complete number of student helpers" (p. 48).

18. Even the Missa was performed with only one bassoon except in the "Quoniam" (Movement 11), since there the part reads: "Seqtr a 2 Bassoni." On the other hand, this inscription might merely have alerted players to the ensuing *divisi*.

19. Dürr, *Kantaten*, I, 69. The bassoon part for the Christmas Oratorio is, however, not autograph.

20. Trumpeters and hornists used crooks to adjust the pitch; the timpani could be set to any pitch. Only the trombones played consistently in *Chorton*.

21. Johann Mattheson, *Critica Musica*, vol. II (Hamburg, 1725), p. 235. See also Alfred Dürr, *Studien über die frühen Kantaten Johann Sebastian Bachs* (1951; rev. ed. Wiesbaden: Breitkopf & Härtel, 1977), p. 19; Schering, *LKM*, pp. 58–59; and Mendel, "Pitch in Western Music since 1500: A Re-Examination," *Acta Musicologica*, 50 (1978), p. 13.

22. With the exception of BWV 52 and 172, nearly all Leipzig bassoon parts are called *Bassono*.

23. Ulrich Prinz has explained the matter with an emphasis on the nomenclature in "'Bassono' und 'Fagotto'" and has reached substantially the same

conclusions; we differ only with regard to the reliability of the names. While he proceeds from the nomenclature, I consider pitch more important. As a result, he postulates two instrument types while I argue for three distinct instruments.

24. Dürr, *Studien*, p. 71.

25. "Man betrachte mir doch den Greuel, wenn manchesmahl Instrumente, die in Kammer-Ton stehen, als: Waldhörner, Fagotten u.d.gl. andere accompagniren sollen, die da Chor-tönig sind, dabey entweder diese oder jene transponirt werden müssen." Johann Mattheson, *Das forschende Orchestre* (Hamburg, 1721), p. 426; see also Mattheson, *Das neu-eröffnete Orchestre,* p. 267.

26. Fuhrmann, *Musicalischer Trichter,* p. 92.

27. Only by this conclusion can one avoid the uncomfortable suggestion that Bach himself, in a group of autograph parts, would go to the trouble of differentiating a special bassoon part but copy it consistently in the wrong key. By assuming the bassoon was always tuned in *Cammerton,* Dürr was forced to conclude that the player "possessed sufficient skill in transposition." Since no other wind parts require players to transpose at performances in the Weimar *Hofkirche,* it is unlikely that Bach could have expected the bassoonist—one of the least respected members of the orchestra—to transpose his parts.

The case of Cantata 23 also sheds light on this question of transposition. The piece was originally composed at Cöthen in C minor (*Cammerton*), but Bach performed it in B minor (*Cammerton*) at his Leipzig audition because he needed to settle on A minor (*Chorton*) for the new trombone parts. The string parts were left intact, and the players simply tuned down the half step. The keyboard players and bassoonist thus required new parts. Three original parts (which resurfaced in 1976) included an organ part in A minor (*Chorton*), a cello part in C minor (to sound in B minor *Cammerton*), and a part in B minor (actual *Cammerton*) entitled *Basson. (e Cembalo)* (see Chapter 2). The fact that the bassoon part was the only one in B minor confirms that Bach's bassoonist was not expected to transpose.

28. Mattheson, *Das forschende Orchestre,* p. 434; see also Brandt, "Fragen zur Fagottbesetzung," pp. 66–67, 71–72.

29. On this point see Prinz, "'Bassono' und 'Fagotto,'" p. 115.

30. The string parts, now lost, were either transposed to C major or could have been copied in D major, with the players tuning their instruments down a whole step.

31. The first viola line, moreover, is notated in mezzo-soprano clef, which Bach never used in a string part. This betrays Schmidt's French orientation, since the violas in French opera (differing in size but identically pitched) were also notated in this way. See, for example, a page of the score to Marin Marais's opera *Alcyon,* reproduced in facsimile in James R. Anthony, *French Baroque Music* (1974; New York, 1978), p. 122. See also Jürgen Eppelsheim, *Das Orchester in den Werken Jean Baptiste Lullys* (Tutzing: H. Schneider, 1961), p. 33.

32. Gottfried Silbermann built this instrument, apparently the first in Germany designed in *Cammerton.* See Ernst Flade, *Gottfried Silbermann* (Leipzig: F. Kistner & C. F. W. Siegel, 1926; rpt. 1953), pp. 133, 178.

33. Bach, for example, called the virtuoso bassoon part in Cantata 155 "Fa-

gotto." While the bassoon line in his autograph score was notated at composing pitch of *Chorton,* the part, which does not survive, must have been copied in *Tief-Cammerton* because it descends far below the range of the later *Fagotto* pitched at *Chorton.* Prinz's listing of this part in *Chorton* (Prinz, "'Bassono' und 'Fagotto,'" p. 108) is therefore misleading.

34. The existence of two different bassoons at Weimar helps to clarify the performance history of two works. In Cantata 185, two new continuo parts were copied in Weimar after the completion of the first part-set (Dürr, *Studien,* pp. 32–33). The oboe part, playing in A minor (*Tief-Cammerton*) was initially pitted against the strings and bassoon in F♯ minor (*Chorton*). But for some reason (either at a subsequent performance or because of a change to oboes in high *Cammerton*) two new continuo parts were copied in G minor. (The A minor oboe part would then have constituted a part in high *Cammerton.*) The new part-titles read *Violone* and *Violoncello,* but these are mere copies of their exemplars. Since string players could easily tune their instruments up a half step, as the violinists *must* have done, why did the cellist and violonist not follow suit? In fact, to account for these new continuo parts, one must imagine that these players in fact retuned. For only two players—both with fixed instruments in *Chorton*—could not retune: the bassoonist and the organist. Only they would have found the parts in F♯ useless. To retain the use of his *Chorton* bassoon in the performance, Bach therefore needed a new continuo part at the new *Chorton* pitch. (Dürr mentions this possibility, but it conflicts with his previous contention that the Weimar bassoons played in *Cammerton.*) Nonetheless, Bach's refinements in the Weimar bassoon part (see the following section in the text) would not then have been heard at this performance in G. Nor could they have been heard at the Leipzig performance of Cantata 185 in June of 1723, when the performing pitch was in G (*Cammerton*) with a bassoon at the same pitch. Indeed, if Bach's oboe at high *Cammerton* became disabled before the first Weimar performance, it is conceivable that the details of the autograph bassoon part were never realized at any performance.

Finally, Cantata 18 suggests that, once Bach conceived of a work with bassoon, he wanted it present at subsequent performances. In the Leipzig performance of this work from Weimar, Bach added two recorders to double the first two viola parts, transposing the piece from G minor to A minor. The Leipzig organist could still make use of the original organ part (*Violono o Organo*), since *Chorton* at Weimar was made equivalent to *Chorton* at Leipzig. The four violas, on the other hand, retuned their instruments up a whole step in order to play from the Weimar parts. Besides the new recorder parts, the only other new part copied at Leipzig is a *Continuo* part in A. Again, if Bach wanted a bassoonist in this performance, he required a part precisely in this key. Moreover, the fact that the continuo part duplicated the old organ part (partially figured in Movements 2 and 3) seems to indicate that the bassoon shared the part with the harpsichordist, as in the Leipzig performance of Cantata 23.

35. Dürr, *Studien,* p. 236.

36. Of the pre-Leipzig works with bassoon parts differentiated by octave, three others are written at the upper octave to the continuo (BWV 21, BWV

131, and BWV 208), while two play at the lower octave (BWV 18 and BWV 31). In BWV 172/1, the bassoon part alternates between doublings at both the upper and lower octave to the continuo.

37. Jürgen Eppelsheim, however, notes that Bach could have used a 16-foot instrument, such as one by Andreas Eichentopf of Nordhausen dated 1714, presently housed in the musical instrumental museum at Leipzig (No. 3394). See *J. S. Bach: Life, Times and Influence,* ed. Barbara Schwendowius and Wolfgang Dömling (New Haven, Conn.: Yale University Press, 1984), p. 137.

38. The partially autograph score for the St. John Passion (P 28) dating from ca. 1735–1742 included the following inscription over a *divisi* in the continuo part for the opening movement: *Violoncelli e Bassoni.* Apparently Bach envisaged a performance of the Passion with two bassoons.

39. In assessing the role of the *bassono grosso* in the St. John Passion, one must be aware that the part was not a newly prepared one but, in effect, merely a series of autograph *tacet*-markings superimposed over a full continuo part used at an earlier performance. Doubtless Bach undertook this arrangement in great haste. Perhaps he wanted to create a part similar to the one in the Mass in which he had reworked the bassoon's participation in the choral movements. Although the more ponderous sound of the *bassono grosso* may account for the extent of the *tacet*-indications, the Mass and the Passion still share a feature in common: Bach excluded the bassoon from the most lightly scored movements.

40. For analyses of similar concerto movements, see my article "Bach's Concerto Ritornellos and the Question of Invention," *The Musical Quarterly,* 71 (1985), pp. 327–358.

V. The String Instruments in the Continuo Group

1. C. P. E. Bach, *Versuch über die wahre Art das Clavier zu spielen* (Berlin, 1753; facsim. Leipzig: VEB Breitkopf & Härtel, 1976), vol. 2, p. 3.

2. See Tharald Borgir, "The Performance of the Basso Continuo in Seventeenth-Century Italian Music," (Ph.D. diss., University of California, Berkeley, 1971), p. 2. The crucial words "beim Solo," as Borgir notes, were omitted in William Mitchell's familiar translation (New York: Norton, 1949), p. 173.

3. In Cantata 196, for which no original sources survive, Bach's limited cello part reflects a similar pattern to that found in Cantata 71.

4. Borgir, "Performance of the Basso Continuo," pp. 128–134.

5. Similarly, the doublings in the second gamba part at the end of "Es ist ein alter Bund" (mm. 179–183) provide a powerful impetus to the musical exegesis. Given Bach's careful attention to the disposition of the instruments, the addition of a cello to the continuo would make nonsense out of the "disappearing" parts in mm. 182–184.

6. The principal *Violoncello* part for Bach's Leipzig audition piece—Cantata 23—was already copied in Cöthen.

7. Among those few exceptions from works performed later, the part designations are either in Bach's hand or were copied from a special indication in an autograph score. These include the motet "Der Geist hilft unsrer Schwach-

heit auf," BWV 226 (1729); the Missa, BWV 232¹ (1733); Cantata 97 (1734); the first part of the Christmas Oratorio, BWV 248¹; and Cantatas 8 (1735–1750), 100 (1735–1750), and 195 (1748).

8. This also suggests that two string players shared one part even when the part-title ("Violino 1," "Violoncello") indicated the singular.

9. Borgir, "Performance of the Basso Continuo," pp. 135–154, 172–183.

10. Jürgen Eppelsheim, *Das Orchester in den Werken Jean-Baptiste Lullys* (Tutzing: H. Schneider, 1961), pp. 40–42, 49–51, 56, 62–63. See also Mary Cyr, "*Basses* and *basse continue* in the orchestra of the Paris Opéra, 1700–1760," *Early Music,* 10 (1982), pp. 155–170.

11. Daniel Speer, *Grundrichtiger Unterricht der musicalischen Kunst,* 2nd ed. (1687; Ulm, 1697; facsim. Leipzig: Edition Peters, 1974), pp. 206–207. Instead of the F named for the third string, Speer mentions that it can also be tuned as an E.

12. In a treatise entitled *Musikalischer Schlissl* (MS., Library of Congress, Washington, D.C.) written in 1677, the Austrian composer Johann Jacob Prinner (1624?–1694) appears to suggest that the violone might be a transposing instrument when he states that "these fiddles represent the pedal or the Sub-bass of the organ" (p. 44). In fact, when explaining how to tune the instrument, Prinner gives pitches in normal bass clef (and the usual letter notation) and tells the player to tune an octave below this. But this evidence may be misleading. Prinner calls his two instruments the Violone and the Basso di Viola. The first has five strings (F′ A′ D F B♮); the second has six (G′ C F A d g). Both, he says, read from the same clefs. Yet when he illustrates the actual notes to be played, transposition seems out of the question. For example, in an F-clef situated on the highest line of the staff—Prinner calls this "low bass clef" (*Tüeffer Bass*)—an ascending scale begins with C D E, all three notes playable only at pitch. It would seem, therefore, that the players did not ordinarily assume that their parts were to be transposed down an octave. I am grateful to Reinhard Goebel for providing me with a copy of Prinner's text.

13. Johann Beer, *Musicalische Discurse* (Nürnberg, 1719), p. 12. Again, there is no mention of the cello. Earlier Heinrich Schütz had called for a "Violon" as the sole string accompaniment to his *Musicalische Exequien* of 1636 and provided instructions for its use, implying a nontransposing instrument. See Heinrich Schütz, *Neue Ausgabe sämtlicher Werke* (Kassel, 1956), vol. 4, pp. 3, 8.

14. Translation by Kenneth Cooper and Julius Zsako in "Georg Muffat's Observations on the Lully Style of Performance," *MQ,* 53 (1967), p. 233. The French original is quoted in Jürgen Eppelsheim, *Das Orchester in den Werken Lullys,* p. 56.

15. Michael Praetorius, in the *Syntagma Musicum* (Wolfenbüttel, 1619), pp. 44–46, describes the violone as a large viola da gamba or contrabasso da gamba but also mentions an even larger "Viola da Gamba Sub-Bässe" that transposed an octave below notated pitch, even though it was tuned only an octave below the tenor viol.

16. Sébastien de Brossard, *Dictionaire de Musique* (1703; Paris, 1705; facsim. Hilversum, 1965), p. 221.

17. Johann Mattheson, *Das neu-eröffnete Orchestre* (Hamburg, 1713), pp. 285–286.

18. Johann Gottfried Walther, *Musicalisches Lexikon* (Leipzig, 1732; facsim. Kassel: Bärenreiter, 1953), p. 637.

19. Joseph Friedrich Bernhard Caspar Majer, *Museum musicum* (Schwäbisch-Hall, 1732; facsim. Kassel, 1954), pp. 79–80. This treatise appeared just after Walther's *Lexikon,* which the author cites in the preface. Majer's G-tuning indicates an F-string as the only possibility.

20. Johann Philipp Eisel, *Musicus Autodidaktos* (Erfurt, 1738), pp. 47–51.

21. Johann Joachim Quantz, *Versuch einer Anweisung die Flöte traversiere zu spielen* (Berlin, 1752), chap. 17, sec. V, par. 3, English trans. by Edward R. Reilly, *On Playing the Flute* (London: Faber, 1966), p. 247. Reilly notes that only in the French text does Quantz provide a footnote stating that the "Contraviolon" or "grosser Violon" was an instrument with four strings tuned, from bottom to top, E-A-D-G. Presumably, then, this instrument was so common in Germany that he thought it superfluous to give its tuning. For the history of the violone after mid-century, see James Webster, "Violoncello and Double Bass in the Chamber Music of Haydn and His Viennese Contemporaries, 1750–1780," *JAMS,* 29 (1976), pp. 413–438.

22. Although frets appear to have been more or less standard on all violones, evidently some players did without them, a practice that Quantz deplored. See Quantz, *Versuch,* chap. 17, sec. V, par. 4.

23. Jon W. Finson, "The Violone in Bach's Brandenburg Concerti," *The Galpin Society Journal,* 29 (1976), pp. 105–111 (hereafter cited as *GSJ*); see also later correspondence regarding this article by Ralph Leavis, *GSJ,* 30 (1977), pp. 156–157 and by Richard Maunder, *GSJ,* 31 (1978), p. 147. Maunder is the only writer to suggest the possible use of a so-called Quint-bass playing at pitch in Brandenburg Concerto No. 6. Earlier references to Bach's violone include Charles Sanford Terry, *Bach's Orchestra* (London: Oxford University Press, 1932; rpt. 1972), p. 121; Hans T. David, "A Lesser Secret of J. S. Bach Uncovered," *JAMS,* 14 (1961), p. 222; Alfred Dürr, *Die Kantaten von Johann Sebastian Bach* (Kassel: Bärenreiter, 1971), p. 68; Adolph Meier, *Konzertante Musik für Kontrabass in der Wiener Klassik* (Giebing über Prien, 1969), pp. 27–28; Alfred Planyavsky, *Geschichte des Kontrabasses* (Tutzing: H. Schneider, 1970), pp. 103–104; Francis Baines, "Der Brummende Violone," *GSJ,* 23 (1970), p. 85; Baines, "What Is a Violone?—A Note Towards a Solution," *Early Music,* 5 (1977), p. 175.

24. Ralph Leavis, correspondence in *GSJ,* 30 (1977), p. 156.

25. The most important contributions to the dating of the Brandenburg Concertos are (in chronological order): Heinrich Besseler, "Zur Chronologie der Konzerte Johann Sebastian Bachs," *Festschrift Max Schneider zum 80. Geburtstag* (Leipzig: Deutscher Verlag für Musik, 1955), pp. 115–128; Heinrich Besseler, NBA VII/2 (1956), KB, pp. 23–28; Johannes Krey, "Zur Entstehungsgeschichte der ersten Brandenburgischen Konzerts," *Festschrift Heinrich Besseler* (Leipzig: Deutscher Verlag für Musik, 1961), pp. 337–342; Martin Geck, "Gattungstraditionen und Altersschichten in den Brandenburgischen Konzerten," *Die*

Musikforschung, 23 (1970), pp. 139–152; Alfred Dürr, "Zur Entstehung des 5. Brandenburgischen Konzerts," *BJ,* 1975, pp. 63–69; Ulrich Siegele, *Kompositionsweise und Bearbeitungstechnik in der Instrumentalmusik Johann Sebastian Bachs* (Neuhausen-Stuttgart: Hänssler, 1975), pp. 151–153; Hans-Joachim Schulze, ed., *J. S. Bach. Brandenburgisches Konzert Nr. 5, Faksimile der Originalstimmensatzes* (Leipzig: Edition Peters, 1975), pp. 5–10; Hans-Joachim Schulze, "Johann Sebastian Bachs Konzerte: Fragen der Überlieferung und Chronologie," *Bach-Studien,* 6 (1981), pp. 9–26.

26. In this chapter, the violone in G refers to the small six-string instrument tuned G′ C E A d g (F may substitute for the E). The violone in D refers to the larger six-string (possibly five-string?) instrument tuned D′ G′ C E A d, an octave below the viola da gamba. The violone in C (the "violone grosso") refers to a four-string instrument tuned an octave below the cello, C′ G′ D A, or, alternately, in some species of fourths.

27. Alfred Dürr edited BWV 1050a in a supplement to NBA VII/2. See also KB, p. 3. This early violone part had played the low C♯ where Bach later transposed the part up.

28. Quantz, *Versuch,* chap. 17, sec. IV, par. 5; English trans., p. 243.

29. Hans-Joachim Schulze, "Frühe Schriftzeugnisse der beiden jüngsten Bach-Söhne," *BJ,* 1963–64, p. 68. The hand is J. C. F. Bach's, who copied from the now-lost original score to BWV 1050a at the time his father's estate was settled in 1750.

30. Christopher Hogwood, working from the argument in my 1980 dissertation, has recorded this version of Concerto No. 5 with 8-foot violone on a recording issued in 1985 as L'Oiseau-Lyre 414 187-1.

31. NBA VII/2, KB, pp. 57–58.

32. Nor are Concertos 2 and 5 (in their early versions) the only works in which Bach used a violone without the cello. The instrumentarium list in BWV 1044, the A-major triple concerto, is virtually identical to that of BWV 1047. The title heading in the extant set of parts, copied by Bach's pupil, J. G. Müthel, reads: *Traverso, Violino certato, Violino Primo, Violino Secondo, Viola, Violon e Violoncello* in addition to the concerted harpsichord. This seemingly reversed ordering of violone and cello occurs nowhere, to my knowledge, in any Leipzig work.

33. At these points, the conventional modern scoring with double bass borders on the grotesque.

34. NBA VII/2, KB, pp. 73–74.

35. Octave doubling, despite an 8-foot violone, was clearly on Bach's aesthetic agenda. Less than two weeks after the performance of Cantata 71, he recommended that certain repairs be undertaken on the organ in the St. Blasius Church in Mühlhausen. Included in his suggestions was the incorporation of a 16-foot Fagotto stop "which is useful for all kinds of new ideas and sounds very fine [*delikat*] in concerted music." BR, p. 59; original in *BDok,* I, 152–153.

36. No evidence of a violone appears in BWV 4, BWV 106, or BWV 150.

37. NBA I/35, KB, pp. 39–43.

38. The only other pre-Leipzig reference to the "violono grosso" is found in

Brandenburg Concerto No. 1. Here Bach added the instrument to the score after he named the other instruments. Is it only a coincidence that the Sinfonia, BWV 1046a, one of the earlier versions of the concerto, is commonly proposed as the companion to Cantata 208, serving as the instrumental introduction and dance postlude to the cantata? However, as Hans-Joachim Schulze observes in "J. S. Bachs Konzerte," the Sinfonia that accompanied BWV 208 would not have included the slow movement transmitted in the source to BWV 1046a. Although the secondary source that preserves the earlier version makes no mention of the violone, the connection between the Brandenburg concerto and the cantata seems too striking to dismiss lightly. On the other hand, Hans-Joachim Schulze's inquiry into the dating of the Brandenburg No. 1 has, with good reason, rejected the attempt to place any forerunner of BWV 1046 with the 1713 performance of Cantata 208. Rather, his suggested dating of the "Brandenburg Sinfonia" together with the 1716 performance of Cantata 208 in Weimar is more plausible, although this would preclude establishing a connection between the violone grosso and Weissenfels. In any event, the violone grosso appears nowhere else during the Weimar years and must therefore be treated as anomalous.

39. There is no documentary evidence of a violone in the Weimar Capelle. Terry (*Bach's Orchestra*, p. 4) lists Johann Andreas Ehrbach as "Violonist" but is probably in error. The only document in which his instrument is given lists Ehrbach as "Violinist" (see *BDok*, II, 55). On the official membership rolls of the court orchestra, he is named merely as *Cammer Musicus* (*BDok*, II, 62–63).

40. Cantata 132 presents a related example. In the first movement Bach differentiates between a reduced bassoon part at the upper octave and a violone and cello at the lower octave, so that the opening measures of the first aria already imply an octave differentiation. A further octave duplication between the cello and violone would be senseless. The third movement also alludes to a violone at pitch. Here the violone is a reduced cello part. However, Bach never notates the part in Cantata 132 above the cello line as he did in the Brandenburg Concerto No. 4 but, instead, either duplicates it exactly or emphasizes the notes in its lowest range at pitch.

41. A violone part and a continuo part for the viola da gamba survive from Bach's arrangement of a solo cantata by Francesco Conti (1682–1732) entitled "Languet anima mea." See Yoshitake Kobayashi, "Neuerkenntnisse zu einigen Bach-Quellen," *BJ*, 1978, pp. 55–58.

42. The duplicate continuo part for BWV 134a contains three sets of rests (mm. 136–148, 182–211, 235–250) in the middle of this final choral movement. The "Violoni" marking thus corresponds to a resumption of activity after several measures of rest. Alfred Dürr reasoned that this continuo part was the violone part and, from the plural designated in the score, assumed that more than one instrument played. However, comparing this source with the autograph score for Cantata 194 reveals that the plural embraced all string basses, including the cello. While the second of two bass lines is left unspecified—the first is for the bassoon—the autograph wrapper for a set of parts used in a performance in 1724 lists the continuo instruments as "Bassono, Vio-

loncello e Continuo." And in Movement 1 of the score, Bach refers collectively to the two lines as "Bassoni e Violoni." The label in Cantata 134a may well refer to cellos or to the cello and violone together: all are, in Walther's sense, *Bass-Geigen.* The NBA (I/35) adds the violone retroactively to all the previous movements as a result of this misunderstanding.

Other sources also designate both the cello and the violone by the collective term. Christoph Graupner, Bach's competitor for the post of Thomas-Cantor, used the word "Violone" in a part-set for his Leipzig audition piece in 1723 to denote a string bass part. A duplicate part, also entitled "Violone," suggests that the cello played from the part labeled with a generic term denoting string bass. This can also be seen in Johann Gottlieb Goldberg's cantata "Durch die herzliche Barmherzigkeit" and in Bach's arrangement of Pergolesi's *Stabat Mater,* both of which contain complete part-sets that include only a violone without mention of the cello. The Goldberg cantata, which Bach performed in his last years, appears in *Das Erbe Deutscher Musik,* 1st series (1957), vol. 35, with critical commentary by Alfred Dürr on pp. 126–130. Dürr discusses the sources for the Pergolesi arrangement in "Neues über Bachs Pergolesi-Bearbeitung" in *BJ,* 1968, pp. 89–100.

43. Though not specifically designated, the continuo fragment from BWV 137 was probably for the violone since a second cellist would have played from the main continuo part.

44. Terry, *Bach's Orchestra,* pp. 17–18.

45. The secondary sources for Cantata 149 suggest that it too had contained another part similar to those found in Cantatas 78 and 137. See NBA I/30, KB, pp. 106–109, 177. The *Violono grosso* part contains a simplification of the continuo line in Movement 2 resembling the one in Cantata 78 and must never have been entered in Bach's score. Bach may have thought to use the term "violono grosso" in Cantata 149 after he consulted the score to Cantata 208: the opening choral movement of Cantata 149 parodies Cantata 208 (Movement 15), which likewise had called for a "Violono grosso."

46. I am grateful to Joshua Rifkin for pointing this out to me.

47. Bach had planned another cantata for this day, "Siehe, eine Jungfrau ist schwanger," but—possibly because he was too involved with the composition of the St. John Passion—never composed it. Instead, he substituted (somewhat inappropriately) Cantata 182, despite the fact that the congregation's wordbook already contained the text for the other cantata. William H. Scheide, "Zum Verhältnis von Textdrucken und musikalischen Quellen der Kirchenkantaten Johann Sebastian Bachs," *BJ,* 1976, pp. 79–94.

48. A Leipzig cello part for Cantata 31 exemplifies an identical procedure undertaken by an anonymous copyist. Here the consolidation was even more extreme, since the Weimar cello part had been marked *tacet* in five movements. It is also likely that the Weimar cello part was given to a violone player at Leipzig, even though it was never relabeled. The Bach-Gesellschaft editor of Cantata 31 did not realize that the two surviving cello parts stemmed from two distinct versions of the work and misleadingly called the Weimar part "Violoncello 1" and the Leipzig part "Violoncello 2."

49. David, "Secret," p. 222. Not that either shared arrangement was convenient for the violone player; but numerous paintings from the period depict cellists or violonists looking over the shoulders of keyboard players at seemingly uncomfortable distances (see, for example, *International Repertory of Musical Iconography (RIdIM)*, series B/9). In the case of dual accompaniment, one can easily imagine the cellist sharing the figured part with the harpsichordist, while the violone player shared the unfigured part either with a bassoonist or a second cellist. According to J. J. Quantz's directions for seating, a cellist and a violone player should sit on either side of the harpsichordist. Quantz, *Versuch*, chap. 17, sec. I, pars. 14–15.

50. Terry, *Bach's Orchestra*, pp. 19–20. See also Schering, *LKM*, p. 131.

51. Spitta, II, 774.

52. *BDok*, III, 180.

53. BWV 12/7, BWV 172/6, BWV 18/5, BWV 165/6, BWV 162/6, BWV 155/5, BWV 31/9, BWV 185/6, BWV 161/6, and BWV 70a/6.

54. Other references to Bach's Leipzig violone appear in the scores of secondary sources for Cantatas 80, 110, 174, 191, and 105 and the early version of the Magnificat (BWV 243a).

55. Although BWV 147/7 presumably derived from the Weimar version, BWV 147a/3, no score of the earlier piece survives except for the first movement. See Dürr, *Zur Chronologie der Leipziger Vokalwerke Johann Sebastian Bachs* (Kassel: Bärenreiter, 1976), p. 59. Perhaps the switch from a small to a large violone caused the new version to have been entered in the Leipzig parts for the performance in 1723.

56. A continuo part for the St. John Passion, performed around 1728–1731, includes the marking "senza violone" in Movement 20, an aria for tenor ("Erwäge") accompanied by two muted violins, but this was probably because Bach wanted the viola da gamba to play continuo without the cellos and violone.

57. On Bach's special use of the viola da gamba in the three sonatas, see my remarks in the Afterword to the Peters edition of BWV 1027–1029 (Leipzig: Edition Peters, 1987).

58. The exception is a Cöthen continuo part for Francesco Conti's solo cantata, "Languet anima mea." The Weimar score had called for a cello, but for the first Cöthen performance Bach had two continuo parts copied: *Viola da gamba* and *Violone*. It is likely that the special cultivation of the gamba at Cöthen by both Bach's employer, Prince Leopold, and his friend Christian Ferdinand Abel accounts for its role in this work and in Cantata 199. See Kobayashi, "Neuerkenntnisse," p. 56. (Consider also the Brandenburg Concerto No. 6 in this regard.) On the other hand, in Cantata 205 written for Leipzig, Bach wrote an obbligato part for the gamba without adding any extra duties in the continuo group.

59. In Bach's violin sonatas with harpsichord, on the other hand, the gamba appears as an optional accompanist in an apparently authorized manuscript copied in 1725 by Johann Heinrich Bach ("col Basso per Viola da Gamba accompagnato se piace"). See Hans-Joachim Schulze, *Studien zur Bach-Überlieferung im 18. Jahrhundert* (Leipzig: Edition Peters, 1984), p. 115.

60. Jürgen Eppelsheim, in the chapter entitled "The Instruments" in *J. S. Bach: Life, Times and Influence,* ed. Barbara Schwendowius and Wolfgang Dömling (New Haven, Conn.: Yale University Press, 1984), p. 133, believes there is "no doubt . . . that the viol is meant to participate not only in the Sinfonia but also in the performance of the instrumental bass of the following movements." But he cites as evidence the gamba part for Cantata 76, which was in fact marked *tacet* in all but its obbligato movements at its first performance.

61. One may also legitimately question whether Bach instructed the oboes not to play in the tenor recitative (Movement 34), given the chordal accompaniment in the gamba part. No corresponding *tacet*-indication appears in the oboe parts, but the composer could have easily instructed the players to leave out their parts in the recitative. The greatest problem in omitting the oboes is the resulting counterpoint between the gamba's uppermost notes and the vocal part: there are too many unisons where it would have been easy for Bach to write another third on top of the chord. The parallel unisons in m. 8 are particularly ungainly in this regard.

62. An identical reference structures the bass line to the second movement of the Italian concerto, Movement 2.

63. It is also conceivable, given the reference to the "special instruments," that the lute also accompanied in the succeeding aria with the viola da gamba and two violas d'amore. No source, however, gives any indication of this possibility. In any event, the lute was present only for the first and second performances of the Passion in 1724 and 1725; in later performances it was replaced by an organ or a harpsichord. See Mendel, NBA II/4, KB, p. 97. Mendel also cites Hans-Joachim Schulze, "Wer intavolierte Johann Sebastian Bachs Lautenkompositionen?" *Die Musikforschung,* 19 (1966), p. 37, who points out that both the copyist of BWV 997 and BWV 1000, J. C. Weyrauch, and his lute teacher, Adam Falckenhagen, were in Leipzig during 1724 and 1725. One of them probably played the lute solo.

64. The one known exception is Bach's score to J. C. Schmidt's motet, discussed in Chapter 4, in which the figured continuo line reads *Organo ô Tiorba.* As mentioned earlier, the score surely reflected Bach's exemplar and not the parts he prepared for his own use.

65. Cited in Spitta, II, 854.

66. According to Walther's *Lexikon* (p. 174), among other sources, the *colascione* or *colachon* was a lute of Turkish origin with two or three strings. The Neapolitans, he adds, pluck its strings with a plectrum or with a feather. As he describes it, the instrument would be utterly unsuitable for continuo playing. *The New Grove Dictionary* (1980), vol. 4, pp. 523–524, adds to the confusion.

67. Mattheson, *Das neu-eröffnetes Orchestre,* p. 279. Cited in Terry, *Bach's Orchestra,* p. 19.

68. Cited in Spitta, II, 862.

69. The engraving is from *Unfehlbare Engel-Freude oder Geistliches Gesangbuch* (Leipzig, 1710) and is reproduced in Schering, *LKM,* facsim. II. It depicts Kuhnau conducting with a paper roll in his right hand, and, to the left of the organist, a violonist and a lutenist. Both string players are playing instruments with six strings. There is no cello present.

70. Mattheson, *Das neu-eröffnetes Orchestre,* p. 279.

71. Ernst Gottlieb Baron, *Historisch-theoretisch und practische Untersuchung des Instruments der Lauten* (Nürnberg, 1727; facsim. 1965), cited in Arnold Schering, *Musikgeschichte Leipzigs,* II, 423.

72. The entry on Falckenhagen in *The New Grove Dictionary* is somewhat unclear on this point. See Hans-Joachim Schulze, "Bachs Lautenkompositionen," p. 37.

73. Gleditsch, who died in 1747, is supposed to have composed twelve partitas for the lute, all of which have been lost. Cited in Terry, *Bach's Orchestra,* p. 142 and in Schering, *Musikgeschichte Leipzigs,* II, 419, although Schering cites no source for this information.

74. See Hans-Joachim Schulze, "Bachs Lautenkompositionen," pp. 36–37. As Schulze mentions, Straube is named in Jacob Adlung's *Anleitung zu der musikalischen Gelahrtheit* (Erfurt, 1758), as "a lutenist and a well-trained keyboard pupil of Capellmeister Bach's" (p. 722). He is also identical with Dürr's "Hauptkopist G." See Schulze, *Studien zur Bach-Überlieferung,* p. 120.

75. At 21 Reichsthalers, this lute was valued at seven times the amount of a corresponding viola da gamba and slightly more than the smallest harpsichord in the collection. See *BDok,* II, 492–493. Bach's own estate was settled only in the autumn of 1750. Hoffmann's will (drawn in 1748) bequeathed his own personal instruments to five of his "dear friends," who included Johann Sebastian Bach and Johann Christian Weyrauch. *BDok,* II, 449.

76. The closest association between Bach's orchestra and the lute is the letter of recommendation (1735) for Johann Ludwig Krebs, in which Bach "obliges him with a testimonial concerning his accomplishments at our School" and notes that he "distinguished himself here particularly *in musicis,* having qualified himself in respect to the clavier, the violin and the lute, as well as composition." *BR,* p. 135; *BDok,* II, 139. But in contrast to the letter for Wild, which connects the harpsichord directly with the performance of church music, Bach characterizes Krebs's lute playing more as an educational achievement. The testimonial for Weyrauch, moreover, does not even mention the lute by name. *BDok,* II, 135–136.

77. Cantatas 6, 41, 49, 68, 85, 115, 175, and 183 have clearly designated violoncello piccolo parts, while the solo in Cantata 180, which survives only in score, may be for the viola.

78. The words *pro Violincello piccolo* seem to have been added later.

79. Winfried Schrammek, "Viola pomposa und Violoncello piccolo bei Johann Sebastian Bach," *Bericht über die Wissenschaftliche Konferenz zum III. Internationalen Bach-Fest der DDR* (Leipzig: VEB Deutscher Verlag für Musik, 1977), pp. 345–354. See Schrammek, pp. 350–351, nn. 1–5, for a list of earlier references to the debate.

80. Both are also distinct from the cello with five strings that is required for Bach's sixth cello suite. Cellos with more than four strings were not exceptional. On this point, see the section on the violoncello at the beginning of this chapter.

81. Certain internal musical evidence suggests that Bach wrote for both four-string and five-string instrument types. The range of several of the ob-

bligatos does not require the low C string, and, in Cantata 85/2, the quadruple stop in m. 9 would naturally have been repeated in m. 27 with four notes if the instrument had possessed a low C string.

82. According to Walther in the *Lexikon* (1732), the "shoulder viola makes a great effect in accompanying because it can penetrate sharply and purely express the sounds. It is fastened with a strap on the chest and is thrown, as it were, onto the right shoulder and therefore has nothing that retards or hinders its resonance in the slightest" (p. 637).

83. The term "violoncello piccolo," on the other hand, appears nowhere in the theoretical descriptions of the eighteenth century. Schrammek, "Viola pomposa und Violoncello piccolo," p. 353, n. 15.

84. Compare Jürgen Eppelsheim's comments discounting this point in *J. S. Bach: Life, Times, Influence*, p. 131. Eppelsheim's explanation that the pomposa was merely a member of the continuo section and hence required no special mention is a little too disingenuous, particularly considering the striking coincidence of parts for the violoncello piccolo, the date Bach is supposed to have invented the viola pomposa, and the utter absence of any mention of the pomposa in the Bach sources.

85. This led Hans-Joachim Schulze to suppose that the violoncello piccolo parts were initially written for Georg Gottfried Wagner, who participated in Bach's performances from 1723 to 1726. Wagner left Leipzig for Plauen on November 16, 1726, only two weeks after the last of the set of obbligatos (for Cantata 49) was performed. Yet three of the part-sets in question (for Cantatas 41, 6, and 175) show evidence of use at a later performance, and there is every reason to believe that all the pieces with violoncello piccolo solos were performed on several subsequent occasions. Schulze, in his *Studien zur Bach-Überlieferung*, p. 114, n. 453, notes that the later violoncello piccolo part for BWV 6 may well have been copied by Johann Heinrich Bach, which would date the later performance to Easter of 1727. Bach therefore did not stop using the instrument after 1726, a point which the late *Continuo* part for BWV 234 also confirms.

86. It may seem odd that any part called "violoncello" should be played on an arm-held instrument *da braccio;* yet Walther's description of the shoulder viola, the *viola da spalla,* occurs under the entry *Violoncello.* Evidently he considered the low range of the instrument a more important feature than the position in which it was held.

87. *BDok,* III, 469.

88. Schrammek ("Viola pomposa und Violoncello piccolo," p. 348) considers this its fundamental purpose, according to an anecdote recounted by Johann Adam Hiller concerning Franz Benda and Pisendel, who played duets accompanied by the viola pomposa. At the same time, he grants that Bach may well have used it for the solos labeled "Violoncello piccolo."

89. Quantz, *Versuch,* chap. 17, sec. IV, par. 6; English trans., p. 244.

Index to Cited Works of Bach

BWV 4: 53, 252n36

BWV 5: 62

BWV 6: 33, 35, 38, 48, 174, 232n73, 257n77, 258n85

BWV 7: 51, 136, 156–157

BWV 8: 250n7

BWV 9: 62

BWV 10: 164

BWV 11 (Ascension Oratorio): 95–96, 242n45

BWV 12: 119, 158, 231n69, 255n53

BWV 14: 243n48

BWV 17: 53

BWV 18: 90, 113, 119, 125, 134, 155–156, 241nn39, 40, 248n34, 249n36, 255n53

BWV 19: 244n56

BWV 21: 123, 134, 248n36

BWV 23: 33, 38, 42, 113, 117, 134, 233nn76, 77, 247n27, 249n6

BWV 24: 51, 103

BWV 25: 223n19

BWV 26: 41, 61

BWV 27: 244n56

BWV 28: 51

BWV 29: 67–68

BWV 30: 95, 237n8, 242n44, 244n56

BWV 30a: 74, 95, 100–102, 105, 243n51

BWV 31: 51, 90, 119, 123, 134, 249n36, 254n48, 255n53

BWV 33: 62

BWV 34a: 244n56

BWV 36b: 244n56

BWV 38: 51

BWV 39: 244n56

BWV 40: 6–8, 51, 223n19, 244n57

BWV 41: 41, 174, 257n77, 258n85

BWV 42: 61, 62, 117, 127, 131, 164

BWV 43: 243n48

BWV 44: 113, 117

BWV 45: 53

BWV 46: 51, 244n57

BWV 48: 223n19, 244n56

BWV 49: 64, 244n56, 257n77

BWV 51: 244n56

BWV 52: 53

BWV 55: 53

BWV 56: 53, 244n56

BWV 58: 95, 242n44

BWV 59: 53, 57, 244n56

BWV 60: 223n19

BWV 61: 119

BWV 62: 162–164

BWV 63: 53, 113, 120, 124, 244nn56, 57

BWV 64: 53, 55, 56

BWV 66: 117

BWV 68: 257n77

BWV 69: 95

BWV 69a: 117

BWV 70: 113, 117, 223n19, 244n56

BWV 70a: 255n53

BWV 71: 113, 119, 132–133, 134, 135, 151–153, 249n3, 252n35

BWV 73: 68, 223n19, 244n56

BWV 74: 244n56

BWV 75: 117

BWV 76: 168, 256n60

BWV 78: 157, 161, 162, 243n55, 254n45

BWV 79: 54

BWV 80: 15–16, 255n54

BWV 81: 55, 223n19

BWV 84: 54

BWV 85: 53, 244n56, 257n77, 258n81

BWV 87: 54, 244n56
BWV 88: 53, 55–56
BWV 89: 55, 223n19
BWV 91: 244n56
BWV 94: 62, 95, 242n46, 244n57
BWV 95: 61, 95, 96, 97
BWV 97: 58, 62, 95, 97, 117, 136, 164, 250n7
BWV 99: 62, 243n55
BWV 100: 62, 136, 158, 164, 250n7
BWV 101: 51, 62
BWV 102: 244n5
BWV 105: 255n54
BWV 106 (Actus Tragicus): 133–134, 166, 167, 252n36
BWV 107: 244n56
BWV 109: 33–35, 48, 231n71
BWV 110: 244n56, 255n54
BWV 115: 257n77
BWV 116: 53, 244n56
BWV 119: 117
BWV 122: 244n56
BWV 124: 41, 51
BWV 125: 41, 244n56
BWV 127: 244n57
BWV 129: 62
BWV 130: 61, 62
BWV 131: 119, 133, 248n36
BWV 132: 119, 231n69, 253n40
BWV 134a: 151, 156, 253n42
BWV 135: 245n3
BWV 137: 157, 254n43
BWV 139: 62, 244n56
BWV 140: 113, 244n56, 246n15
BWV 147: 51, 116, 135, 161, 244n56, 245n12, 255n55
BWV 147a: 151, 255n55
BWV 149: 246n15, 254n45
BWV 150: 252n36
BWV 152: 167
BWV 154: 223n19
BWV 155: 119, 123, 231n69, 243n48, 247n33, 255n19
BWV 161: 255n19
BWV 162: 113, 119, 134, 135, 156, 255n19
BWV 165: 151, 255n53
BWV 166: 53
BWV 169: 67
BWV 170: 64, 67, 244n56
BWV 172: 113, 118, 119, 123, 134, 135, 249n36, 255n53
BWV 173: 117
BWV 173a: 151, 156
BWV 174: 116, 244n56, 255n54
BWV 175: 174, 244n56, 257n77, 258n85

BWV 177: 62, 113, 117, 246n15
BWV 178: 54
BWV 180: 257n77
BWV 182: 134, 135, 157, 231n69, 254n47
BWV 183: 244n57, 257n77
BWV 184: 53, 55
BWV 184a: 134
BWV 185: 90, 113, 119, 123–124, 134, 156, 242n42, 248n34, 255n19
BWV 186: 117
BWV 191: 255n54
BWV 194: 117, 253n42
BWV 195: 55, 69, 165, 244n56, 250n7
BWV 196: 151, 153, 249n3
BWV 197: 95, 237n8, 242n44
BWV 198 (Trauer-Ode): 15, 19, 30–31, 32, 69, 167, 169, 170, 172, 226n33
BWV 199: 113, 119, 123–124, 134, 156, 168, 231n69, 255n58
BWV 201: 69, 244n56
BWV 205: 158, 255n58
BWV 207: 244n57
BWV 208: 117, 151, 153, 241n37, 249n36, 253n38, 254n45
BWV 210: 164
BWV 213: 244n56
BWV 214: 164, 244nn56, 57
BWV 215: 113, 244n56
BWV 226: 42, 53, 126, 158, 249n7
BWV 232 (B-minor Mass): 53, 113, 117, 118, 123, 125–126, 246n18, 250n7
BWV 234: 172, 258n85
BWV 240: 51, 164
BWV 241 (Kerll Sanctus): 45, 48, 69, 70, 113, 126, 136, 158
BWV 243 (Magnificat): 117, 255n54
BWV 244 (St. Matthew Passion): 3, 26, 33, 40, 73, 74, 75, 86, 95, 97–102, 105, 169, 227n33, 243n55, 246n15
BWV 245 (St. John Passion): 19, 26, 33, 40, 99, 113, 117, 125, 127, 168–169, 170, 225n33, 228n44, 249n38, 255n56, 256n63
BWV 246: 237n8
BWV 248 (Christmas Oratorio): 42, 117, 118, 136, 244nn56, 57, 58, 246n19, 250n7
BWV 249 (Easter Oratorio): 243n55
BWV 250–252: 22
BWV 997: 256n63
BWV 1000: 256n63
BWV 1027–1029: 167
BWV 1044: 252n32
BWV 1046–1051 (Brandenburg Concertos): 142–151, 156, 251n25
BWV 1046 (Brandenburg Concerto No. 1): 142, 143, 151, 253n38

BWV 1046a: 253n38

BWV 1047 (Brandenburg Concerto No. 2):
142, 149, 150, 151, 153, 252n32

BWV 1048 (Brandenburg Concerto No. 3):
142, 143, 150–151

BWV 1049 (Brandenburg Concerto No. 4):
142, 143–145, 146, 151, 161, 253n40

BWV 1050 (Brandenburg Concerto No. 5):
142, 146–149, 151, 161

BWV 1050a: 146, 149, 151, 252n30

BWV 1051 (Brandenburg Concerto No. 6):
142, 150, 151, 167, 251n23, 255n58

BWV 1055: 69

General Index

Abel, Christian Ferdinand, 255n58
Adlung, Jacob, 68, 235n105, 257n74
Altnikol, Johann Christoph, 146, 149
Art-Fiddlers, municipal, 117, 156

Bach, Anna Magdalena, 164
Bach, Carl Philipp Emanuel, 20, 58, 62–63, 64, 69, 70, 89, 132, 158–161, 231n67, 234n90; and conducting, 16, 32, 226n33; and recitatives, 84, 86, 102
Bach, Johann Christoph Friedrich, 252n29
Bach, Johann Heinrich, 53, 255n59, 258n85
Bach, Johann Ludwig, 44–45, 53, 113, 117
Bach, Johann Sebastian, 2, 6–9, 109, 231n69, 245n14; and the harpsichord, 25–26, 40; as continuo harpsichordist, 30–31, 32; as conductor and violinist, 31–32; as organ soloist in cantatas, 64. *See also* Memorandum to the Town Council
Bach, Wilhelm Friedemann, 64, 84, 227n36, 232n73, 235n101
Baines, Francis, 251n23
Basse de violon, 138
Bassetto, 2, 60, 132, 172
Bassoon, 108–118, 131, 133; pitch, 118–123; in Bach's Weimar parts, 123–125; in Bach's Leipzig parts, 125–127
Baumann, Thomas, 237n11
Baumgärtner, Johann, 234n92
Beer, Johann, 137
Bellermann, Heinrich, 13
Benda, Franz, 258n88
Beyer, Johann Samuel, 23
Bodenschatz, Erhard, 22
Borgir, Tharald, 132, 133, 136, 249n2
Brandt, Konrad, 116, 246n15

Brewer, Barbara, 245n10
Brossard, Sébastien de, 139, 140, 166

Cammerton: definition, 7, 118–119; figured continuo parts in, 8, 16, 48–58; parts with *tasto solo* markings, 60
Cello. *See* Violoncello
Chorton, 7, 11, 118–119
Christiane Eberhardine, Queen (of Saxony), 30
Chrysander, Friedrich, 13
Colascione, 170
Collegium musicum (Leipzig), 30, 117
Colochon, 170–171
Conti, Francesco, 253n41, 255n58
Corelli, Archangelo, 127
Cues, for short accompaniment, 76, 89–91
Cue staves, in parts for recitatives, 8, 55–56
Cyr, Mary, 250n10

Dadelsen, Georg von, 4, 235n101
Dart, Thurston, 4
David, Hans T., 229n52, 233n85, 251n23
Denner, Johann Christoph, 111
Dual accompaniment, 8, 12, 13–17, 18, 19–22, 25, 27–28, 38, 41, 48, 57–58, 225n33, 227n33; as controversy, 10, 12–23, 225n33, 231n68; as convention, 68–71
Dürr, Alfred, 4, 120, 234n92, 235n101, 243n50, 246n19, 247n27, 248n34, 253n42; views on dual accompaniment, 38, 42–43, 226n33, 232n73, 233n82; views on the bassoon, 116–117

Ehrbach, Johann Andreas, 253n39
Eichlern, Christian Gottfried, 25

Eisel, J. P., 141
Eppelsheim, Jürgen, 247n31, 249n37, 256n60, 258n84

Falckenhagen, Adam, 171, 256n63
Finson, Jon W., 251n23
Fougeroux, Pierre Jacques, 78, 84
Franz, Robert, 12–13
Freiberg (cathedral), 23, 69
Fuhrmann, Martin Heinrich, 111, 120

Gasparini, Francesco, 238n19
Gerber, Ernst Ludwig, 174
Gerlach, Carl Gotthelf, 31
Gesner, Johann Matthias, 17, 28–30, 230n54
Gleditsch, Johann Caspar, 171, 257n73
Goldberg, Johann Gottlieb, 254n42
Görner, Johann Gottlieb, 30
Gottsched, Johann Christoph, 30, 230nn59, 60
Graun, Johann Gottlieb, 87
Graupner, Christoph, 233n75, 254n42

Hahn, Georg Joseph Joachim, 81, 105
Handel, George Frederick, 13, 15, 16, 78
Hanslick, Eduard, 13
Harpsichord, 10–11, 27–32, 40, 58–68, 70; controversy, 12–23; use in churches, 23–26; parts for, 32–58
Hasse, Johann Adolph, 87
Heinichen, Johann David, 76–78, 80, 82, 87, 91
Hiller, Johann Adam, 88, 258n88
Hoffmann, Johann Christian, 171, 257n75
Hogwood, Christopher, 252n30

Keiser, Reinhard, 44
Kellner, David, 54, 78–80
Kerll, Johann Kaspar, 44, 45–48, 113, 126, 136, 158, 171
Kirchbach, Carl von, 230n59
Kirnberger, Johann Philipp, 11, 153
Kittel, Johann Christian, 16, 17, 28, 30, 31, 56, 69, 70, 224n15, 225n33, 229n52
Klein, Johann Joseph, 87
Knüpfer, Sebastian, 227n34
Kobayashi, Yoshitake, 253n41
Köhler, Johann Friedrich, 230n54
Kollmann, Augustus Frederic Christopher, 87
Krause, Christoph Gottfried, 82
Krebs, Johann Ludwig, 171, 257n76
Kuhnau, Johann (Thomas-Cantor), 16, 21–22, 23, 119, 170, 233n19, 230n64, 246n17
Kuhnau, Johann Andreas, 6, 7, 33, 38, 157, 168, 232n71

Leavis, Ralph, 251n23
Lully, Jean-Baptiste, 84, 137, 245n6
Lustig, Jacob Wilhelm, 83, 91, 239n24
Lute, 31, 170–172, 230n61

Majer, Joseph Friedrich Bernhard Caspar, 140–141, 251n19
Marais, Marin, 247n31
Marshall, Robert L., 222n13, 223n18, 234n88
Mattheson, Johann, 2, 21, 238n15, 239n24; and the harpsichord, 15, 16, 24, 69–70; and the bassoon, 111, 120, 245n7; and the violoncello, 135, 139; and the violone, 139–140, 141, 166; and the lute, 170–171
Maunder, Richard, 251n23
Meier, Adolph, 251n23
Meissner, Christian Gottlob, 7, 35, 41, 61, 232n71
Memorandum to the Town Council, Bach's (1731), 135, 156, 171, 246n17
Mendel, Arthur, 232n71, 246n21; and dual accompaniment, 58, 225n33, 229n52, 233n78; and recitative accompaniment, 73, 90–91, 241n38; and the lute, 256n63
Mizler, Lorenz, 81, 85, 230n60, 239n21, 240n31
Mohrheim, Friedrich Christian Samuel, 58–60
Muffat, Georg, 138–139
Müthel, J. G., 252n32

Nagel, Maximilian, 171
Neuhaus, Johann Gottlieb, 25
Neumann, Friedrich-Heinrich, 73–74
Neumann, Werner, 30–31, 225n33, 230n60, 243n52, 244n57
Neumeister, Erdmann, 76, 125
Niedt, Friedrich Erhard, 77–78, 80, 87, 89, 106, 221n3, 238n15
Nikolai-Kirche, 16–17, 19, 25–27, 40–41, 227n34

Organ parts, 11, 58, 63–68
Organ repair hypothesis, 19, 21, 26–27, 40, 44, 51

Palestrina, Giovanni Pierluigi da, 44, 48
Penzel, Christian Ferdinand, 55, 149, 151
Peranda, Marco Gioseppe, 44
Pergolesi, Giovanni Battista, 44
Petri, Johann Samuel, 84–85, 89, 105, 227n36
Pisendel, Johann Georg, 258n88
Planyavsky, Alfred, 251n23
Platen, Emil, 74, 237nn8, 9, 242n44, 243nn48, 51, 244n58

Praetorius, Michael, 235n105, 250
Prinner, Johann Jacob, 250n12
Prinz, Ulrich, 245n5, 246n23, 247n29, 248n33
Prixner, Sebastian, 87

Quantz, Johann Joachim, 69, 231n67, 239n26; and the violone, 141, 232n72, 251nn21, 22, 255n49; and the violoncellist, 149, 175–176, 232n72, 255n49

Rameau, Jean-Philippe, 84
Recitatives, 3, 55, 236n2; execution of continuo parts in, 72–107. See also Short accompaniment
Reilly, Edward R., 251n21
Richter, Bernhard Friedrich, 224n20, 235n101
Rietz, Julius, 3, 227n33
Rifkin, Joshua, 223n18
Rolle, Christian Carl, 236n109
Rost, Johann Christoph, 225n28
Rousseau, Jean-Jacques, 69, 83–84, 85, 91
Rust, Wilhelm, 60, 235n97

Scheibe, Johann Adolph, 105
Scheide, William H., 254n47
Schering, Arnold, 73, 117, 234n92; views on the harpsichord, 10, 19–22, 30, 58, 60, 69, 225nn26, 29, 31, 33, 229nn50, 52, 234n92, 235n97
Schmidt, Johann Christoph, 113, 119, 120–123, 245n10, 247n31, 256n64
Schneider, Max, 18–19, 224n21
Schrammek, Winfried, 40, 172, 258n88
Schröter, Christoph Gottlieb, 85–86, 91, 235n105, 240n31
Schulze, Hans-Joachim, 222n10, 223n19, 232n74, 246n17, 253n38, 255n59, 256n63, 257n74, 258n85
Schütz, Heinrich, 237n11, 250n13
Schweitzer, Albert, 223n5, 224n20
Seiffert, Max, 17–18, 20, 58
Short accompaniment in secco recitative, 9, 72–75, 105–107; witnesses to, 76–89; use of quarter notes in notation, 78, 91, 99, 100, 103, 105; evidence of in Bach's continuo parts, 89–103, 105
Sicul, Christoph Ernst, 15, 21, 30–31, 225n33
Silbermann, Gottfried, 225n31, 247n32
Smit Duyzentkunst, Ingrid, 74
Speer, Daniel, 137, 250n11
Spitta, Philipp, 3, 4, 14; views on the harpsichord, 13–17, 24, 30, 58, 224nn15, 20, 229n52

Springsfeldt, Gottlob Christian, 24–25
Stölzel, Gottfried Heinrich, 81–82
Straube, Rudolph, 171
Swanton, Philip, 235n105

Tacet-indications, 2, 58–63
Tasto solo, 42, 67
Telemann, Georg Philipp, 44, 80–81, 82, 84, 89, 105, 239n24
Terry, Charles Sanford, 3, 19, 21, 113, 116, 229n52, 253n39
Theorbo, 123. See also Lute
Thomas-Kirche, 16–17, 25–27, 40–41, 158, 171, 225n28, 227n34, 229n52, 230n64
Thomas-Schule, 21, 22, 28, 48, 55, 171, 224n15, 230n54
Town-Pipers, municipal, 117, 156–157, 171
Trombone, 245n3, 246n20
Türk, Daniel Gottlob, 86, 87, 89, 235n105

Ulrich, Bernhard George, 117

Viadana, Lodovico, 235n105
Viola da gamba, 134, 166–169
Viola da spalla, 174
Viola pomposa, 172–174
Violoncello, 35, 38, 132–136, 149, 175
Violoncello piccolo, 172–175
Violone, 35, 136–137; German descriptions of, 137–142; in Brandenburg concertos, 142–151; in early Bach works, 151–156; in Leipzig works, 156–165; types used by Bach, 165–166
Vivaldi, Antonio, 125, 127
Voigt, J. S., 82

Wagner, Georg Gottfried, 258n85
Walther, Johann Gottfried, 1, 42, 111, 135, 140, 141, 155, 251n18, 256n66, 258n82
Watteau, Jean Antoine, 111
Webster, James, 251n21
Westrup, Jack, 73
Weyrauch, Johann Christian, 171, 256n63, 257n76
Wild, Friedrich Gottlieb, 2, 27, 56, 69, 225n33, 229nn49, 50, 257n76
Williams, Peter, 74, 90, 106, 226n33, 227n35, 241n38
Wolff, Christoph, 232n74, 233n77, 234n87

Zimmermann, Gottfried, 117